RESPECT

chaps, an almost mythical grouping of criminals whose ethos includes: professionalism in the pursuit of crime; loyalty to others of their kind; hatred of any non-cooperation with authority; and courage. Many aspire to membership, few qualify.

'Foreman, friend of the Krays, dubbed by the press the "British Godfather", has been privy to some of the most sensational criminal events of the century'

The Bookseller

'One admits that this book does have its place as a piece of modern social history'

Marie Ross, *Publishing News*

'Full of authoritative revelations from one who knows what went on, because he was in it up to his neck, not a bit-part player or a hanger-on looking in from the fringes, like too many of these "I was there" authors . . . he has broken the criminal code of silence and lifted the lid on some of gangland's secrets. His absorbing life story charts how he made the transition from ingenious but ruthless armed robber to true gangster status. It is easy to see how he became one of the most feared characters around.'

Sunderland Echo

RESPECT

Autobiography of Freddie Foreman – Managing Director of British Crime

by Freddie Foreman

with John Lisners

arrow books

This edition published by Arrow Books Limited 1997

7 9 10 8

Copyright © 1996 Freddie Foreman and John Lisners

First published in the United Kingdom in 1996 by Century

Arrow Books
The Random House Group Limited
20 Vauxhall Bridge Road, London SW1V 2SA

Random House Australia (Pty) Limited
20 Alfred Street, Milsons Point, Sydney,
New South Wales 2061, Australia

Random House New Zealand Limited
18 Poland Road, Glenfield
Auckland 10, New Zealand

Random House (Pty) Limited
Endulini, 5a Jubilee Road, Parktown 2193, South Africa

The Random House Group Limited Reg. No. 954009

randomhouse.co.uk

A CIP catalogue record for this book
is available from the British Library

Papers used by Random House are natural, recyclable
products made from wood grown in sustainable
forests The manufacturing processes conform to
the environmental regulations of the country of origin

ISBN 0 09 969951 6

Printed and bound in Great Britain by
Cox & Wyman Ltd, Reading, Berkshire

Acknowledgements

I wish to thank all the following people who have contributed to the writing of this book. Firstly, Ian Atkinson and Frank Kurylo for persuading me and John Lisners to write my story. Also Mark Booth and especially Liz Rowlinson for her patience with me; also Nicky Eaton, Tracey Jennings and all the other staff at Century Books. Many thanks to my friends and associates who sent photos and attended my book launch, also to the members of the press who publicised my autobiography. To my Janice who helped, encouraged and supported me; lastly to my son Jamie and his wife, Carol Harrison, who I owe a great deal for her valuable assistance in the completion of the paperback.

Contents

Contents

Prologue

Throughout my career, publishers and authors repeatedly approached me to write my memoirs. Until now, I resisted all their efforts to persuade me. I considered the time was not right and many events were, I felt, best forgotten. Furthermore, to discuss incidents and episodes about which I had always remained silent in a long career of villainy was totally alien to my nature and upbringing. The chaps don't talk.

Why then change a habit of a lifetime? Having reached the end of my career I have had time to reflect on the past and to read a number of books which have mentioned my name and the role I played in various criminal enterprises. Many of these have been inaccurate. Inevitably, rumours have been turned into fact and speculation has been presented as truth.

Now is the time to set the record straight. The chaps who were part of my life and are no longer with us would have had no qualms about appearing in this book. And the chaps who, like me, have survived the years have encouraged me to tell it the way it was.

As I unlocked the doors to my mind, memories came flooding back. To some readers my story may well serve as an historical record of a colourful era in the London crime scene. For me, it is more personal. It has given me the opportunity to analyse the events that shaped my life. To explain to myself why I took such drastic measures as I did. Was it to prove myself as a man or express anger through feeling rejected as a child? Or was it through living in dangerous and exciting times which began in the Second World War? When the four idols in my life were my older brothers who had joined the armed forces and fought for King and Country and held me spellbound with heroic tales of battle?

My environment as a boy was not of my choosing. There were few opportunities for people from my part of south London. At eight I was brought up with death and destruction. Did that have a bearing on my behaviour? With hindsight I sometimes wonder whether or not I was a case for treatment. I look back and say: 'You should never have done that, Fred!' After much soul searching I came to the conclusion that I wanted 'Respect'. I craved it at any cost. And for many years, it cost me dearly.

· 1 ·
Kidnapped

They came, mob-handed, for me on the morning of Friday 28 July, 1989. Black Friday – as I now call it. The Guardia Civil sprung me and swagged me off to Malaga nick then banged me up in a Spanish cell with a load of smack-heads and low-lifes. About a dozen, all like animals in a cage.

As far as the authorities were concerned, I was responsible for what the Spanish press described as the *robo del siglo* – ROBBERY OF THE CENTURY. Five of us were named and secretly photographed in our luxury villas. The sneak pictures of the 'Famous Five' were published internationally.

The Spanish coppers couldn't get me legally so the bastards kidnapped and drugged me. They did this by tossing the rule book out of the window. I can see the irony of it now. They reverted to my tactics: off with the gloves and anything goes. You don't expect that from law enforcement agencies. They should be setting examples, ha! ha!

Although I had not yet stood trial for Britain's biggest cash robbery – the £7 million hold-up at Security Express' HQ in the City of London, the Spaniards expelled me on the basis of a whispering campaign. Spain has a long history of inquisitions and abuse of human rights.

Four years earlier, Johnny Knight and Terry Perkins stood trial for this robbery at the Old Bailey and were jailed for twenty-two years. Now the Guardia Civil were intent on expelling me to face the music in Britain. Even

1

if that meant snatching me off the street, shoving me inside a cell, and slinging me on the next plane to London.

The first sour notes of this scenario were played at ten in the morning as I walked to the car-park of the El Alcazaba, a luxury development in Puerto Banus, Marbella. I had bought several apartments there with profits I made in America from a gaming machine business. To keep myself busy whilst in Spain I bought a share in the Eagles Country Club situated in Aloha.

I lived the life of Riley in a warm Mediterranean climate, amid palm trees, beautiful beaches and lovely ladies. Sun, sex and sangria, as people like to call it. It was all there for the taking and I made the most of it. Life was unreal. Since my arrival in Spain in 1983, the Costa del Sol had been round-the-clock pleasure. I had gone there to retire at the age of fifty-one, although I still had unfinished business in America and some loose ends to tie up back in England. But that didn't present a problem as I'd been back home several times without getting arrested.

Black Friday began as another day of pleasure. The pool at the Alcazaba sparkled in the morning sunshine. The palms and gardens, beautifully kept and rich with flowers, turned the development into a colourful oasis. Millionaires from around the world were attracted to it. My apartment was a big duplex facing the sea. Behind it were the rugged and beautiful Ronda mountains.

July and August are the hottest time in Andalusia and I had dressed comfortably in shorts, T-shirt and sandals and was set to visit my wife Maureen who had medical problems and was in a private clinic near Marbella.

I didn't notice anything unusual as I walked to my car. Had I been more observant then I might have seen a number of unfamiliar faces lurking about. Policemen in all manner of disguises had descended on my paradise. They were everywhere. Hiding behind trees, pretending to sweep pavements, or just sitting in cars. As I opened the door of my British Rover Sterling, they pounced. Suddenly I was being arrested by a group of plain-clothes officers and whisked off to Malaga police station.

I didn't struggle or resist at this time because this had happened so many times before. I had not committed any offences in Spain and had nothing to fear. I had also employed several lawyers on whom I could rely if the going got tough. Even so, every time a major incident happened, the Guardia would take me in for questioning – every time they fished anyone out of the sea or someone was washed ashore, usually minus their head and hands, it was always me they questioned.

Raymond Nash's daughter had been kidnapped in Spain and they had me in the nick over that. 'British criminals,' I bluntly told them, 'don't do this sort of thing. We don't kidnap little girls. That's not our style. Your people, or other Europeans may do that but not us.'

They didn't like that remark. But I was proven right. Marbella was tipped upside-down and they finished up arresting two Italians and two Spaniards.

On another occasion, a Canadian businessman renting Billy Smart's luxury villa, was murdered. He'd been shot through the head in his car which had then been set alight. He was cooked like a bit of roast pork and police found his charred remains in the mountains behind us. I knew the guy with whom he shared the villa. I'd been there for a couple of parties and it was a beautiful place, done out like a circus tent with a large swimming pool in the garden. Anyway the police came around on a Sunday asking me what I knew about the incident as if I had something to do with it. With that they pulled out a folder containing horrific photographs of this guy. 'Do you mind!' I said. 'I don't want to look at them. I'm going to have my Sunday dinner in a minute.' (Maureen had just cooked me a lovely roast leg of pork!)

With the constant questioning, I was beginning to feel persecuted (which was nothing unusual). At the same time I had a number of legal actions against me by different provinces intent on expelling me from the country. Pressure to get rid of me was growing by the day but, as I had done nothing wrong here, the courts would not sanction my expulsion. Thank God!

Although the Spanish had been told I was a suspect in the Security Express raid, the British police had no evidence against me. Nevertheless Scotland Yard clearly hoped that the Spanish could boot me out on the strength of the whispering campaign and that I would go on the run. Scotland Yard thought I had a dodgy passport because they'd found an application at Petty France (the passport office in London) in the name of Walters, a pseudonym I had used to apply for the passport. They figured if they could get me on the run I would be arrested for passport offences, giving grounds for extradition. But of course I'd already destroyed the dodgy passport – too smart for that!

Unfortunately for both of us, the police had also tried to link me with Ronnie Knight. Ronnie, an old mate who had been married to the actress Barbara Windsor, liked the convenience of the Alcazaba and bought a small apartment there. His main house in the hills of Mijas was too far to drive after partying in Puerto Banus. When Ronnie's brother was convicted of the Security Express robbery, police checked the names of all the tenants at the development and put Ron's and mine together, hence guilty by association.

So there I was, slung into the cells at Malaga with the low-lifes around me. I called for my lawyer but the police ignored me until I became such a nuisance that they sent over an interpreter to quieten me down. I was urgently demanding that he call my lawyer who was literally across the road from the police station. 'Yes, okay, okay, Mr Foreman,' he promised.

Some minutes later, several policemen came downstairs to take me away. I refused to leave and held on to the barred door preventing them from pulling it open, insisting once more that they call my lawyer. The other English and Spanish prisoners joined my stand and helped keep the police at bay.

The Guardia responded by summoning the interpreter again. This time he approached me, smiling: 'It's all right, Mr Foreman. You can come out now, your lawyer is waiting upstairs.' I didn't think he would tell me wrong, so when they opened the gate I walked out. But as I got to the stairs they jumped me, the bastards. They grabbed my arms and legs and hung on to my clothes. As I struggled, more of them joined in. In all there were about a dozen Guardia trying to get me to a car outside the station.

'You fucking liar,' I shouted at the interpreter. 'There's no lawyer!' With that I hooked on to the stair railings and clung on for dear life. 'I'm not going anywhere till my lawyer arrives.'

I knew the bastards were as desperate to get me to the airport as I was to stay. They were frantic in their efforts to separate me from the banister. With so many of them it was only a matter of time before they cuffed me up and got me in the car.

They shoved me into the rear seat, a guard on either side. Two more were in the front. But I wasn't going without a fight. Once we were underway I threw myself forward, trying to make them crash so I could make my escape. I was desperate. I knew that if they got me to the airport and on to a plane I'd be on my way back home to England facing a twenty-two-year sentence. Can you imagine me and four Guardia squashed in a poxy Seat car – sweating, swearing and swerving at 100 mph along the Marbella–Malaga Carretara. They'd stop at nothing!

In the meantime, my son Jamie and my daughter Danielle had gone to the nick to find me. On learning what had happened they went straight to my lawyer Juan Carlos Ramirez Balboteo whose sister, a local judge, issued them with a habeas corpus writ and joined the chase to catch up with me at the airport. Served with the writ, the police would have been compelled to bring me to court again before throwing me out of the country.

The Guardia took no chances. They had me firmly pinned to the seat of the car and drove straight on to the tarmac to a waiting plane. But as they opened the car door to haul me up the passenger steps, I broke free and made a run for it and crashed past Customs and Immigration, straight into the terminal among all the passengers waiting to catch their flights. Everyone looked with open mouths, rooted to the ground. Some pointed and stared.

As the police grabbed hold of me again, I shouted: 'They're kidnapping me!' I was causing mayhem, creating as much commotion as possible while uniformed Guardia with guns and sticks surrounded me. If I'd had a free hand then I would have grabbed a pistol and held them until my lawyer arrived, but I couldn't shake the handcuffs. Again they hauled me to the steps of the plane and for a second time I broke away. This time, wet with sweat, they chased me around the wheels of the plane, cursing with frustration. It was like the Keystone Cops all over again.

Eventually they picked me up – it took about six of them – and they carried me up the aircraft steps. I waited till they got about half-way and thrust my leg under a supporting rail and, with a tremendous heave, pushed backwards. We all toppled over, landing in a heap at the bottom. This time they got the right hump. Grabbing my arms and legs, one of them started laying into me. Another tried to strangle me. One little fat bastard, I'll never forget him, was letting rip with a torrent of Spanish abuse, whilst punching me in the bollocks.

I could see the pilot looking out of the window, stretching his head around, worried about the commotion. 'Right,' I thought, 'the more I perform the better the chance of him refusing to take me.' Two policemen were already down, taken to hospital with injuries, and the rest of them were red-faced and dripping sweat. Alas, they got me inside the plane and threw me face down on the floor, collapsing on top of me. Like them, I was exhausted. I lay on the floor with my arms still behind my back and turned my head upwards to see a male steward and two stewardesses.

The male steward was attentive: 'Would you like a drink, Mr Foreman?' I was parched and grateful for his kindness. He poured a drink into a plastic cup and held it for me.

'That's very kind of you,' I said, gratefully.

Soothingly, he replied: 'Drink it all, drink it all,' tipping up the cup to ensure it all went down. But the penny dropped. It was cold, refreshing with a bitter aftertaste.

I looked at him and said, 'You bastard, you fucking done me, you've doped me right up.'

Apparently all planes have sedatives for people who run amok. The steward smiled and gave a little look that said: 'Yeah, I've done you good and proper, no more trouble from you.' He was right.

I could feel myself going right away. But I was still arguing. I called for the pilot and although I couldn't see who I was talking to I was saying: 'I'm not going to go. I'll fucking stop you. You won't fly this plane back to England.' A voice replied that we were going to Morocco. 'Bullshit,' I said.

It was obvious we were going back to England, but I was trying to fanny them: 'You are taking me to London and what you are doing is totally illegal and you will all wind up in serious trouble. This is totally illegal!' (A tryer to the end – that's me!)

When that didn't work I again threatened to wreak havoc on the plane. But I could feel the drowsiness coming over me and knew I'd be going over any minute. Just then I got a massive panic attack. Paranoia set in.

Why were there no other passengers on board? Were they going to fly off with just me and dump me somewhere in the Mediterranean?

I hovered between sleep and a drowsy consciousness. They had lifted me on to the seats and I could hear what sounded to me like the muffled rage of the jet engines flying me away from my paradise.

I lay across three seats, my arms still pinned behind me and the steel handcuffs working patterns in my back. My hands were numb through lack of circulation.

I tried to reassure myself: 'I'll wake up in a moment and everything will be all right. It's just a dream. People are trying to rouse me but that's all part of this nightmare. I'm slipping back into unconsciousness. It was that bloody steward. There's a bitter taste in my throat . . . how can this be happening to me?'

How could it? I had fought and won all my legal battles against expulsion in four different regions: Andalusia, Madrid, Seville and Barcelona.

What's going to happen to me now? I'm looking at a twenty-two-year prison sentence. I'll be leaving jail in a wooden box or struggling out on a zimmer frame. This is it. My life's finished! They were taking me away from my palm tree paradise to the cold reality of Brixton Prison. What evidence have they got to throw at me? They must feel confident to go to the trouble of kidnapping me and taking me back in this manner, taking a right liberty.

I was drifting through this nightmare, seeing my life flash by me like the passing clouds. 'Think positively.' I said to myself, 'Go back to the carefree days of my youth, where there's still a future.'

My mind wandered back to south London. To Sheepcote Lane where life was an adventure. I was born there on Saturday 5 March, 1932, the youngest of five brothers. The last thing my mother wanted was another boy! But here I was unwanted but loved. My father was from Irish stock and my mother from a middle-class London family. Father's family was huge. There were about thirteen children: six sisters and seven brothers.

Every part of London had one street where villains came from and in our area it was Sheepcote Lane. Other streets in the area were similar but ours was notorious. For example Cable Street in Stepney, east London. Number 22 was a terraced house, two-up and two-down. You stepped from the street straight into the front room. The kitchen was at the back and upstairs, and we five brothers shared one bedroom. We were poor but happy. A lot of exciting things happened in those days.

The week's highlights came on a Saturday night. Poor as they were, the family would hold legendary parties after the pubs had closed. As kids we weren't allowed inside the pubs, but we'd linger about and wait for the action which usually began after the last drinks had been served.

We were rarely let down. Differences of opinion and heated exchanges would always arise, leading to the eagerly-awaited spectacle of a bareknuckle fight. This would take place on the street outside The Flag pub and from time to time my father would be one of the combatants.

My brothers would let me watch others fight and hoist me on to a window-ledge outside the pub from where I would get a glimpse of their heads and shoulders throwing punches. If they fell to the ground and rolled about, someone would take the part of referee and break them up so they could shape up and start again. The drunken crowd would form a circle, shouting and encouraging their respective mates into action, and were oblivious to the blood and sweat that sprayed in their direction. There was a lot of drunkenness around, and snuff-taking was also popular with older people. My grandmother, and others of her age, would take it on a regular basis, like people do coke today, and you could identify the snuff-takers by the brown stains under their noses and on their smudged handkerchiefs. From a little boy's point of view it was disgusting, especially when the old girl tried to kiss you.

Some parties at our house would finish up in much the same way as the pub evenings. They would begin with song and dance and sometimes end in a fight. Two of my father's sisters were on the boards at the Upper Brixton Empire and part of their repertoire included clog dancing and singing popular tunes around the piano. Lizzie Mayne, my aunt, was a lively entertainer. Her special number was 'There's a Blue Ridge Round My Heart Virginia' which my father, a little worse for drink, would follow with a rendition of 'Are We to Part Like This Dear?' which he sang to my mother.

We kids used to sit on the stairs and enjoy the mixed procession of people including boxers, market traders, vendors and musicians wandering in and out of our tiny house.

Musicians were always welcome and from time to time just for the crack (joke), the Salvation Army band would be invited to play. Huge wooden firkins of beer would arrive on willing shoulders as well as quart bottles of brown ale, four to a crate. Later, to help soak up the alcohol, big doorstep sandwiches filled with cheese and mustard pickle and large jars of pickled onions would appear and be wolfed down. As the evening wore on and my old man became more spirited, he would disappear to the pigeon loft in the back garden with a crate of ale and two or three of his favoured cronies. They would sit there telling each other stories until one of the wives dragged them out to join the party.

The loft had been built by my brother Wally, the second oldest, and it still holds poignant memories today. A big tom-cat once got in there and slaughtered all Wally's prized pigeons. Some time later my mother heard a horrendous commotion in the garden and ran outside in a panic. Wally had caught the offending cat, swung it around in circles by its tail and projected it across three neighbouring gardens, never to be seen again.

With the reduced pigeon population, the loft became a useful watering-hole for my father and his friends. But having drunk all their liquor, they'd return to the house and the fighting would begin. The old man's regular opponent was his brother-in-law Johnny Wicker who was as tough and as game as he was.

The pair would be at it hammer and tongs, battering the daylights out of one another with bare fists. They were constantly brawling and had fought each other so often that their contests had become a game of one-upmanship, win one, lose one, call it a draw, it went on and on, party after party. They never got fed up with bashing each other. I did not enjoy these spectacles, seeing my father bloodied and hurt. These times were violent and very physical – proving one's manhood in those days was an essential part of survival.

My father was christened Herbert Albert Foreman but his brothers called him Sonny. Confusingly, my mother called him Alf and he called her Lou, short for Louise.

I never discovered whether my father spent time in a civilian jail. If he did we were never told, although there were periods when he was not around. In those days judges or stipendiary magistrates didn't give long sentences. You'd get two to three months for assault and battery, or for beating up the police which was done on a regular basis. The coppers were quite into it themselves and would return for a 'straightener'.

Hitting a police officer was acceptable. Talking to one was not, even if he had the misfortune of being a relative. My mother's brother, Ted White, who ended up being Chief Constable of Durham would drop in to see my mother if he was on a job in London. But on the rare occasion that he visited us my father refused to acknowledge his presence, let alone speak to him. He'd put on his hat and coat and walk out of the house. No self-respecting citizen of Sheepcote Lane would ever be seen in the company of a policeman.

My father's hatred of authority was universal and led to a spell inside a military prison before I was born. Like my four brothers, he too had fought for King and Country and joined the Army at seventeen. Previously he'd been apprenticed as a blacksmith but when his arm was shattered by German shrapnel in the Battle of the Somme, it put an end to his blacksmith career. He returned to Aldershot where he fell foul of a sergeant major. The sergeant poked him with his stick and my father, a young man with lots of spirit, lost his rag and whacked him with the butt of his rifle. Rather than face a court martial, he made his getaway by stealing a bicycle and cycling all the way home to London.

They eventually caught him in the bar at the Super Palace at Princess Head, Battersea, and there was a hell of a fight. He was battered and unceremoniously dragged down to one of the Military Police wagons and then off to the nick.

After a further period in barracks he was sent back into action, though not to the front line. His injuries at the Somme prevented him from using a rifle and he was packed off with a pistol to Ireland as part of the peace-keeping force. My father was of good Irish stock so you can imagine this didn't sit well with him at all – but he had little choice.

I take after him. I can't stand being told what to do by people who abuse authority and that has got me into trouble. While in custody all I have ever demanded is that which anyone else is entitled to: to be treated fairly and with civility and to be spoken to like a human being.

My old man used to say, 'A little civility costs nothing', and these words have stuck with me throughout my life. As a young child, I can remember he once took me for a special treat to a café where he bought me a meat pudding and two veg. He couldn't afford one for himself and by the time my food was served, it was quite late and they began clearing up.

As I got stuck into my meal this guy came around and started sweeping. Dust went everywhere. Then he began putting chairs on tables, ignoring the fact that I was a customer. My father asked him to stop but the geezer either ignored him or made a rude comment. That was too much. My father looked menacingly at him and said: 'Put that fucking broom down and wait for my kid to finish his meal.'

At this point I was getting embarrassed and trying to eat my food as quickly as possible because, knowing the old man, it looked like being a right fight any second now. But the man took my father's threat seriously and stopped clearing up.

My father wasn't a man who would take liberties nor did he expect them to be taken. But he never laid a finger on any of us five boys, although the threat was always there. Mum would give you a clump, but not viciously. And never around the head. When she got the hump with you, you'd run for the coat rack and cover yourself with the heavy, khaki greatcoat from the First World War. She'd then get down and smack your legs, the only exposed area she could find.

Those days we were so poor that in winter, us boys would huddle together in bed sharing the greatcoat and a couple of blankets for warmth. Gas stoves were still a luxury and there was no electricity in the house.

As the youngest brother, there was a considerable gap between our ages. Herbie was older by twelve years, Wally by ten, George by eight, and Bert by five. Herbie was the only one to have the luxury of a single bed to himself, but shared the same small bare room.

We made do with gas-fired mantel lamps above the fireplace. They would spit and splutter, occasionally making gentle popping sounds and throwing moving shadows on to the wall. Huddled together around the cooking range, toasting bread whilst listening to favourite programmes on our pride and joy, one crystal set radio – happy memories!

If you were the youngest, bathtime could be a dirty affair. The ritual cleansing took place on Friday nights when the tin bath was carried in from the yard and set up in the kitchen. The older boys jumped in first so I always ended up in a tepid bath with scum floating on top – not such happy memories!

Our toilet was in the yard next to the big, wooden coal bunker. Years later, after they had demolished the house, we discovered railway sleepers in the foundations. The house had probably been built on a disused railway track. In front of our place was a brick railway embankment leading to the Southern Railways trucks and wagons which were shunted and left above some stables. Locals in Sheepcote Lane would break into these on a regular basis and nick saleable goods. Ignoring natural caution, they would then pitch a stall and sell the goods on their front doorstep.

Nice cars were a target for us local urchins. We'd jump on to the running boards for a game and honk their horns in innocent fun.

This was our street and we didn't like outsiders. They'd interfere with our football and cricket and another game called bridge where as many boys as possible would leapfrog on your back and cling on until you collapsed under their combined weight. If nothing else, the game built up your strength.

My immediate family were to be amazed that I developed strong bones and a marked physical presence because, as a very young boy, I was sent to a nursery suffering from malnutrition. I had rickets and they put me in callipers to keep my legs straight and fed me all this cod-liver oil, malt and egg custard. A nurse would go around to everyone with a big spoon of enriched vitamin mixture which you had to take and lick clean.

As poor as my parents were, they would not have anyone say I was undernourished and did everything to make sure I got enough to eat and exercised my little muscles. Mum used to have a mangle which, with great effort, I turned in order to squeeze dry her washing and she'd say: 'My, you're a strong little boy, Freddie,' as I swung on the handle and struggled to pull it round. She used to go to Shaftesbury Welcome, a church hall run by a charity, where they'd sing a few hymns and say some prayers, and on their way out, the mothers would get a quarter of tea, a pound of sugar and a packet of biscuits. It was a hard life.

Living at Sheepcote Lane was like being part of a permanent fairground. Horse-drawn carts would constantly rumble past our house, scattering chickens as they went. Street traders came with candy-floss and choc-ices. The knife sharpener would loudly announce himself and out you would run with all your mother's knives.

Another horse-and-cart man with a small hand-driven carousel would play music as you sat in tiny wooden seats and rode slowly around a central glass dome with two figures, like a wedding couple inside. The kids loved it. This was real pleasure.

Billy goats chased kids down the lane, and every now and again you'd see policemen grappling with men resisting arrest. Someone else would come with trays of muffins on his head but the coloured man was the most exotic attraction. Prince Monalulu was coal black and an expert on the horses. Barefooted children followed him down the road, a mystery Pied Piper from foreign lands. The street was fascinated by him. 'Aah got a horse,' he'd begin and then write out little betting slips and give a rundown of horses he claimed would win races.

That would tickle my grandmother. She was a terrible gambler. She'd have betting slips in every available vase. 'Just for reference,' she'd say. Granny Foreman was born

Stacy Flynn, of good Irish stock. She was a real fighter. She would regularly fight her neighbours on Saturday nights after leaving The Flag pub.

Almost everything imaginable was offered for sale in our street. From goats' milk to stolen motorbikes, huge blocks of salt, accumulators for radios – if you were lucky enough to own one – and vinegar by the pint. You were amazed and fascinated at the polished brass of the gypsy caravans at the bottom of the road. These caravans were spotlessly clean inside and out.

As a treat, you'd be sent with a tray to the local butcher and return with specially cooked pease pudding and faggots with saveloys on the side. It was a lovely meal consisting of mashed peas made into a thick paste with brains, herbs, and saveloys. You can still get it today in Bermondsey. Other than that we'd eat a lot of breadpudding. Meat was a luxury for Sundays only and for afters my favourite was rhubarb and custard – we'd fight over who licked clean the custard basin.

Our heroes were the faces on cards given away with cigarettes. They were usually boxers like Welshman Tommy Farr, British and Empire champion, the German Walter Neusel, Ben Foord, South African champion, and Jack Doyle, the Irish champion. We'd swap these with other kids as you would stamps. I remember listening to the Tommy Farr/Joe Louis fight in America in August 1937. At five years of age I still remember vividly being gathered around our crystal set and excitedly awaiting the verdict. We all felt that Tommy Farr had won on points but it was a home-town decision.

All the entertainment was in pubs and you might be lucky enough to see singers and vaudeville acts at the Grand, Clapham Junction and the Princess Head in Battersea (where the Army had nicked my old man). The famous blind jazz pianist George Shearing lived in Alfred Street, near The Flag pub, and used to walk past our house with his mother on the way to school.

Although we were Church of England, my father never believed in religion. But he had a strict code of morals that he stuck to all his life. He was a proud man who would not accept charity. If he was down to his last penny he'd stay out of the pub rather than accept drinks he couldn't afford.

At home, he would never curse, and moral issues were spelled out in black and white. You would never steal from neighbours or your own, or from people as badly off as yourself. And a cardinal rule was that you never trusted a policeman or told them anything. I stuck to that code throughout my career as a villain. My targets were always large financial organisations or stores. I never broke into houses or mugged people.

In spite of the poverty in our road, doors were left open because most people respected these unwritten rules – unlike today.

My biggest treat during those early years was to persuade mum to allow my brother Bert to take me to a Bela Lugosi film about the living dead. For weeks afterwards I paid a terrible price for this indulgence by having nightmares about zombies.

As one of the older boys, Herbie was always going to the pawn shop with something of my father's and then retrieving it a week or so later. The old man's suit used to get hocked as regular as clockwork.

Looking back on it, I realise how impoverished my parents were in those times. Thankfully that era came to an end when the boys were old enough to work. From then on, we started to live reasonably well.

Our standard of living had vastly improved, not just from the better housing but also from increased income brought into the household by my older brothers. Herbie, who now lives in Sydney, Australia, worked at the Eccentric Club in Ryder Street, St James. He started off as a lift boy, and graduated to the billiard room as billiard marker. He got Wally a job replacing him on the lifts, while George worked at Whitehall Court, an exclusive apartment block on the Embankment next to the National Liberal Club.

Many famous names used the flats at Whitehall Court during the week, returning to their country bases at weekends. Among them: George Bernard Shaw, Mr John Dewar of the whisky family, Sir David Llewellyn and Sir Ernest Tate from the Tate and Lyle sugar family. Sir Ernest was a mean old boy and George, whose wages were then ten shillings a week, was never tipped by him for shepherding his girlfriends into the lift up to his apartment. Most of the other gents were always generous to the hired help. Lord Wakefield from Wakefield Oil used to give half-crown tips every week, enormous money for those times, and John Dewar generously had delivered a whole lamb, turkeys, boxes of shortcakes and hampers at Christmastime and a white five pound note. What a good old man he was. Even though he only had one leg, he was always smiling.

In 1939 when I was seven, Sheepcote Lane was pulled down and we moved to a brand new block of flats at 32 Croxteth House, Union Street, Wandsworth Road. This was luxury compared to before. Our new home was a three-bedroom council flat which had electricity and a bathroom and wash basin – 'thank God no more tin-baths'.

One day my father took me to a boxing match at Blackfriars Ring near The Cut on the south bank of the Thames. Also at around this time, just before the war started, my brother Herbie did a bit of amateur boxing. There were pictures of him in the local newspaper with Kid Bessel from Bristol who used to come and stay at our house and they'd frequently go down to Blackfriars ring to watch the big fights and they'd tell me all about them. I had been fascinated by the sport from before I could walk, when I had watched the bareknuckled contests outside The Flag pub.

· 2 ·
Hard Times

I was a product of the war years. We grew up with a strong sense of loyalty, bravery and honour instilled into our psyche – even at the risk of death. Although I was too young to fight in the war, the lesson was drummed in: if captured by the Gestapo, you would never reveal information no matter what the outcome. The public were continually brainwashed. Everywhere you looked, on trains and buses were slogans like: 'Be like Dad, keep Mum', and 'Careless talk costs lives', and 'Walls have ears' etc., etc.

In the struggle to survive within our own little world, the 'enemy' became the authorities and the lessons from brainwashing we received as children applied to them. Cossers in particular. My father's refusal to talk to police, let alone acknowledge them, was virtually inborn in the family.

As kids, we practised our reading on these public propaganda signs which were not exclusively directed against the enemy. They also advised on the nation's health: 'Coughs and sneezes spread diseases. Trap the germs in your handkerchief and help to keep the nation fighting fit.'

We also learned to be street smart, to survive without food, and to take care of ourselves in a fight. We lived just for the day. Tomorrow we could be blown to bits.

The English are a barbaric and warrior-like race although the public only recognises this attribute during wars. Young men in particular need to let off steam and prisons would have far fewer inmates if the authorities helped youths channel their energies in positive ways.

I am a warrior. I would defend England to the death if need be, and I admire the fighting spirit for which we have been recognised throughout the ages. I remember reading a Roman soldier's account of the bravery of a British warrior fighting with Queen Boudicca when she rose against the Romans. The soldier sliced the British warrior through the jaw with an axe. A lesser man would have fallen but not the Briton. He tucked his beard into his mouth, holding it with clenched teeth and came back on the attack with his jaw wide open.

Nothing has changed since then. We proved it during the First and Second World Wars and in the Falklands. We are a fighting nation and I'm proud of the fact. Even Hitler said give me the British soldier and a German officer and I'll conquer the world. That inbred loyalty which wins battles and keeps alive national pride is also evident in prisons. The men I served time with would sacrifice their liberty to stay solid with you.

Having been brought up in a violent era I have learnt to understand some of the forces which dictated my actions. Obviously I went over the top on a number of occasions and I would put that down to the madness of youth.

Although young men at the time never considered the implications, if someone died as a result of a fight you could very easily find yourself facing a murder charge. And in the 1950s and 60s the death penalty was still in force. In spite of that you continued to risk life and liberty in doing violent battle with others.

As young men we had no fear. Nobody wanted to lose their freedom or their life but there was literally nothing that could frighten us. Physical pain was something you accepted as inevitable and confidence inspired by youth made you think you were infallible.

If you took part in a serious fight and someone got

hurt, you would take every precaution to avoid arrest, but at the crucial point of battle, nothing could deter you, particularly if your foe was a liberty-taker.

Violence and bloodshed had been commonplace in my formative years. At the start of the Second World War, our family were among the privileged first to be moved into the brand new block of flats in Croxteth House, Wandsworth Road.

The only downside – which became obvious to us a couple of months after moving in – was the location. Opposite us was a projectile munitions factory identified to the enemy by Fifth Columnists. As a result it – and the surrounding area – became a target for German bombers. Next to the factory was a foundry and we would watch a small train carrying the white-hot, glowing shells for storage on a concrete base across the road. In winter we kids stood close to the shells for warmth. The factory was targeted many times during the war but only hit twice. Instead, most streets in the area were wiped out by bombs missing their mark.

War films were constantly being shown at the movies. War was part of our lives. My first memory of it was watching an aerial dog fight high above London on a clear summer's day. The sky became a spaghetti junction made up of vapour trails from Spitfires and Messerschmitts. At first, nobody took any notice. It was only when the black-out sirens sounded that we were warned to get under cover to avoid fallout from shrapnel.

From our first-floor window at Croxteth House I would watch the WAAF girls practise putting up barrage balloons filled with helium gas to deter bombers from flying too low. As the war progressed we lived in daily fear of bombs. Other than being killed outright by a direct hit, windows and doors represented the greatest threat of injury; flying glass could be a killer and so could a door ripped off its hinges and sent flying through the room. We were advised to cover the glass to stop it shattering or, if the windows were blown out, to staple transluscent material in their place until workmen could be sent to make repairs.

There were six concrete shelters at the back of our flats with bunk beds littered around. When the bombing started, people would pour into them bringing their bedding and food. There were no toilets, just tin buckets behind a tarpaulin sheet for about forty people. Even then I thought it was quite degrading to hear the sound of adults urinating all through the night. The refuge the shelters provided was awful. There was no privacy. From a dark corner you would hear couples carrying on their sex lives, grunting and groaning: 'Ooh, you're hurting me Joe,' – I would be trying to see through half-closed eyes what was going on but couldn't work out why two people should be lying on top of each other facing the same way.

All my older brothers joined up and fought in the war. Watching them go was a stirring experience. Young men dressed in uniform with kitbags and rifles making their way down to sign on at Parliament Square, Westminster, under the gaze of Big Ben.

Their first steps to war began with a march across Westminster Bridge amid the fanfare of brass bands and cheering crowds. The younger kids followed them all the way to Waterloo Station. But they didn't know what they were letting themselves in for. Later the young servicemen were to say it was safer being with the Forces than facing the Blitz in London.

Wally, who was in the territorials, was awaiting a posting abroad. Herbie had already joined the King's Royal Rifles (my father's old regiment) and George was in the Navy. When the bombing got too bad, I was evacuated with my brother Bert. The people who billeted kids got about fifty pence a week per child so that was quite a decent amount of money. But it was horrible for me.

The first time I was sent away I was given an apple, an

orange, a bar of chocolate and a gas mask in a cardboard box with a string around it. You never went anywhere without that. My name-tag was attached by safety pin to my coat, and we said a tearful goodbye to my parents at Waterloo Station.

Bert and I arrived at Woking and were taken to a church hall. We sat on the floor while people walked about picking us out like cattle. 'I'll take him, not that one . . .'

An official replied: 'You can't separate them, they're brothers.' But they did. Bert was chosen by a nice family. They had a lovely home and later wanted to adopt him. I was left on my own feeling totally rejected. Out of a church hall full of young kids, I had endured the pain of watching each one being chosen by a host family, wondering when my turn would come. When they took my brother away, my heart sank. How could they leave me? Why not take me? What was wrong with me? I was heartbroken.

Evacuees were generally looked down on. Eventually, an awful woman with five children of her own picked me out. Now that Bert had been taken away from me I felt completely alone. I was as miserable as arseholes. The woman's place was dirty. We all had to pile in the same bed with her sons. One morning I woke to find myself and the sheets covered in blood. This kid I was sleeping with had TB and had been coughing up blood throughout the night.

To wash me, this woman would try and get me to stand in the sink with no clothes on. I didn't like it. There was no relationship within that family. The old man never acknowledged us. There was no conversation and very little to eat. At least at home in London there was love, cleanliness and food. I was billeted for only one reason, to supplement the family income by fifty pence.

My mother visited me there to see if I was all right. Hoping she'd come to collect me, I ran over to her expectantly and she leant over the fence at the school playground saying: 'Look at the state of you, Fred.' And then, to my embarrassment, in front of the other kids, she spat on her handkerchief and tried to clean me up, washing my face and my ears. She even came back to the house with me and and I remember thinking as she viewed the dirt and squalor – now she'd surely take me home, but she didn't. The bombing in London was still too heavy.

Now I was really miserable again. She'd left me a second time. But then a month or two later, I was walking home from school and looked up the country road to see my father standing there. I just ran up to him. He put his arms out and I grabbed him round the waist. 'Come on, Freddie,' he said gently. 'I'm taking you home. If the Germans bomb us, we'll all go together.' He came back to the house, collected my bits and pieces and we went home to London – I was overjoyed.

Unfortunately the pleasure of returning was shortlived. London was still being heavily bombed so I was evacuated for a second time, to Earthlingborough, Northampton. Herbie arranged it for me. While on leave from the Army, he had met a girl called Judy who was to become his wife, and he'd asked her parents to billet me. I'll never forget the journey to King's Cross Station. I sat silently on the bus, my heart breaking at having to leave my home and family and live once again with strangers.

I liked Judy's father but her mother was not that keen on having me stay. They were middle-class and owned a shoe shop. A south London cockney kid was not really their cup of tea. Next door to them lived a nice young lad with whom I had got on really well, but when his parents noticed that he started talking like me, they stopped us playing together. That's the kind of neighbourhood it was.

I was grateful to move away from them to a family called York who were bakers. I went out on deliveries with Mr York and enjoyed a new freedom. While I was staying there, Herbie arrived in a Bren gun carrier chewing up the street and leaving deep marks in the bitumen. Then Wally came to visit. He was an Army despatch rider, wearing trousers with leather inside, big brown boots, and a .45 gun in his belt. Their visits were the highlights of my stay.

The Yorks were upset when I left. Although they had a son and daughter of their own, they had grown quite attached to me. The curious thing is that I always kept myself apart. In winter the family would gather around the fire and invite me to join them but I would sit on a hard-backed chair on the opposite side of the room, listening to the radio, thinking how pleased I would be to get back to my own family. I hated being sent away and missed my parents and brothers. Nobody could take their place.

After Northampton, I was evacuated twice more to Hove, Brighton. The house where I stayed was on a hill facing down to the sea. One day I saw several dray horses shed their load as they bolted down the hill and crossed the main road, crashing through a grocery shop window. The whole episode was very messy but I watched, fascinated, as police held down the horses while a man in a suit put a metal frame on each horse's forehead and killed them with a spike and club hammer. Those images stay with you for life. For a boy of ten, I saw far too much blood and guts.

Mrs Freeland, my Hove billet, was quite a fat lady who sold her body as a sideline. She used to tart herself up with rouge and bright red lipstick then march out to the seafront in her white strappy sandals to earn a bit extra while her husband was away on nightshift. She always made sure she was back before he returned.

Mrs Freeland's son and I once nicked a whole tin of chocolate biscuits and sat in bed eating them until we felt really sick. We did quite a bit of nicking and I became a dab hand. In London during one particular air raid, I took the old battered pram in which I used to fetch coal from Nine Elms coal yard and put a brick through the window of a grocery shop in Wandsworth Road. We loaded the pram with Australian canned fruit and made a dash back to our flats. My parents would not have approved, so me and my mates ate it in secret in the bomb shelter till we made ourselves sick.

After Brighton I was determined not to be sent away again. There was a lull in the bombing, due to the Germans having lost most of their planes. But new and more dangerous missiles were imminent – the V1 and V2 rockets. The government at first misled people about the V2 bombings. To avoid panic, propaganda was spread throughout the media, putting the blasts down to gas explosions rather than the rockets which were killing thousands in central London.

As frightening as the bombing was, it was also fascinating. I will never forget the sight of a young woman caught in a bomb blast under an arch. When I noticed her, she was picking herself up off the middle of the road, her clothes had been blown away and her stockings were in shreds. I watched as she tried to hide her modesty. For a twelve-year-old it was a very erotic scene and the first time that I had laid eyes on a semi-naked woman.

Large numbers of civilians were killed by doodlebugs and rockets and you would see young children whose limbs had been torn from their bodies, and rows of dead people laid out on the pavements, some killed in shelters, others pulled out of their wrecked houses. Tragically a bomb scored a direct hit on the King's Arms one night killing nearly all the customers, including several of our neighbours who were having a pint.

My parents were lucky to have four boys survive the war although there were moments when they feared the worst. I can remember Lord Haw Haw's propaganda programmes on the radio. In spite of the fact that he was a Nazi propagandist, he pulled a large audience. One particular night we heard him say: 'Germany calling, Germany calling. This is Lord Haw Haw speaking . . . The Fuhrer's Navy today sunk the minesweeper *Fitzroy* in the English Channel. All hands were lost . . .'

George was on that boat and we were all convinced he was dead. My mother burst into tears. My father was visibly distressed but kept a stiff upper lip. I sensed their tremendous sadness. Over the next day or two, we waited with anguish for the knock on the door when the official telegram would bring the bad news.

Days later, I was leaning over the balcony, deep in thought and looking down at the square when I saw a figure coming into the housing estate in a boiler suit and a sailor hat. As the figure loomed larger I couldn't believe what I was seeing. It was George! My George! He was alive. I couldn't contain my excitement. I could hear mother washing up in the kitchen and shouted to her, 'Quick Mum, it's our George. He's alive!' Mum rushed out disbelieving me but wiping her hands on her apron as she joined me to look over the balcony into the square.

'Georgie!' she cried out. George, a big grin on his face, waved his arm cheerfully and my mother rushed to the top of the stairs and hugged him and cried with joy. The old man got out the hard stuff and that night it was down to the local Portland Arms for a good session.

George told us the story of how his ship had struck a mine and went down in four minutes. He had just finished his duty-watch in the stoke hole. The ship had capsized and he crawled out hand over fist, upside-down along an escape ladder and jumped into the North Sea. He'd managed to get into a life-raft but had to go back in the water again to make way for a petty officer with an injured back. He was in the water for two hours before they were rescued by HMS *Elgin*, another minesweeper, and taken to Great Yarmouth. All his possessions were lost and he and the other seamen were given fresh clothes and two weeks' compassionate leave. But they were recalled after only a week and sent off to Mombasa, East Africa, on the *Stirling Castle* troop carrier. While he was out there, George joined the cruiser HMS *Mauritius*. It was a notorious ship. They had more arrests on that ship than on any other in the British fleet. At one point there was nearly a mutiny on board.

A book could be written about my brother Herbie who fought in eleven different countries for King and Country and escaped death on a number of occasions. He was one of twenty-two of his battalion of 600 to survive a drop into Arnhem.

We kept an open house in those days to whoever was a friend of the boys. They would come to Mum's and stay on their short home-leave. During black-outs, I would lead friends of my brothers to the local pub when they came on leave to stay with us. I knew my way there blindfolded. One was Bertie Chapman, a pal of George's.

An inevitable problem arising from the war was the amount of armoury entering the country. My brother Herbie brought home Lee Enfield bolt action .303 rifles, and his mates would bring back pistols and knives as souvenirs. My brothers presented me with German bayonets and daggers, which I proudly showed to my friends.

Herbie and Wally, both paratroopers in the First Airborne Division, had access to all kinds of weapons, including knuckle-dusters. They even had dyed-blue, wooden bullets which had been used to save on metal. Everywhere you went in the less gentrified areas of London, metal railings had been pulled out to help the war effort. The middle- and upper-classes living in areas like Belgravia and Knightsbridge were spared this inconvenience.

Schools, when lessons were not interrupted by bombs,

were run on a very strict basis. They caned you and battered you for the slightest misdemeanour. I was always
in trouble and very nearly expelled for letting off some
fireworks.

The bombsites around us were ideal for fighting. All
around were tunnels and wasteland where mock battles
would be fought. Fireworks represented live ammunition although, on some days, real bullets were used. I
broke into a shed next to the temporary school and
nicked all the smoke-bombs and crackers belonging to
the Army and let them off in the girls' lavatory. The
school notified the police and three of us responsible for
this outrage were dragged to the front of assembly and
given a terrible dressing down by the headmistress. 'You
are nothing but Nazi children! Hitler's children! Nazi
youth!' she said venomously.

This was too much. I protested. 'I've got four brothers
fighting the Germans. I'm not a Nazi!' One of the problems with school was that by the time I was fourteen and
showed an interest in learning, it was time to leave. But
even so, they could have encouraged my natural ability
in art, the only subject in which I excelled.

My art reflected my environment. I drew battle scenes,
tanks, artillery, aircraft and scenes of carnage. I had an
artist's eye for detail. I could tell a Wellington bomber
from a Lancaster, a Hurricane from a Spitfire, a Heinkel
from a Messerschmitt and could identify enemy tanks. I
drew gory fights where death came at the point of a bayonet or a bullet.

Those images were true to life. I was getting the violence down on paper. My reputation began to spread.
Schoolkids went out of their way to see what I had
drawn and offers were made to swap comics for my art.
I started to take this further and drew my own action
comics. This led to a fight between two pupils who
argued over what I was drawing one day.

One of the kids punched the other in the face, and a

pencil he was holding went right through the victim's rosy cheek. I got the blame for that and it alerted the teacher to my art. He took my drawing and examined it in detail. I probably had about one hundred figures on it: Germans and British troops, action scenes involving tanks and aircraft, buildings being blown up, barbed wire, killings. A lot of work had gone into it. The teacher summoned his colleagues and examined it. 'This is one sick little bastard,' they must have said.

But it was a comment on the times. There were always guns in the house, German Lugers, old service revolvers, Japanese swords and crudely made scabbards and Arab daggers. I used to love playing with them.

In spite of my bad school record, I had a grudging respect for Mr Nye, who regularly beat me with the cane. Although he had a withered arm he had this amazing robotic capacity to administer six of the best while speaking to the rest of the class at the same time. Unlike other teachers he would pay me compliments for my sporting abilities. I won all the races at school and he would tell everyone: 'That boy's got shoulders on him like a horse.'

At one point I remember seeing a parachute come down. Men ran to it, prepared to lynch the German pilot who'd dropped these bombs on us. But instead of a German, there was a landmine attached to it and a couple of streets were blown up.

Towards the end of the war, my father was on warden duty when a doodlebug hit us late at night. My mother and I were in the shelter and my father came down, his face covered in brick-dust and blood trickling from his forehead. he'd been blown up in the blast and came looking for us. 'I'm all right Lou,' he told my mother. 'But we've lost everything.' Croxteth House was reduced to rubble and we were moved first to a two-roomed temporary accommodation in Wickersley Road, Battersea, and then moved to Usk Road, at the top of Clapham

Junction West Hill. Our balcony overlooked the railway.

Bertie arrived home on leave in his Navy outfit, all nice and white. Whenever one of the boys came home they'd be cooked a special breakfast of bacon and eggs. While mum was preparing this treat for Bertie, there was a terrific explosion.

As mum walked to the kitchen the blast lifted up the thick lino from the floor, stopping the door, which had been blown off its hinges, from hitting her in the face. Soot blackened the flat and all you could see of Bert was his white teeth and eyes, looking like a Kentucky minstrel. 'Oh Bert, look at your eggs and bacon!' said mum. She was more concerned about the pile of soot over his eggs and bacon then the fact the front of the flat had been blown away. The V2 had dropped on the other side of the railway embankment, shielding us from a blast that had killed many others.

Croxteth House was rebuilt and we moved back again. Most of our personal belongings and family 'treasures' were lost. We had to make do with very few possessions. Furniture was non-existent. You had to improvise tables and chairs from tea chests: THESE WERE REALLY HARD TIMES.

· 3 ·
Your Country Needs You

The slogan before and during the war was: Your Country Needs You. Now that the war was over *you* needed the country. I was young enough not to be disillusioned with the way the system worked and old enough to be aware that those with nothing got nothing. My four brothers, and our father in the First World War, had been willing to lay down their lives for their country. When the war was over, they got very little in return. On being demobbed, you had the choice of either a Prince of Wales checked suit, or a blue pin-striped suit and a gratuity of about £60 to £80.

Everybody you saw those days was dressed in the check suit and I could sense some of the bitterness and resentment that accompanied their paltry reward. My brothers George and Wally were only skilled at killing Germans, so the jobs they were offered were quite lowly: digging trenches at the top of Northcote Road and building prefabricated houses mostly made of asbestos. The boss didn't like them so they got the sack after two weeks. My brothers then put their money together and, with a little extra from my father's meagre savings, bought a stall, and a horse and cart.

They parked it on the corner of Princess Head, Battersea and sold fruit and vegetables with a sideline in logging. I helped them although I was still at school, and we went scavenging on bomb sites, dragging out old rail sleepers, cutting them up with large cross-saws, then chopping them up into bundles to sell as firewood. I was in my element working with my brothers.

But a freezing winter and an impoverished neighbourhood did not make for good business, so George went back to work doing what he was used to in the Navy. He shovelled coal off barges on to a conveyor belt in the Thames for Nine Elms power station. That was a terrible job, breathing in all the grime and dust in a hold full of coal. You could see the lines from this tough existence etched into his face. Even though he was a good-looking chap with fair skin and blond hair, he was ageing prematurely. There must have been a couple of kilos of coaldust in his lungs and he still suffers with his chest today.

The war had done nothing to dispel our mistrust of uniforms, coppers and authority in general. You trusted no one. Not even the officers. They shot you in the First World War and they, in turn, were executed by the soldiers. Shot in the back. My father told me about that. So when our lot came out of the Army and saw someone thieving, they would look the other way as long as the victim wasn't one of their own. That attitude was very prominent in the period after the war.

We had lived on the edge. A German bomb could have ended our existence at any moment but we felt that youth was invincible. We were too busy enjoying the excitement and exhilaration of discovery – and Milky.

Milky Big Tits was a good sort. Big busted with blonde hair down to her waist and nice long legs. Just the type of girl I always fancied. I was fourteen and a virgin when I met her. Milky (her real name was Olive) was a couple of years older than me. She was brazen and adventurous. Nobody could wish for a better introduction to manhood than spending some sticky moments with a girl as eager to please as she was.

Milky went beyond the call of duty. The more we indulged the more she enjoyed it. The backdrop to this nonsense was anything but romantic. We just had a kiss and cuddle ending in a knee trembler against a brick wall within the compounds of a bombed-out school at Larkhall Lane, just around the corner from our old council flat in Wandsworth Road, which was being rebuilt.

'Catch me and I'm yours,' she'd say. From time to time she would allow one or two other boys to catch her but she was physically able to resist our advances if she didn't fancy the outcome.

Sharing these sexual encounters with mates extended Milky's horizons even further. After I'd had my wicked way, I would talk her into letting a pal have a go. Without too much persuasion, she would say: 'All right, but just this once.'

Then they would start queuing: Johnny Brindle, Ronnie Mitchell, and the Long brothers: George, Teddy, Tommy and Jimmy. Jimmy was only a little kid, probably about nine or ten. When it came to his turn, the big boys would shove him to the end of the queue and Milky would snort: 'He's too little. He can't do it!'

But little Jimmy was determined. 'Yes I can, yes I can,' he'd insist. Every time he was pushed out of the queue he'd race to the end and wait patiently for another chance.

Taking pity, we'd plead: 'Come on, let him have a go. At least he'll shut up.' Eventually she'd relent but it was all over in a wink and none of us ever discovered whether Jimmy had made it, or not, or whether Milky was aware of the fact.

Milky, like the rest of us, had experienced the ravages of war. Two years earlier, a bullet had smashed through a brick and grazed her breast, so perhaps enjoying life meant more to her. I had to laugh at the memory of us boys and Milky sitting around a bonfire together with our trusted black mongrel, 'Gyp'.

With the war, very few schools were left standing and I left at the age of fourteen, with few qualifications, and got a job with South Western Railways as a driver's mate delivering goods in London and all over southern England. We started off with an old Iron Horse, a three-wheeler petrol-driven truck which you would hook up to a horse-box and take the horses to different stables. We then graduated to a Bedford truck which had tarpaulin sheets on the back and could hook up to trailers, some with containers already loaded. The jobs were diverse. We could be delivering fruit to Covent Garden one day, and gold to the Bank of England the next. Sometimes we'd take a load of metal drums filled with coins to the Royal Mint. When delivering bullion, we were paid an extra £2 on top of our £5-a-week-wages for the heavy work involved.

Alfie, my driver, was not backward when it came to nicking loads of fruit from the market. We'd take luxury items like lovely Cape grapes and peaches and fruit. Those days you never saw anything like that at local shops, and down it would go under the seat in the front cabin of the truck, hidden by a blanket. Alternatively, we'd deliver a load and damage some of the parcels, pulling out some of the contents, like shirts perhaps, from the middle. Everybody was doing it. Crane drivers in the docklands would always drop a load on purpose. If it was a crate of whisky, they would nick a few bottles of Scotch that had remained intact and write off the whole load.

Never had my senses been so aroused as by the sight of all the gold we had volunteered to collect from King's Cross when I was still a lad of fourteen. We backed the Southern Railway Iron Horse, with tarpaulin sides and a sheet at the back with leather straps to close it from prying eyes, right up to the railway carriage. Inside was a fortune in wedge-shaped gold bars, two on the bottom, two across, one on top, neatly packed so you could get your fingers underneath each precious bar. All together the load would have been worth several million pounds.

And all we had guarding this lot was a fourteen-year-old boy (me), two coppers, and a government official next to Alfie, the driver, who was one of a family of well-known greengrocers in those parts. We would drive from King's Cross to the Bank of England in Thread-needle Street or, if we had coins, we took them to the Royal Mint on the north side of Tower Bridge. Snatching the gold would have been the easiest bit of work ever for anyone with a little bit of enterprise. I fantasised even then about nicking it. At today's prices, each bar would have fetched £100,000, and I lovingly cradled those bars like I would a child. The deliveries were made on a fairly regular basis and because of the heavy work were unpopular, and word quickly got around because everyone was asked to volunteer. It would have been easy for us to tell someone where it was coming from, but those days, people weren't that way inclined. They didn't think of thieving big lumps of money. But for me, a seed was sown.

My next job was at Pannet and Eden as a warehouseman. They were based in Wandsworth and did herbs and stuffing as well as hair cream and associated products. One job involved carrying hundredweight sacks full of breadcrumbs up ladders and stairs, which built up my strength. Another part of the job was handling 56lb boxes of lard or fat intended for the stuffing – so my mother's family and friends were never short of hair oil, mint sauce, stuffing or lard. Nor were many of the women working in Pannet and Eden. I would wrap chunks of lard in greaseproof paper and slip it into their open handbags. I never charged them a penny for this although a number showed their appreciation in different ways, usually among the empty sacks in the loft above the storage rooms. We were still on ration books shortly after the war and limited to only about an ounce of lard per person, per week, so I became the most popular young male among forty-five women workers.

People always go on about men on building sites, but

you have to see it to believe what women get up to in factories. The old ones were the worst. They'd grab your dick and get a little too excited. If you gave them a playful kiss, you'd get a tongue down your throat.

With a wage of £4.50 a week I'd nick anything to make up for the hard work I had to do. A good line was women's make-up which would get you a few quid on top of your wages. I stayed at Pannet's for about a year, the longest I've had in any job and eventually got sacked when someone grassed me up for giving cooking lard to one of the women. The sack came out of the blue, but it didn't worry me very much and I went to work for Stevens and Carter, a scaffolding firm.

The only person to be really upset at my abrupt departure from Pannet's, was a lovely spinster of about forty called Gladys. She cried when she heard I'd been dismissed. Gladys lived with another, more elderly woman. She was tall and thin with dark hair swept back and wore glasses. While she was no beauty, her nature made her a lovely person. She didn't have a bad word for anyone and was always kind and laughing. Gladys had a lovely little twinkle in her eye and I think she got quite attached to me, not sexually, you understand, but in a maternal way, like an affectionate aunt. I used to chat to her quite a lot, and we got on well together. I would help her tie parcels and lift them off the bench after she'd packed them up. She talked to me about life in general and liked to see me enjoying myself.

Gladys was well aware of what I was up to with some of the young girls working on the factory floor. She became my accomplice and would leave me in the warehouse with the girls, shut the door, and say: 'You two stay there . . .' I last saw Gladys when I was fifteen and was very upset some years later to learn that she had committed suicide. I was too sad to ask the details, but she must have been a troubled soul or very ill to do that. But years later a very strange set of events took place.

Gladys made what I can only describe as psychic contact with me during moments of great stress. I was thirty-seven years old and in the depths of despair after being charged with the Frank Mitchell murder when Gladys 'spoke' to me. I could hear her voice saying: 'It's all right Fred. Calm down. Take it easy. It's going to be all right.'

Gladys came to me again when I was kidnapped and brought back to England from Spain and I know she is always there to help me in times of crisis. She's lovely, my Gladys. A guardian angel sent to comfort me in times of need. I hope and pray she is now at peace and that I won't need her services any more.

Her death, like the death of my parents, possibly affected me more than it might otherwise have done because I was never able to mourn for them. I was unable to attend the funerals of my father, mother and sister-in-law Nellie because harsh prison rules would not allow me out. Tommy Wisbey also had a tough time after he was jailed for the Great Train Robbery. While he was doing his thirty years he lost his teenage daughter, Lorraine, in a car accident and was not allowed out to attend her funeral. I was godfather to his other daughter Marilyn and he was godfather to my son Gregory.

At that time I was unable to grieve their loss with the rest of the family and, somehow, your mind doesn't accept they are dead if you don't go through the ritual of a funeral service. I still wake up at times and, just for a moment, think I must go round and see if the old man and mum are all right. And then it slowly dawns on me that they are no longer here . . . but back to my youth.

Scaffolding was considered a macho job and attracted strong young men including ex-soldiers. We were all south London men working on a site at Hatfield College, near the Armstrong Siddeley aircraft factory in Hertfordshire. The college had received deliveries of a large amount of sheet copper in packs of one hundred-weight rolls, and I immediately saw the potential of nicking it. The rolls were stored under lock and key in a large metal bunker at the back of the site next to some woods accessible only by a dirt road.

To help me with this enterprise, I engaged the services of an elderly man called Fat Joe and his partner Claude, an evil-looking bastard with dark, slitty eyes. Fat Joe weighed about twenty stone and he and his partner owned the right vehicles to get the load away. They told me they would be able to sell the metal in Croydon.

An ex-guardsman who was supposed to be minding the site was more often than not in the village pub with his big bastard of an Alsatian dog. The man was a bully and very unpopular with the locals and some of our lads who had already had punch-ups with him. I timed the robbery for when he was at the pub. We drove up the dirt road and knocked off the paddy (padlock) to the steel shed, then we loaded up two big old cars, a Ford V8 shooting brake and a Chrysler. It was all dense weight but we cleaned most of it out. The operation was a success and proved to be a nice little earner.

Next day when I returned to work, enquiries about the theft were already proceeding. Stevens and Carter scaffolders didn't suspect me but, as I was sitting eating in the canteen, the guard's Alsatian walked up to me and started sniffing me out. As if that was not enough, he then plonked himself down in front of me and sat staring at me. Never suspecting anything, my workmates made a joke of it: 'Are you sure you never nicked it Fred?' they asked and then jokingly said: 'Look at the dog watching you!' The bloody animal looked as if he was about to spring on me! This went on for a few days but, thank God, only the dog sussed me out.

While working as a scaffolder, I had a relationship with a little firecracker called Joyce who was separated from her husband. There were other girls too who were quite saucy, nearly one in every block on my estate, and I used to cop for quite a few of them. But Joyce was a bit special. I'd met her at a party and took her outside for a drink on the balcony. She was more forward than I expected. She took off her knickers, put them in her handbag and, without waiting, undid my trousers and jumped on me, wrapping her legs around my waist, and clinging to my neck. Then she started bouncing up and down like a bloody rabbit. It had never happened to me like that before. My mother poked her head around the door and caught us at it while I was banging away like a good 'un. Later she warned me to stay away from that girl. But I found her a sexy little thing and she knew a lot more than I did; she taught me a thing or two.

Joyce was a little bit on the tarty side. She was very attractive with a nice body and cheeky eyes. I used to take her down a dark alleyway and she was quite happy having it there, as anywhere. Our relationship thrived until I saw her with another guy walking down the same alleyway which I thought was special only to us. But obviously I was wrong. She was not true to me but I was infatuated with her. I was with Lennie Sunbourne, a relation of mine, when she walked past. I hadn't seen her at first because I was buying a cup of tea and a hotdog sandwich at a stall. Then Lennie pointed her out and I pretended I didn't care. But, of course, I did. These things brew in your mind. She was heading for our alleyway.

I went down there just as they were coming out again and chinned the geezer. He went spark out. I then gave her a backhander and called her a fucking slag. My ring had sliced open the geezer's cheek and Joyce got down on her knees to help him. 'Look what you've done!' she cried.

I told Joyce not to come near me any more and walked back to the flats. A short time afterwards, I heard an ambulance siren and then a worried Lennie tapped on my door: 'Did you do him with a brick, Fred?' he asked. 'He's in a hell of a state, never regained consciousness.' I had a right dodgy night worrying about the cossers coming round. But it had only been one punch, a right hander. The guy never grassed me to the police so I was okay.

Later, Joyce came to my local and tried to make up. I was nearly tempted but I blanked her completely. I was hurt and felt she had done the dirty on me. In fact, she was just a lively and lovely girl who worked in the button factory and was a good little jiver.

Anyway, there were always plenty of other girls about but I must admit Joyce was a bit special. I had quite a lot of romantic little flings, as you can imagine, and I know that there are one or two little Freddies about, but I can't go into details as I don't want to embarrass anyone who may be married with a family. The last thing I want is to cause any problems. But I often feel that I would like to hire a hall and get all my old friends and family together for a big nosh- and drink-up and chat about old times and see the kids who have grown up.

Enough of that and on with the story. I retired from scaffolding after falling from a second-floor level. Although I landed on my feet, I got pinned to a plank of wood with this rusty old nail. It went right through the sole of my shoe and into my foot. I was taken to Hatfield hospital and given antibiotic injections. My leg felt like a war was going on inside. It throbbed like fuck for about a week. This was a good time to leave the scaffolding job. Winter was also coming on and scaffolding wasn't much fun in lousy weather. I went to see George who was still shovelling coal and told him he had to stop that and do a bit of work with me.

We met a guy who said we could earn good money for a few months' work pile driving. We needed two extra men to make up the work team, a steel fixer and another to control the pile driver and change the sections over as the holes for building foundations got deeper. It was a bit like drilling for oil. A big crane smashed down these metal and concrete tubes deep into the ground, some twenty-five feet or so till it hit rock bottom. Then I would slip the steel cage that I had fixed and that fell to the bottom and the steel rods would stick out of the top, ready for the concrete. Once that was poured in and set, the foundations would be solid enough for blocks of flats or flyovers.

I suppose that's how the stories of Ginger Marks's disappearance came about and speculation that he had been buried under a flyover. Mind you, if you did stick someone down one of those holes, they would have to pull the whole building down to find anything, so it's not a bad idea, and it did cross my mind on one or two occasions years later.

On most Saturday nights, we'd go to the dances with big band sounds. All the town halls had English bands like Vic Lewis, Ted Heath and Ivor Kerchin playing American big band music. I remember seeing Ted and Barbara Andrews and their daughter Julie singing on stage at the Grand, Clapham Junction. Most of the upcoming stars would appear there: Peter Sellers, Harry Secombe, and Michael Bentine.

Harry Secombe's farmyard imitations would bring the house down, as would Sellers's impersonations of film stars. The Grand would also put on boxing exhibitions with the likes of Freddie Mills and Frankie Hough. The entertainment industry had started up again in a big way because during the war large numbers of people were prevented from congregating in one place in case they were bombed. Manpower was at a premium.

We enjoyed the sounds of Ted Heath and his orchestra, the Squadronairs, Vic Lewis, and the Ray Ellington quartet. My mates at the time included Patsy Toomey, Lennie White, Jimmy Turner, Tommy Wisbey, Tony Reuter, Jacky Cramer, Arthur and Teddy Suttie, Billy Adams, Freddy and Dinny Powell, who we called Nosher after his father who was a horse trader at the arches behind the Elephant and Castle.

I was also a member of the Battersea Boxing Club run by a Mr Hall. One of his trainers was old Billy Whitely, the same one who used to come to parties at my parents' house and load me up with pennies. I introduced the gang to the club because they were all pretty keen to learn as we often fought with other gangs in the streets.

I had problems with a gang down the Wandsworth Road so we got together to sort them out. During one streetfight, a guy jumped out of an upstairs window onto my back while I was battling with his brother. He was a lot older than me and looked well-muscled in his Navy white vest. But I think he must have regretted coming home on leave from the Navy because some of us beat the shit out of him. We really fancied ourselves at the fight game. Patsy Toomey would ask: 'Who's the best fighter around here? Go and fetch him and I'll have a straightener.' On one occasion we were at a stall down the World's End in Chelsea. Patsy challenged this guy and I held their coats. There were five of us and about thirty of the other gang.

Everyone crowded around to watch the fight with cups of tea in their hands. 'Patsy, you better win this one,' I said to myself. But he came unstuck and the guy he was fighting had him pinned down and sat on his chest punching his head in. I couldn't stand seeing my pal hurt so I interfered. I pulled the guy off and smashed his head against the kerb and the next thing I heard was running feet followed by blow after blow smashing down on me. They were laying into me with their boots. I rolled under a parked lorry and got up on the other side. 'All right,' I said, 'let's make this one-to-one.'

One stepped forward and said: 'I'll have him.' We started to fight and, being a strong kid, I held my own for a long time until, exhausted, we both ended up on our knees facing each other, still punching it out. By mutual agreement, whispered in each other's ears, we'd had enough. That signalled an honourable tie-breaker. We stood up and shook hands and everybody went back to have another cup of tea. In a way, it was history repeating itself. We began where our fathers left off.

The dance halls and pubs also became a major venue for our brawling. We'd go into the pubs and bars, get tanked up and if anyone tried to chat up any one of our girls you would have a row and the place would degenerate into a free-for-all. Going to dance halls in different parts of London was like going to a football match and meeting the other team's supporters. If it was the Lyceum, you took a pitch in the corner and no one else was allowed there apart from us south London and Elephant and Castle boys.

Before the end of the night, there'd be a row and the girls would get excited and want to go home with you afterwards. It was all very macho stuff. The next day we'd dissect the fight and revel in our victory and relive the finer moments. Sometimes the fights would turn quite serious and tools like starting handles would be brought out. You'd also end up respecting one or two of the opposition and get pally with them in the future.

One of our gang had been to a wedding in Dulwich and a crowd of lads had bashed him up and taken liberties with him. He asked for a bit of help and as we were prepared to travel anywhere for a good row, we offered to sort things out for him. It was the done thing then.

With adrenalin flowing, we descended on the other gang at a youth club. A few got injured and the club was wrecked, but that was as much the fault of the other gang as it was ours. The main principals in this fracas, including me, got away while some of the lesser fry got nicked and stuck up all our names. A couple of days later I was dragged off to the nick, charged with assault, GBH (grievous bodily harm) and affray.

The police found a few coshes, made from steel rungs from a barber's shop chair, and a thick woollen sand-weighted sock belonging to a friend called Francis. I was too young to be put in Wormwood Scrubs prison so they put me into Stamford House Remand Centre, where a few of the warders were nonces. They were into young boys and at the same time were sadistic bastards who wanted to beat the shit out of you with canes and thick pieces of wood.

Police raised such a hue and cry over this case that it went to the Number One Court of the Old Bailey. It should never have come to trial let alone been heard in the Central Criminal Court. What a ridiculous waste of public money and police time. I was only sixteen years old and already I was in the most famous court in the land! Such treatment served only to elevate me in the eyes of my peers. The trial in 1948, heard by Sir Gerald Dodson, the Recorder, was full of comic moments. The prosecutor ran through a list of weapons and then held out Francis's smelly sand-filled sock at arm's length, turning his head away from it as he spoke.

Each time he used the phrase: 'and one sand-weighted sock', we lads in the dock – there were eleven of us – all repeated the phrase with our heads down, whispering the words with the QC: 'and one sand-weighted sock'. Then we went redder and redder, exchanging looks and stifling giggles and fits of laughter.

The judge bound us over and fined us £5 each. We were also ordered to be taken down to the cells at the Old Bailey to experience 'the feel of life behind bars'. Sir Gerald said: 'This experience should serve as a lifelong lesson. When you come out, look up to the sky and be thankful you can see it.'

I wonder if he was aware that we had already spent time in prisons and remand centres awaiting this trial as well as many hours in the cells under the Old Bailey awaiting his Lordship.

With all the practice we were getting inside and outside of the ring, our little firm got quite skilled in the art of fighting. I took Nosher's brother, Freddie Powell, down to the Battersea Boxing Club. Having a heavy-weight champion from the Army join your local club was a feather in your cap. He had several fights for the club and then turned professional.

The club officials got the horn when they saw Freddie who was a big sun-tanned 6ft 3in heavyweight. He was a real crowd-pleaser. Nobody left a show until they had seen him fight. The promoters always put him on last to keep the crowd and atmosphere alive. Nosher and Fred are still friends of mine today.

In my teens, I was a light welterweight at about 10 stone 3lbs. Patsy was two or three pounds lighter and Lenny White was only 9 stone 9lbs. We all gave our best in bouts but did very little training: a couple of times a week at most. The rest of the time we'd go to the big bands, drink beer and go out with the girls. We would also train at a number of different centres: the Budekai Club where I learned a bit of Ju Jitsu, and at the Battersea Boxing Club (Latchmere) and Joe Jones's gym in Islington.

On Sunday mornings we'd go to Jack Solomon's gym in Windmill Street, Soho. He ran a nursery for just a few young amateur boxers. And what an experience it was. Nat Sellers was the trainer then and Jack Solomon the fight promoter. He was a lovely man who was never without a big cigar in his mouth. Apart from American pros, we had people like Freddie Mills, George and Tommy Daley, Joe Carter, Tommy McGovern and Alby Hollister. Most of the active fighters in London worked out at Jack Solomon's gym at one time or another. Exhibition matches were put on about once a month between ourselves and could turn nasty if you got hurt and sought revenge on your sparring partner.

Stewart Grainger often came to Jack Solomon's. He was then a budding young actor in all the Gainsborough films with Margaret Lockwood and would comment on our fights. He said of me: 'Young Freddie Foreman is similar to Freddie Mills in his line of attack', and handed out a prize of dressing-gown and shorts. My father and brothers would proudly watch the proceedings from small wooden benches.

We kids were all protégés of Bud Flanagan of the Flanagan and Allen comedy duo. Bud was a nice old boy who used to give us free tickets for his West End shows and treat us to slap-up meals in Victoria before taking us to see his Crazy Gang show at Victoria Palace. We had some tough contests when we did the rounds at the bath fights. These were boxing matches arranged at venues like town halls and local baths. Our opponents were from other clubs and the three Armed Forces. We fought all over London. I must have had about thirty fights in all at venues which included Nine Elms (lots of times), Tooting Bec, Manor Place, Victoria Park, Bermondsey baths, Seymour Place baths, Shoreditch Town Hall and Grange Road baths. Fights were held nearly every week in those days. I had a few wars with opponents much older than myself, old timers who had been around for years. I was only in my mid-teens and they were in their late twenties and early thirties. It was quite hard work some nights because you could end up fighting three different opponents.

You might arrive for a novices competition at 6.30pm, fight an hour later, then go in the ring with the second opponent at 8.30pm and, if you got through the first two, then go on to the final at about 11pm. And during all those excruciating hours your black eyes would puff up more and your swollen nose become sorer and sorer. I had a couple of nights like those, only to get beaten in the final. I was so disappointed. I had set my heart on a beautiful cup and lost it to a guy I should have beaten.

At one fight in Nine Elms baths, two MPs (military police) had to bring an Army champ to fight me (apparently he was doing some chokey [imprisonment] in the stockades). He was all tattooed up, muscles everywhere.

A right hard bastard. It was only a three round fight in the welterweight division. A great but damaging fight. I really felt the pain afterwards. The girls we knew from the dance halls were there and they screamed the place down. It was the best fight of the night and they loved it. I gave as good as I got but he edged in on points.

Some years later, during a prison spell in Wandsworth, I ended up in the same cell with Joey Carter whom I had seen at Jack Solomon's. He was featherweight champion of south London and had fought Ronnie Clayton for the British featherweight title but lost in four rounds. Then Tommy McGovern got nicked for receiving and was sentenced to six months. I had the two of them in my cell! I felt sorry for Tom as he was basically a very straight person and couldn't handle prison life. It seemed like the end of the world to him.

Tommy was an ex-lightweight champion of Great Britain. All he and Joey talked about was boxing and as I was quite well up on the subject it renewed my urge to do a bit of training and fighting again when I got out. Soon after my release I turned professional under the experienced eye of Tommy Daly, training at the Thomas-à-Becket in Old Kent Road, south-east London. Tommy Daly's son John was later to become a well-known film producer working with David Hemmings in their company Hemdale Productions. Tommy got me fit with plenty of sparring and road work. I would run around Brockwell Park, Herne Hill, down to Camberwell Green, along to Loughborough Junction, under the arch and up Shakespeare Road and finish off in the park again. Then I'd run up Milton Road with my knees up to my chin for the last ten, as fighters call it, get indoors and do my mat work. Sit-ups, elbows to knees, all stomach work, wrap up and sweat it out. I got really fit. Tom used to put me in with a light heavyweight for three rounds, then a middleweight and a welterweight to speed me up. I was really banging hard even with the big sparring gloves. I caught the light heavy a shot and wobbled him after two rounds one day and they said enough. I didn't take liberties in sparring because we were in there to help and learn from each other.

When I had my medical, the doctor held his stethoscope to my chest and kept looking up at me making 'um, ah' sounds. He got me doing press-ups and listened to my heart again, saying: 'Very strange, very strange.' I wondered what the problem was. Perhaps there was something wrong with me and he was frightened to tell me? Years later, when I was in Full Sutton Prison, I discovered what it was. I have a very slow heartbeat: the average beat for a person is seventy and mine is only forty-five and that is very much in my favour. Thank God I've got something going for me. I had never been a smoker either so that worked in my favour as well.

All the local fighters from south London trained at the Thomas-à-Becket: Henry Cooper, George Cooper, Freddie Reardon, Dave Charnley and Charlie Tucker. Dave Charnley wound up British champion. Also Peter Waterman, Eddie Hughes, the Auld twins from Bermondsey and Fred and Dinny Powell.

Tommy had fixed me up with a guy from Croydon called Del Breen for my first professional fight at Manor Place baths. Del was experienced. He'd had about twenty pro fights, winning the last four on knockout so I was cannon fodder. Stan Baker was the promoter. Topping the bill were Henry and George Cooper, Dave Charnley, Freddie Reardon and Charlie Tucker. Then there was Del Breen and little old me on the undercard.

It was Tuesday evening, 23 November, 1954. Normally boys were given a few easy ones to get their confidence up and not get too hurt for about six or so fights. That's the general rule of a manager. Tom may have had second thoughts about pitting me against Del but even if he had wanted me to pull out, it was too late, because I had sold so many tickets. I was quite well-known and already had a bit of a reputation as a street-fighter.

The place was packed. I looked at Del. You could see every muscle in his body. He was a fit man. The first two rounds were all Del's. I couldn't match his experience. In the third he caught me with a good shot. I fell back on the ropes and the crowd went wild. I came back strong at the end of the third and caught him with a left and right hook, bang on the chin. I felt it go right up my arm to my shoulder. He went down right in his corner.

The crowd went wild. I was the underdog of all underdogs and I'd knocked him out, I thought. But just then the bell went and he sat in his corner, his seconds feverishly working on him. They lifted him up and pushed him out for the fourth round. The baths were buzzing. He boxed his way out of trouble in the fourth and I couldn't get a good shot in. His head cleared and his experience came to his aid. We both gave it our all for the rest of the fight. It was a war. Toe-to-toe stuff that the boxing crowd love to see. The final bell went and it was all over. Del won on points. If the bell hadn't gone in the third, I would have won. That's the luck of the game. The money started to pour into the ring. The seconds picked it up in a towel. I got £12 for the fight and £25 in nobbins (tips thrown in by an appreciative crowd).

Ernie Derfield, a promoter, was on the phone to Tommy. 'We want your man on our next show; he's a good ticket seller and crowd-pleaser.' So that was my moment of glory in the fight game. All the fighters up and down the country have had similar fights to mine. I hold out my hand to them for their courage and heart because it takes a lot just to step into a ring.

My rating in the *Boxing News* went into the six stars so I would never have an easy fight, only wars with experienced fighters. They reported on the match and said: 'Promoter Stan Baker can have every reason to be satisfied with the attendance and crowd-pleasing bill of fare in his first venture at Manor Place baths. Three former ABA champions Freddie Reardon, Henry Cooper and Dave Charnley all won their bouts and gave promise of great things in the future . . . "Nobbins" were showered into the ring after the first bout of the evening, in which Del Breen, Croydon (10–11), outpointed Freddie Foreman, Walworth (10–11 3/4) over six rounds. These two threw everything but the bucket at each other. It was Foreman's first pro bout . . .'

Stan Baker was asked about his best undercard fight and he mentioned mine. In the book *Down Memory Lane with Stan Baker*, he said of the fight: 'It was right at the end of 1954 when I put on my first bill there. I had three ABA champions on the undercard, Freddie Reardon, Henry Cooper and Dave Charnley. Henry's brother Jim boxed in one of the six-rounders and Charlie Tucker topped the show against Hanley's Tommy Higgins. The entire bill cost me £300. Do you know what I paid Cooper? – twenty quid!

'One guy who deserved to be paid 100 notes was Freddie Foreman, who had his one and only pro fight, against Del Breen. Best supporting scrap I ever saw! They hit each other with everything but the corner buckets. Nobbins were still coming in five minutes after the fight ended. After such a fistic baptism Freddie never again drew on a glove.'

As it happened, I did go back into training intending to carry on with the fight game but fate had other ideas in mind. The promoters wanted me on the next bill. I fought as a middleweight and was in really good shape, so much so that my trainer Tommy Daly made me a sparring partner to top fighters. I sparred with Peter Waterman who was British welterweight champion and even got into the ring with cruiser weights who I was bowling over with big gloves. Unfortunately, I had no sponsors to pay my bills and I still had to put food on the table for my wife and son. To support my boxing career I had to continue thieving. Unfortunately I got nicked and another stretch in prison ended my pro career, at least in the ring.

I sometimes wonder whether things might have turned out differently if I had done National Service. My brothers talked me out of joining up; the war in Malaya and Korea was beginning and the brothers thought that as four of them had survived the Second World War, this time the family might not be so lucky. The problem was how to get out of it when I was in such peak physical condition. We decided I would become mentally deficient and my brother George organised a medical certificate requesting a deferment on the grounds of my 'schizophrenia'.

We went down to Chelsea Barracks, George leading me by the hand and complaining that he had to take the day off work to accompany me. My mum, who was not party to the proceedings, asked incredulously if I was going out of the house in my present state. My hair was unkempt, I had Bert's clothes on (he was much smaller than me) which were tight-fitting with bits of wool hanging out of an old blue jumper and some sticking plaster on my face. I had deliberately cut myself while shaving and was a complete mess. On top of what I was wearing, I'd donned an old air raid warden's overcoat. When we got to the barracks I meekly did as I was told by George, not taking any interest in the surroundings but staring, open-mouthed, through the window. George bullied me: 'Get over there and sit down. Get your socks off and hurry up, don't take all day.' Watched by the Army personnel, he then took my socks off himself. They must have thought: 'We've got a right nut here.'

George never let up for a moment: 'All he does is sit watching out the window seeing them trams run by. He won't do anything. He just sits staring.' The Army doctors said they would give me a deferment for some months before making a final decision. George had a go at them: 'I've got kids to support,' he complained. 'I can't spend all my fucking days here. He's a fit boy. He did a lot of boxing and sparring but fucked up his brain. He's a bit scrambled.'

We had to come back a second time. Following George's excellent tuition, I again sat on the edge of the seat, gaping open-mouthed, and the medical board obviously thought I needed help. 'This young man needs some treatment,' they told George. They granted me Grade 4, which exempted me from doing National Service, and recommended that I attend Cane Hill mental institution in Surrey for electric shock treatment! Maybe they were right.

In some ways I regretted not doing National Service with my mates. Lots of my friends were sent all over the world, like Micky Regan who went to Suez and Freddie Puttnam who went to Malaya. Patsy Toomey and Lenny White joined the Army and became PTIs and fought in the Army Boxing Championships so, in a way, I later felt that I had missed out.

Money was in short supply and most of my friends had secure jobs in Smithfield meat market, Spitalfields, Billingsgate and Covent Garden. Being a market porter was quite the 'in thing' to be those days, and although I did it for a short time, I had bigger ambitions.

At around the age of eighteen I teamed up with a load of girls known as the Forty Thieves. You virtually had to be born into it to become a member of this gang. All the girls were hoisters and followed their mothers' footsteps in professional shoplifting. My job was to graft with girls like Mae Mae Cooper, Annie Revel and Nellie Donovan, and make sure they got away after shoplifting from top stores like Harrods. You would bump into the guy who was going to give them a pull, or give him a right hander if he got too clever. We met the girls in the local pubs. Their mothers, all from the Elephant and

Kennington, were the original Forty Thieves. Though they had cockney accents, they knew how to talk lah-di-dah, putting on the upper-crust voice whenever the situation demanded. They wore their clothes better than titled ladies and really looked the part. They were stunning girls, well-known throughout London.

When they got nicked, they got it hard. Some of these girls were sent to Holloway for two to three years, even though they were mothers with children. They were not treated gently but they were tough and did their lump of bird. Like fellas, they risked their liberty every day of the week to get a pound note.

A lot of them were scarred up because they could also be vicious bastards and were often in fights and rows, cutting each other up. When they let their hair down they were totally outrageous. Sexually, some of them were hot stuff. People who live on the edge can be. As I've said before, they lived life to the full and knew how to make a man happy. When they tired of their man, they'd kick him out and move on to the next one. They were real characters. I still see a few of these lovely ladies, beautifully turned out and probably still grafting. It's in their blood.

They used to call shoplifting 'clouting', which was the name for an undergarment. Old English for drawers. The amount of goods they could stash away in bloomers under their dress was unbelievable.

Working with the girls was only a part-time activity. It was fun to do and I enjoyed the company of these larger than life ladies, each of them a colourful character in her own right. But there were bigger prizes to be had.

· 4 ·
Spencer Park

I'm moving on too quickly here. Let me go back and tell you of my teenage years at Wandsworth Road which were amongst the happiest of my life. At eighteen, while still living at my mum's, I became a full-time thief. My social life was exciting and fulfilling and I was fit and ready to take on the world.

My mates Lenny and Patsy loved staying at my place, mainly because my house was the general meeting place and also local girls joined us for sexual adventures in the drying rooms at the top of the block. We used to hang around the entrance to the flats late at night while Rosie, one of the girls I fancied, would come by. I'd greet her and offer to escort her home. Of course there was a diversion. A gentle tug on the arm would be enough to change direction and I'd lead her up to the drying rooms. Her protests were never meant to carry much weight and we'd soon be at it with a knee-trembler against the wall. Lennie used to tail me off minutes afterwards. The routine was: handkerchief out of the pocket, wave it so Lennie could see, and give a little cough to signal the changeover. Rosie would act startled: 'Who's that?' I'd tell her it was my mate Lennie and a little indignantly, she'd threaten to go home. But the thrill of a further sexual adventure was too strong and she stayed. Lennie would slip up behind and take over from where I'd left off. This became a right regular occurrence.

I was worried about my George's health shovelling coal and breathing in all that dust in the barges. Even though he was older than me, I suggested he pack the job in and join my little firm. 'You'll be dead in five years if you don't,' I warned. The pollution outside the power station was bad enough. A fine layer of coal-dust covered the roads and footpaths so when you walked down Nine Elms Lane to the power station you left a trail of footprints. I couldn't bear to think what this did to my George's lungs and reckoned his chances of survival would be better with me. In those days there was no social security, so you only had two choices: to work or to thieve. I thought thieving was the lesser of two evils.

After working with the Forty Thieves I progressed to the jump-up. This involved stealing the goods from a commercial traveller's car or from a lorry and driving them to an arranged meet where they were loaded into another van and sold on my behalf. I bought a 500cwt Ford van and, through trial and error, taught myself to drive. Driving licences were provided by our friend in County Hall.

Just after the war there was good money to be made from the black market in rationed goods. The profits were better still if you didn't have to pay for the rations in the first place. The canteen at George's power station catered for hundreds of people and was given a large allocation of tea which was very much in demand.

Every three or four months they would get eight to nine chests, some of which would probably go to other canteens. You could get double the price for it on the black market so I said we had to have it and asked Lennie and George to help. We broke into the building, made our way to the canteen and got the tea chests out without any problem. It was a good night's work.

The night watchman was alerted to us but it was nothing to tie him up which took only a few minutes. Much better than battering him unconscious. People are normally so surprised and shocked by a sudden hold-up or threat that they freeze and are easily subdued.

George said he earned more from that night than
working for several months at the gasworks, and that
convinced him to turn his job in and join me. Soon we
had organised people in different factories to sell our bits
of gear to their large workforces, and people began
approaching us with orders for items in demand. I was
always being asked for spare lorry wheels with plenty of
meat on the tyres. They came to between £10 and £20
each which was a lot of money then. We stored the tyres
in George's house in Wickersley Road until we broke the
floorboards bouncing tyres into the backyard. The final
straw came when we broke the staircase – George's Rita
was not amused.

We used to nick anything and everything. We'd follow
a travelling salesman and as soon as he went into the
house selling goods on the never-never, the jump-up
would happen. You'd use a screwdriver to open the
quarterlight window of his motor, up went the catch,
open the door and start the car up with a flat key and
drive off. Lenny or George would follow in our van to a
quiet street, preferably a cul-de-sac with a wall on either
side, and load up the gear and leave the salesman's
motor there.

We got plenty of Twining's vans loaded with tea
chests and a couple of drivers even let us have all their
goods by parking up outside a café. While they were
having a cup of tea we'd jump-up and drive it away.
Some drivers would approach us, asking if we'd rob
them for a percentage of the take. One of my relations
offered to let us have his truck which we 'nicked' from
him at the Lyons Corner House by the Tower of
London. Offers were coming our way all the time.

If we sold our goods at factories we'd have to wait
until the end of the week before we got our money. This
became a bit of a hassle so we found a buyer in Chelsea
who stored the gear in a garage adjoining a vicarage. We

first met Fatty Sid the Yid in the local pub and he gave us an address to deliver our goods. We said we would bring a van full of clothing the next day at about 2pm.

'I'll be on the corner waiting for you,' he said. We drove there as arranged, only to see the old vicar standing on the corner. I went around the block again hoping he'd go away, but he was still standing there with Sid the Yid at his side, gesticulating and mouthing: 'Come on!' I refused to drop off the clothes, pointing at the vicar. 'Don't worry about him, it's the vicar's garage! He'll be in for a pair of grey flannels in a minute.' After that, Fatty bought all our gear from us in bulk.

The jump-ups improved as time went on. You progressed to lorry loads of tea, cigarettes and cloth, and buyers from all over London started to spring up. You could sell anything then, and people would place orders for the next time you got a load. Nobody grassed you up in those days. They would rather buy something cheap.

Mum was getting a little worried about my activities. Even when I was working for Pannet and Eden I would tell her to help herself to my wage packets if ever she was in need of money. She would open the wardrobe and find £50 in notes and all my wage packets unopened. Once she found a .45 revolver stuffed at the back of the drawer: 'Oh, you do worry me Fred,' she once said but never brought the subject up again.

My father knew I was thieving but left these things unspoken. He was grafting as a taxi driver now. He'd done his 'knowledge' – on a bicycle, learning all the short cuts along the back streets of London. The hansom cab which he drove had no sides or protection from the weather and like many drivers, he finished up with rheumatism in the elbows and joints. Years later, when in his late seventies, he had to have operations for plastic elbows: he'd suffered badly.

George and I would take our goods to the various markets where we had contacts. But with a busy schedule, I was seeing less and less of Patsy Toomey who worked in Covent Garden. Patsy had always been very possessive of our friendship and was now becoming unreasonably jealous. He wanted to be in on the action and felt he wasn't, even though we'd given him gear to off-load on our behalf. Patsy's personality was undergoing a change – his moods became excessively brooding and violent, as I was soon to find out.

I had gone with George to the Nell Gwynn café in Covent Garden. It was packed to capacity. You got very good food there, and George and I and a couple of porters sat at a table for four in an L-shaped section of the café. I was about to get stuck into my baby's head and two veg (this was a meat pudding – a speciality of the house) when Patsy walked in. I looked up and greeted him, 'Hiya Patsy.' He didn't reply. Instead he smashed me full in the face with a left hook. I crashed backwards over the table behind me and rolled onto the floor. I was up on my feet like a shot and steamed straight into him with blood pouring from my nose. We'd been the best of pals, stood together, fought together, protected each other. We'd been like brothers. Now he was laying into me – and Patsy could have a fight.

All the customers cleared the area and became spectators. People outside hearing the commotion came in and stood on tables and chairs to get a better view. As we battled, everything around us got wrecked: mirrors, pictures on walls and chairs. We really went at it. I finished up getting him in a stranglehold on the floor. His face was in my stomach and he was kicking his legs like a man struggling to stay alive.

'Fred, don't choke him, he's gonna be dead. You're killing him,' someone said. But I wouldn't let go and still had a cross-collar hold. My old judo was coming in handy and he was gasping away, going blue in the face. They pulled me off him – not a moment too soon. He was already semi-conscious and closer to death than I'd realised. By now the police had been called and just before they arrived we were hustled out to the pub next door.

We used to drink in there and the governor let us use the toilets to clean up. While we were washing, George and some of the porters came down and told us we were silly boys to fight like that when we'd been such good friends. I gestured at Patsy: 'Talk to him about it.' Any thoughts of a reconciliation were abandoned when George picked up a leather cobbler's knife with curved blade and wooden handle. They were a common and lethal tool for cutting people those days. Sharp as a razor. When I saw that, my blood boiled. The blade had been meant for me. I went to do Patsy there and then in the toilet with his own knife. I turned to him: 'You'd fucking use this on me?' With that he broke down and started to cry saying he was sorry but thought I had dropped him out and that I didn't look on him as a best friend any more. He was convinced I'd blown him out and replaced him with my brother George.

My anger gave way to pity. I felt really sorry for him. It became obvious to me he was mentally ill. Afterwards I could never feel the same about him again. What can you do with people like this? He was paranoid. Psychotic. After all we'd been through together and the close friendship we'd had, it was all destroyed on that day. And although he'd never used the knife on me, I knew the intention had been there and that is mainly what upset me. Maureen, whom I was courting at the time, couldn't believe Patsy and I had been fighting each other.

From then on, we went our separate ways. Years later, Patsy worked as a minder for Oliver Cutts who owned a string of petrol stations and put small animal zoos into them as a publicity gimmick.

Patsy was always getting into fights and rows. As he

got older he became bigger and heavier. He once had a row with a taxi driver taking him to a pub in Covent Garden after he'd been drinking in the West End. The cabbie stopped outside Bow Street police station sounding his horn. When police came running out, Patsy knocked two of them out, but then got overpowered and dragged into the cells. He finished up with a twelve-month sentence and was sent to Wandsworth. He was always being carted off to the nuthouse for one reason or another. One time it was for trying to strangle his wife, Margie (a lovely girl). Some years later he came to my pub, the Prince of Wales, when he knew I'd had a bit of aggravation. 'I'm with you Fred,' he said, brandishing a shooter which he'd pulled from his pocket. 'I want to sign on the firm again.' I told him to put his gun away. I thought, there was no way I'd have a loose cannon like him about me. It was all very sad. Patsy was a lovely guy but, as I say, he was a sick man who needed help but never got it. In 1983 Patsy died of lung cancer in St Thomas's Hospital and I often think of him and feel sad.

When I was eighteen going on nineteen, I was introduced to my future wife Maureen Puttnam, on a blind date arranged by my friends Sammy Osterman and his girlfriend Joanie Winters. Sammy worked in the print and he and Tommy Wisbey, who was to become one of the Great Train Robbers, were old mates. Tommy worked for his dad who had a bottle factory in Cook's Road, Camberwell. His girlfriend, Renee Hill, whom he later married, was related to Joanie who was also a good friend of Maureen's.

The girls aroused Maureen's interest in me. They said I was always spending money like water and treated my women well. I wasn't such a bad-looking chap either. We got on fine together and she was an absolutely straight girl. No funny business at all. It was ages before we made love and in my way I respected her for that.

At my age, I didn't feel ready for marriage but all my

pals had girlfriends and were getting married so you just seemed to follow suit. Maureen must have had marriage in mind. I let her down two or three times on dates and once she came around to my house demanding to know why I hadn't shown up. She was a strong girl. Our courtship, like our marriage, was volatile. She was very possessive and jealous and I couldn't look at another girl without upsetting her. We were always rowing, sometimes even in the street.

There was a reason though: she had a very unhappy childhood and needed a lot of security, love and affection. She lived with her aunt Lizzy who had a heart of gold. Whenever Lizzy was out of the house, we'd have a kiss and cuddle in the front room. We did all our courting there and also in the back row of the Kennington Odeon Cinema.

Inevitably, Maureen fell pregnant with my Gregory and we got married at a church in Walworth Road on a Monday, which was the most convenient day for market and street traders. The wedding party was an all-day affair held at Tommy Wisbey's sister-in-law Janie Shaw's place, a four-storey home in Walworth Road. It was a good day out and everyone enjoyed it. Maureen was given away by her uncle Joe because her father had been killed falling off the back of a lorry crossing Waterloo Bridge. He had worked the smudge (camera) in Trafalgar Square, taking pictures of tourists until given the fateful lift by a grocer friend.

We set up home in Milton Road, a wide, tree-lined street in a very desirable part of Herne Hill, south London. Maureen gave up her job as a presser once we got married, but she always pulled her weight. However fiery our relationship was, she would always support me in my work. I used to joke that she believed manual labour was a Spanish wrestler, but she was never frightened of hard work really. When I got nicked she went straight back to work at Waterloo Station on the tea and buffet cars. The job was handed down to members of the families and it kept her going while I was in the nick. She was also very protective of me and never frightened to weigh in physically on my behalf.

Shortly after my kidnap Maureen walked into a restaurant bar in Spain. Sitting at the table having breakfast was none other than the Spanish translator who, on seeing Maureen, greeted her with an airy, 'Good Morning Señora Foreman.' Maureen promptly chinned him, sending him sprawling. Before he had time to compose himself she was restrained by friends and staff from finishing him off with a heavy glass ashtray.

In the past, I've had to do a bit of ducking from Maureen myself. When we had the Prince of Wales pub in Lant Street and a flat on the Brandon estate, Kennington, she threw flowerpots at me from the fourteenth floor after a row. Another time I had a brand new Citroën DS 19. It was a lovely car, painted in racing green. I'd been out with George, Bertie Blake, Buster and Tommy Wisbey and got home late. She steamed into me and I legged it back to the car, dodging a hail of stones, bricks and small change from her handbag which dented the car roof. From the fourteenth floor these missiles were as dangerous and deadly as bullets, causing sparks to fly off the pavement, nearly penetrating the roof of my new car. (I hate to think what they'd have done to my skull.)

But I could be just as angry towards her. On one occasion I was several hours late for Sunday lunch. When I arrived home from drinking after hours with the chaps, the roast smelt wonderful but Maureen had retired to her bedroom with the Sunday papers. 'That smells lovely,' I complimented and went to the dining room expecting her to serve up the food. Maureen came into the kitchen and without a word to me, opened the oven, took out the roast and went straight out the back door to the yard while I sat expectantly with my knife and fork at the ready. Instead of a steaming hot roast being delivered on my plate, I heard the sound of a knife scraping the serving plate as she emptied the lunch into the dustbin. She then trotted back in disdainfully looking past me and went straight back to the bedroom and her newspapers.

I was incensed. I went to the yard, picked up the dustbin, carried it to the bedroom and emptied the contents over her as she sat fully-clothed on the bed. I then walked out of the house and returned to my cronies and carried on drinking. When I returned home a couple of days later, we were sweet as pie to one another. Childish really, but that was typical of our early days together.

Even before we married, Maureen had witnessed gang fights involving me and our friends. It was all part of life in those days. The Harrises picked on Sammy Osterman outside a pub in Camberwell New Road one Sunday morning. Sammy got a glass in his face as a result of this feud with the Harris family. A terrible fight followed and unfortunately the feud went on for several years.

Tommy ended up working with them after the feud and one of the brothers with whom I had a straightener, even came to my wedding. Later in our careers we'd drink together and help each other out if there were any problems. Many of my early rivals have over the years become solid friends and we still drink together on occasion.

Families like the Harrises, Frasers, Brindles and Carter brothers were well-known in our area for feuding. The wars between the Frasers and Carters were legendary. (If you want a good read, Frankie Fraser's book *Mad Frank* will tell you more about these times.)

On one occasion, the row was between the Harris family and Tommy Shaw, the bookmaker, involving bets and street pitches. Tommy was a generous man with a charming personality and was a very successful bookmaker. If you were short of a tenner, he'd give it to you.

Curiously enough, when bookmaking became legal in Britain, licences were only given to those people who could prove they were in the business. So for some, the only acceptable proof entitling them to the much sought-after licences, was to prove they had broken the law and had convictions for betting!

One of my mates at around this time was Horace 'Horry' Dance. He was an old friend from Battersea and lived in a nice, respectable street just off Clapham Common. His mother was one of those well-spoken ladies who would proudly show you a photograph of her Horry immaculately turned out in his cricket whites surrounded by the rest of the team. The bit she didn't reveal was that the photograph was taken in borstal.

Horry was a well-known face and married a beautiful girl called Barbara. But he was a right handful. Always in trouble and getting nicked for assaults on police. He had a powerful BSA Thunderflash motorbike on which we went to work. I would do a snatch on a nightsafe while he would wait down an alleyway or round a corner. We'd make sure the numberplates were covered up and we disguised ourselves with pilot helmets and goggles. (There weren't any crash-helmets in those days.) After the snatch we'd roar off. There were rich pickings to be had. We robbed furniture stores like Times Furnishings where the day's takings might be left in a drawer just minded by an office girl. The money piled up from people bringing in their monthly instalments for goods which they'd bought on the drip (HP).

Later on we nicked a Vincent Black Shadow motorbike (this was the fastest motorbike on the roads) and used that to snatch money off managers and cashiers as they went to put cash in nightsafes. Indirectly I gave some of it back when I bought a Times Furnishings bedroom suite – for cash.

There was nothing Horace wouldn't do for you. He was once in hospital with peritonitis when he heard that

I'd been nicked. He pulled out the tubes connected to his stomach, got out of bed immediately and went to the police station to bail me out at Catford magistrates' court. That's the sort of chap Horry was.

And there was nothing he wouldn't steal. Wherever he went, he carried a screwdriver and nicked everything he could take home. He bought three houses and built a fourth one entirely from stolen materials. There was a violent streak in the family too. His wife Barbara, who helped him build the house, was involved in a hilarious brawl with Horry's mum and dad. The argument began inside the house and spilled out into the garden of a lovely suburban street with neighbours peeping through curtains at the commotion. The garden became a battlefield. Both sides picked up stones, bricks and gardening tools – anything they could lay their hands on. They used metal dustbin lids as shields to protect themselves against the missiles (you can imagine the din).

For all that they were lovely people and good friends. I didn't see Horry for years and then learned the sad news that he'd taken his own life with an overdose.

In the early days, Horry had introduced me to some heavier people who were into bigger paydays than we were getting. For me it was like serving an apprenticeship. I was continually progressing up the scale with more experienced people to whom Horry had sung my praises.

One of Horry's past acquaintances was 'Mad' Mo Jones. When Mo came out of Wandsworth Prison after serving five years, he called on Horry's mother. We reckoned there might be a problem because he and Horry had a fight some time ago and so we tooled up. To my relief the meeting was amiable. Mo was with another chap I knew, Lennie Morgan, so we all shook hands.

This was a relief, as Mo Jones was a fearsome man. He was built like a brick shithouse and had a nasty temper with it. Mo had just got out of jail for cutting up a copper's face. He was always tooled up and had a terrible reputation in and out of the nick.

I was invited to work with him and Lennie and another chap called Bertie Blake. We did a few post offices, tie-ups, and pay snatches. Those days there were still trams and trolleybuses and there was one evening when Mad Mo actually did a raid on a tram! Believe me, this was a one-off in the annals of crime. We had been waiting for the cashier of the Super Palace Cinema at Clapham Junction to leave the building with the day's takings. We missed him and someone pointed out that he was getting on a tram. Mad Mo jumped on the same tram and we followed. He walked down the gangway looking from left to right for someone holding a cash bag. When he found him, he asked the chap if he was the cashier.

The geezer confirmed he was and Mo grabbed him out of his seat and said: 'Give me the fucking money!' The poor chap handed it over without hesitation. Mo had that effect on people.

Something was bound to give and it happened in an unexpected way. Mo raped Lennie's girlfriend Rose, a good-looker with a voluptuous body. He went around to her place and threatened her with a knife to her throat and then raped her. She came screaming and crying to Lennie to tell him what had happened. Bertie Blake and I were unaware of this when Lennie called us for a meeting at the Prince's Head pub.

When I got to the pub, Mo Jones was already there. He bought me a drink and I sat down with him. Mo and I waited an hour for Lennie and Bert to arrive, whilst having several drinks together. Bert then put his head through the door of the pub and waved me outside. He said Lenny wanted to show Mo something on his own and we would meet back here later. Bert took Mo to meet him as arranged. I didn't think any more about it and waited for them to return. As far as the customers and publican were concerned, I was the only identifiable person with Mo that night.

Our fashion those days was to wear gaberdine rain-coats with epaulettes. It was the Robert Mitchum look – given currency with the film *Build My Gallows High*. Your hair was slicked back with gel meeting in a duck's arse at the back of your nut – the DA haircut. The look was big and baggy and worst of all, easily identifiable. Lenny was wearing an identical gaberdine raincoat to mine.

Bert returned to the pub once more and again beck-oned me outside. Lennie Morgan was there with his coat collar turned up. 'What's going on?' I asked.

'I've done Mo! I've killed him,' Lennie replied. He opened his coat and I could see he was smothered in blood.

'Fuck me!' I said. 'That's naughty.'

Lennie kept talking: 'He's gone to my home while I was out and fucking raped my Rosie with a knife to her throat. She was in a right state. She's still in bed and can't talk.'

I commiserated with him: 'The bastard deserved it,' I said. 'Rosie's a lovely girl.'

Rosie had the voice of an opera singer and could sing songs from all the shows, specialising in Ivor Novello tunes. Lennie was one of the chaps and well-respected. He was then about thirty and I was still in my teens. He asked me if I thought Horry's mother would give us a change of clothes. At that time Horry was away doing nine months for GBH on a copper in Wandsworth. It seemed all of our friends or acquaintances were in and out of Wandsworth then. I went around to Mrs Dance and she was a good old girl. She had a big fire going in the grate and we burnt all of Lennie's clothes. Mrs Dance gave us a fresh set belonging to Horry. We then cleaned out all the ashes and left.

But I began thinking about the implications. If Mo was dead I would have been the last person to be seen with him. I'd been sitting with him in the pub for several hours having a drink and then gone out with him, although I had come back afterwards. But it would still not look good if people recognised me. I started to visualise reports about me: 'Young man with hair slicked back, latin looks, wearing gaberdine coat, wanted for murder . . .'

Later Lennie told us what he did. He took Mo to Spencer Park, which is close to Wandsworth nick. It was pitch black and was bordered by a row of large, fashionable houses. Apparently Lennie pointed to a house. 'That's the one we're going to screw,' he said, stepping behind Mo and pulling out an iron bar. He smashed Mo over the head several times. Mo held up his hands for protection but Lennie kept bashing away. Lennie left him in a crumpled heap with his head split open and bleeding profusely. Nobody could survive an onslaught like that. Or so he thought.

For two days there was no mention of Mo. We had been looking in the newspapers for a murder report and were understandably concerned since we risked getting hung for a lady's honour. Then we read a report that screams had been heard in the park and police found a considerable amount of blood indicating someone had been seriously injured. But there had been no body found.

Bert got a message from Mo's sister to call around to her house in Garratt Lane, Wandsworth High Street, about a mile from Spencer Park. Bertie was shitting himself when he went to see her. He pretended to be shocked to find Mo lying in bed with towels around his head. Mo was not to be fooled. His piggy eyes were alert. He told Bert that he had been led into a trap.

Mo's look said that he would kill him if he had the strength. Then he took the towel away from his head and Bert said the wound was like looking into an open mouth. They had to take Mo to hospital or he would have died. He had two or three brain operations and several hundred stitches in his nut and hands. All his fingers had been crushed and broken during the attack.

Amazingly he had crawled and dragged himself away from the spot to his sister's house leaving a trail of blood. But he wouldn't let her call the police. He said nothing. That was the way it was then and always will be in our world.

I'm a great believer in fate. I always felt I was destined for something more and I feel I've had a charmed life. Some of that luck, I reckon, must be down to Gladys, my guardian angel, who watches over me all the time.

Years later Lennie was doing nine months in Wandsworth when who should come into the metal shop but Mo Jones. They looked at each other and immediately ran around the shop searching for tools. They were ready to kill each other. But they missed their chance. A screw saw what was happening and rang the alarm bell. They weren't given the chance for a return contest and both were dragged down the block.

Many years later I saw Mo myself when he was an old man. He was shrivelled, and the tramlines on his head from the operation were clearly visible and his skull was concave where it had been smashed. There were a lot of little saucers in his head.

It was only four months after Lennie's attack on Mo that we were out with Bert, Rose and Sylvester, a stall-holder, and a lovely old guy who was a street bookmaker called Jack the Pie. We started out on a pub crawl and ended up at The Surprise in Vauxhall Bridge Road. We were in high spirits. The pub was packed and Rosie, Lennie's girlfriend, was sweetly chirping away some Noel Coward tunes at a grand piano in the corner. We boys were near the door laughing and playing around with Jack Pie, riling him about all the money we had lost to him over the years.

He took it all in good fun. But then we took it a step

Spencer Park

further and grabbed Jack and tied him to a chair with our scarves and sat him on the tramlines in the middle of the road. It was about 10pm and trams used to come up there at speed. Poor Jack suddenly got scared but we were close by, ready to drag him away as a tram approached. 'This is what you get for taking our money,' we shouted to him. The tram driver was frantically trying to slow down, winding the brake handles at a furious speed and donging the warning bell with his foot. He was convinced he would run over Jack. We dashed out and scooped Jack away with only seconds to spare. It was all boys' stuff. Highly spirited antics inspired by plenty of gin-and-tonic and scotch on the rocks.

Excitement over, we went back into the pub to hear Rose finishing her number and giving it the big one (she always finished her songs on a high note) when a load of coppers arrived from Peel House, a section house for training coppers which was only two streets away. A fight started and spilled out into the street, and one copper had a stranglehold on Lennie from behind. I pulled him off and cracked him one on the chin. The copper staggered back on his heels right across the pavement. His back hit the railings gate and he disappeared down the basement steps. Oops! Very nasty.

Now, all hell broke loose and everyone headed in different directions. I had three coppers chasing me up Vauxhall Bridge Road, intent to kill. I was running out of puff at the foot of Vauxhall Bridge and just made it onto a departing tram. My legs were gone. I couldn't step up off the platform. I looked around gasping for breath. The coppers were straddled in a long blue line a short distance away. One determined bastard, bent on getting his man, was closing up on me as the tram stood waiting to go.

The tram conductor came down the stairs, sized up the situation at a glance and without a moment's hesitation gave the word for the tram to continue: 'Dong dong,

71

fares please.' Magic words! He looked at me and winked.

'Thanks mate,' I said, as I flopped down on the seat. The tram left the coppers labouring for breath and kicking the air in anger and frustration.

Unfortunately, Lennie, Bert, Jack and Sylvester were all arrested and received time for assault on the police. Lennie told me afterwards that when they were arrested, they were taken down to the nick and all of them were pressed (a polite word for it) to reveal my name. But they all stood up, strong men, solid men, and wouldn't tell the police anything.

At the magistrates' court, the coppers came to give evidence swathed head to toe in bandages. Lennie got nine months, the others three and four months.

As each of them was released we had another piss-up and a good laugh. Lennie, like me, also had a brother called George who had some good contacts in the car business. George was keen to get some muscle on his firm and wanted to include me in everything. He told me that he had a man in County Hall who could get brand new car log-books and stamps. Would I like to go into business with him? I jumped at the chance: 'When do we start?' I pulled my brother George in on the action and got myself a set of twelves (keys). They would open most of the cars we had targeted for nicking: Ford Prefects and Austin A40s. If the key didn't fit, then two screwdrivers were all you needed to break in through the small quarter-light side window with very little damage done.

My job was to nick the cars and then drive them to Tunbridge Wells and park them up. My George would follow and take me back to London. A car dealer he knew in town would put them in his showroom furnished with a log-book and all the right details. They started to go like hot cakes. George and I were doing very well. In fact the lock-up garages were full and I was told not to nick any more for a while. The price of a Ford was then about £900 and it was £1200 for an Austin. Our whack was £200 and £250. Great money in those days. But all good things come to an end.

The showroom sold a Ford to a man who was very knowledgeable and he spotted a number behind the sun visor that shouldn't have been on that particular year and model. He called the police and the dealer was arrested. They traced the log-books back to County Hall but nobody grassed on our firm. The wartime propaganda – that golden rule that insisted on silence – still held good.

Georgie Morgan's next scheme was counterfeiting and we had a load of white fivers printed up. But that was short-lived. His relation who did a bit of work for him, nicked a parcel of the dodgies and went to Wandsworth dogtrack where he got himself nicked. Then on top of that George Morgan got nicked and it all blew up in our faces. It was now time for me to move further up the ladder and try something new.

· 5 ·
Firm Friends

Villainy relies as much on sound business practice as any other enterprise. When our profitable car-stealing scam came to an abrupt end, we had to switch operations and find new products to market. Luxury items, such as washing machines, spin dryers, television sets and radiograms, were very much in demand in the early 1950s, but their high cost put them out of the reach of many people.

A little market research showed it was a business that couldn't fail. All I needed was a small Ford van, a white dust-coat, a pencil in one ear, papers in my top pocket and a lot of front. Dressed to deceive, I would then walk into shops, target a fridge or washing machine, which would often be just inside the door, and walk out with it. If a salesman was standing there, George would act as a decoy and lead him away to the back of the store to look at carpets or other goods. With one lift, a deep knee-bend is all it took, I'd have the object of my choice up and out of the shop and into the van. The back of the van would be padded with a mattress covered by a blanket to avoid damaging or scratching the goods. Once I was out of the shop George would be minutes or seconds behind me. It worked like a charm.

It was only later when you were delivering the goods to customers that you realised how heavy they really were and wondered: 'How the fuck did I lift that on my own?' But during the robbery your adrenalin worked like a wonder-drug and provided extra strength.

We sold the goods at just one third of their shop price and consequently couldn't get enough to satisfy all our customers. Client families even gave us orders for their married daughters and sons. The list was endless. It gave us a lot of pleasure to see how happy we made people when they got something new. The Foreman brothers were doing very nicely. There was no violence, nobody got hurt and we were giving pleasure to people who couldn't otherwise afford these luxuries. I'm a saint, ain't I?

While this was going on, I was continually on the look out for more ambitious projects. On one of our shopping expeditions shortly before Christmas, we found a store in Clapham Junction which could easily be burgled by tampering with its steel shutters. It was an ideal night for the robbery because a thick fog had blanketed London. I had already borrowed a large van from a market guy in Covent Garden and told him to scream if anything went wrong, otherwise we'd return the van the following day.

Everything went to plan. We got to the store at night, up came the shutters and in we went while the night watchman was fast asleep in his office. In no time at all we took what we wanted and had the pick of each department: washing machines, carpets, Hoovers, curtains. We began loading up the van. Just as we'd finished loading, a guy walked by out of the fog. We decided to move away very fast so George went to get the back-up motor parked around the corner. Meanwhile I finished packing and locked the van doors. I stayed in the van and waited for George.

All of a sudden a Wolseley police car screeched around the corner and stopped bang in front of me. Three cossers piled out of it and jumped on me. 'Gotcha! You're nicked!' they said, pinning me to the shutters.

'Not if I can help it,' I muttered and struggled as they tried to hold me down. In the skirmish that followed, I came clean out of my jacket leaving them wondering where I was. They were still holding the sleeves which had been turned inside out as I legged it into the pea-souper.

I could hear them coming after me and looked desperately around for a hiding place. Nearby was a car with a tarpaulin over it. I got underneath the canvas and slid on to the bonnet and lay across the windscreen. The Wolseley drove round and round the block searching for me. They were obviously quite upset with me!

I was thankful they had no dogs with them. I stayed hidden for more than an hour and by the time I made a move it was getting light although the fog had not fully cleared. I had to get to the nearest and safest port of call because I was very noticeable in just a shirt on this cold winter morning. Who could help me out? I almost spoke the answer out loud: 'Jack Pie, the bookmaker. The one we'd tied up and put in front of a speeding tram. That's it, he's nearby.' I made my way there and knocked him up. 'Jack, Jack, open the door, let me in. Hurry up I'm freezing my balls off out here!' Jack was as good as gold. I cleaned up and borrowed some fresh clothes and then caught the bus home to Maureen who had been worried out of her mind.

George had been inside my house telling her that he couldn't find me. He didn't know what had happened. As I arrived, he was just leaving and about to get in his car. The police, in the meantime, had gone around to the Covent Garden man, who owned the van, and held up my jacket to ask him if he knew who I was. He told them nothing but later joked: 'I could see you standing there, Fred. It was your shape.'

You can get away with an awful lot when you're fit and young. I remember one time when George and I were desperate for a bit of money and targeted the cashier's box at a Dorothy Perkins store. The ladies kept putting the big £5 notes into a wooden box but it was one of those boxes where you couldn't pull your hand out if your fist was clenched. A bit like the monkey and coconut syndrome.

I boldly walked up to the cashier and shoved my hand inside this box but couldn't get it out because I'd grabbed a load of notes. Exasperated, I pulled so hard the whole top came off so I just stuffed my pockets full and legged it to George who was waiting in the getaway car. (Desperate times call for desperate measures.)

I wasn't so lucky, though, when I was grassed by a pal of Horry Dance. As I said earlier, Horry had been ill in hospital with peritonitis and suggested I continue working with a pal of his who was really a plumber and had a big motorbike with a sidecar. He was basically a straight man but had sold lots of gear for us. Horry had assured me he was okay so we went to Catford and heisted loads of gear into the sidecar which he took back to his place. But we'd been sussed and the next morning proved disastrous for me.

At the time I had an Armstrong Siddeley car which I parked in the next turning to my home in Milton Road because I'd lost my licence and didn't want people to see me driving it. The Armstrong was a beautiful car. Coach-built and fast. An ideal car for our sort of work as people never suspected it was driven by villains.

On the morning after the robbery, I was in bed and heard a knock on the door. It was the police. I didn't even have time to get dressed. Annie Revel of the Forty Thieves lived next to us and I raced out the back, over the wall and up the side of her house, vaulted the gate and took off down the road. The cossers were still standing at my door and saw me go by like a flash in my underwear.

I got to the Armstrong Siddeley and lay down on the front seat but someone spilled the beans and told the police they'd seen me get in there. The cossers opened the door, gave me a few whacks with their sticks and got me out. I ended up getting nine months at Greenwich

Magistrates' Court.

By this time Maureen and I had our first child, my Gregory, who was born in the St Thomas's Annex. Our home in Milton Road was nice and comfy. Everything had been paid for. But with me away, Maureen went to work at the tea bar at Waterloo Station and met June, Buster Edwards's wife. Buster, who later became one of the Great Train Robbers, was godfather to my second son Jamie.

Prisons were a much tougher regime in the 1950s. While I was in Wandsworth I was sent to work in the woodshed. There were all manner of particles floating in the air, lit up by sunbeams. Concerned for my health, I told the screws I wasn't going to injure myself breathing in all these impurities. Working there was like being on a production line: there were big electric bandsaws and rows of guys chopping up wood on a conveyor-belt system.

To make my point a little more effectively, I went to the screw sitting on a platform overseeing the work and buried my chopper into his desk. He got frightened and I told him to put me down the block: 'I don't care where I go. Just get me out of here. I can't stand the saws any longer.' They gave me a job in the hospital which suited me for a little while until I realised what that involved. There was shit everywhere, on straitjackets, mattresses, floors and all over the walls. You couldn't clean the place. The 'patients' had blocked the toilet cisterns with books and the place was covered in excreta. Even their porridge bowls were filled with the stuff. This was the first time I had seen people so mentally deranged and dis- turbed. (I never doubted my sanity after that experi- ence!)

I requested a cleaning job on the wing. A screw was approached on my behalf and I was given the Number One job on the landing, which meant you were in charge of the cleaners and handed out the razorblades every morning and took them back after they'd been used.

Other privileges followed. I was given extra food. The best grub was goulash which you could make into a nice sandwich although it was a bit greasy and looked like bread pudding. You were always starving in those places and couldn't wait for the next meal. People who came out of prison in those days were instantly recognisable by their prison pallor: a grey sallow look.

I was in Wandsworth with Georgie Cornell and Jackie Cramer. They put you three in a cell – there was safety in numbers in case of rapes and assaults. Prison was clean, not like today. Cells were inspected, everything had to be correctly hung up, and sheets folded like in the Army. It was all very regimental.

But there were always fights. I got put down in the block over a fight with a gypsy kid and his brother. Each landing had its own food orderlies and they used to come around with buckets of tea and soup. Each prisoner had his metal plate, tin mug and cutlery made from cheap tin. The knife's serrated edge had been folded over and beaten with a hammer and probably would have failed every hygiene test in the country. Now they issue them in plastic.

The tea orderlies would come along past your cell. Three of us would hold out our tin mugs and then quickly produce a water jug for a top-up. Other orderlies would give you a cob of bread and dinner. They would be followed by the screw who would come up behind and bang you up for the night. This all happened at breakneck speed because it meant the screws could go off duty as soon as it was done.

This gypsy kid wouldn't top me up saying he didn't have enough tea, but he still had enough to give a second helping to his mates. Next time he came around I told him to go to the next cell and I'd get my tea from the guy following. He refused to move on so I whacked him and knocked him out (a hungry man's an angry man). The tea went all over the landing floor as I sent him sprawling. I then dragged him into the cell by his ankles but was stopped by Stevens the screw, a hard-faced bastard, from inflicting more damage on the gypsy.

The screws told me I was nicked and marched me straight down to the block. In the morning, the governor gave me nine days: three days on, three days off. The diet was a jug of water and a cob of bread. You were left in the block without belt, shoes, tie, or braces, and made to sleep in an empty cell on a wooden bed. You could only take your bedding in at 5.30 at night and it was freezing. To keep warm you had to lay down by the hot pipe. You were allowed library books but they were crap. To pass the time, you did press-ups and walked round and round the cell like a caged animal. Warders kept looking at you through the door and all the time you got hungrier and hungrier and angrier and angrier!

The first three days are the worst. After nine days your stomach shrinks so much that you lose your hunger and seem light-headed.

My battle with the gypsies was not yet done. After I'd been down the block I was out in the exercise yard. The two brothers sniggered and took the piss. Although we had to be three paces behind each other, I got close to the gypsy and at a blind spot I did him again. This time, he ended up flat on his back in a shrub. That livened him up a little and let him know it was not all over. But the screws found out and I was sent back down to the block again. They really had it in for me. Nevertheless, they couldn't prevent the clock from going round.

On my release, although my Greg was only a little boy, he looked at me as much to say: 'Where have you been? Why did you desert me?' And I felt I had, as these were the most important months of a child's life.

Whilst Maureen worked at Waterloo Station during the day a cousin, Renee Darling, looked after Gregory in Baylis Road. It was named after Lillian Baylis who

founded the Old Vic theatre which was at the end of the
road where Buster worked in a florist's shop for Adie
Warner, a gay chap who lived with his mum and always
wore a trilby hat. That's when Buster and I became
friends. On his demob from the RAF he'd found it hard
to get a living so he went to work as a florist.

After my release it was suggested by Maureen that I
might try going straight. I considered it, but not for long.
In fact I went straight back to grafting with Joe Carter,
my old cellmate. Joey and I used to do the windows:
smash them and grab all the gear in the early hours of the
morning. You'd either reverse the car into the window
or you smashed it with a heavy object.

One night we were involved in a terrible chase around
Streatham. There were about three patrol cars in front
and another three behind when police cordoned off the
road and made us stop. As they approached the car we
took off again like something out of Brands Hatch,
crashing patrol cars as we escaped. They gave chase
because they knew we had been grafting in the area and
had been waiting for us at around five in the morning
while we were on our way to Wallington. We were eventually cornered for a second time when Joe drove into a
cul-de-sac after being rammed in the back by a police
car. We both ran off in different directions.
Unfortunately, Joe climbed over a garden wall and fell
through the roof of a chicken coop where he was
arrested. I managed to escape over several garden fences
and made my way home. Joe wound up with nine
months for stealing a car, resisting arrest and driving
without due care and attention.

With Joe away I had no full-timers on the firm.
Pressure was put on me again to go straight and get a job
so I spoke with Tommy McGovern who fixed me up
with a porter's job at Smithfield meat market. I used to
collect Tommy at about 4am on my way from Herne
Hill. He had a flat at 'The Horns', Kennington. Although

I tried not to, it wasn't too long before I strayed off the straight and narrow again.

The wages at the meat market were so poor I had to have a little extra so I saw a pal who had a fiddle going with a big cosmetics firm. I took gear from him on credit and sold it at a good profit. It helped supplement my wages. Once I even had a van-load of nicked policemen's boots and sold the lot to the market porters. They went down a treat and all the porters were running around in nice soft coppers' boots.

Although there were some great guys working there, Smithfield was not for me. I had been my own boss since my job as a scaffolder and couldn't stick working for someone else. That's when I started my little firm with Buster Edwards, Tommy Wisbey and Billy Hart.

As with all the firms I have been involved in, ours was democratic and flexible. I would still do work with George if he put something up, or with anyone else I knew and trusted, like my brother-in-law Freddie Puttnam.

Freddie worked for a gown firm and told me he was due to collect the firm's wages. Our plan was to snatch the money and I would clump him in the process so he wouldn't be a suspect. It had to be done right so I gave him a few whacks and he had to have a couple of stitches. Obviously there was someone with him so we had to make it look realistic. He was a bit overzealous and grabbed my leg as I made my getaway. Hence the stitches.

You had to laugh. Later he put his share of the hold-up money into a home fishtank which had a decorative treasure chest and diver. Freddie wrapped the money in waterproof packets and stuffed it underneath the treasure chest in the gravel on the bottom of the tank. I had warned him not to buy anything new as he would be suspected of helping in the raid. Sure enough, two months after the snatch police came around unexpectedly and asked him about his new radiogram. 'Where did you get that Fred?' they asked. He was able to pull out a payment book showing he was buying it on the never-never. Freddie got married and was able to pay for the wedding out of our little touch. After that there were no more visits from the police.

George and I were always open to fresh opportunities like the one that presented itself at George's own workplace. Geo Harding & Co had converted an old prison in the Borough into a large warehouse on different levels. George got friendly with the night-watchman, a lovely old rogue George falsely introduced everyone to as Digby Morton. George has a good sense of humour and was always giving people nicknames. The real Digby Morton was one of the top fashion designers of the time and this old watchman was the complete opposite. He resembled a tramp. He had the face of a tired hound-dog, a bulbous nose mapped with blue veins that looked ready to burst, and a knobbly head on which he balanced a battered trilby. Wrapped around his body, and held together by a belt, was an ageing and stained raincoat, and to complete the picture, he shuffled around in boots that were several sizes too large. You would expect to see him on a park bench rather than in an office with a bunch of keys rattling at his side. So this was Geo Harding & Co's night security officer. His wage was a pittance. It was a case of who is going to watch the night-watchman?

We used to meet Digby at the pub about half-past nine at night. You had to get him pissed so that he'd go back to the warehouse and leave the back door open for you to sneak on to the premises. But our timing with regard to his drinking had to be more precise than our thieving. If you got him to the pub too early he would get too drunk to do anything. If we left it too late, he wouldn't be pissed enough to do as we said.

When it came to drink he was a sly old fox. He used

to draw it out to the last minute. 'I think we can have another Guinness now,' he'd say, just as it was coming to closing time. Then he'd add: 'Can I have a drop of scotch, George?'

Anxiously looking around, George would respond, 'How many times do I have to tell you, Digby, not to come into the pub rattling those fucking keys.' People knew he was a night-watchman and he'd stand out a mile drinking with two rascals like ourselves.

Eventually he'd make a move and we'd follow. He'd unlock the door and leave it an inch ajar. He'd then walk off to his cubbyhole where he had a primus stove for making tea. We knew what time the police came around to check the back door. Once inside we'd be selective about the goods we took. We made parcels with cardboard boxes and filled them up. You could get away with up to £500 worth of gear, a lot of money then. We did it once or twice a week but you had to be careful. If they'd caught us filling up the car round the back, the night-watchman would have been nicked and, even if we'd managed to escape, we didn't want that to happen because he would probably have talked. We treated him quite well. Digby always got his booze paid for and a nice bit of money on top.

With the amount of goods we were getting, we decided to get our own outlet rather than selling the goods through others. George, who was the driving force in this enterprise, called it the 'Larkin's store' – all the goods for sale were down to larking (that meant it cost nothing). We got a bit flippant in a way.

One night Freddie Puttnam asked us to a party but we'd already made a meet with Digby to get another load at the warehouse. Not wanting to miss either opportunity, we seized both. By the time we met Digby, we were already pissed. Nevertheless we filled up the car with the stolen goods and returned to the party once more, parking the motor in a square by the block of flats near Lambeth Walk. In our inebriated state, we left one of the back doors unlocked although we'd put a blanket over the gear. While we enjoyed a nice drink, someone who came to the party told us that two cossers were examining the car with a torch.

One of the policemen went to Kennington Road nick for reinforcements, the other kept guard under a porch nearby. We had to get rid of the car lively. George and I strolled over to it, unlocked the door and were about to drive off when the cosser came up: 'Excuse me sir, is this your car?' he asked.

'Oh fuck off! Leave us alone.' We went to drive off but the copper bravely threw himself over the bonnet of the car and as we drove off he was desperately trying to smash our windscreen with his truncheon.

We roared through the square from Lambeth Walk into Kennington Road, dodging a load of metal posts on which people strung their washing-lines. We drove through this obstacle course until the copper was shaken off. The gear was then taken to a lock-up in Herne Hill and we returned to the party for another drinking session. It had been a nice bit of work, regardless of the slight hiccup.

As was to be expected, Digby got less reliable as time went by. On one occasion he had one too many and was so paralytic he passed out in the warehouse without leaving the door ajar. There was nothing we could do to wake him up from his drunken stupor. All you could see of him through a crack in the door was his pair of boots lying half-way up the passageway so it was a wasted night.

All good things come to an end and Digby finally got sacked for being drunk on duty. He came by to see George a few months later and said he had a job in the City. George gave him a few quid and we went for a meet outside St Paul's Cathedral. He gave us another fanny about being a night-watchman again and hit us for

£20 or more. Of course he was unemployed and had us right over.

George said: 'I bet I know where that bastard is. At the Elephant and Castle kip-house!' And that's just where he'd gone. He was sauntering his way to the kip-house as we waited for him. I grabbed him and threw him in the doorway. We let him go because he said he had no money and was desperate. He was too old and sick for me to batter so I just kicked him up the arse and sent him on his way. The last we heard of him was that he'd pegged over from the booze. Well, it was only a matter of time.

George recruited an unusual storeman for the Larkin's store – a housing estate caretaker called Bert. The man looked after the goods and stored them all over the flats and cupboards of the housing estate in Lambeth. Even an old air raid shelter in the grounds was full of Larkin's goods. The Larkin's store was doing well and Bert, a stocky man with pebble-glasses and a fat gut, with an angry disposition and a know-all attitude, was now on the firm.

The kids on the estate thought he was a tyrant and used to run off shouting: 'It's Bert the caretaker!' whenever they saw him – Bert wouldn't allow the kids to play or enjoy themselves – but my Greg and Jamie were used to him. They'd seen him at our parties and at Nell and Johnny Fitz's place which was on the same housing estate. Now that Bert had substantially increased his income, Bert was getting pissed more often. He was a real know-all handyman and had every tool that was ever made – all down to the council.

When George took over this shop in Larkhall Rise, Clapham, it had previously been a wet fishmonger's with a yard containing a brick smoke-hole. We wanted to pull the smoke-hole down to make more room so we could drive a stolen lorry and trailer into the yard. To assess the job, all three of us, George, Bert, and myself got up

Freddie at 2 years old.   Freddie's father.

Family group – parents' visit to Brighton to where the boys were evacuated: (from left to right) Albert (father), Freddie, Louise (mother) and Bert (brother).

Wally in Sheepcote Lane.

The five brothers – Wally *(top left)*, Herbie *(top second right)*, George *(middle right)*, Freddie and Bert *(bottom row)*.

Freddie's brothers in WW2 – *(clockwise from left)* George, Bert, Wally and Herbie.

The family outside Croxteth House in the War: *(left to right)* Herbie, Wally, George, father and Bert.

Billy Adams, 'Quiet' Jim Turner and Freddie (16 years old) at Roehampton open-air swimming pool.

BELOW LEFT: Herbie with Albert Bessel.

BELOW: Freddie boxing at Jack Solomon's gym.

Freddie and Patsy Toomey at Jack Solomon's gym.

Freddie, Maureen and Gregory on Orry's motorbike.

Freddie (18 years old) with future wife, Maureen.

Freddie and Maureen's wedding –
(left to right) Renee Wisby, Nelly
Puttnam, Maureen, Freddie,
George, Freddie's mother and
father.

Freddie and Maureen.

Hopping in Kent – boys' stag night *(left to right)* Tommy Wisby, Freddie,
Georgie McDonald, Ronnie Winters, Sammy Osterman, John Cosham
and chauffeur.

Freddie and eldest son
Gregory in 1954.

(Left to right) – Maureen, Jamie, Gregory,
Danielle and Freddie.

(left to right) – Gregory (top), Jamie, Danielle, Maureen and Freddie.

(*left to right*) – Charlie Kray, Reggie Kray, Terry Allen, Ronnie Kray, Barnie Beal, Freddie, Johnny Fitzgerald, Buster Edwards. (circa. 1962).

Charlie Kray, Reggie Kray and Freddie at the Double R Club.

Maureen and girlfriends at Freddie's Prince of Wales pub charity bike race. (circa. 1963).

Freddie Puttnam's wedding to Jeannie in the late 50s. From *(left to right)* Maureen, FF, Freddie Puttnam, 'Butcher' Payne, Jeannie, Fred's foster Dad, Jeannie's Mum Jessie, Ethel Puttnam, and baby Tina.

George Raft (American movie star who played gangster roles and ran the Colony Club in London; barred from entering Britain in 1967), with Maureen, Ronnie Kray and Freddie.

Dorchester Boxing Evening – *(left to right)* Freddie, Maureen, Johnny Mason, Lennie White (with glasses), Dell Rudell ('Ding Dong'), Ronnie Everett (with their wives).

Freddie and Terry Waller (ABA Boxing Champion) – Freddie presented the best Boxing Writer's award.

(Left to right) Chrissie Regan, Micky Regan, Barbara Windsor, Ronnie Knight, Maureen and Freddie (1966).

(Left to right) – Joe Scala, Bernie Coleman, Freddie and Fred Scala – the Scalas took Charles Forte under their wing.

The chaps' gym: *(left to right)* Mark Row (ex British Middleweight champion), Phil Landrigan, Ronnie Oliffe, Maureen, Freddie and Dave Chandley (British Lightweight champion).

(Left to right) Henry Cooper, Ronnie & Charlie Kray, 'Red Faced' Tommy, Reggie Kray, FF, Jim 'The Bishop' Wicks, Sulky from the Astor Club.

Alfie Gerrard – one of the firm.

(Left to right) Mick Regan, his wife Chrissie, George Raft, Maureen, at FF's Prince of Wales pub.

Freddie in the West Indies.

Freddie Puttnam, Stevie Ellison, Richard Hennessey and Peter Hennessey.

Freddie in Maidstone Prison with a few of the chaps.

(Left to right) John Mason, Freddie, Ronnie Everett and George Foreman.

Freddie, George and friends at a London party.

Janice, Freddie's girlfriend.

Herbie at Arnhem circa. 1965 *(second from right)*.

Jamie and his wife, Carol Harrison (Freddie's son and daughter-in-law).

Danielle (Freddie's daughter), and children Santi and Freddie.

Freddie's brother George and his daughters Tracy, Janet and friend Anna.

(Left to right) Kathleen, Janice, Barbara and Freddie at a party.

(Left to right) Jimmy Allen, brother George and Charlie Wilson in Marbella.

Ronnie Kray's funeral in East London, 1995. Freddie paying last respects to Ronnie Kray with fellow pallbearers: Johnny Nash, Reggie Kray, Charlie Kray, Teddy Dennis, Alex Stein, and Laurie O'Leary.

Freddie and family (left to right) – Barbara Fitzgerald, Tina, Carol, Jamie, Pat, Freddie, Danielle, Mo, Gregory and Lisa.

Maureen and Danielle with Freddie's grandchildren, Freddie and Santi.

Noelle Kurylo, Freddie, Helen Keaton (actress) and Frank Kurylo.

Maureen.

Freddie's son Jamie, with son Alfie and wife Carol.

on a high wall at the back of the sloping roof which was a little dodgy after years of smoking haddocks and kippers.

Bert the know-all loud-mouth said: 'Now look fellas, don't walk across the roof any-old-how, step on the main beam that supports the roof here, and here,' he said stamping on the roof to emphasise his point.

At that precise moment, there was a loud crack and the sound of splintering wood and clattering tiles. Bert made a partial disappearance through a hole in the roof, leaving only the upper half of his body visible. The know-all expression had changed to a look of terror. A further crack was heard and the rest of Bert followed through the hole. As he crashed twenty feet to the floor below, a cloud of black soot rose up and mushroomed like a mini Hiroshima. All went quiet. George and I had been comfortably and safely perched on the wall and had to bite our lips to stop ourselves laughing in case it was serious.

We got down to Bert who was moaning and groaning with pain and lying in a crumpled heap looking for all the world like one of the black and white minstrels. He was white-eyed, red-mouthed and groaning for an ambulance. George leaned over to him: 'What's the number, Bert? Do I ring 999? Is that it?'

Bert was outraged. 'Stop fucking about, George. I've busted me ribs, ring 999.' Later, George made to get in the ambulance with him when it arrived but Bert refused. 'He'll only try and make me laugh and it fucking hurts like hell.' Afterwards, he wouldn't speak to us for months and sulked something rotten. Silly know-all bastard! As if it was our fault he fell through the roof!

It all came to an end when my George got grassed up and sent down for three years in Wandsworth. During his sentence, he was approached and asked if he would help Bruce Reynolds get an automatic pistol into Wandsworth Prison. Bruce was doing three-and-a-half years and was concerned about his family. He wanted to get out as quickly as possible and George thought he was helping in an escape attempt. But Bruce had a different plan in mind. He wanted time off for good behaviour and his plan was to hand in the gun to the authorities and earn special remission. He was going to say he found it in the brush shop.

They got George the gun through an outside working-party who were supervised by a screw called 'Yogi Bear'. The prisoner with Yogi was Speeby, a one-time friend of Joe Carter. He was on the same wing as George and came into his cell at afternoon tea, gave him the automatic, and legged it. George put the gun under his pillow. Where else could he hide it? And he says to this day his bottle has never been the same since. Every time someone walked past his cell door, his bum was making buttons. And they were coming by every few minutes: screws, and other prisoners returning from labour. You can imagine how little sleep poor George had that night. The next morning after slop-out and breakfast, when the prisoners were assembled on the 'Wandsworth centre' (this was the centre of the prison block where warders scrutinised and counted all the assembled inmates before sending them off on work parties – standing there was an ordeal for every prisoner), George stood there with the gun in his back trousers feeling like John Wayne. He was never so glad to get to work in his life. He hid the gun in the storeroom until they came to pick it up two days later. Bruce's scheme didn't work as he'd already approached a screw previously about getting a gun in but this screw had thought better of it. Some people obviously didn't like what he'd done and he paid dearly for it. Although I have never discussed this episode with Bruce, either then or now, the facts may have been a little different, but I have always believed that this was the true story. It has been locked away in my subconscious all these years and when the problem arose with Mitchell and the Twins, I considered it pay-back time, as Bruce has always been a friend and a well-respected thief – solid, loyal and one of the chaps.

On his weekly visit to the bath house, Mad Frank Mitchell stabbed Bruce in the back puncturing his lung. He was found slumped in a bath full of water which was slowly turning red. Frank Mitchell was nicked and sent to appear at Marylebone Magistrates' Court, on a charge of attempted murder. Bruce never grassed on him and Mitchell was acquitted. It took thirteen coppers to get Mitchell out of the dock when he remonstrated at the magistrates' court.

My firm of Buster Edwards, Tommy Wisbey and Billy Hart was formed in 1956. Tommy, Billy and I had been friends since our teens when we went to pubs and dance halls together. Buster used to sell my gear at his florist's in Waterloo and when we became friendlier, he asked me if he could come in on the action. So I took him out to work and he became a thief. In a way I corrupted him. He'd been a straight bloke. He had worked as a cook in the Air Force and, on being demobbed, started his own window cleaning business and eventually worked as a florist until finally he became a criminal with me.

Billy came from the Elephant, Walworth. There were a lot of thieves from there and neighbouring Bermondsey which was part of the docklands. Although people from those areas may have been a poorer class on the social scale, their fathers earned good money in the docks. Every docker had a radiogram, TV and fitted carpets in his front room. They lived a good life because they earned that extra bit of money. When the docks folded, all the families of the younger men were used to a bit of luxury and inclined to go out and get big money, so you found that most of the armed robbers were from that area. Unfortunately, the prisons are full of those young men serving long sentences because they got a taste of the good life.

· 6 ·
East Enders

Our firm had made good contacts throughout London so we were always being told about little bits of work that would keep us busy. The core enterprise now included using skeleton keys to break into shops and emptying the premises but had extended to snatching wages if the opportunity presented itself.

The skeleton keys which we had specifically made up would open most shop doors and not many businesses had alarms fitted in those days. It was all trial and error. We'd pull up outside the shop in a transit van and try the key in the lock. If it didn't fit you'd blacken the key by smoking it up with a lighted match and reinsert it into the lock and wiggle it about to see where it needed filing. Then you'd go back to the van and file it down. Normally that would do the trick and, flop, over the lock would go.

We would then return to the store and walk around inside the shop trying to set off hidden alarms. You'd then lock up again and keep observation from a safe distance. If the police arrived you knew it was belled to the local nick.

We did shops all over London, the best ones being Grays and Stones electrical stores, though fashion shops were also a good touch. We even robbed the first of the Mothercare chain of shops which probably helped set them up. Not only did they receive publicity, but they were also able to claim insurance on losing all their stock. Privately, someone from their firm said it was the best thing that could have happened to them. With the money to buy fresh stock it gave them a good start and they opened up further branches. (So you see how we helped people in those days.)

We always did our research. Generally we'd watch the shop one week and return the next. We'd find out how many employees there were and when the last one was due to leave the premises. You'd see him or her come out and lock up the premises. Then you'd follow to make sure the person got on a bus or in a car.

We'd then go back, pull up in front of the shop as bold as brass, and go inside. I'd usually wear a pin-stripe suit to make it look as though I was the manager, and the others would be dressed in overalls or white dust-coats.

You never faltered, even if the cossers walked by which they occasionally did. You just carried on not taking a blind bit of notice. Then we'd fill up the van and drive off to my lock-up in Herne Hill. We always had a high-speed back-up car like a Zephyr, Ford Zodiac or Consul.

One bit of business in the East End which had been recommended over a drink was a menswear shop. We fitted it up and went to work getting all the gear into large sacks. Having cleared the shop out, Billy went to fetch the van. While we were waiting for him, Tom, Buster and I heard this tap-tapping sound coming from a stairway.

The noise came in stops and starts and was disconcerting because we had watched the staff leave and had been in there for at least half-an-hour getting everything packed up by the door. We just had to find out what the noise was and crept upstairs to investigate. Peeping through a crack in a door we had gently opened, we were astonished to see an old Jewish boy with his back to us sewing away on a machine. He must have been stone deaf.

We closed the door again and tried to stifle a laugh.

Tommy was a notorious giggler. For a second, we were going to slam the door on the way out but thought better of it. We often wondered what happened when the owner came back and found the shop empty but the old boy still machining away in his own little world.

I met my pal Charlie Kray through selling our crooked gear. Charlie was connected with Stan Davis, a big buyer of our goods. Stan would take the lot from us and collect it from a garage or safe-house and pay cash on the nose so we would take a little less but eliminate the risk of putting it about. Charlie was a good man to do business with and safe. We acquired a lock-up over his manor in Old Ford Road as well as our own in south London so we didn't have too far to travel after each bit of work. It was good money for a year or so.

As we got to know each other better, I used to go over and drink with Charlie and the Twins. Over the years I'd seen Charlie and the Twins at boxing shows and gyms and they had quite a reputation in the amateur fight world. Charlie and I hit it off straight away. He brought his wife Dolly over to my place because he liked how we had decorated it and wanted to show her. She also got on well with Maureen and while we had little Gregory, they had their son Gary. Dolly was always given first choice of any kiddies' clothes we'd nicked before they went to the rest of the punters.

They were frequent visitors and when everything came on top for me and I had to go on my toes, Charlie and the Twins helped me out.

Charlie always tried to talk a bit of sense into his brothers but they wouldn't listen. They were ambitious and wanted to go places fast. They had an aura about them that people recognised. I always found them polite and well-mannered. You could take anybody into their company and they wouldn't embarrass you.

Violet Kray, their mother, was lovely. She'd make cups of tea and sandwiches and loved the kids when you took them around – a really nice lady. She wasn't a bit like they portrayed her in the film with Billie Whitelaw. She'd never say she wanted to cut someone's throat. That wasn't her style. She was a very gentle woman and, of course, she loved the boys to death.

Their old man couldn't handle them at all. There was nothing he could do when they went out in the yard and beat the shit out of each other. In the end, he took no notice of them.

Their home was a typical east London, cockney house. Violet kept it immaculately clean and extended a warm welcome to visitors. The Twins were just like other young kids growing up except for this overpowering ambition. Charlie had a kind of calming influence and encouraged them in the gym.

The Twins initially helped their father out selling gold in the street but they didn't like that. They wanted more out of life. You didn't need a lot of money to start little businesses then, one of which was the Double R Club which also had a gym above it, and the pool hall.

It was after Ronnie had been to Wandsworth for GBH that the Twins seemed to become more violent in their dealings. While he was inside, Ronnie chinned a couple of screws and they moved him to Epsom where they could keep him indefinitely in the nut-house.

I was invited a couple of times to join the Twins when they were being wooed by Billy Hill and Jack Spot. Both of them wanted the Twins on their side because they had an army of heavies around them. Had they wanted to, they could easily have mustered an army of about twenty to thirty guys. If there was trouble or they needed to intimidate somebody they could arrive mob-handed with these ugly looking bastards with big Mars bars down their faces. Some were massive – twenty to twenty-four stone in weight. Tommy Brown was known as the Bear and tipped the scales at nearly twenty-five stone. All were streetwise guys who knew how to handle themselves.

The Nash brothers were also coming up at this time and the Krays were friendly with Johnny and Jimmy. Billy Hill was trying to coax them over as well. Billy Hill would ask the Twins and their friends to show some strength at race meetings and pay them money. They asked me to do a bit of growling at race meetings – because arguments often arose over the best pitches – but I was a thief and this sort of work was not really my scene.

It was different with Charlie. He and I went to Billy Hill's card games as minders. You could eat and drink what you liked and you stood about in case of trouble. But there was never any problem. The people who went to these spiels very rarely got violent if they knew who was minding the business. Clients included people from Mayfair and Kensington. In those days, gaming was illegal but people loved to gamble. Billy Hill cleaned them out. 'Red-faced' Tommy – he always had flushed cheeks – used to handle the cards and do the business during the game with a special deck. Billy Hill's wife Gypsy and other pals of his used to sit in the card games as part of the scam and when the night ended we'd cut up the money. Charlie and I used to come home with a few hundred pounds for a night's work. Some very posh people would turn up. There was a naval commander, titled people, including baronets, Lords and Ladies and other top-ranking members of HM Services. The naval commander, despite owning a Rolls-Royce, welched on a gambling debt. His was visited by the Twins' firm who dispensed summary justice by embedding two pickaxes into the door panels of his Roller.

I never robbed poor people or broke into homes. We robbed only businesses and factories and did jump-ups with lorries. We considered that respectable and honest thieving. Not like today's mugging of old ladies and young girls. We treated and looked after women and paid good money for presents and clothes for our friends and family. We never nicked cars to go joyriding. We nicked them to go to work and get a living. It was a business and no one felt ashamed of what we did. We stole money to live well but ultimately our intention was to earn enough to go into business and go legit – stop having to risk our liberty.

Like everybody else you wanted to own your own home and car and have money in the bank and provide a good education for your kids, something I never had. Whichever way I earned my money my sole aim was to provide for my family. I sent my Greg and Jamie to Oakfield College in Dulwich. Later, when we returned from the East End, the boys attended Christ College, Blackheath, and Jamie, who got the acting bug went with Danielle, my daughter, to the Italia Conti Academy of Theatre Arts.

Charlie's partner Stan the fence did quite a lot of business with my brother George and George would also buy things off Stan – until he got nicked with Stan's goods. He'd bought a load of Prestige knives from the man and, without warning, his flat was raided by coppers.

We figured it must have been Stan who grassed him, because the next thing I knew, they were raiding one of my lock-ups and certain things the copper said could only have come from Stan. Inside the garage, they found one of my vans full of stolen gear and I went up for trial at the London Sessions. Fortunately I had a friend called Albert Connell, the local bookmaker, who acted as an intermediary between me and the police. Albert associated with them but there was never any harm in it. He was a solid man and if he could help you in any way, he would. I asked for his help and he arranged for us to have a meet with them in a Streatham club owned by Edie Clements. It was nice food and we had a good time. At the trial I was found not guilty. It was a good result but quite expensive.

After that episode, Charlie split up with Stan.

Most of the shops we robbed were probably very grateful to us for the insurance they could claim though I don't say this in mitigation of what we did. We had no regrets.

We had a good run with our robberies but London was getting too warm so we ventured out into the sticks. It took longer to get home with the goods but the work was the same.

Until we went down to Southampton, most of our jobs went smoothly. I had some relatives on the coast and found a couple of nice shops to do. On one particular occasion we stayed overnight and did the shop early in the morning. There were four of us: Tommy, Billy Hart, Buster and myself. We got there bright and early. The doors had two deadlocks, top and bottom. In the middle there was a Yale lock which had to be knocked off with a heavy screwdriver. We went to work and all went well. I must mention here that when carrying out the TVs and other goods, you couldn't wear gloves. It would have looked very suspicious all four of us wearing black leather gloves. So every item we touched had to come out with us and that had to be the rule. At the back of the shop was a warehouse full of goods packed in boxes which made it easier for us to get more goods on to the van. There was no wasted space.

On show in the shop was a lovely Decca walnut radiogram, a type we'd had before and which we knew was a very popular seller. As we liked keeping our customers satisfied, Tommy said: 'We got to take that one Fred. I know someone for it.' We filled the van to the brim, locked up the shop and drove away, sweet as a nut.

About five miles down the road we could hear the Zephyr hooting the Ford van and then drawing alongside to stop us. It was Tommy. He said we had left the radiogram behind with his prints all over it. It had been moved right next to the doorway and they were bound to print it up. I said: 'Okay, jump up here and I'll go back with Buster and pick it up. You carry on and we'll catch up with you on the road.' Leaving a print behind was like leaving your name and address.

Buster and I went back to the shop. One guy was already setting up his paper stall next door and another was cleaning the shop's windows. We went straight to the front door, spun the locks off and snapped the Yale back with the screwdriver as quick as a flash. We then got the radiogram into the boot of the Zephyr. I stood in the entrance and held up my trade board and wrote down bollocks for the benefit of the window cleaner and the paperman. We drove away feeling okay about it and put our foot down once we got out of Southampton and even caught up with the van, overtaking it and giving a relieved Tommy the thumbs-up sign. We got back safely, changed the plates of our transport, and set about selling the gear.

A few days later, Tommy asked to borrow my new Ford 5cwt van, a nice little motor for business and running about. Tommy had to deliver some of our goods to one or two customers who had ordered items.

Apart from working with us, Tommy still used to stand out on his father's pitch and collect racing bets. His old man was an SP bookie and had a sideline running a bottle-washing business with Tommy's brother. The bottle factory was in a yard down an alleyway and Tommy would stand at the entrance so that if police came he could run down the back and escape over five or six back gardens of adjoining houses.

The police were always trying to nick you for illegal betting and it became a sort of game with lookouts down each end of the street who would give a good whistle if anyone came along who looked suss. The cossers would use every ploy imaginable to catch people. They came disguised as dustmen, milkmen, postmen, tramps and even old ladies. Once they jumped on you they held on and a police Wolseley would come tearing round the corner. Other police would emerge from hideouts, whistles blowing and causing mayhem in the neighbourhood.

And after all that fuss Lambeth court would fine the offender £2.50 or, if you had six or seven previous, it would double to £5. Anyway, Tommy had my van with some of the gear from Southampton parked outside the gate when police sprung to arrest him for gambling. After he got nicked, they searched the van and found the stolen goods which they traced to the Southampton robbery. He was then further charged with handling stolen goods. They had put Tommy on an ID parade but neither the window cleaner nor newspaper seller could pick him out because fortunately it was me and Buster who went back.

The van, however, was traced back to me and there was no way I could afford to be nicked and go to Southampton. They would have put me away for a five-year stretch, so that's when I went on my toes over the water to the East End. Charlie Kray and the Twins found the nice little flat in Adeline Grove right opposite the Blind Beggar pub run by Jimmy and Patsy Quill who were lovely people. The local greengrocery was owned by Laurie O'Leary. He was one of the pallbearers with me at Ron's funeral and had been manager to Doris Stokes, the clairvoyant, and to various pop groups. He also ran a club in Swallow Street, Piccadilly, in which Beatle George Harrison, TV personality Alan Freeman and Sir William Pigott-Brown, the former two-times amateur champion National Hunt jockey had an interest in. It was called Sibylla's after society girl Sibylla Edmonstone of Duntreath Castle, Scotland who was also involved in the venture. Although an exclusive club with a restricted membership of only eight hundred, I was always welcome at the club.

Laurie did me a great favour years ago. Like many friends from the past, he gave my son Gregory a job at the Exhibition Club while I was in prison. Laurie was a loyal and trusted friend of the Krays and myself.

Charlie's wife Dolly was a marvellous help in getting Maureen over to join me from south London when I was on my toes in Adeline Grove. She really helped a friend in need. All wives and mothers in our circle are like that. Adeline Grove was just around the corner from Sidney Street, made famous by Churchill when, as the Home Secretary, he led troops to the famous siege of Sidney Street when they shot 'Peter the Painter', a terrorist who threatened to bomb the Royal Family and Houses of Parliament.

It was quite a wrench leaving Milton Road. My Jamie was only a little boy and Gregory was in Oakfield School and it was a shame having to pull them out of a familiar environment and family home to follow me to the East End. Gregory had to start a new school although he was getting on fine at Dulwich. But what could I do? It was too dangerous to stay across the water where I could be spotted by local police who knew me on sight, so it had to be done. I couldn't be without my kids.

So anyway, I was on my toes for a couple of years. The kids went to local schools and Buster and June from south London and Dolly used to come over nearly every day. We had a very good social life with all of our East End friends, but Maureen was a bit homesick for south London. It didn't matter much to me because I was in a new environment which I liked. Crossing over the Thames was like going to another country in those days.

My Greg also must have had a hard time in the East End school because he couldn't help but speak posh so he got into lots of fights, poor kid. Jamie was too young to really know the score. Ronnie, Reg and Charlie used to pop around and I would go to the Double R Club, the pool hall, the Blind Beggar and many other pubs in the area. It was mostly Jewish food over there and you got all these characters like Sammy the Yid, Nobby Clarke, Bill Ackerman, Limehouse Willy and Leslie Berman. They were all part of the organisation, working at the local spielers. I used to pop in there to pass the time but never played cards.

I became a regular at Bloom's, and Kossoff's the bakers for my fresh bread and bagels on Sundays. It was a new way of life coming from the south side and it was to be a turning-point in my career because I met up with some other chaps I'd previously known but had not worked with: Alf, Ron and big George.

The flat in Adeline Grove was the same flat the Twins had used when Reggie and Ron traded places at Epsom prison and Ron went on his toes. I had it decorated out by John Doland, a very artistic fellow who had a well-paid job as floor manager of a large commercial enterprise by day and sometimes worked as a barman by night. He was gay and had a part-time job as barman at the Double R Club and years later came to work for me at the Prince of Wales. But really he should have been an interior designer.

I asked Ronnie King, an old friend, to come and look after my home in Milton Road, Herne Hill until I returned. Things always worked out better if you allowed as much time as possible between the offence and getting nicked. Time is a great healer. Another advantage with time is that IDs wouldn't stand up so well and with any luck, witnesses may have moved.

I'd met Alf, Ron and big George on other occasions at Paddy Onions' and Alf's car site at the Elephant and Castle a year or so before and they were interested in why I was living on this side of the water. I told them to keep in touch as I had plans for a bit of work later if they were interested. I knew Big George was good with the old fizzer, cutting open safes and that there would be some big prizes. Later, as we became more successful, we recruited two more chaps.

Micky Regan and Patsy O'Mara were experienced, courageous and reliable. With Mick's arrival the team was now complete and there was no stopping us. An added bonus was that he became a lifelong friend. You couldn't wish for a better team.

· 7 ·
The Comeback

The East End marked a new stage in my career, a graduation. Banks, post offices, bullion, wages and payrolls were now the target. I had progressed to a bigger and heavier firm.

Buster Edwards was still grafting with the shops and a bank firm known as the Bowler Hat mob. Tommy Wisbey was in prison over the Southampton job. The new firm liked the way I worked. I was a hard grafter and could drive any sort of car or lorry and handle myself if there was any trouble. If any of the firm got into difficulties, each one of us was 100 per cent loyal and dependable. You wouldn't leave anyone behind. If we got nicked, we got nicked together.

This was no job for weaklings. You had to be powerful to pick up oxyacetylene bottles, heave them on your shoulder and carry them up fire escapes, over rooftops and lower them into the well of a building. We would have to cut our way into banks and other buildings by sawing through iron bars, knocking down walls, or cutting through joists above a ceiling. We had a few disappointments but the paydays were very good.

We planned our operations carefully, paying close attention to detail. While our inside information was usually spot-on, we never totally relied on it. We would sit in the back of a van outside a bank, factory or post office, and observe the target premises from holes drilled into the sides of our vehicle. If the windows of the target building were high, we'd come back with a furniture van to get a better vantage point. We did things then that police do in surveillance today. I lost count of the number of places we robbed. Over some months, it seemed to run at about one a week.

In the 1960s, wages were moved around on backs of lorries to factories, power stations and office blocks. Some six or seven members of staff would be chosen to guard the wages. They got a few extra pounds in their pockets for this and were armed with coshes and police truncheons. They thought it was a big giggle until a lorry or car smashed into their vehicle, sending them sprawling in a heap in some quiet street through which they had to pass. Then they would be confronted by five or six masked men standing over them with pickaxe handles. Fortunately for them, no one was in it for the violence, only the money.

As far as our firm as concerned, the less violence the better. We'd never batter people till they were on life-support machines: we just got the money and went. The element of surprise and the method of attack were the best possible way to ensure this. Usually they were so surprised they had their mouths wide open and we'd be gone before they knew it.

Of course there was always the Mackeson man. Remember the stout advert? A chap dressed in a boiler suit, muscles bulging, an iron girder on his shoulder with the Mackeson balanced on it. Macho employees who imagined we were stealing their personal money would sometimes have a go and would receive a tap here and there or a clump on the shoulder or legs, never on the head. They were only workers trying to get a bit extra to take home. Besides, our information for the bit of work usually came from inside so we didn't want to hurt one of our own.

It was all very business-like. We had nicked fast, reliable cars to get away with and were cool drivers. There was never any panic.

Micky Regan, from Clerkenwell, was a big powerful man, six feet four inches tall with excellent credentials and experience. Big Georgie came from Canning Town, a good man with a torch. He could cut open anything. He was a good worker and, like the rest, older than me and more experienced. People like Big Tommy Sullivan were always available to give us more strength.

Alf Gerrard was also from Canning Town. He and I got on like a house on fire. Big Ronnie was an excellent grafter as well as a good coach. He could drive anything. He knew all about cars and lorries and could repair them if they broke down. Although he had fingers like bananas, he could deftly pick up the smallest screw without fumbling or dropping it. Big Ronnie was always a good family man. He was never into clubs or gambling but was more interested in family life and being with his children. He's a lovely man who I've been very proud to know.

Patsy was about six feet tall but of nondescript appearance. He was a right asset because he could walk into places or stand outside a hit and not draw any attention to himself. The rest of us would be hiding in the van and on his signal, usually a tap on the side of the van, we would spring out and do the business. His job was to always make sure he got the money bags.

Whenever we did a bank or vault job, I never did the burning open, that was left to Ron and Big George and Mick. Me and Alf used to cop for anyone who came back to check us out. We'd wrap them up and make sure it was safe to carry on.

Sometimes you had to work between security shifts so you did things like pin-up the door – put a matchstick in the door so you would know when it was opened and, if possible, time the openings. That had to coincide with cracking the safe. We could tell from the make of the safe exactly how long it was going to take to open it.

We varied our operations so that there was never a

definite pattern and we'd go up and down the country, cutting and burning open vaults, wrapping up staff and snatching payrolls. Other firms were working at the same time as us and our democratic organisation would allow any of us to join them on specific jobs. Buster and my friend Lennie were still with the Bowler Hat gang. Ronnie Scrutton and Micky Kehoe had their own firms. From time to time I would also work with other pals like Billy Ambrose, Jerry Callaghan and Big Tommy Sullivan, who also had his own firm but was always available if an extra man was needed.

We were fearless, loyal, skilled and determined to win. We'd met through introductions and got to know each other better through having a drink. You always get the belly of a man by having a drink and watching how he behaves. Whatever shortcomings there were in any of us you'd find out over a drink. But we'd served our apprenticeship in villainy and now you couldn't have wished for a better, more reliable group of men.

Each one of these men was strongly individual with a colourful history.

Alf was a neanderthal with a heart. He'd lay down his life for you but if someone got on his wrong side they'd be in trouble. He was built like a brick shithouse, as wide as he was tall. He loved his food. He once told me how he swallowed a chicken bone while devouring the whole bird. 'Fuck me, Fred,' he'd say, 'I've swallowed this chicken bone and had to fish it out of my arse.'

His other love in life, apart from food, was his dogs. Alf ran a scrap-metal yard in some arches with a big smelter to melt down gear and had a couple of dogs guarding the place, one a mangy long-haired Alsatian. A young guy of about thirty worked for him at the yard and tried to emulate Alf by acting tough and doing a bit of growling around the place. He was a bit of a bully really although Alf found him a good worker, and strong. There were a lot of rats in the arches and Alf's worker was trying to poison them, although he was told not to do so if the dogs were around. Defying Alf, he put the poison down and the next morning Alf came in to find the Alsatian dead. 'What did I tell you!' Alf said, brokenheartedly, to the young geezer.

'Well, he was only a mangy old dog anyway,' replied the young bully. Alf got hold of his dog and shoved him into the furnace.

He then turned on the young guy and said: 'Mangy old dog was he?' Crash! He punched him straight in the forehead with the club hammer. The bruise ballooned immediately and he then grabbed this fella and made to throw him into the furnace after the dog.

While Alf loved dogs he didn't know how to treat them. He was too brutal. He only respected his dogs if they had a go at him or threatened to bite him. I went around to his house in Green Lanes, London on one occasion, and found a hell of a commotion going on. I had just walked into the large entrance hall which led to stairs and a first-floor gallery when his wife Margie screamed out at me: 'Stop him, Fred, stop him! He's killing Tiger!' As she pleaded with me, Tiger, a vicious Boxer with the build of a Bull Mastiff came flying over the gallery rail and crashed down on his back on the tiled floor below. Growling ferociously, his legs slipping on the marble floor as he raced to scramble back upstairs, Tiger shot up to the bedroom. I followed to find the dog in a crouched position on the bed snarling at Alf and waiting for an opportunity to spring on him.

Alf was in a rage. He held a four-by-two timber high above his head ready to bring it down on the dog's head: 'That fucking dog, Fred, he won't do as he's told. I told him not to get on that fucking bed and the bastard still gets on it.' Whack! Whack! Whack! He brought the stick down on Tiger. After that he couldn't handle the dog any more so we had to ship him out to the country.

About six months later we had cause to visit the farm

late at night in pitch black conditions and, as we got out of the car into the yard, we could hear growling in the darkness. A heavy deep growling. Understandably, I hesitated getting out of the car – I didn't fancy getting my nuts chewed off! – and Alf started laughing saying: 'It's that fucking Tiger, he thinks I'm coming to take him back.' I exercised caution, staying in the car until the new owner put him away.

Whenever we went to the pub in Alf's Jaguar motor car, there'd be a scramble to get in the back seat when we came out. Alf was a terrible driver. He couldn't drive slowly if he wanted to. He even knocked his uncle down in the garage by lurching forward when the poor fellow had squatted down in front of the vehicle. When they pulled him out, slightly stunned, he had the Jaguar marque emblazoned on his forehead from being hit with the bumper!

Nothing in the world rattled Alf. We were on a bank job in Manchester once and had to sneak through a mortuary. Bits and pieces of bodies from accident victims were slung into metal coffins. I tried not to look but Alf would say: 'Come over here and have a look at this one, Fred.' He'd have been quite happy to sit down alongside a coffin and eat a roast dinner. But for all that he had a heart of gold and he'd never let you down.

Together we must have created a menacing presence. If we ever walked in anywhere, people would draw in their breath and say mind how you go with them two. He was an animal. You didn't fuck with Alf. But for all that he had a sense of humour. We once kept watch on a security van while Alf was parked outside a butcher's shop window. He was drooling over sides of beef and legs of lamb in this butcher's shop as two young girls walked past. They thought he was drooling over them and said: 'Drop dead grandad!' Alf saw the joke and fell about laughing.

With his enormous appetite, Alf would eat six to eight

pies and mash at Cooks' Pie and Eel shop in The Cut next door to the Young Vic. They had the best pie and mash in London. He was always interested in food, more than sex, and ended up owning the Blue Plaice fish restaurant employing as his assistant chef, Eddy Watkins whom I'll mention again later. I took Maureen to his restaurant on one occasion and we got there before opening time. Maureen, as always, had dressed to the nines when she went out with me. Alf popped his head around the door of the kitchen and said he'd be with us in a minute. He came out wearing his white cook's outfit covered in blood, a knife in one hand and a big conger eel with its head half hanging off in the other. It was like a scene from the *Texas Chainsaw Massacre* and put Maureen right off her food. 'I think I'd prefer a Chinese meal, Fred,' she whispered.

'What's the fucking matter with her?' he growled as we slipped out of his restaurant. 'See you later Alf,' I replied, chuckling to myself.

Alf was intuitive and always had a sixth sense about people and jobs and was a good judge of character. Like Big Ronnie, if he got bad vibes on a job, we'd pull off. Both of them were proven right on many occasions. Ron, particularly, was our eyes. He'd weigh up a situation and if he didn't fancy it, he'd pull off. No questions asked.

We once unintentionally kidnapped a cosser who happened to be a top Flying Squad officer. Alf and I had been out all night looking at business and were driving along the Embankment by Chelsea Bridge. He'd been asleep in the back and I noticed a car had copped us. Our motor had Irish plates but it was straight. I told Alf to wake up as I knew we'd get a tug. I reached over and locked the front passenger door and my own door and just as we stopped at traffic lights, four coppers ran from their car trying to get into ours. Only one managed it, he was the governor. I took off and drove down a side-street while the other cossers ran back to their car. Now the officer was scared: 'I'm Chief Inspector . . . of the Yard,' he protested. Alf was giving him a terrible time in the back and had pinned him against the door with his feet. Eventually his colleagues found us and tried to take us to Scotland Yard.

We protested. How were we to know the geezer who'd jumped uninvited into our car was a Flying Squad officer? It could have been anybody. Reluctantly they had to let us go.

Alf once got into a row with a load of fellas and was heavily outnumbered. They had surrounded him and were closing in to do him. He copped for one and got his head under his armpit and dug his two fingers into the socket of the geezer's eye, threatening to pop it out onto his cheek. He growled: 'Are you going to fuck off all of you or do I blind him?' So that finished that one-sided row. If you were fighting him – it was all or nothing – Alf would rip your jugular out, as Stan Thompson found out in the nick. Alf was always going to win any way he could.

Neither of us feared any man or any thing. You just didn't give a shit, you knew what your capabilities were. You would know if there was any heavy work that needed to be done, you were quite capable of doing it. There was no limit to what you would do. People knew that, so you held that bit of fear and respect and it was true of the situation at that time.

I was also a bit of a nut in those days. Looking back, I did things then that I wouldn't dream of doing now.

Sadly, I was away in America in 1980 when Alf died. He was on his toes in Brighton, wanted again for some robbery or other. Unfortunately, he ate something which caused internal bleeding. His stomach slowly filled up with blood but he didn't want to go to hospital as he was on the run. By the time he agreed to see a doctor it was too late. He collapsed in the hospital lift and died from internal haemorrhage. It was a sad way for him to go and ironic that he died from his own passion in life: food.

After that, his son Nicky followed in his father's footsteps but was not up to it. He was a bit of a lump like Alf and had a few rows with people. He shot a few people, cut a few people and did all the usual stuff growing up. In June 1982, his killers lured him to a party and blasted him with a shotgun through the windscreen of his car. (This would not have happened if Alf had still been alive or if I'd been around.) Afterwards, apparently they threw up with nerves in their getaway car so it wasn't the mark of professional assassins.

Nicky's distant relation by marriage, Tommy Hole, was later charged with the murder but acquitted. He, like the others, had feared Nicky and what he was capable of doing.

Tommy Hole was serving time for armed robbery when I was returned from Spain. We were together at Full Sutton prison although I didn't know Tommy or his father who was also doing time. It was a terrible atmosphere because Tommy knew that Alf had been one of my best pals.

I knew the full strength of it and Tommy got really paranoid. He had only four months of his sentence left to do but his paranoia got worse by the day. I don't know what he thought I'd do to him. But the next thing I knew, he cracked up and was shipped to Parkhurst where his father was doing time. He accused everyone of trying to kill him and one day his father walked into his cell to find him strung up. He'd topped himself. The old man cracked up after that, went loopy, and wound up in Broadmoor. A very sad story but I hear that the old man is home again now – time heels all things!

Patsy O'Mara was a true-blooded Irishman even though he spoke with a cockney accent and came from Finsbury Park, north London. He and Mick Regan used to do safes together, knocking off the rivets with a hammer and chisel. Patsy was well-read, intelligent and argumentative – but really good company with it. He had this great advantage of looking like a bank clerk or an office worker. He was slim and dressed conservatively. No one would ever take him for a pavement artist or a thief like the rest of us.

If he was in a row Patsy could handle himself and he was game for anything, even pulling the trigger if need be. He also liked his drink. One night, he had a bit of an argument with some people at a party. He got mad and took his shotgun and blew out all the windows in the house. Patsy didn't give a fuck about anyone.

I once took Patsy to see Fred Coffey, the firm's GP. He was another lovely Irishman – as were most of the firm's GPs. Patsy had a ruptured belly button, it was like a golf ball and Fred Coffey told me to bring him into the surgery at Paddington. I was sitting with him when Dr Fred told him to drop his strides and get on the couch. He lay there chatting away – Patsy was a good conversationalist – while Dr Fred slipped on his rubber gloves and spread Vaseline on his finger. He gave me a wink and told Patsy to put his knees up: 'This won't hurt a bit,' he said.

And all of a sudden, Patsy was doing a wrestler's bridge raising himself by his head, catapulting his stomach into the air and shouting: 'NITTO! Fred. NITTO!'

Dr Fred had inserted two fingers into Patsy's arse. Patsy screamed with surprise at this unexpected intrusion. 'Hold on Patsy,' Dr Fred said, seeing Patsy's eyes watering. Apparently this rupture was caused by his excessive drinking – and poor Patsy needed an operation.

I knew he was a big drinker but didn't realise how badly it had got to him. Patsy, me and Ronnie Everett had all bought caravans in Hastings and during the school holidays I would send Johnny Fitz and Nellie with their kids and my sons to the caravan for the summer. Patsy would start drinking with Johnny at about 9.30am and continue throughout the day.

But he never let drink interfere with his work. Fitzy was a good drinker too and popular because he could sing all the old music hall songs. Patsy sang Irish songs and the pair would get paralytic together.

Sometimes he went a little over the top. He and I were in a bar in the Tin Pan Alley Club (owned by Jimmy and young Frank Fraser – our families go back over forty years) once, when Patsy picked an argument with two geezers in the corner. On this occasion he had his arm in plaster so it was left to me to sort them out. He was such an argumentative bastard but I loved him.

Big George was from Canning Town. A big lump of a man and as tall as Micky Regan, he was very muscular with a granite face and carried oxyacetylene bottles as if they were light as a feather. He was a good-natured man and a very good worker. He had a curious habit of stretching his arms out to shorten his jacket sleeves every time he sat down. His size and bearing contributed to his frightening appearance. What a formidable team! Big Mick, Big Ron and Big George – all the same size. Then neanderthal Alf and me, and wild Patsy.

While I was on my toes at Adeline Grove, I got nicked at an illegal spiel in Limehouse. Maureen had been in the car waiting for me while I walked inside for a few moments and all of a sudden the place was surrounded by police vans and cossers. Everybody got nicked, including me. Apart from being a police station Arbour Square was also a magistrates' court where small fines were given.

But then they started fingerprinting everybody and that was a different story. I had already given a moody name of Freddie Puttnam. They insisted on keeping me there so finally I gave in and thought I might have a chance to get away before they checked my prints.

Alas, in court the next morning I went up and got my fine in the name of Puttnam. Together with thirty to forty others out of the spieler. My George also came to court in case I needed to come away a bit lively, so as I walked out of the dock there were two coppers waiting for me at the back of the court. I recognised them. 'Hullo Fred, we've been looking for you for a long time. Come on, it ain't going to be too bad.' Fortunately, but unbeknown to me Maureen had done the sensible thing and had got in touch with Albert Connell, the bookmaker go-between, to do whatever he could. We were all sensible that way. We knew the routine and were usually one step ahead.

I went along with the coppers to the car-park and as we got around the corner, instead of three of us, there were suddenly four. George had fallen into step and was marching alongside, his hand in his jacket ready to pull out a big cosh that was down his trousers. Looking sideways at me and then George, the coppers asked: 'Who the fuck is he?' I turned to George and told him we were going to the nick and I'd be okay.

But George had been willing to have a row with the coppers, put the cosh about and spring me. He'd said: 'You sure mate?'

I replied: 'See you later, George,' and he reluctantly walked away. At the nick I was kept in the cells for a couple of hours and then one of the guvnors called me into an office.

'Where've you fucking been, Fred? We been looking everywhere for you. You been in the East End? That's a bad manor to be in, Fred. You're a south London boy.' The copper told me that he'd see whether they wanted me in Southampton and would play it by ear.

He got on the phone and his conversation went like this: 'You know the guy we're looking for, I got him in custody. Freddie Foreman. Are those witnesses still available? But how are they going to deal with it after two years? Do you want me to deal with it or do you want to be fucked about with it down there? I've got him for receiving. All right, leave it to me, I'll deal with it then.' He put the phone down and said that was that, did I want to put my hands up to receiving? To me that was a good result. I got three months and being sent back to Wandsworth prison was like going back to a mother's womb. Good old Albert had done the trick again!

The firm were upset by my departure because we had business to do and work to complete. Now that I was no longer on my toes, Maureen wanted to return to south London to be near her sister Nellie and Johnny Fitz. Buster and June and Renee and Tommy Wisbey were on the other side of the water so we took a flat in Vauxhall Walk, a council estate, right next to Lambeth Walk. John Doland (interior designer) came over and made the place look presentable and Maureen spent far too much on it for a council flat, but it did look nice. Now that I was back in south London I could get involved again with George and Buster although I was still working with the other firm.

Using some of my profits from the pavement work, we got premises in Lambeth Walk and turned it into a drinking club with entertainment and live music.

The club opened in 1958 and was an instant success. Johnny Fitz was one of the barmen, Ronnie King on the door and George and Buster helped run it. Jock the piano player was at the keys most nights and Bertie Blake did the cabaret. The building was long and narrow and a potential deathtrap because we only had one window half-way down the club. Before it was inspected for fire regulations, we knocked a hole through the back wall and put in a door leading to a supposed fire exit. In fact it led straight into Sainsbury's private goods depot – this did the trick but as soon as the inspection was over, we had to brick it up again, leaving the door on show complete with Emergency Exit sign – thank God we never had to use it.

The premises were licensed and luxuriously fitted-out. The place was cracking away but it also drew a lot of attention when people left late at night. They made a lot of noise, laughing and joking and waking up neighbours so we knew it was only a matter of time before police raided us. We got nicked a couple of times for after-hours drinking and that's when I got to know Frank Williams, a detective inspector from across the road at Kennington police station. Albert Connell knew him well and arranged a meet. He became a good contact and helped me out on a number of occasions.

Upstairs at the club, Joe Carter ran an SP office so that was another string to our bow. It was a good little earner. Even so we were one of many clubs in the area. The Richardsons had their club in Camberwell, there was the Bungalow Club in Brixton and Ronnie Scrutton ran the Chase Club at the Angel.

You could go from one club to another and see the same faces. We could easily tell which pavement firm had a touch on a particular day by the way they were celebrating in the afternoon. They'd be walking around with bottles of vodka or scotch. Money just flowed. There were always loads of tarts and birds on week nights. Friday was chaps' night and wives were only allowed on Saturday and Sunday nights. (We were only being fair!)

We had terrific times. All the women would dress up as flapper girls on Roaring 20s nights. On other nights we'd have fancy dress parties and lots of music and drink. Like all club owners you had plenty of trouble indoors with wives and girlfriends. I worked hard on the pavements by day and played hard in the club most nights.

Johnny Fitz's wife, Nellie was a lovely lady but a real little firecracker. She'd come down to the club and drag him home if he was drunk and stayed out late. Apart from her being mad at him for drinking, she was as good as gold most of the time.

While Joe Carter had an SP office above our premises,

Micky Regan ran one upstairs above the Chi Chi drinking club at the Angel. All the chaps used to use the club which was respectably run by two women, so nobody took liberties. People from all over London drank there. Mick's offices were run by his sister Pat, a lovely person, his brother Maurice, a cousin Danny and Nobby Clarke, his board man. Mick would help out on the phones when we were not doing other business.

We never knew the reason for it, but Mick's premises were attacked by a gang led by Peter Langton, a local face, who was making a name for himself on the manor. But he only got as far as the stairs. He charged up to Mick's SP office with six or seven of his gang, looking for trouble. A violent row followed. They'd come tooled up with a few bayonets so at the end of the fight there were several broken arms, cuts and bruises shared out on both sides.

As Mick was one of the firm, I got tooled up when I heard about the trouble and went over there to him straight away and slept on his settee that night for support. Later our firm went for a cruise and toured all the little pubs to find those responsible.

Late one night I had one of the gang responsible in my sights and we stalked him through the back streets of Islington. Fortunately for him he got to his street door just in time. Years later I met him under different circumstances and found him one of the nicest chaps you could meet. But that's the way it was in those days. You couldn't sit on the fence, you had to declare who you were with, friend or foe, and I was with Micky Regan, come what may.

We drove around for weeks in two cars looking for other members of the gang. We had spies and finger men out visiting all the pubs and clubs with orders to report to us immediately if they spotted any of them.

Several weeks went by and I was in the corner of the Walk Inn having a drink with Ronnie Kray. The club was packed out on this particular night. Ronnie said to me: 'Don't look now Freddie, but there's that geezer Langton at the corner of the bar. I'm with you if you want to sort it out.' Langton was with two of his friends. I told Ronnie I'd sort it out myself another time, I didn't want to involve the Twins; it was the firm's row, but then Buster, who was behind the bar, said Langton wanted a word with me.

He offered me a lorry load of booze he'd nicked and I said I might be interested if he gave me a breakdown of what he had and came back to see me the next day. I got in touch with Mick immediately and let him know that we were going to get a visit from someone he badly wanted to meet again.

Langton arrived for the meet with two of his guys and I had Alf Gerrard, Big Ronnie, Big George, my George and Buster with me. I stalled for a bit and told him a buyer was coming over who'd probably have the lot off him.

After about half-an-hour and a few drinks later, Mick walked in and the blood drained from Langton's face. The two guys with him didn't know what was going on as they hadn't been part of the row. Langton looked around, there was only one way out: the window. Alf warned him that if he made a move he'd be a dead man. 'Don't even think about it,' Alf said.

Langton looked at me: 'You too, Fred?'

'I'm afraid so,' I replied.

One of Mick's people backed a van to the club door and I said: 'Whichever way you want to go out of here, you're going now.' The other two guys were crapping themselves. I told them it had nothing to do with them and to sit down in the corner with my George and Buster while the rest of us dealt with Langton. I then gave Langton the choice of walking out or going out feet first.

'Will it be bad?' he asked. I told him he would have to wait and see and that it was up to Mick. He walked to the van and we roped him up and blindfolded him. The place we were taking him to was our flop (a farmhouse) a couple of hours' drive away in the country, and by the time we got there he was starting to talk gibberish and was obviously in a state of shock.

I asked Mick what he was going to do. Mick had an iron bar and said that he would just do his legs. I said: 'I'll anaesthetise him and put him out of his fucking misery.' It was more out of mercy than anything else. I hit him on the chin and knocked him out, breaking his jaw. Mick sat him up against the wall and propped his knees up to his chin and gave him a few good whacks with the iron bar.

Langton started to come round and began pulling down his blindfold. 'Pull that fucking blindfold down and you're not going to leave here,' I warned him. We put him in the van and on the way back he was talking gibberish again.

We got back to Myddelton Square at the Angel and pulled him out. I stuck a tenner in his top pocket for a cab fare and left him on the pavement. He couldn't walk or do anything. Both his legs were busted. It was no surprise he just disappeared off the scene. Everyone knew he'd been taken for a ride, but he never came to the front again or tried to be a name. The other people involved with him went to ground and never surfaced for six to twelve months. On one or two occasions we got the motor out and went looking for them but they had vanished.

Twenty or so years later when I went to the A & R Club for a drink (Mick and Ronnie Knight owned it) Mick told me I'd never believe who was drinking there. It was Peter Langton who he said turned out to be a really nice guy. Langton told Mick it was the best thing that could have happened to him. It set him on the straight and narrow and he'd never done a day's bird since. He bought us drinks and said we had treated him right and taught him a lesson. We all shook hands and that was the end of that episode. It shows that the short, sharp lesson sometimes works!

A similar comeback was taken against somebody who'd been in prison with George and who I helped out. John Speeby was a tall, flat-nosed ex-soldier who had a pension for wartime injuries. On his release from prison, he came to the club and I gave him a job as a sort of handyman and caretaker at one of my investments: a house facing Clapham Common. He was provided with his own well-furnished room complete with television and all the comforts of home. A relation of mine, Billy Owen, had recently died and as he was the same height and build as Speeby, I gave him all his wardrobe. Speeby had never looked so smart in his life.

One day I received a call that all the tenants' rooms had been broken into, and their money and valuables stolen. Dear old Speeby was missing. I was sick. The tenants had called the police who now asked me to attend the local nick. The house had been one of my private investments and now my cover was blown. I remembered Speeby's snide remarks: 'You're doing all right for yourself, Fred.' I went through his room and found an old pension book under the paper in his cupboard drawer. It had the days and address from where he collected his pension. I pulled out one of my vans and got hold of Ronnie King. I told Ronnie I wanted him to 'Old Bill' a guy for me and get him in the back of a van. The day I picked Ron up from Milton Road, he came out with a long object wrapped in brown paper. 'What's that Ron?' I asked. He told me it was a shovel. 'I don't think it will come to that Ron,' I said. 'But, just in case, we'd better take it with us.' (I didn't want to hurt his feelings.) Anyway, pretending he was Old Bill, Ron went into the post office and made a few inquiries for me. We were told that the gentleman in question usually came about ten to collect his pension so we didn't have long to wait.

Speeby arrived shortly after and the anger inside me swelled when I saw how smartly dressed he was in my Bill's clothes and Crombie overcoat. He strode about as though he didn't have a care in the world. 'Out you go, Ron,' I said.

Ron pulled him lovely. He has a nice speaking voice and can pass for anyone in authority. Speeby climbed into the back of the van like a lamb to the slaughter.

I had my back to the door and was leaning over the front seat. Ron closed the back door as I turned round to face Speeby who was now sitting down. His face drained of all colour. He tried to compose himself: 'Hullo Fred . . .' Before he could speak another word I smashed his face with a thick rubber cosh.

I said: 'You mongrel bastard, after all I have done for you, you rob me and my house and old ladies and nurses. You're going to die you bastard.' Whack! Whack! I belted him good and proper. 'Get those clothes off, you mongrel bastard!' I tore at his coat and shoes and kept whacking him as I did it. As each item came off, I went through his pockets and found pawn tickets for left luggage lockers at railway stations. I took him to pawn shops in Lambeth Walk, Walworth Road and Waterloo Station, and to all the other places where he'd pledged my tenants' belongings and I redeemed the goods. Pitiful things like picture frames and bits of tom, even clothes. His pockets bulged with pawn tickets. Every time I got back into the van I'd give him another whack.

I took him back to Spencer Park where Lenny Morgan had battered Mo Jones. It was winter and icy cold and all he had on was my Billy's pants and socks. His face was swollen and his eyes were like slits. He looked as if he'd just done fifteen rounds with Henry Cooper. I threw him out the back of the van and he staggered towards a clump of trees and walked smack into one. I returned to the house and, much to my enjoyment, put all the goods in the hallway and let the tenants sort out their belongings. The house had been a nice little investment, but now it would have to go. It had cost me quite a few pounds to get back the tenants' stolen items but to see the pleasure on their faces was worth every bit of the money.

Some years later I heard Speeby was sentenced to another ten years. The bastard deserved all he got. The world would be a better place without people like him. I loathe petty criminals stealing from their own kind and from people who have nothing worth stealing but whose goods mean a lot to them. Sentimental objects can never be replaced and I have no time for muggers, house-breakers, pickpockets or joyriders. Nor for conmen who take advantage of another's trust in order to steal their money.

The Walk Inn was taking too much of a toll on our lives and we were considering giving it up. As I said before, we were continually in the doghouse with our wives and families so we thought we'd have an insurance coup. I had a word with a friend of the family who worked as an assessor and on inspection of the premises he said there was too much concrete and brick for a good fire so we had to think of other solutions. In the end the problem solved itself.

Buster, who was getting drunk all the time, drove into about six cars one evening, writing off his own in the process and leaving a gaping wound in his head. The blood just poured out. He came into the club and we thought this was the final straw. He was getting into too much trouble through the Walk Inn. I had just had a touch and money was no problem so we thought we'd smash the fuck out of the bar, smash all the mirrors, the chairs and juke box, all the stage lighting and plants. We literally wrecked the place. We then got Buster to go around and flick his head up and down leaving huge streaks of blood splattered across the walls. He was a bit masochistic in this way but I thought the world of Buster and sadly miss him to this day. I only wish I could turn the clock back.

Anyway, having smashed the place up, we called the police and Buster sat there with the gaping wound still oozing blood. Frank Williams, the station DI, came over and we said we'd had a bit of trouble from a gang across the water.

He looked at Buster and said: 'I know who that is. It's Porky Bennett's gang.' I'd never heard of him at that time, although he came from Bethnal Green, which was the Twins' territory. I later found out they'd had a few rows in clubs over the East End.

So I told DI Williams: 'I don't know who the fuck it was. I just got here. We've had enough of this, Mr Williams, we're going to call it a day!'

He said we were going to lose our licence anyway so we put in a claim and my insurance man got us a nice few grand plus loss of profits. We had turned defeat into victory. Now we could get back to normal with our families again.

· 8 ·
Pavement Artists

The post office would have to reorganise security and bring in a host of procedural changes as a result of our enterprise on the pavements. We were known as pavement artists because of the speed and efficiency with which we relieved post office and security vans of their valuable cargoes. Basically, it meant hanging about on a pavement until the target stopped off for a pick-up or a delivery. We'd strike then and it would be all over in minutes. It was a highly lucrative business.

Thursdays were the busiest day of the week. That's when pensions were paid. I would dress up as a postman in trousers with red stripes, badges, the whole gear. We already knew through inside information which PO van would leave a particular sorting office with bags of cash. The van drivers were never told what they would be carrying and security was surprisingly lax considering that there could be up to £20,000 in cash, a lot of money in the late 1950s.

I'd be lurking on the pavement, waiting for the van to arrive. The driver was usually alone and I'd cop for him as soon as he opened the sliding door. In most cases, I'd drag him into the back of the van and wrap him up with some rope. Alf would jump up with me and go through the sacks of mail and find the four or five registered bags that had to come out. These were normally identifiable by a perforated edge on the label.

Ron would drive us away with another van or car tailing us. It was all over in seconds. We would drive the van

to a predetermined spot, usually a dead turning or somewhere you would be least noticed, dump the motor, and be
off in the getaway car. We always prepared thoroughly in
advance and noted stopping times, delivery times, routes
and escape routes. The operation went like clockwork and
we used to average one a fortnight.

The hauls were mostly cash but we also got insurance
and postage stamps. You could sell the insurance stamps
to business firms for one third of their face value. Mike
Harris and his partner Reggie Isaacs had people lined up
all over London who'd buy them. He even sold them
back to post office workers who'd flog them across the
counter and get back the face value. Our 'sales force' had
been established over many years and everyone was on
an earner. They were all part of an established organisation and you knew they could be trusted.

Eventually, the authorities must have sussed what was
going on because they started perforating stamps and
putting codes on them for certain areas. But that didn't
stop us. We cracked the codes quickly and made sure the
post office in Southwark wasn't selling stamps destined
for, say, Carshalton. Once when we raided a sorting office,
we had nearly half a million pounds' worth of stamps, all
coded – with our organisation it was no problem.

When things began to hot up too much, we switched
to banks and sorting offices. The PO had begun counter-
measures by putting two men into the vans. When that
failed to stop us, they installed bullet-proof glass and
panic buttons which immobilised the vehicle – but even
that never stopped us.

Our getaway vehicle used for bank and post office
raids was a Vanden Plas limousine. The boot held all our
readies: pickaxe handles, coshes and spare clothing, and
we had false plates fitted for the occasion. The cap-wear-
ing 'chauffeur' sat alone in the front, while the rest of us
hid on the floor. We used that car for a long time. It was
reliable, and we considered it a 'lucky' car.

The layout of a north London sorting office had been accurately sketched for us. Our information was that on a certain weekend there would be a load of cash coming in which would be stored in a strongroom and would amount, by today's values, to several million pounds. Our plan was to enter the building before the weekend and stay overnight in one of the recreation rooms for which we had a spare key. Planning this operation took several weeks. By the time we were ready for the robbery, most of our gear had been smuggled inside the sorting office and hidden in lockers and cupboards.

Instead of bringing in conspicuously large oxyacetylene bottles, we converted much smaller oxygen bottles which we stole from St Thomas's hospital in south London. We entered the building via the loading bay dressed in authentic post office attire and made our way along passageways we'd memorised from the sketch to an upstairs recreation room. We brought with us our bags and sandwiches and walked about purposefully and confidently as though we were part of the staff. Once inside the recreation room, nobody would disturb us because it was locked up over weekends.

At about 9pm on the Saturday, when only a skeleton staff were in the building, we covered our faces with scarves and made for the strongroom. On the way, we met a security man who put up a bit of a struggle. He was a copper type, and got whacked a bit and then tied up. Another two security men gave no trouble at all and we tied them up and left them in the strongroom. The cutting gear was not needed because we managed to get a key. It was an Aladdin's Cave full of cash. We sorted out all the registered bags and filled up two trolley-loads of high-value parcels filled with money and valuables. On the way out we bumped into two more night-workers. We copped for them and wrapped them up with a bit more string and left them on the loading bay. All that lay between us and riches were the exit gates.

They were bolted with chains secured with padlocks and we sent Paddy O'Nione (Paddy Onions) and Big George to open up so we could toss everything into our van which was already standing by, engine running, ready to drive into the loading bay. Alas, this was where things started to go wrong.

We had used somebody in the country to provide a lot of our equipment and he was a penny-pinching bastard and had brought cheap cutters even though he'd been given plenty of money to buy the best heavy-duty gear. As a result, Paddy and George had difficulty cutting the chains and were a bit slow. Mid-way during this little operation, a cosser walked by the gates on the footpath outside. Instead of fannying it out Paddy fucked up. He panicked and brought attention to himself by overreacting to the copper's presence. As far as the cosser had been concerned the sorting office was lit up and everything looked normal. Meanwhile, we were making our way there with the trolleys full of cash. But the copper, alerted by Paddy's behaviour, ran from the gate and blew his whistle.

Me and Alf were not willing to go empty-handed. Our van was outside revving its engine like fury. The gate was still shut but there was a gap at the top just large enough for us to squeeze through. We tried throwing bags of money through this opening but they were too fat. We then pushed a couple through but things were getting too hot and, reluctantly, we left the skips and narrowly squeezed through the gap ourselves.

We changed cars in north London and then went to our lock-up in Kennington. We had a nice stow for the cars off Clapham Road, left them there, and went back to my place in Vauxhall. Paddy said he'd had enough. He wasn't going to do this any more. After what happened, we didn't want him. Our haul was only a few thousand and a bit of tom. But it should have been millions! C'est la vie!

Some months later, four of us did the place again. I was

masked on this occasion and scared two of the security men shitless when I walked in on them. With the light behind me I must have looked a menacing sight. I had them both on the floor in an instant, and Alf joined me. We put a bit of rope around them. I asked one how many more were in the building. 'Two more,' he said. We went stalking for them and Alf copped one, head under his arm, a tap on the head, and frogmarched him to another room.

'Where's your friend?' He didn't know and we couldn't go to work until we found him. All of a sudden we heard a toilet flush. He was in the khazi so we got him when he came out.

He told us where the keys to the strongroom were and we got in without a problem. This time we made our exit from the building through a side-door, sweet as a nut. It was a good bit of work. We got a lot of cash from pay-rolls sent through the post, and some tom – rings, watches, and other jewellery in transit for Hatton Garden. Although it had been a good bit of work, it was a little disappointing as they hadn't stored as much cash and stamps as we'd hoped. That was all down to the last episode which must have scared the shit out of them.

After another aborted job in which we lost quite a few tools, we went up to Manchester where a bit of work had come our way in one of the Big Four banks. To get at the back of the bank, we had to go through a locked car-park and then into another yard belonging to a funeral parlour. That's where Alf pointed out the accident casualties in their coffins. After we'd got inside the premises, a security man arrived with two Alsatians and let the dogs loose in the yard. They made a hell of a fuss by an open window through which we'd entered with all our oxyacetylene equipment. With all the commotion we couldn't go on, so we quickly collected up all our gear and got out of there.

The police put a cordon around Manchester thinking we'd head south, and this caused us to go a long way round. We tried to fox them by doing a detour around country lanes. But hours later we ran out of petrol and had to wake up a lorry driver sleeping in his cabin. We gave him a tenner and got him to drive us to the nearest garage for a can of petrol and we were then able to return safely to London.

We had a bad run, one disaster after another, but that's how things went sometimes. Christmas was coming up and we hadn't earned any money for quite some time so we raided a postie van in south London. Most of our tools were lost on aborted raids and we had to make up new pickaxe handles to go to work. All you needed was some rope which you put on each side of the handle and then wound black adhesive tape so you could carry it easily on your wrists. The hitting end was also taped up to soften the blow. It was a good tool.

Armed with these tools, we got into the back of the van. The security men put up quite a fight but the situation got worse with the arrival of reinforcements. These were made up of local builders and scaffolders who joined in the mêlée. The bastards got a bit brave and put up quite a fight. The security guards were not the ordinary run-of-the-mill guards either, so we had a terrible row with them. Afterwards my bollocks were black and blue. As we made our getaway, a big petrol tanker came up and blocked the road. We had to go up the pavement to get around it. Big Ron was a good coach and we just scraped through a narrow gap.

As we did so, they threw everything at us, from bricks to scaffolding poles, but we escaped and were back in the money again. Me and Alf finished up going to Harrods and spending £600 on toys for the kids.

Some villains panic when their liberty is at stake but we always prided ourselves on our professionalism which included never doing any real damage to innocent parties. We had targeted another sorting office on the outskirts of London. We knew that there'd been a delivery of quite a lot of cash and we struck late at night when we expected only about six to eight staff on duty. We waited by the vans in the yard when one guy came out to do the perimeter security and let the last van in. We copped for him and got his keys but he struggled violently and made a lot of noise. A housing estate was next to the perimeter fence and the commotion threatened our safety.

Big George, Mick and Patsy had already gone inside to wrap up the others so I told Ron to take his hand away from this noisy geezer's mouth so I could knock him out. What happened was that his false teeth had slipped half-way down his throat and he was choking and fighting for his life. He was as good as gold after Ron delicately fished out the small plate with his banana fingers! After that things ran smoothly and we had a good payday.

At one stage we were competing with the banks in a race against time to get at their vaults. They had commissioned a leading safe manufacturer to provide new safes before we had an opportunity to crack their old ones. All the major banks, after seeing their vaults busted open with square holes through great thick doors and cages, and their deposit boxes plundered, realised they would have to renew their antiquated hardware and fit the most up-to-date security systems.

With all the heavy work we had been doing, we were strong as bullocks. Our 'equipment' included about six suitcases and several oxyacetylene gas bottles weighing two hundredweight each. We used to lift these up and throw them over our shoulders and then climb fire escapes and ladders and scamper across roofs.

We used walkie talkies – as there were no mobile phones then – and we had become so professional we even had smoke extractor fans to get rid of the burning smell. One night we did a factory while staff were on duty. Dressed in boiler suits, we made our way along a river towpath, clambered over an outside wall, and got into the office block containing the vault.

We were told that there was no night security because

the whole place was alive. But the vault door was on view to all the working staff milling about in the yard outside. To block off the view, we came prepared with a large tent which we built in front of the vault door and set to work with the cutters. While we were waiting for the vault doors to cool down after being torched, there was time for a flask of tea and sandwiches. Big Ron and me were facing some porthole swing doors and saw a face skip away from one of the windows. Ron rushed after him. There was night security after all! He rugby-tackled the guard who smashed his torch into Ron's face. I sat on the man's chest and told him to behave himself or he'd get hurt. All he said was: 'You'll never get away with this,' and then fainted. We dragged him back to the vault room and roped him up. We then got the money and left him protesting wildly: 'You'll all hang,' he screamed. 'I'm going to die.' He passed out again. But it was all a sham. There was quite a large air vent in the vault door after we'd been at it so he had nothing to worry about. Nevertheless, we packed our suitcases in a hurry as we didn't know if the night security guard had to check in and, if so, how often. If you could possibly avoid it, you never left gear behind because of the expense, the risk of prints and the bother of replacing it. Because of our need to get away quickly, we just threw everything into our suitcases leaving us short on space. So we stuffed all the money that was stolen into the legs and body of Alf's boiler suit, making it look like a bonfire Guy Fawkes with no head, tied and knotted at the neck and ankles. We left in two Ford Zephyrs for our safe-house in north London where we would cut up the money.

I found a spot to park the Zephyr in between two other cars. It was a bit tight, but I managed to squeeze in and was just about to get out of the car when two plain-clothes policemen came out of the darkness and began asking questions about the numberplate and ownership of the car. I gave the details and told them to leave us alone. I locked the car door and started to walk away when one of the clever bastards shone his torch into the back and saw Alf's boiler suit torso. 'Hello, hello,' he said. 'What's this then?' Well, all hell broke loose. One copper was laid out and I drove down the road with the other silly bastard lying across my front windscreen, right across the bonnet, flashing his torch into my eyes.

I said to Alf: 'I'll have to stop and you get out and bash this silly bastard.' At which point, I braked hard. Alf got out but with the rapid stop, the copper had disappeared over the back, ripping off the windscreen wiper as he went. That got rid of him. We drove to a friend's flat where we could walk through different blocks of the estate out of sight with our headless dummy which Alf and I were holding up like a drunk, and phoned the rest of the firm to tell them of the change of venue. We'd had a narrow escape, but it all ended well and we cut up the money whilst Alf tucked into a rabbit stew.

As an offshoot to our main business, Paddy Onions, Alf, Brian and Peter Loughran organised a smuggling enterprise bringing in watches from Switzerland. It got so lucrative we had our own special brand made up called 'Moodoo' watches (a joke on moody watches), which were gaudy and garish. The chunky ones with lots of gold, bangles and stones in them were sold in Brixton. The ladies loved them. For gentlemen we had a 'slimline' watch which was quite plain-looking. They were genuine Swiss watches, made to order but shipped in without paying tax and duty. We had good contacts with some fishermen and smuggled them in on a fishing boat at Newhaven. The captain would pick up the gear off the coast of Belgium and then Paddy would sail out to meet him in a dinghy and bring the watches into Newhaven in a holdall. Small fortunes were made and some of us bought houses with cash from the profits.

On one particular day, the Customs were waiting to smash this enterprise. Brian was the coach, Alf was there minding and Paddy had the gear. Customs men had disguised themselves as fishermen and they had an attractive undercover lady officer who chatted up Paddy on a train journey to Switzerland showing off her legs and putting him in promise land. He'd already taken her out for dinner and she'd intimated that next time they met he'd get his leg over. But the next time he saw her, he was a million miles from getting his leg over. He was in the dock in the Old Bailey and she was giving evidence for the prosecution.

When Paddy sailed into Newhaven, the fishermen asked what was in his bag as they were talking downstairs over a cup of tea in a harbour canteen. Paddy's reply was: 'Cock-a-doodle-doo, it's got nothing to do with you.' That expression was later repeated at his trial, provoking great laughter.

Those days Customs were quite gentlemanly in their business and were used to people responding in like manner. But not our team. When the officers confronted them with the words: 'Good morning gentlemen, we're Customs Officers. You're under arrest!'. 'Bollocks!' came the reply as the three rushed out to their Jaguar getaway car and took off. A Customs Officer stood in front of the car for a brief second but thought better of it when he realised they would not stop.

A chase ensued and, unfortunately, the Jaguar's accelerator cable broke. That didn't stop our men. Alf opened the bonnet and lay across the engine, bringing the bonnet back down on top of him, and held the broken accelerator arm together so they could escape. They threw all the bags containing the watches, approximately £40,000 worth, into a farmer's ditch and covered them over as best they could. Unfortunately the next day the farmer decided to clear his ditches and found the watches which he handed in to the police. When the three appeared before the magistrate at committal proceedings in Lewes Magistrates' Court, we watched the prosecution's car arrive and followed it at lunchtime to the local pub. While they were having a bit of lunch and a few jars we stole their briefcases with the evidence. We got all the prosecution's phone numbers and found out how they had done their investigation. Amazingly, they had gone as far as bugging a public phone booth outside my flat in Kennington. This was 1960 so you can imagine what they get up to today.

When Alf was tried, the jury got him off the more serious charges because they all lived in the Isle of Dogs and were sympathetic to an East Ender. He went down for nine months. Paddy got five years.

Those days you had no privileges like today. There were no phonecalls home to your wife, visits were only allowed once a month and then you could only shout through thick, dirty glass and would have no physical contact. It was bad. No home leave, nothing.

If any of the firm were ever unavoidably detained in prison, we'd still cut them in their whack whenever we had a touch. It was our rule although not a lot of firms did as we did. We looked after wives and children when their men were away and out of circulation.

Around this time we were offered some work in Ireland by an Irish connection who had worked in London and done some time in British jails. We were in a quiet period but holding a good amount of money. The Irish firm said they had access to a bank and keys in Drogheda, Co. Louth, just thirty miles north of Dublin on the east coast of Ireland. Did we fancy going over? We liked the sound of it. In case we were stopped and questioned over there, we had the plausible excuse that we had come to look at betting shops.

It was just before the British government had decided to cash in on SP betting itself. Betting shops were given a trial run in Ireland for a year or so before they were allowed in England.

The four of us went out in pairs. Me and Patsy O'Mara on one flight, Micky Regan and Big George on another. Big George had already been there earlier to look at the safe and said it would only take half-an-hour to cut through it. The Irish firm had been given a shopping list of equipment necessary to burn open the vault and they already had access keys to let us inside the bank. All of us used pseudonyms when we booked into Dublin hotels on arrival. 1 stayed with Patsy at the Gresham Hotel under the name of Roberts and the other two booked in under false names at the Moria Hotel.

We were met by the Irish firm and did a little more negotiating on how to go to work. The bank was in an industrial area and all our equipment was stored in a tomb of a church graveyard adjoining the bank. One of the priests had enthusiastically entered the plot and had agreed to bring the loot to England for us wearing his dog collar. That would ensure he wouldn't get a pull by police or special branch. The scheme was looking better and better. We asked the Irish firm to hire a car and gave them some money to organise it. We then drove down to look over the bank. Everything went according to plan and we were pleased with the arrangements. On returning to Dublin, we passed through a small village. Four large men driving through a quiet country village was not too clever but we had nothing on us to worry about. The keys to the bank had been lodged with someone local and everything was above-board, or so we thought.

A lone Garda Siochaina (guardians of the peace is their fancy name, but in reality they're just the local cossers) waved us down. Next thing, twenty armed Gardai were all over us. They appeared from behind walls and hedges and arrested us and took us to the local nick. We gave our false names.

It turned out that Zebedia, the geezer whom we paid to get the car, had tried to earn himself some pocket money and instead of hiring it, had borrowed the car from his girlfriend. The problem was that she was two-timing Zebedia, and lent him a car belonging to her other boyfriend who turned out to be an Irish policeman! That explained why they flagged us down. They had recognised their colleague's car and were convinced the four heavies inside had stolen it. Can you believe it? This could only happen in Ireland!

Thank God they had not been on our tail when we went to visit the bank but now they wanted to know what we were up to. They didn't buy our story about visiting betting shops and didn't believe we had given our proper names. They had got in touch with the girl who lent the car and she said that she had not laid eyes on us before, nor had she allowed us to use her car. So, now we were nicked, fingerprinted and asked for our proper names. We tried to fanny our way out but they said: 'We're just as clever as Scotland Yard, you know.' We couldn't get in touch with Zebedia so they banged us up.

As our prints were on their way to London, there was no point in maintaining our false identities any longer so we told them who we were, but that caused further complications. I was okay with a name like Foreman and a cockney accent, but Patsy, Mick and George all had Irish surnames as well as cockney accents so once again the Gardai thought we were trying to have them over.

'Do you take us for idiots?' They hit the roof when we insisted Patsy O'Mara, George Cahill and Michael Regan were Englishmen. The CRO (Criminal Record Office) files confirmed our names but, even so, it was off on remand to Mountjoy Prison charged with stealing a car.

It was a terrible prison, fifty years behind the times. Filthy wooden floors in the cells, knives and forks made from old tin hammered into shape and corroded with age and encrusted with food. You couldn't use them without risking death from food poisoning. The diet was potato soup, potato soup, and potato soup. The winter was freezing cold and there was no heating in the cells. You could hear the mice scrambling under the bed. After 5.30pm when the lights went out in winter, it was pitch black. The cons had no vests or underpants. They were lucky to have buttons on their shirts and they had no woollies or jumpers apart from old blue-dyed army battle dress as the warmest piece of clothing.

We were in nice cashmere overcoats, suits and ties, in spite of which we still froze. Rather than being locked up in these conditions for twenty-three hours a day we asked to be put to work in the woodshed, a Nissen-style hut without sides in which we sawed sleepers and logs wearing our overcoats for extra warmth. A bell rang every quarter-of-an-hour or so and warders and cons who observed the faith would kneel and cross themselves. The screw supervising us was a fat little Hitler complete with moustache.

Patsy, after being constipated for a week, asked the screw for some toilet paper and, accompanied by him, went in search of a khazi but they had all frozen over. We watched the pair of them inspect each toilet in turn, pour cold water, then hot water down the pan, and even try and break up the ice with a four-by-two timber. It was hilarious seeing them shake their heads, and discuss frozen crap. The screw remarked, 'cold water won't shift that'. This went on for half-an-hour and frustration grew between the two men. They then returned, with a bucket of boiling hot water which promptly split the basin in two. Patsy had had enough and said he'd gone off having a crap. The screw nosed up to his face and said: 'You shit when I tell you!'

Patsy responded: 'I'm not getting frostbite in my bollocks for you or anyone else.' The pair then stood nose to nose swearing at each other, until the bell rang again, and the screw dropped to one knee and crossed himself.

My old friend from London, Jim Murray, came to our rescue. He had an interest in a small hotel in Dublin. Jimmy was a good friend for whom I had done a favour in Soho a year before. I'd visited his club with the Twins for a late-night drink. Tony Mellar, who was later shot by his partner, tried to take over Jimmy's club and sent in some heavies on the night we visited. It was a clip joint with nice-looking girls and run properly by members of Jimmy's family. All of a sudden several guys tipped over chairs and tables and started a rumpus. Reg got one of them just in time before he smashed a huge ashtray on my head. We laid out all five of them and dragged them downstairs to Wardour Street, where we left them on the pavement, neatly laid out side by side.

Jimmy was grateful for that. He was a real character. He once hired the Festival Hall for St Patrick's Day celebrations and laid on a red carpet with Irish pipers and the Ted Heath band. He had a lovely house in Clapham overlooking the common. I would go there for parties and he invited a mixture of showbiz people, villains and titled gentry. Lord Moynihan, despite his title, was lower than a sewer rat although he was a frequent visitor to these parties. However, I never liked him and as events were to show, he revealed himself as a treacherous, deceitful informant. I also saw people like Peter Rachman, the notorious landlord, Raymond Nash and actors and musicians.

Anyway, Jimmy arrived at Mountjoy with style. As remand prisoners our food could be brought in and Jimmy delivered it to us using silver service from the kitchens of the hotel. The screws hadn't seen anything like it. A lawyer, aptly named Mr Blood, was engaged to represent our firm. My London solicitor, Tony Block, had earlier telephoned Maureen to ask if she knew where I was. She responded as she'd always been briefed when authority rang: 'He's just gone out to buy a newspaper.' Tony said I must have gone a long way then because Fred was in Mountjoy, Ireland. So Maureen came with Ding Dong (Dell Rudell), a close friend who handled a lot of my business. Patsy's people came with a little Jewish guy called Solly Lautman from the East End. He was in the shmuttar game (rag trade), manufacturing clothes, and we needed a lot of bail money which he brought with him.

The court appearance in Drogheda was like something

out of a farce. The place looked nothing like a court-room. At one end there was a table and chair and, at the other, a big roaring fire. The room was full of people all talking excitedly. The magistrate, a one-armed chap, wanted £10,000 bail in cash for each of us. They could-n't believe it when we piled this king's ransom on the table. It looked like the Great Train Robbery money. I think it was probably the highest bail ever demanded for charges of being in possession of a car without the owner's consent. Let's face it, you could buy a beautiful house for £5000 those days. We made front-page news with headlines referring to us as the 'London Gangsters in Dublin' and were treated like celebrities. Crowds had turned up for the court appearance.

We were each sentenced to nine months, suspended, and were ordered not to return to Ireland for five years (which would have been much too soon for me, anyway).

There was a footnote to this story. Zebedia tried to leave Ireland from Shannon airport when he heard that it came on top for us. Thinking the worst scenario, he got himself kitted up in the priest's outfit, hat, glasses, dog collar, and bible under his arm, the whole bollocks. Zebedia had form as long as your arm so the Gardai recognised him straight away and kicked his arse into a patrol car and arrested him. That idiot could have got us all fourteen years if we had been nicked a day later doing the bank! Another lucky escape!

After the Irish fiasco, we all went into the betting shop business. I was not able to acquire a licence myself so I put my brother-in-law Johnny Fitz up for it, as he knew the game and had worked for different bookmakers at the races as a clerk. Another relation of mine, Jack Darling, also had a bucket and sponge job at the dog-tracks which was a job handed down to family members over the years. It was like a pension. You were paid tips for washing down the blackboards and keeping an eye on the bookie, giving protection.

While I was setting up my betting shops I was asked to help resolve a conflict which could have led to wars between some of the biggest London firms. It involved the Nash brothers, one of whom had been charged with the murder of Selwyn Cooney, who was shot dead in the Pen Club in Duval Street, Stepney. The club was owned by two pals of mine, Billy Ambrose and Jerry Callaghan, who were recruited from time to time to join in some pavement work with our firm. On this weekend, 6 and 7 February, 1960, Billy Ambrose had been paroled while serving a ten-year sentence for robbery with violence. (Jerry and Bill both had a good touch robbing a pen company and that's how the club got its name.) There was a fight in the club involving the Nash firm which included Joey Pyle, Johnny Reed and Jimmy Nash on the one hand, and Jerry Callaghan and Billy Ambrose on the other.

Unfortunately, the barman Selwyn Cooney got shot in the head and Billy Ambrose got a bullet in the stomach. A few of the others had bottles smashed over their heads. Billy, in spite of his wounds, took Cooney's body out of the club and put it on the pavement before driving himself to hospital.

Later Jimmy Nash was arrested for the shooting and looked like being hanged if he was found guilty so we had a 'sit down'. Both sides needed someone to negotiate so I was called in for Billy Ambrose, and the Twins for the Nash brothers. To make sure no villainy was done I had to guarantee that Billy and Jerry weren't setting them up for an ambush. The Twins, in turn, made sure the Nashes didn't come tooled up and blast Billy and Jerry. We held the meeting at Vallance Road and pledged our help. It was a case of us against the authorities.

Fortunately, Jimmy was acquitted of the murder and got five years for GBH which was a good result. It's a pity that politicians and heads of state can't settle their differences as effectively as we did.

· 9 ·
Good Times

Harold Macmillan, Britain's Prime Minister, was right when he told the nation in the early 1960s: 'You've never had it so good.' Those years were some of the most lucrative in our career. Continuing success from pavement work and robbing banks and post offices meant I could now begin to invest money into straight businesses like the betting shops, and clubs and pubs. Ironically though, Scotland Yard kept putting obstacles in the way of me 'going straight'.

When my brother-in-law Johnny Fitz (Fitzgerald) applied for our first betting shop licence in Lower Road, Bermondsey, we were heavily opposed. At the hearing in Walworth Road Town Hall, half a dozen coppers crashed in like storm troopers and accused Johnny of being: 'a front man for Frederick Foreman, a known criminal'. Well as it happened, I knew the mayor, Bill Gates, who was chairman of the Licensing Board. I had raised money for his favourite charities and Bill, wearing his mayoral chain, was photographed in the local newspaper arriving at my pub, the Prince of Wales, in his Rolls-Royce. In response to objections from the police he pointed out, quite rightly: 'It is Mr Fitzgerald who is applying for the licence, not Mr Foreman,' and he granted the application.

My mini empire was expanding rapidly. My pub, the Prince of Wales in Lant Street, Borough, where Maureen and I lived in an upstairs flat, was proving very popular. The area was famous. One of Lant Street's noted residents was Charles Dickens who had lodged there when his father was in Marshalsea Debtors' Prison, which used to be around the corner. The house Dickens stayed in had been demolished but one of my locals, Terry Fermature, brought me Dickens's old lock and key which I proudly displayed in a glass case in the Prince of Wales.

I had another flat on the fourteenth floor of the Brandon estate which was a prestige block when built and included members of parliament among its tenants. We used it as a quiet little bolt-hole which only close friends knew about. I had also invested in a house converted into five flats facing Clapham Common, and we still had the house in Milton Road where Ronnie King lived.

Over a short period of time, we built up a chain of betting shops. In addition to Bermondsey, I owned another with Tommy Wisbey and Billy Gorbell in Borough Market, one in Brixton run by Reggie Isaacs, another in Rotherhithe New Road, and two in Croydon. The most successful was the shop at Nunhead Lane, Peckham, where one of our punters was Ronnie Corbett, the TV comedian who lived around the corner.

It was managed by Ding Dong with my George and a young chap Kenny behind the counter. I would occasionally chalk runners up on the board and pay out the winnings on days when it suited me. It was a very good front after I'd done a bit of pavement work as it provided me with the perfect alibi. I'd get back there as fast as possible and be chalking up more winners for everyone to see. They'd be so absorbed with betting they never missed me while I was out and would later swear blind that I had been there all the time.

Whenever there was a big robbery, police would telephone around and ask to speak to whoever appeared on their list of suspects. If I wasn't there, Maureen or one of my staff would tell them I was 'just around the corner buying a newspaper' or 'busy chalking up winners'.

Around the corner from my pub in Marshalsea, I also bought a twenty-year lease on a large building which I turned into a gym on one floor with a boxing ring, punch bags and the usual boxing apparatus, a disco in the basement, photo agency at the top and an SP office on the other floor. The Marshalsea gym was christened 'The Chaps' Gym' by boxing commentator Reg Gutteridge.

Mick and Big George had also gone into the betting shop business with large premises in Poland Street (which they eventually sold to Ladbroke's for a small fortune), so they were semi-retired and with Alf doing nine months and Ron away for three years in prison, it left just Patsy and myself to make up a firm. We pulled in another two men who were good workers and had been with us on several big jobs whenever we needed extra help. Big Tommy Sullivan was one of them, he was another big lump who was capable of any work that had to be done.

A little job which came up at this time involved a guy called Charlie who put up the work and insisted on making one with us 'just for the crack'. The money came down Silvertown Way in a taxi and we waited on the corner. Our smash-car overtook the cab and forced it into our street where we were waiting on the pavement. We smashed the cab windows to cause confusion and ripped open the doors for Patsy to grab the money bags with no trouble. It was done right outside an electrical firm. Our escape van was in place and we dived headfirst into it, lying flat while the wheel man put his foot down and tore off at high speed. But Charlie came unstuck. Unused to this kind of adrenalin-pumping exercise, he became very excited as we took the cash bags and the silly bastard stood upright in the back of the getaway van, shaking his fist and laughing at the workers who came out of the electrical firm to see what was happening. They heard the commotion and all the shouting and windows smashing. Within seconds, the street had come alive with people.

As we'd clambered on board, the wheel man was urged: 'Go, go, go!' But Charlie, in his excitement, failed to hold on as the van took off and went flying through the back doors, falling flat on his face in the middle of the road. Our driver was already in second gear when we shouted for him to stop. 'Hold on! Hold on for Charlie!', as the van roared on down the road. Now that we'd gone, all the bank clerks, security men, the taxi driver had got brave and ran towards Charlie. We screeched to a stop. Charlie was a long way back down the road and limping badly as the mob got closer and closer. Our driver reversed backwards at speed and just managed to get back there before the mob grabbed him. We dragged Charlie into the back of the van and told the silly bastard to lie down as we sped off once again. After that he became known as 'Hold On Charlie', and this was shortened even more. So if anyone asked after Charlie in the future, they'd just say: 'Have you seen Hold On?' A new nickname was born that day.

It was a nice payday. We cut in the other two of our men who were otherwise indisposed.

Another venture we considered getting into around this time was the bookshops in Soho. People like Jimmy Humphries, Bernie Silver and the Greeks and Turks were making a fortune from this type of business. But you had to clear this sort of enterprise with the Old Bill so they wouldn't come and nick you all the time. Our introduction here was through Mick. Regan had saved a couple of coppers by getting them out of trouble after they were nicked for something and owed him a favour. We were told to see one particular cosser and we met up with him at a Soho pub. This man was puffing away at his pipe saying: 'Yes, we might be able to work this out. All I need is a body now and again. You scratch my back and I'll scratch yours.' This was silly talk to someone like ourselves.

It was Patsy who said to him: 'How would you like that pipe stuck right up your fucking arse?' Needless to say that was the end of our little venture into the West End. It just shows you: nobody could work in that business without giving up bodies. It makes you wonder about people who have businesses there and are allowed to reign.

In my next attempt at building up a 'legal empire' we got together and formed the Bookmakers' Guardian Association, an insurance company catering to the interests of betting shop owners. I rented a lovely suite of offices in Regent Street, close to Piccadilly and the Stork Club, and had them professionally furnished and decorated. Ding Dong fronted the organisation and Major Collins, a very well-known bookmaker, Jimmy Lane and Johnny Parry were made directors as was my brother-in-law Jimmy Puttnam who bet under the name of Jack Ray. Jimmy was credited with being the first bookmaker to take bets on away meetings. He had a moody phone on his pitch in Tattersall's and he rigged up a bell which he could press with his foot and then answer, pretending to get the odds from the other race courses. Punters would then place bets with him accepting his moody odds.

So, our proposed insurance company would take care of bookmakers in court, lend them money for new premises and insure their businesses. They would be represented by our retainer, the one-armed barrister William Rees-Davies, QC and MP who was known as Dracula in the House of Commons for his habit of sweeping through the House wearing a black cloak. Rees-Davies, who at the time represented Thanet in Kent, was instrumental in drawing up the gaming law for street bookmaking. His father, Sir William Rees-Davies, was formerly Chief Justice of Hong Kong. Dennis Wheater and Brian Field, well-known criminal lawyers, were our solicitors and also board directors.

Both were later arrested in connection with the Great Train Robbery.

We paid for a full-page advertisement in the *Sporting Life* to publicise the company and sought £5 insurance for the first shop and a lesser figure for every subsequent one. To give the enterprise a kick-start, we had to create a little tension and of course, the only thing to do was to go around and set light to a few of those bookmakers who tried to win unfair advantage over little shops by paying out on the fourth horse. By doing that, they used to crucify the business for the other smaller businesses so we considered them fair game, though we always made sure the shops were empty and there were no livers above before giving them the old fireworks.

About six bookmakers went up in this way. I remember one shop where we poured a mixture of fuel through the letterbox. Our lookout warned us that a cosser was coming down the street so we went away for a little while. We had been experimenting with a mixture of petrol and oil to give us enough time to get away before the fire took hold. On this occasion the mixture had been too rich and by the time we returned, all the fumes had built up and when we threw in a lighted rag, the whole shop blew up and windows shattered. Fortunately we were behind a solid old door, otherwise we would have been blown across the street. One of our target shops was let off the hook because when we checked it out in the dead of night, we found the manager having a right old rump across the office desk with a female member of staff.

The response to our advertisement was unbelievable. Bags of letters flowed in requesting to join the association. Word had spread almost as quickly as the fires. Although I had not been linked to the arson attacks, rumours had started about my involvement by the fact that Ding Dong was managing the organisation. Major Collins then pulled out and the lawyers were having trouble getting a board of directors together because after a couple of fires, their bottle went and their arseholes fell out. They didn't want to be associated with it. They should have stood their ground and said those fires were nothing to do with us. Instead they lost their nerve. Gus Dalrymple from the *Sporting Life* then started making himself busy writing articles about the Bookmakers' Guardian Association and his reports were taken up by national newspapers who wanted to know who was behind this venture.

I don't know why they were so worried. The original BPA, Bookmakers' Protection Association, which we were virtually copying, had been started by three local businessmen, a butcher, publican and builder – so why not have one like ours? Police also began taking an interest when mailbags full of cash from prospective customers began flowing into my Regent Street offices. Our new company would have been a goldmine. After the initial villainy it would have been a straight business, but it was not to be.

The loss of that enterprise was disappointing but the shops and pubs were doing really well. The Prince of Wales, considering that I had only paid £5000 for the pub, was probably the best investment I ever made. The whole place was buzzing and jam-packed with people. I would buy the latest hit singles from the A1 store in Walworth Road, songs like: 'Sitting on the Dock of the Bay', and Chris Montez's 'The More I See You the More I Want You', and 'River Deep Mountain High'. As the top singles came out I was the first to play them. At times I had to bolt doors to stop people coming in. There were many marriages made from that pub because so many young people found a kindred spirit. Many of those relationships grew and have survived to this day.

The cellars would be stacked full to the brim with booze, and crates would spill over into the yard. I earned more money out of that little pub than any other straight business I had ever invested in. As my reputation grew, so the business got better. Everyone loves a face.

The Peckham betting shop became the head office and from there we were interacting with all the other shops. George also opened up a minicab office in Peckham, a small café next door, and a 'Shush' club, a speak-easy or drinking club, down the street. Our customers would gamble their money in our shops, use George's minicab firm, eat at his café, and then go to his 'Shush' club. It acquired its name from people asking George for its address and he'd put his finger to his lips and say: 'Shush'. Those little clubs were unbelievable. You could drink around the clock and people said they had the best time of their lives in them. We had a piano and dancing and we could move the club within a day if it was discovered by the licensing authorities. George was in his element in the Shush clubs. Always the party man he loved entertaining people and enjoying himself whereas, although I liked socialising, I probably appeared more sullen and menacing to those who didn't know me. People warmed a lot more easily to George while I kept a distance. I was always in the background, a bit heavy, but people knew they couldn't fuck with George because I was there. I'd find people who misbehaved and bar them. Bertie Summers, a long-time friend, together with Ronnie King were on the door. Johnny Borsch was another one who minded for us.

I was also very friendly with Ronnie Oliffe from Bermondsey. His family were dockers, a good little family. There were five or six brothers, and they were a force to be reckoned with. Ronnie was good at running spiels and we had several in partnership in the Marshalsea building and the Old Kent Road.

I was asked by Bernie Colman, who owned a chain of south London pubs left to him by his father, to be his partner in the 211 Club in Balham. Bernie was involved with the MCC and went all over the world with the

England cricket team. Now he needed someone strong behind him. A good friend of mine, a district surveyor called Ronnie Stafford, introduced us. Local villains, including someone involved with the Nash brothers, were trying to muscle in on Bernie but once he told them I was his partner, they left him alone. We agreed that I would run the casino upstairs and he would run the bar and restaurant on the ground floor. The 211 Club in Balham High Road was a lovely property. Known as Hamilton House it had at one time belonged to Lady Hamilton, Lord Nelson's fancy bit, and was later turned into an embassy. Inside was a magnificent ballroom and gardens. The venue attracted people from all over London.

We laid out a small fortune doing the place up. We had French roulette tables, a crap table, three blackjack tables, a *chemin de fer* table and the decor, arranged by Maureen who was good at interior design, was Regency style. Fred and Joe Scala, two friends who started their career in this country making ice-cream in Fulham, took care of the casino.

The 211 was a posh place. Staff were dressed in dinner suits and we had glamorous croupier girls who wore low-cut dresses. Clubs were the rage at the time. The Krays, the Nashes and I each carved a share from the Colony Club in Berkeley Square, Mayfair. It was run by George Raft, the American actor who starred in early gangster movies and was swooned over by most women who met him. Patrons at the Colony included Frank Sinatra and Robert Ryan. Dino and Eddy Celini ran the casino and the real owner was the MD of American crime, Meyer Lansky.

I was involved in several clubs with the Krays including a share in the Starlight Club off Oxford Street. The Colony went on for a couple of years and was a good earner. George Raft, who had Mafia connections, wanted us to keep a low profile. He didn't want faces to frighten away guests. In those areas it was not the done thing.

I asked George Raft to officially open the 211 Club and he first came to my pub in a chauffeur-driven Rolls in the company of Ronnie Kray. While we were drinking at the bar, I asked George who, in his opinion, was the main man in the prohibition era and he replied without hesitation that strangely, the main man was an Englishman by the name of Owney Madden from Leeds who was raised in Wigan and became known as the Duke of the West Side. He owned the Cotton Club and was well involved with bootlegging. George Raft rode shotgun on his expeditions.

Anyway, back to the story. We were then chauffeured in a convoy of stretch limousines to the 211 Club where we were joined by actors, bookmakers and fighting personalities. George Raft was very impressed with the layout and did his celebrity bit in style while photographers snapped pictures of him playing dice and meeting local celebrities such as Barbara Windsor and the *Carry On* team whom I had invited for the opening. Mick Regan, Ronnie Knight, Ronnie Oliffe and the rest of the chaps who were on hand every weekend to help sort out any aggravation were also invited.

While I owned a number of gambling premises I was never a gambler myself and discouraged my friends from this habit, knowing it was always the house that would win.

When punters left the 211, they'd inevitably move on to my George's late-night drinking club in Clapham South called the Red Sail. Coppers caused panic once by coming around after hours one Sunday afternoon. George quickly ushered everyone out the back and then let the coppers in by the front door. All they wanted was to give him his late-night licence for a hospital charity do. The police were not aware that the fifty drunken revellers standing at the bus-stop had just emerged from George's back door.

George's lease for the Red Sail was in the names of Mr Green and Mr Brown. Our Polish landlord, who had been a secret agent during the war and was always worried about us, had a heart attack while on a holiday beach. His dying words to his wife were: 'Don't forget Mr Green and Mr Brown, they're behind with their rent!'

'Saturday Night Cowboys' were our biggest problem at the 211. They were workers who were in straight jobs during the week and who let loose on Friday and Saturday nights when they came in mob-handed and thought they could get away with doing as they pleased. They had to be taught a lesson to stop them picking fights, smashing glasses and upsetting other customers. My own team included Johnny Cook, Lenny White, Ding Dong, Ronnie King, Ronnie Oliffe and his brothers Joey and Danny, and quiet Jimmy Turner, which was enough to keep most people in line. But all the same we had to teach these mugs a lesson.

One of the people who gave us problems was a fellow called Johnny Hanlon from west London. On one occasion he and a few of his mates who were publicans and their wives and girlfriends who should have known better, were making a nuisance of themselves. So I took his drink out of his hand and told him to leave. As I put it down he made a move on me but didn't take into account Ronnie Oliffe who was leaning against the wall minding me. Ronnie pole-axed him with a right to the jaw and he was out before he hit the ground. I grabbed a shillelagh hanging behind an office door and put it about a bit lively. Billy and Mary Gorbell were also there and had some German *swaschenbachers*. These consisted of metal springs with a steel knob on the end that came out of a metal rod and wrapped around the victim's head. An old pal Tommy Flannagan who was playing the roulette, saw the fracas and quickly joined in – it was promptly sorted.

Years later I met Hanlon at the doctor's when I was doing my ten for McVitie in Wormwood Scrubs prison. He looked at me and asked: 'Are you Fred? Freddie Foreman? I'm Johnny Hanlon.'

I said, 'Oh yeh, do you want to step into the recess?'

'No, no, no,' he replied, and asked me if he was out of order that night. I told him he was, he apologised and we shook hands there and then.

Some years later in Spain there was a consortium of publicans who came over to see me with a spokesman and wanted rid of him for a price. I told them I was not a paid hitman. 'I don't do those things for money,' I told them. Hanlon would wreck pubs and was such a nuisance that publicans gave him money just to go away. He's still around, all twenty stone of him.

One night I had a terrible cold and was home in bed trying to get over it with a bottle of scotch which I don't normally drink. The club rang to say they had trouble and would I please come over. I tried to get them to sort it out themselves but they insisted I come as they couldn't handle it. I instructed them to get the main troublemaker, a tall geezer, bigger than the others, and the rest of them downstairs to the bar. 'Give them a drink and say Fred's on his way and he wants to talk to you.' I then put a suit over my pyjamas and, although it was late, Ronnie Oliffe was still running the spiel at the Marshalsea so I asked him to pick me up and run me to the 211.

When we arrived, the manager had been told to hang about near the troublemaker and nod in his direction when I walked in. I went up to the geezer and asked: 'Now what's this all about?' Without waiting for a reply I knocked him spark out and asked the rest of his gang if they wanted some. I told them never to come here again and then dragged the big fellow across the floor into the toilets. I got my shillelagh and lifted his legs up to his chin while he was still out cold and battered his legs. 'That's for getting me out of fucking bed, you cunt.' And

I'm belting him with the stick. I gave his legs a good hammering. He would feel the effects the next day when he woke up. Ron told me I was getting a bit carried away so I stopped and we got his pals to take him home. I was really pissed off dealing with these mugs. Week after week the same thing. When would they learn to behave in my club and place of business?

Throughout my life I've had a revulsion to liberty-takers and bullies. In the eyes of the law and society, I am recognised as a villain, but I have always strived to be quiet, polite, and well-mannered. My father's belief in civility was ingrained in me. Whatever club, pub or betting shop I owned, I treated people decently and with the same respect as I expected from them. When that respect was not returned I would get very angry and the response could be severe.

On one busy weekend evening there was a disturbance in the bar downstairs. Our staff had become anxious because a gang of about a dozen guys, some of them very ugly with punched-in faces led by a bloke I called Flat Nose, were causing mayhem.

My mate Micky Regan and I were upstairs. I grabbed a tool from the office and Mick and I raced downstairs to find them leaving. Mick suggested we wait until they were all outside and then deal with it. At that stage we didn't know what had happened but our blood ran hot when we saw a young girl who was knocked spark out and her jaw broken. She was only about seventeen and Flat Nose, obviously an ex-fighter, had punched her lights out.

Angrily, Mick and I ran out of the club following the gang who were getting into several cars with their women. Flat Nose was shouting directions to his friends so they could meet up at another venue. They were on the other side of the road and I waved my arms signalling to him that I wanted a word. Flat Nose and his partner both stood on the far kerb beckoning for us to come over. But as we got closer, the sight of big Mick and myself was a bit formidable so they made a run back to their car parked in a side street. We followed, swiftly crossing the road as the two guys pulled out pickaxe handles from the boot of their car. 'Come on then,' they sneered, smacking the handles into the palms of their hands.

It was the wrong move for them. I pulled out the equalizer, a .38 pistol which I had grabbed from a hidey hole upstairs in the casino. They froze. 'Just drop the sticks,' I commanded. The pickaxe handles clattered to the road.

'There's no need for that,' they said.

'No need for that?' I retorted angrily. 'After what you just did to that little girl!' Crash! I gave Flat Nose a right to the jaw. Mick went for the other one who, with fists raised, was dancing around the street doing a Cassius Clay. I laid into Flat Nose and pistol-whipped him five or six times around the head and then put the gun into his shoulder and pulled the trigger. Unknown to me at the time, the bullet didn't go clean through him as I would have expected but ricocheted off his shoulder blade and travelled around his body missing several major arteries and his heart, before emerging from his side. Apparently that often happens when someone is shot at close quarters.

While I was sorting out Flat Nose, Mick had chased and caught 'Cassius Clay'. They sparred for a little bit and when he'd had enough of that, Mick battered the granny out of Cassius and tossed him over a hedge onto someone's front garden.

After I'd shot him, Flat Nose had dropped to the ground like a sack of potatoes. I then went over to where Mick had tossed Cassius and got to him just as he was picking his face off the ground. I put my knee into the middle of his back and grabbed his hair and pulled his head back whispering in his ear: 'If I ever see you out here again, this is what you're going to get.'

With that, I put the barrel of the gun behind his ear and let one go. Blood splattered everywhere as the bullet took his ear right off and the blast from the explosion burnt him all over the face. Covered in blood, we returned to the club and cleaned up in our private bathroom. Then I sent Ding Dong Dell, one of the firm, to check out the two guys. Apparently the one whose ear had been blown off managed to stagger to the car and drive Flat Nose and himself to the local hospital. We then sent another member of the firm to check out their ward and report on how badly damaged they were. In the meantime, the young girl with the fractured jaw was taken to the same hospital.

Police were called but no statements were made. Both Flat Nose and his companion had been spoken to on my behalf. They understood that all they had received was a 'taster' and it would not be a good idea to take it any further. We never heard from them again.

On one occasion at the 211, Jack 'The Hat' McVitie, who was losing money, pulled a knife on my croupier and then, when he realised I was on my way upstairs to speak to him, threw it under the table. It landed where a friend of mine, Bobby Neil and his wife were dining. Bobby was an ex-lightweight boxing champion. I knew Jack: he was on the Kray firm but they told me he was unreliable. He had taken money to kill Leslie Payne but never went through with it and still spent the money. Anyhow, he was a loudmouth. He went around saying he was going to kill the Twins and boasted that he had tried to run Ronnie over. He'd also gone to the Starlight Club where Micky Regan and I had some roulette and blackjack tables. He held up the place and made all the guys drop their strides. He was a bit of a nut and lived in a shithole with no furniture. When he was high on drink and drugs, he would fire his big .45 gun into the chimneybreast.

I came up behind him and asked him what the problem was. 'Misbehaving again Jack? Come with me, I just want to talk to you.'

He looked at me and replied: 'What, and get a fucking bullet in the head?' I told him I'd go downstairs and when I got back in ten minutes I didn't want to see him there. When I returned upstairs to the casino, he'd left. Later I mentioned the incident to Ronnie Kray who bollocked him for causing trouble in my club.

When the gaming laws changed in the mid-60s, restricting gambling to the West End, we lost our licence so I took all the units out of the 211 and opened an illegal casino in Strood, near Rochester, Kent.

The Colony Club also closed down and George Raft was stopped from entering Britain. Nevertheless, we did further business importing one-armed bandits from the Americans. I had a van-load of machines given to me by this nice American guy called Dave Dick, and another called Gabe Foreman, my namesake. I took loads of machines off him although a boat-load of them were smashed up by police and Customs. Even so, lots of little cafés and clubs on both sides of the water had one-armed bandits working day and night bringing in plenty of cash for the firm. But another era was coming to a close.

I was just getting over my birthday celebrations (5 March, 1966), playing the part of mine host in the bar of the Prince of Wales. I was feeling just a bit tired and jaded, well in fact completely knackered. It had been a really hectic week, the POW was busy every night and this particular night, 7 March, 1966, was no exception. The place was already packed, when in walked Peter Hennessey, Billy Hayward, Billy Gardner, Dicky Hart, Johnny Perry, Duggie Horn and several others. They were all nice guys who as well as being regular customers that spent well, behaved well and gave me no trouble, were all good friends of mine. The drinks were flowing and Billy Gardner, a larger-than-life character and brilliant raconteur who'd once won the first prize on Michael Miles' TV show *Double Your Money* on the subject of boxing, was on good form.

The conversation turned to the new club that had just opened in Catford, called the 'Mr Smiths and the Witch Doctor' (a very strange name). Billy Hayward and his brother Flash Harry had pubs and clubs in that area and felt it was their manor. If anyone opened a similar business they thought, and rightly so, they should be consulted and given a share in the new enterprise. Especially as the club owners had come all the way down from Manchester to take bread out of their mouths. Paddy McGrath and Owen Ratcliffe, the new owners of 'Mr Smiths', had a number of clubs up north and felt there were rich pickings to be had down south; but Catford was not one of them. There are only so many drinkers and gamblers to go round late at night. The West End was full of these sort of places but in south London there were only so many printers to cater for, so you can understand the rivalry.

I had my own place the 211 Club in Balham to worry about. You see the West End had all the licences, so when punters stepped outside, they could walk straight in to another club, casino or restaurant. Everywhere was still open, the West End was buzzing. But step outside in Balham High Street or Catford at 2am in the morning, and it was deadsville, not a soul in sight. That's why all other clubs and casinos in the sticks were doomed to failure.

Unfortunately Paddy's and Owen's other big mistake was to go to old-time villains Billy Hill and Albert Dimes, who were not the right people to get advice from. They didn't know fuck-all about what was really going on in London, or who was who. There were a lot of very dangerous firms around, armed robbers, who didn't give two fucks about names or reputations, and even felt, 'how did these old villains get their reputations anyway?'

when they had not done anything on the scale of villainy as the men who were active at that time. If Paddy and Owen had come to me I would have told them forget about Catford, keep your money in your pocket and go back home to Manchester.

Getting back to my story. Come closing time we had all enjoyed the night's drinking, when Peter and Billy asked me to go with them to Mr Smiths. There was no talk of any trouble or that Eddie Richardson and Frankie Fraser were going to be there that night. The invitation was to carry on drinking and take a look at their new watering hole. I declined their offer saying 'another time, chaps'. I had hardly slept since my birthday and I still had to attend to business at the 211 before trying to grab some well-needed shuteye. At 11 o'clock we went our separate ways. I drove to Balham, and Peter, Billy and the others all piled into several motors and headed for Catford. After spending a few hours at the 211 Club I returned home and crashed out. I was awoken by a quiet tapping outside and a few gentle rings on the pub door. I threw on my dressing gown and opened the upstairs window. Through the darkness I could just make out a crowd of men. At first I thought it was the Old Bill, but it wasn't the rat-a-tat or continuous banging of the police, it was more polite and gentle. I called down, 'Who is it?' and heard Peter Hennessey's voice. 'It's me Fred. Can we come in, we need to speak to you for a minute?' I knew that something was seriously wrong. They told me the full SP, how the Richardsons had come down to take over the club, which they considered was their domain. Frank and Eddie had arrived firm handed, so when Jimmy Moody arrived with even more reinforcements, it was time for Billy and Peter to send out for some tools. When you have two firms facing each other tooled up ready to settle old scores and grievances, it's gonna escalate into a full-scale war. With 15 hard men involved there had to be a few casualties . . .

My visitors told me that they thought Frankie Fraser, Dicky Hart and Harry Rawlings were dead, and that Eddie Richardson and Ronnie Jeffreys were wounded. A .45 revolver and two shotguns had been used, leaving blood and bodies everywhere. They needed advice and a safe house. I got dressed and told Maureen not to worry, to go back to sleep, and took Peter, Billy Gardner, Duggie Horn and John Perry on to a safe house, telling them to stay put until we could find out what real damage had been done. Then we took Billy Haywood to one of my doctor friends. His head was gaping from a bayonet wound. After a few weeks I managed to get Peter Hennessey, Duggie Horn and John Perry to go into Catford police station, and admit that they were there on the night, but that they had left before any trouble started – that would explain why their names were in the members' visitors book and why the bar staff and hat check girl could identify them. This having been done, no charges could be brought against them. They all walked. Only Billy Hayward went down for eight years for affray.

It took a bit longer to get Billy Gardner off the hook as he had been identified as one of those brandishing a shotgun. The police still wanted him bad. I had to keep him holed up in my brother-in-law's flat for about four months, then move him down to a campsite in Battle just outside Hastings, where I owned a caravan. In those days many houses still had outside toilets and a tin bath hanging up on the scullery wall but this had all mod cons (toilet, bath and TV) so he didn't have to show his face too much on the campsite, just venture out occasionally at night. This he did. Only one night he ventured into the village pub. After a couple of hours plying the locals with drinks and regaling them with his jokes and stories, 20 gin-and-tonics later he returned, paralytic drunk and staggering around the campsite firing his shotgun into the air shouting: 'I'm the man who shot up the Richardson gang!' This did *not* please me. I had to send three 'chaps' to drive all the way down there to rope him up till he was sober. Bill apologised for his bad behaviour and I forgave him. After all, he was a good, loyal and solid man, who after spending months on the mattress had just got drunk and let off a little steam. Eventually, through good friends of mine, Bill was given a job working in a Portsmouth casino. As time went on, Mr Smiths was no longer a problem for Billy Gardner. However this was not so for Frankie Fraser, who was arrested and charged with affray as he lay almost bleeding to death, his leg shattered by a .45 bullet.

Five people were shot that night but apart from the tragic death of Dicky Hart, they all miraculously survived. Billy Hayward received eight years, and Henry Bottom a five. Frank Fraser was tried separately for the Dicky Hart shooting, found not guilty, but received five years for affray. Ronnie Jeffrey, Harry Rawlings, Jimmy Moody and Billy Stayton were all found not guilty. But Eddie Richardson, who was attacked and also shot on that fateful night had to endure a retrial, only to be found guilty and receive a five-year sentence. Personally I thought that on all the evidence he should have walked. If a man is challenged to a fight, he's entitled to defend himself. To be blasted with a shotgun, arrested while lying in hospital, and then sent to prison for five years – where's the justice in that? Eddie has had some raw deals in life. Later he got another ten years for the torture trial which brought it up to fifteen. As if that wasn't enough, due to a drug-related offence, Eddie was sentenced to a further twenty-five years. Isn't it about time someone gave him a break?

I knew both camps and was sorry that the night at Mr Smiths had ended in such carnage. If I had gone with Peter and Billy, perhaps, only perhaps, I may have prevented the events that took place. On the other hand, knowing myself, I would have been right up at the front, and the body count may have been higher. Then again . . . Who can tell what fate has in store.

· 10 ·
Battle of Bow

I learned early on to keep a low profile. The last thing a successful firm wants is for the Old Bill to come mosey-ing around or to lay itself open to an informant fingering you after a big job. You can get away with an awful lot in life if you don't shout about it. That said, our work nearly always attracted widespread publicity, not least for the huge rewards offered for information leading to our arrest and conviction. If there had been a competi-tion for front-page splashes in national newspapers, we'd have won hands down. But unlike some flash vil-lains who couldn't resist flooding the bar and mouthing their latest victory, we knew when to stay shtoom!

As with other trends in society, crime has a distinctive pattern of evolution and we did our bit in shaping the criminal landscape. To this day the public has never been told the full story of what happened in the Battle of Bow when a bank clerk shot and killed a member of our firm. His death was never recorded. Police and newspaper reports only said that a robber had been wounded and might need 'urgent medical attention'. They didn't reveal that an unarmed man had been shot in the back of the head. Had they done so, there would have been a public uproar. It was a crazy situation. On the one hand police were not issued with guns, while on the other, an ordi-nary bank clerk was allowed to discharge a lethal weapon in a busy London road during rush hour traffic!

Neither the Home Office nor Scotland Yard were pre-pared to reveal the full facts of this major incident because of the potential political scandal. Nevertheless it became the turning-point in determining Home Office policy on the use of weapons and security, particularly as related to guarding bullion.

The legacy of our actions, and the actions of other firms like ours, has been the growth of a billion pound security industry giving employment to thousands and inevitably making our task more difficult in the process. (I wish I had bought shares in the security industry.)

Members of our firm had planned the Bow theft over a period of months. As a rule of thumb, most big raids usually involved detailed planning based on inside information. Experience taught us to assess such information and to weigh up the likelihood of success.

Thursday 14 December, 1961: a cold, drizzly day, wisps of early morning mist rose like steam from the wet, cobbled roads. The mist had almost cleared by the time the wages van came into view in Carter's Road, at the junction with Bow Common Lane near the east London gasworks.

The firm had been in position for some time. They'd rehearsed their roles for weeks. Now, flushed with excitement and the thrill of the chase, they were counting on an early Christmas present. At today's values, the snatch, if it came off, would be worth more than £2 million.

The target bullion van had been hired by the City bank of Glyn Mills to deliver large sums of money from their head office in Lombard Street, to the East End. This was a regular trip. The van set off about 8.45am with the driver, Edward Banks, two guards, Fred Dighton and Ron Harman, a bank official called Bill Shelton, and City of London police constable Ted Buckle and Flash, his German Shepherd guard dog.

Their first drop was in Wapping High Street, then on to Bow, to the gasworks. The firm, already familiar with the route, delivery times and the number of people in the van, were in place for the ambush.

One vital piece of information, however, was missing. The robbers had not been told that the two bank clerks guarding the payroll were *armed*! Dighton and Harman were each carrying a loaded .22 Beretta pistol with five rounds of ammunition. And they were both crack shots.

The proposed ambush was relatively straightforward. It would take place in Turner's Road at the junction of Bow Common Lane. The target van would be rammed by the first vehicle, another van would park across the road cutting off access from behind, and a third vehicle would come up alongside to create a diversion while the second vehicle wrenched off the bank van's rear doors.

Three members of the firm lay in the back of the diversionary vehicle. It was a very long lorry with the side cut out and a tarpaulin sheet hanging down one side. The driver kept watch for the target van through his side mirror and had no verbal contact with the others. The target vehicle was a solid old van. Brown in colour it had two very small windows along the side and another two on the back door.

The firm's second vehicle was a print van with a reinforced iron rail welded into the back to strengthen the chassis where a hook and chain were secured. The ram vehicle, manned by two of the robbers, was positioned in front of the target van ready to jam on its brakes and reverse into the bank van at the predetermined spot near the junction. All the gang wore heavy coats with hats and scarves and industrial facemasks ready for the smother-up (disguise). Pickaxe handles with rope and taped ends to provide grip were at the ready.

Everything had been planned with military precision. Lorries and vans had all been stolen, false numberplates fitted and modifications made. Each member of the team had been carefully chosen.

Now, as the time for action drew nearer, the tension mounted. The gang's excitement was measured by short puffs of breath visibly hitting the cold morning air.

At 9.45am the big brown van turned a corner at the bottom of Turner's Road and came up behind the open lorry which sped forward to keep abreast. Had they tumbled that something was amiss? The firm's other lorry, some way in front of the target van, braked suddenly and then hit reverse gear. The bullion driver must have shitted himself to see the lorry reverse at speed making a head-on collision unavoidable. Crash! Lorry and van shuddered to a stop as they collided. The gang's open lorry then hit the side of the bank van, making a sickening scraping sound exaggerated by the ripping of metal. On impact, the three raiders in the back were thrown about like rag dolls. Scrambling to their feet, they made their way to the side of the van and ripped away the sheet of tarpaulin to expose the windows of the bank van.

Tooled up with small iron crowbars, they smashed the glass windows to create confusion inside. At the same time, the robbers in the print van reversed against the two rear doors, smashed the back windows and passed an iron hook and chain through them. On securing the chain, the signal to drive forward was given. The print van revved up and lurched forward, wrenching off the two back doors of the target van. They went flying into the air before crashing down on to the road.

Meanwhile, the three men at the side of the van had created total confusion among the bank clerks and bank official who were screaming and shouting, running back and forth in panic. But there was to be a turnabout. One of the robbers came face to face with the clerk and was struck by a premonition of danger. His hair stood on end and his blood ran cold. Without a second thought he ducked. A millisecond later, a bullet shattered the glass. His premonition saved his life.

At this point, the plan was going drastically wrong. The firm should have been filling the van with a noxious substance. They were only eighteen inches away from the most daring and cunning part of the entire raid: smashing a hole in the window and blasting in a mixture of pepper and talcum powder to temporarily blind the cashier, security guard and policeman.

Their apparatus was ready: a huge funnel which was fed by a length of copper tubing attached to a three-foot oxyacetylene cylinder to force pounds of the powder and pepper through the broken window. But the driver had misjudged his crash and they were out of line with the nearest window and couldn't work the apparatus.

Instead, they concentrated on the rear of the bank van. Once the doors had been wrenched off, they armed themselves with pickaxe handles and stormed inside. Tantalisingly, half-way down the van they could see brown cricket bags bulging with cash – £122,000 in wage packets: a fortune waiting to be grabbed.

But the scene had become ugly. They were confronted by a snarling Alsatian, and out jumped a 6ft 4in City copper who turned out to be an ex-boxing champ and was as determined and courageous as his dog. He was struck across the head by the driver of the print van who had come alongside. Another robber went for the dog and cracked him on the head. There was a sound of gun shots which nobody heard at first because of the commotion going on.

Still unaware of the danger from the armed guards, one of the robbers, waving a sledgehammer, tried to climb into the bank van with a helping shove from his colleagues. The attempt was short-lived. He came face to face with two guns pointing at him and the guards standing in firing position, legs astride, shouting: 'Come any closer and I'll shoot.'

Risking the warning, he tried to grasp the end of the cricket bags, hesitantly snatching at them. The other raiders egged him on but then the penny dropped. They could see that one of their number had been shot in the

163

side of the head. The badly injured robber, blood pouring from the back of his head, crawled round to the rear of the van.

Meanwhile, the bank clerks inside were still shouting: 'I'll shoot, I'll shoot.' Two of the robbers threw themselves under the van to help their wounded mate. Another, half in anger and frustration, hurled a pickaxe handle into the bank van sending it crashing against the cabin wall and forcing the bank employees to duck as it clattered to the floor.

Two of the robbers then lifted and dragged the wounded man into the print van and clambered aboard themselves. Another robber had also been shot through the arm. At this stage they decided to call it a day. They'd had enough and were ready to pull away.

But it was not over yet. Two of the firm were missing. Where were they? Down the road some fifty yards away a strange ritual seemed to be underway. From a distance it looked like a dance in slow motion choreographed by an odd troupe wearing facemasks and police uniforms. The policeman was twisting and turning, a pickaxe handle in his left hand and, with his right, struggling to hold a robber's neck in an armlock. Next to him, obstinately gripping the second robber's arse with his bloodied fangs, and swinging from side to side as the robber tried to shake him off, was the dog, Flash.

Two of the robbers jumped from the print van to the rescue, one grabbing a pickaxe handle, the other a sledgehammer. Running back past the rear of the open bank van, more shots were fired. Did they really think the raiders were coming back? One of the robbers shouted out: 'I think they're out of bullets.'

The rescue team warned PC Buckle: 'Let him fucking go.' Terrier-like, the copper hung on and was rewarded with a more forceful gesture. A pickaxe handle came crashing down on his head. He looked up: 'You bastard,' he yelled. A second later a sledgehammer went whizzing by and the copper got hit in the back between his shoulder blades. The hammer bounced off and went sliding twenty feet down the road. But still the PC persisted. His dog, like its master, continued to grip the other bandit.

There was only one thing for it. The copper would have to be beaten unconscious. The team laid into him. Five or six good hard whacks on his nut until eventually his knees buckled. Then someone kicked the dog in the bollocks and another robber gave him one on the nose for good measure. The robbers were finally free to stagger back to the waiting print van.

As they did so, the policeman tried to walk away but he just crumbled. He appeared to be walking down a slope, disappearing into the ground as his legs gave way. He finally fell flat on his face and was out cold.

But what a strong bastard copper. Well they used to come big and still do in the City of London. He had to be given credit for his courage. Afterwards he and his dog received a medal. As for the firm, they were all very upset with the morning's work and had to go away and lick their wounds.

Later that day, police issued a statement warning every hospital in greater London to be on the look-out for a wounded man. What happened to the victim was very sad. His death could not be acknowledged and it was the first time a man had been shot dead by the authorities during a robbery. To reveal his name today would only open old wounds for his widow and family. His disappearance was covered up with a story that he had run off with a mistress to Australia.

The problem now confronting all the big firms was that this episode showed the authorities were prepared to use guns while we only had sticks. We needed an equaliser. That became a turning-point for criminals as well as the establishment. The whole of the underworld said: 'Next time, we'll be armed as well.'

Police said that they found a toy plastic Luger gun in the gutter near the van and that the firm was also armed. For some time afterwards, there were a lot of cartoons in the newspapers with pictures of bank vans with cannons, rockets and machine-gun turrets carrying cash through the streets of London. The press also wanted to know how many armed bank vans there were. Under a headline: GUN LAW PERIL IN BRITAIN, the Liberal MP for Bolton West, Mr Arthur Holt, warned the government that the shooting of a bullion bandit by a bank guard could lead to Chicago-style gun battles imperilling passers-by. He wanted the Home Secretary to disclose how many private persons were permitted to carry arms for the protection of property.

The bank guards, it transpired, went twice a week for target practice. Dighton, who fired the shots, thought he had discharged five bullets in all but in fact only four shots were fired. The first two, he explained, had been warning shots at either side of the doors. The second volley hit home.

A director of the Glyn Mills bank, Mr Faulkner, made an astonishing admission. Asked by one national newspaper what would have happened if a robber had been killed, he replied: 'About twenty men at the bank employed as messengers are licensed to use guns. They collect their pistols from the bank before going on payroll and other duties. Each man licensed to carry a gun has regular marksmanship training at a police shooting range. These men are good shots. I think Mr Dighton did a damn fine job and next time I hope we hit two of the bandits.'

Dighton admitted to hitting one of the robbers. He said later: 'I know I hit one man. He yelled and grabbed his left arm. The gang seemed to panic. The whole thing was over in a couple of minutes.' The only clue left by the bandits as they made their getaway in a Jaguar motor car parked nearby, was a blood-soaked piece of gauze torn from a protective facemask.

Since then there have been many cases when a robber
has been killed, particularly at ambushes where police
have been lying in wait for robbers to show up. From
what we have witnessed in recent years, it appears that
police are more keen to have a shoot-out than stop the
robbery. Why not nick the robbers earlier? The answer
must be that they have been given carte blanche to do
whatever is necessary to stop armed robbery.

* * *

I've had a love affair with gold ever since I first handled
it at fourteen. It is a soft, beautiful metal with aphro-
disiac qualities, so nothing could be more tempting or
alluring than the promise of forty solid gold bars, each
the size of a house brick and with a combined weight of
nearly half a ton.

The firm was offered the job in April–May 1963.
Bullion which by today's values would be worth about
£5 million was the prize. Before embarking on it, there
was planning to be done and alibis to be arranged.

It was a nice piece of work from friends in the East
End. There were some complications, however. The timing had to be spot-on and it meant that the firm would
have to be ready and prepared to strike in a matter of
minutes. For week after week they waited for the van to
show up at the right time for its delivery of gold bars.

The ideal time for it to arrive, it had been decided, was
late in the morning, preferably when most of the staff
had left for lunch and only a few would remain in an
upstairs office and at the back of the warehouse.
Importantly there would only be one man on duty to
shut the gate after the van arrived.

In order to be there at the crucial moment, the firm
would have to sit around for possibly weeks on end in a
hired van. That was never going to be easy in the City of
London which was heavily patrolled and a hot area for
any villainy. But after weeks of no go, the van eventually

arrived late and the staff had started to leave the premises for their favourite café or restaurant.

And so on 24 May, 1963, Sharps Pixley & Co., bullion brokers in Paul Street, near Finsbury Square in the City of London, became victim to the biggest gold bullion snatch in London. The *Daily Express* devoted its front page to the theft and called it the 'hottest load of loot since Colonel Blood snatched the Crown Jewels'. Someone, they said the next day: 'is sitting on half a ton of gold bars'. Describing the robbery, the newspaper reported: 'Certainly they went about the grab in deadly professional style. There were four of them in blue overalls. They were waiting in busy Paul Street, Finsbury, when a van carrying the gold from Rothschild's Bank drove up to the warehouse of Sharps Pixley & Co., bullion brokers.

'Two warehouse men had just gone to lunch and Charles Houghton, the fifty-five-year-old porter was alone there. He opened the big double doors and guided the van into the yard. The four men in blue slipped in behind and vanished into the shadows. From the van the crew and Mr Houghton unloaded forty gold bars weighing 27lb a piece and the size of a house brick. Twenty minutes later the van left empty.

'When the men in blue overalls came into the open they had stockings on their faces and coshes in their hands. Mr Houghton was tied to a chair. The attackers opened the gates again and backed in a waiting blue Bedford van.

'Swiftly the gold bars, stamped with serial numbers, were reloaded. When this van nosed into Paul Street, noisy with traffic and drills, no one took any notice. But then the bandits made their first mistake. They turned left and Paul Street is one-way in the opposite direction. People shouted. Cars hooted. But the Bedford roared on regardless and vanished into Finsbury's warren of side streets.'

Curiously, police had been literally round the corner while Britain's biggest gold swipe was taking place. They were investigating a £10 safe robbery!

During the raid, the security man, a big old boy, had picked up a gold bar and tried to hit members of the firm with it. He was given a right hander to slow him down and take the fight out of him. The raid was over in minutes and the firm took the gold to a north London yard, reloaded the bullion on to a tipper truck full of rubble and took it down to the country. A back-up car followed in case of trouble.

When police called the betting shop, I was busy chalking up the runners for the last race. The firm had done a brilliant job, left no clues, no one saw a thing. The security man turned out to be a serious suspect but he was only doing his job and risked getting hurt trying to protect his employer's money. Interpol and Customs throughout Europe had been alerted to the bullion. Everyone was convinced that it was destined to be sold abroad.

Contrary to the press reports, the robbers did *not* go the wrong way up a one-way street. By pure coincidence it was another van which had nothing to do with the robbery. As a result the police were searching for the wrong vehicle. When the firm realised this, Ding Dong took back the van he had hired and asked for his deposit, safe in the knowledge that nobody was looking for the van. It tidied up the whole business.

About a month later, in June, police searched a Dutch motorship in Amsterdam following a tip-off by an underworld source that it was carrying forty gold bars. But the 496-ton *Zaanstroom* was innocent of smuggling. The bullion was safely buried in Britain.

People were buzzing about the robbery. I was even approached by a friendly villain called Mikey Harris. He was well-known, because Billy Hill, the notorious gangster, had taken liberties with him and tramlined his face years before. Mikey said he could get his hands on the gold. He wanted me in on it to give him credibility so that he could have it on approval for a few days and let the people know they wouldn't get conned out of their money. Knowing it was safely hidden away for the next six months to a year, I told him: 'Of course I'd be interested.' It certainly took the heat off me with the criminal fraternity.

A few weeks after the raid, I was having a drink at the Spanish Patriot pub in The Cut, Waterloo, with Tommy Sullivan and Patsy O'Mara when in walked Buster Edwards, Gordon Goody, Bruce Reynolds and Tommy Wisbey. We all had a nice drink and during our conversation I was asked if I would like to go on some work. I thanked them for the invitation but said the firm was having a little rest for a few months.

Once I had refused their offer they didn't elaborate on what they had in mind. It was none of my business but I wished them luck in their enterprise. Three months later, on 8 August, 1963, they had pulled off the Great Train Robbery.

· 11 ·
Panama Gold

In 1963 I was approached by some very serious people to rob Panama's main bank of its gold. My contact was a retired Foreign Office mandarin who was a friend of Churchill and the Royal Family. Whether he was acting in an official or freelance capacity, I will never know, but as unlikely as it sounds, you have to understand the politics of the era to realise the 'tricks' governments got up to then. In the early 1960s Britain was still trying to be an influential player in world politics. After the Suez retreat, its main concern was over Aden and the growing crisis in the Middle East. Julian Amery, a government minister, wanted to knock the stuffing out of the Egyptian leader, Nasser, who was set on taking the British base there.

Prime Minister Macmillan was persuaded by Julian Amery and Billy McLean, Conservative MP for Stirling, to give unofficial backing and finance to royalists opposing Nasser's troops. To this end, Amery and McLean, former Special Operations Executive Officers in the war, set up an operation run by David Stirling, founder of the SAS, to help the royalists by recruiting ex-SAS mercenaries. Because Sir Alec Douglas-Home the Foreign Secretary preferred appeasement to conflict, the war against Nasser became a secret war involving SIS (the Secret Intelligence Service which later became MI6).

Further afield in South America, the Foreign Office turned its attention to Russian influence in Cuba, and central South American politics. How could a professional robber play a part in these Machiavellian plots? The answer is that 'anything goes in international politics'. The bizarre plot in which I almost became a player, involved Britain's most famous ballet dancer Dame Margot Fonteyn and her Panamanian ambassador husband Dr Roberto 'Tito' Arias. It was hinted that I would be doing a service for Queen and Country.

A well-connected friend of mine who had organised the sale of bullion in Switzerland for our firm, asked me in April 1963 if I'd be interested in some overseas work. He said an acquaintance who had been in the government wanted to hire a team of top professional safe-crackers and bank robbers for a job for which they would be handsomely paid.

At the time, Dame Margot Fonteyn was consistently in the headlines. In February she received international accolades after performing at Covent Garden in *Swan Lake* with Rudolf Nureyev, and then in March with Ashton's new ballet *Marguerite and Armand* at a Royal Ballet Benevolent Fund gala. She and Arias had married in Paris in 1955, having met each other years earlier when he was a student in Cambridge. In 1956, she had been made a Dame of the British Empire and he'd become Panamanian ambassador to the Court of St James, resigning two years later when he fell out with the Panama government. The Panama Canal joins the Pacific and Atlantic oceans and had been a virtual protectorate of the USA, jealously guarded for its strategic position. But the country was always having revolutions and counter-revolutions. The Arias family had been very influential. Tito's father had twice been the country's president and Tito had harboured ambitions to follow in his father's footsteps. His uncle Arnulfe had been elected president four times and overthrown three times. Internationally, Dame Margot Fonteyn's husband had a wide circle of influential friends, including President Kennedy. Dame Margot had been a guest on the Onassis yacht with Winston Churchill and had dined with the Kennedys.

I was given some of this background detail in a preliminary 'briefing' when I was taken to see the former diplomat at his Wimpole Street flat in London's West End. A lift took us directly into his private lobby adjoining a large study-cum-drawing room complete with antique furniture and a grand piano. He greeted me cordially and told me I had come well-recommended. He was very much an establishment figure and his appearance reminded me of Sir C. Aubrey Smith, the famous actor who starred in films like *Rebecca*, *Waterloo Bridge*, and *Clive of India*. He had white hair and an aristocratic bearing. He was in excellent shape and I estimated he was in his late-sixties or early-seventies. As a young diplomat in the British Embassy in Moscow in 1917 and 1918, he'd helped smuggle the royal family's gold out of Russia shortly before Tsar Nicholas II, a close relative of our King George V, was murdered. I made three visits to Wimpole Street to discuss the plot to steal Panama's gold. This mysterious Aubrey Smith character had impeccable contacts. Photographs displayed on shelves and on the piano included shots of him with Prince Philip, other members of the Royal Family and with Winston Churchill.

My own credentials to him had been further verified by people like Tom Driberg MP, and Lord Manny Shinwell.

The FO mandarin (retired) wanted me to bring a team of five men to Panama City. He was looking for the best mercenary robbers in Britain. We would get none of the gold but would be paid a total of half a million pounds – £100,000 each which in 1963 would make you a millionaire by today's standards. It was an attractive proposition made even more so by the adventurous aspects of the enterprise.

The plan, which would be more fully outlined once we

had accepted the work, involved us entering Panama City separately from different parts of Europe some two weeks before the robbery. We would also book into different hotels. The operation would take effect during a fiesta. All the equipment we needed for the raid would be supplied and we would each be issued with small-arms.

An armed sentry at the target bank would have to be taken care of, and we would have to familiarise ourselves with the route from the city to the port. A truck – he called it a 'camion' (a lorry) would also be provided, together with escort vehicles, and I would have to do a dummy run from Panama City to the harbour, some forty miles away. Our FO man would supervise operations at the bank, after which we would be on our own.

The bullion would be loaded on to a Greek vessel. Apart from the captain and first mate, none of the crew would be aware of the cargo and there was little doubt about what we had to do if there were difficulties: sling the troublemakers overboard.

The night after the robbery, we would lay off the coast at a certain point and pick up three passengers in a small motorboat and escort them to Mexico City. One would be a treasurer of the bank, the other would be Roberto Arias and the third passenger remained a mystery. We were also expected to provide a 24-hour guard on the cargo until the ship reached Mexico. An armoured van would meet us in Mexico City and the bullion would be transferred to the branch of a bank which also had a base in London. We would then return to England and the money we had been promised would be sent to the account numbers we had nominated in whatever part of the world we wanted. I wanted to know a lot more and did some homework in local libraries. I knew the area was a hot-bed of activity and that the Americans would be very suspicious of vessels in the area. I didn't want us to end up cannon-fodder in an ill-conceived plot where we were being used. It was a very sensitive area and we were not sure who was behind it.

As bank robbers, we were easily dispensable and nobody, apart from our families, would care what happened to us. Each of us was told to take out life insurance for our families prior to departure.

I discussed the work with Patsy O'Mara, and we came to the decision that we would concentrate on a job in London which proved to be equally lucrative. Why travel to a distant country where we ran a great risk of never coming back? The others were wary of going into unknown territory. Here in London we knew all the back streets where we could duck and dive, and we had friends with whom we could stay if we had to go on our toes. The money was attractive. For a working-class cockney lad, the thought of instant riches was very enticing. But the downside was the very real danger that we were being used as pawns and would be dispensed with once the work had been done. Apart from that, our new bit of work in London was looking rosier and rosier. As a result, I declined the offer.

In June 1964, Dr Arias was shot in Panama by a 'political' assassin. The official version was that he had stood as candidate for the National Assembly as a Deputy for the Province of Panama. A political colleague, Alfredo Jimenez 'the expressionless one' had asked Arias to register him as his deputy. His refusal resulted in Jimenez shooting Arias five times at point blank range at a busy road junction. Dr Arias survived but was permanently paralysed. Knowing what I did, I wondered if Arias *had* attempted to get the gold which would have been his springboard to power in Panama.

That year, then, was a lucky escape for me. I refused Panama and I had also knocked back the chance of becoming one of the Great Train Robbers and the likelihood of a thirty-year prison sentence. Instead, my firm prospered all the way through the 60s until I was sent to prison as an accessory after the fact in the Jack 'The Hat'

McVitie murder case. In the meantime, we did all we could to help friends in trouble.

The firm arranged for Buster, and later Ronald Biggs, to escape from Britain and get plastic surgery abroad. It was done through my contact who used a former top-ranking Nazi officer to organise plastic surgeons and safe passage through Europe. Austrian-born Otto Skorzeny fulfilled in every way the popular concept of a Waffen SS officer. His face was lean, mean and authoritative. And in common with others of his kind, he proudly bore the status symbol scar inflicted on his face while fencing at university. But the man's enterprise was not in question.

In September 1943 he had led a detachment of men in gliders and landed on a short, inclined slope in front of the hotel on the Gran Sasso Range, Italy, where Benito Mussolini was held prisoner. After a brief battle, he liberated the fascist Italian leader and brought him to Hitler's headquarters in East Prussia. For his bravery and enterprise, Hitler awarded him with the Nazis' highest honour: the Iron Cross. In September 1944 he infiltrated the Citadel of Budapest and forcibly prevented the Hungarian puppet leader Horthy from making a separate peace agreement with Stalin. Then, during the Ardennes counteroffensive in north-east France in 1944, he caused widespread sabotage behind Allied lines. His activities included dressing up as an American army officer with his men as Allied military police and changing roadsigns over a vast area, leading to utter military confusion among Allied convoys. After the war, he stood trial as a war criminal but was acquitted. Now he and his wife Else ran a profitable business as 'fixers' for people all over Europe. Buster invested £20,000 with Otto's wife Else for a share in a holiday complex under construction in Algeciras, southern Spain. Although he got some returns, the whole thing was a rip-off.

Ronnie Biggs escaped from Wandsworth Prison with

a friend of mine, Eric Flower, on 8 July, 1965. They were sprung by Paul Seabourn who drove a furniture van alongside the prison wall and threw over rope ladders, which got them out while other prisoners held down two screws. Although they no longer sew mailbags for the GPO, screws at the prison still hold an unfinished mailbag 'for the day Biggs returns'. I hope that never happens. Thirty years is too long to hold a grudge.

Eric Flower rang me from the 'safe place' he and Biggs were deposited at in Dulwich by Paul Seabourn. He said he didn't think security was as good as it might be. We said we'd be over straight away. I had never met Biggs before although I knew most of the main men in the train robbery. As I've said, Buster, Tommy Wisbey, Gordon Goody, Johnny Daly, Jimmy Hussey and Bruce Reynolds were all pals of mine. They were all from south London and our paths had crossed many times. I felt outraged that they had been given thirty years for the robbery. That was a fucking liberty. Nothing short of barbaric. I still believe to this day that someone probably sweet-grassed them.

Eric Flower was doing a twelve for robbery at the time of the escape. When Alf and I went to the Dulwich flat to see him and Biggs, Paul Seabourn was not too happy. He recognised Alf Gerrard immediately and took Biggs to another room and told him (as Biggs confirmed in his autobiography *Odd Man Out*): 'I know Alfie and I can tell you he's bad news. They're not here to do you any favours and they know you've got lots of dough tucked away. Take this [he offered a pistol which was refused] to look after yourself. You're out, now make sure you stay out. Use this if you have to.'

He was right about one thing. We were there to help Eric rather than Biggs but we had no designs on Biggs's money. We were only doing this as a favour for a friend. We didn't need the money and all 'fees' for services went directly to the parties involved and not us.

We moved Biggs and Flower to a safer address in Bermondsey knowing that Seabourn would be in the frame, as Biggs and Seabourn had been close in prison. I didn't know Seabourn either and therefore had no reason to trust him. We moved Biggs and Flower from Bermondsey after we'd been tipped off that Seabourn had again been interviewed by police. The following night, police raided the block of flats where Biggs and Flower had been staying.

Safely ensconced in one of the firm's safe flats in Camberwell where my sister-in-law Nellie looked after them, Eric and Biggs spent most of their time watching television. My Nellie looked after them for weeks without asking for a penny, or receiving any money. She did their cooking and washing and risked her own liberty without demanding anything. And she knew they were loaded because there was a suitcase stuffed with money behind her sofa. They did not venture out while we arranged passports and travel to Belgium and France for their plastic surgery.

But then Biggs got restless and wanted to move down to Bognor Regis for a couple of months to get rid of his prison pallor and link up with his wife Charmian and his kids. We only agreed reluctantly to this because of the obvious risks. Later we brought him back to Camberwell and arranged for a boat moored on the Thames at London Bridge to take him and Eric to Antwerp. We provided 'seamen's' clothes for them and drove them to the docks. They were to walk through the dock gates where the ship's mate would meet them and hide them both on board. They were given seasickness pills and told that no matter what happened they had to stay in hiding on the boat until told to go ashore. A yellow DAF car would pick them up once they had walked out of Antwerp docks. The passports the firm provided were in the names of Terence Furminger and Ronald King. We did not profit from the transactions and that was the end of the firm's involvement with Biggs. All we knew was that he was possibly in Australia.

Life is full of ironies and coincidences. In 1969, when Biggs fled Australia, Alfie Gerrard, Ronnie Everett and Jerry Callaghan were also there. They'd been on their toes having fled Britain after a fight with police. While in south Australia, they had started a road haulage business and a store and were doing really well driving lorries across Australia. Alfie loved it. But their freedom was shortlived because of the introduction of a satellite TV link between Britain and Australia. Scotland Yard organised pictures of Biggs and members of my firm to be beamed across the Pacific and they were arrested hours after the transmission. Eric Flower was also arrested and they were all extradited to Britain. Eric was sent back to Wandsworth to finish his twelve years and the other three stood trial for assault on police and vehicle theft charges. I was away doing my ten for Jack McVitie. Meantime, lucky Biggs had successfully evaded arrest and was on his way to Brazil and a new life.

Many years later, when I was on my toes in Spain in the mid-1980s, I met a Polish film director called Lech Majewski at the Red Pepper restaurant in Puerto Banus who wanted to make a film on Biggs. I got the pair together and Biggs went ahead with the movie: *Prisoner of Rio*. I don't think it was very good but Biggs made a few bob from it. Majewski and his girlfriend Julia Frankel wrote the script. Paul Freeman played Biggs, and Steven Berkoff and Peter Firth had starring roles. It was released at about the same time as the film *Buster*, starring Phil Collins and Julie Walters.

Buster had escaped the police net in exactly the same way as Biggs and together with June and Nicky, had gone to Mexico and met up with Bruce Reynolds and his family. But life in Mexico was not for Buster. The family missed London and Buster returned to Europe in September 1966 to give himself up. On his way back, he asked me to meet him in Cologne, Germany, to help him with a plan of action.

Just before then, I had been a go-between for several others involved in the Great Train Robbery who were being hassled by Tommy Butler, the Flying Squad chief in charge of the case. By then, Detective Superintendent Frank Williams whom I trusted and who had helped me in the past, was his deputy. Butler was obsessed with catching *all* the men involved.

To stop him pestering the men, I was asked to offer him £50,000 as a bribe. Frank Williams put it to him and Butler seemingly agreed the bribe. I made a meet with Frank to take the £50,000 cash stuffed in two holdall bags to Nunhead Station in south London, close to my betting shop in Nunhead Lane. When I walked into the station with the money, Frank Williams, looking a bit flustered, said: 'Fred, I can't take it. Tommy's backed out.'

I told him it was no big deal and I'd take it back. He offered to act as my minder while I returned the money. 'No thanks, I can manage,' I said and got the fuck out of there.

I returned the money only to go through this business all over again. Frank was obviously keen to get his hands on a nice Christmas present and this time arrangements were made for me to leave the money in a telephone box in Great Dover Street where I could mind it from my brother-in-law's flat. A separate bundle of £10,000 had been left on top to be dropped off at Albert Connell's betting shop. But Tommy Butler didn't want to stop at Albert's. He insisted on going straight to Scotland Yard where he declared the lot. Oddly enough the ones who got away weren't bothered by him any more.

I took Maureen with me when I went to Cologne as she had wanted to see her old friend June and we spent a few nice days together eating at restaurants and enjoying nightclubs. June had been very unhappy in Mexico and wanted to be back home with her family. Buster asked me to make a deal with Butler. I said I didn't trust him and that I thought he would double on him. But I promised to speak to Frank Williams.

I treated Frank and Tommy Butler to a lunch at Simpson's-in-the-Strand, one of my favourite restaurants. We sat in one of the box seats upstairs and I gave them the full treatment. Plenty of fine wine, roast beef, cheeses and vintage port. By the time we'd finished eating they were both relaxed and feeling mellow. All Butler wanted to talk about was cowboy films. He knew all there was to know about Westerns. Frank kept looking at me as if to say: 'Don't upset him, Fred.' Anyway, eventually we got to an arrangement where if, and only *if*, I emphasised, we could put Buster down as a minor participant in the robbery, such as cleaning up at the farm and being paid only a small amount of money, would Butler agree to do whatever he could to get him a lighter sentence. We all shook hands on this and I went and explained it to Buster and got him back into a safe flat in Russell Court, Holborn. He and June shared some days together and I kept in touch with Frank Williams.

Although everything had been agreed, I still did not trust Butler and asked Frank his opinion. Frank said: 'Let's wait until Butler takes his leave. He goes to all the European countries like France and Spain with field-glasses looking on the beaches for train robbers. That's his holiday. While he's away, bring Buster in to me, then I'll be the arresting officer and will be able to give my evidence *after* Butler has given his.' Frank Williams was a good man considering he was a copper. In his Welsh accent, he said he thought thirty years was much too much time for a man to do.

So that's what we did. I arranged for Buster to come to the Prince of Wales pub on 19 September, 1966 while Maureen kept June company. We sat in my lounge above the pub and got stuck into vintage brandy, Camus I think it was. The three of us, Frank, me and Buster spent hours chatting and got plenty of drink down us. I felt really worried in case it went wrong. I didn't like the idea of seeing a man throw himself in, knowing he faced the possibility of a thirty-year sentence.

Buster got up and went to the loo at one time and Frank said: 'He can go if he likes, Fred. If he has changed his mind, I don't really care.'

So I got Buster in the bedroom and said: 'Look mate, if you want to go, I'll take you back to June.' But he wanted to get it over with and said: 'Let's go through with it, Fred.' It was a sad night as he walked out of my pub and got in Frank Williams's car and drove off to the Borough High Street nick where Frank sat Buster right under one of his wanted pictures. Not one copper, not even the Flying Squad team recognised Buster. Mind you he did look different. He had lost lots of weight and the plastic surgeon had done a good job. I visited Buster in Bedford Prison with Maureen and the press were waiting outside thinking she was June. They drove us nuts following us around Bedford taking hundreds of photographs. June was known to the press as the 'Black Rose' and looked very much like Maureen.

I engaged George Stanley, solicitors from Stratford Broadway and we had the trial moved to Nottingham Crown Court. We got the best QC available, a leader of the circuit and a very nice man to talk to – Bernard Caulfield. He was shortly to be made a judge and many years later went down in history in the Jeffrey Archer libel case for his chivalrous commentary on Lady Archer.

Buster and I put together a story that Buster had been at another address at the time of the train robbery. We contrived to say he only went to Leatherslade farm where the money was counted, *after* the event, and that his job had been to burn it down and destroy the evidence. One of the prosecution team was Tom Williams QC, another Welshman who had impressed me and so I

'Bottom of the bill but best fight on the card …'

Evening Standard

42,767 THURSDAY, DECEMBER 14, 1961 ●● 3d.

Crash-helmeted, gas-masked thieves with pepper spray-gun ambush wages van

BANK GUARD SHOOTS £100,000 BANDITS

Five bullets then the gang cry 'Beat it!'

P-c AND HIS DOG COSHED IN BATTLE IN A BOW STREET

By JOHN PONDER

Five shots, a brave policeman and a growling Alsatian foiled eight desperate men from pulling off a £100,000 wages grab in Bow today.

Seven of the bandits got nothing more than a glance at the money. The eighth got a bullet in his arm and lost a toy gun he was carrying.

THIS WAS THE PLAN

It was a simple, daring plan.

Ambush the armoured van—it was from Glyn Mills Bank in Lombard Street, City—couple a chain to the doors and tear them off and then smoke out the security guards with home-made "tear gas" equipment.

This consisted of a cylinder of compressed gas attached to a container full of cayenne pepper and face powder which could be blown at high pressure into the van.

Grab the money and flee.

.22 PISTOL

The timing was perfect. The ambush came off as arranged in Turners Road, Bow. But the raiders didn't count on 48-year-old bank guard Frederick Dighton and his .22 pistol. When he fired they panicked, "Beat it," they're shooting," one of them was heard to say.

This was what Mr. Dighton, of Islington, saw from the van.

"I was in the back guarding the money — wages for gas workers," said Mr. Harmon—another guard, a cashier, Mr. George Shelton and City policeman P-c Burkle and his dog, Flash. We felt the crash as the gang's lorry

● Page Sixteen, Col. 4

LORRY USED TO BLOCK ROAD

RAM VAN

BANK VAN

After the hold-up attempt today, the bank van, its side windows broken, is hemmed in by the lorry and van used by the raiders

PICTURES BY EVENING STANDARD CAMERAMAN WILLIAM ALDEN.

P-c Buckle, his arm in a sling, with alsatian Flash today.

TV tycoons part with some of their TV shares.—PAGE THREE.

WEATHER—Bright periods.—See Page 17

INSIDE NEWS

KATANGA: BRITAIN STANDS ALONE
PAGE SEVENTEEN

Trade "gap" lowest since August
PAGE TWO

P1127 TEST PLANE CRASHES IN FLAMES
PAGE NINETEEN

18 handcuffed men flee jail coach
PAGE SIXTEEN

Amusements Guide
PAGE TWENTY-THREE

THE MINUTE-BY-MINUTE STORY OF BOW GUNFIGHT

● From Page One

backed into the front of our van.

"There was another crash as a second van ran into the side of ours. Then a terrific tearing noise as the doors of our van were torn away by the heavy chain.

"Suddenly the doors were gone and there was a man with a 14lb. sledgehammer facing me. There were others behind him. Their faces were covered with gas masks. They all wore crash helmets. I had my revolver in my hand.

I SAW A MAN RUN

"I fired five times and saw one man run for the gang's van holding his arm.

"My orders are not to leave the money and I did not. Mr. Shelton, who is also armed, had no chance to use his gun. The City policeman—we always take one with us on this wages run on Thursday—got out of the van with his dog.

"He had no chance. They bashed at him with their coshes and they coshed the dog."

P-c Buckle was taken to hospital for treatment as dozens of police arrived and closed part of Turners Road.

Two hours later, under Detective Superintendent James Beale, they had built up this picture of the £100,000 raid which failed:

9.43: The green bank van, carrying the cash in six brown heavy leather bags marked clearly with the name of each gasworks for which they were destined, drove down Turners Road.

In a second or two it would turn into Bow Common Lane and into the main gates of the North Thames Gas Board's works. Then a red lorry—bearing false number plates, police later discovered—pulled out of a side turning in front of the bank van.

FULL SPEED—IN REVERSE

At the junction with Bow Common Lane the lorry stopped—and reversed at full speed.

Said bank van driver Mr. Albert Banks, 60, of Canonbury: "I was trapped in my cabin as the lorry reversed into us and a second later another van crashed into the side of us. Two unmasked men smashed the window of my cabin. The glass cut my ear. I could not get out."

9.44: Three vehicles — the green bank van, the red lorry and the yellow van that crashed into the pay van's side—stood locked in the middle of the junction. The gang attacked the heavy metal chain to the rear doors. The other end was attached to a third vehicle they were using, a Minibus.

9.45: The Minibus shot forward and the chain tore away the barred door.

9.49: First, sight of the money—a neat row of six brown leather bags. But astride them stood Mr. Dighton, his black 32 pistol in hand. He fired the first shot as the first of the raiders tried to get in. P-c Buckle and his dog leapt forward. The other robbers crowded towards the torn-open bank van. And then fell back. Dighton fired again. They fled towards their Minibus as P-c Buckle landed among them.

There coshes — pickaxe handles, bicycle chain, and the toy gun which were later found by detectives — rained down on the policeman's head. He fell into the roadway. The Minibus moved away up Turners Road.

10.5: The Minibus was found abandoned in Rhodeswell Road, Stepney, about a quarter of a mile away. A Jaguar that may belong to the gang was found there, too.

Immediately Superintendent Beale arrived he sent out an all-London alert. Scotland Yard flashed the description of the Minibus to all cars. Hospitals and doctors were asked to report if the shot man was brought in for attention. He is between 35 and 40, 5ft. 8in., broad, clean-shaven and wearing a fawn raincoat.

THE ROUND GOES ON

10.30: Yard fingerprint men swarmed over the three vehicles, still locked together in the roadway. Detectives knocked at every door seeking witnesses.

11 a.m.: Another barred vehicle from Glyn Mills bank arrived and a smiling Mr. Dighton and Mr. Harman helped police carry the money bags into it from the gasworks to which it had been taken by the police.

The wages round was continued with a police-car escort. Afterwards the bank guards, the cashier and the driver went to Limehouse police station to tell their story.

The Battle of Bow was over.

FLASH THE OBEDIENT

P-c Buckle and his dog were in the news earlier this year when Flash nosed a Central Line train at Leighton, just before the doors closed. His master was left behind on the platform.

P-c Buckle, on his way to Cloak Lane police station, had to get a car to Liverpool Street station, where he found four officials trying to coax Flash from the train. He refused to move until he saw his handler.

Flash had made no attempt to get off the train at any of the 12 stations between Leighton and Liverpool Street, the normal stop for P-c Buckle on his way to work.

VAN CARRYING THE CASH — RAM VAN USED BY GANG

CASH BEING TRANSFERRED TO CAR

The scene today after the attempted hold-up.

CROWBAR — PICKAXE

HELMETS

PISTOL

GASMASK

Left behind after the raid . . . in the kerb is a length of chain, on the pavement an imitation pistol.

OXY-ACETYLENE CYLINDER — PEPPER CONTAINERS

Inside one of the bandits' ram vans.

Watkinson gets tough with Strauss

From ROBERT CARVEL

PARIS, Thursday.—Britain will ask NATO to put West Germany in the dock unless the Federal Republic Defence Minister, Franz - Josef Strauss, soon shows signs of willingness to carry a bigger share of the cost of defending the Western Europe.

Mr. Harold Watkinson, defence Minister, will have a show-down with Strauss here tonight. He has invited this argumentative German politician, who always asks for more than he offers, to dinner tonight.

If Strauss is ready neither to pay more towards the upkeep of Britain's Rhine Army nor to take big new arms orders in Britain, an appeal will be made to NATO to find some way of disciplining the Germans.

Rebuff

Mr. Watkinson is hopeful of mutual success this evening.

The Germans had a reverse from NATO chiefs at the recent conference. They did not get their own way over the control of nuclear weapons. A move by Strauss for transferring responsibility for them to European hands was neatly side-tracked.

It was agreed to refer the question on to a committee early in the New Year without saying when things happen after that. There is now great reluctance in the alliance to allow German fingers on nuclear triggers.

The Germans believed in an unprecedented way today. It is customary for statements to be made in turn by Ministers of the different countries. Yet the Germans insisted on having two speeches, one after another.

The first Foreign Minister Schroeder talked about disarmament and the peaceful use of atomic energy. He added that NATO should turn its own tongues.

To everyone's surprise, Strauss then pitched in with a fistful of proposals of his own.

Demanding

He wants NATO to have many more tactical nuclear weapons for defending West Germany's borders. He wants vertical takeoff aircraft developed for use there, too, and he wants the alliance to have its own long-range rockets with nuclear warheads.

Strauss circulated a paper showing how everything must be settled by 1962 he said.

The Secretary - General, Mr. Dirk Stikker, replied that no progress had been made in assigning last year's American offer to supply NATO with five Polaris submarines.

I understand that the NATO Ministers were told that the latest military intelligence reports still suggest Russia will not provoke any incident which would likely lead to a major war.

He hoped that Britain has already decided to withdraw two divisions from Germany as an economy move were authoritatively denied today.

Does the law protect the man who shoots to kill?

Evening Standard Reporter

A security guard is attacked . . . he uses a gun to defend himself and his money . . .

This was the news today that brought important fresh significance to the question: Just how far can a man go legally in defending himself?

And is he prosecuted by the law if he shoots to kill?

Archbold's Criminal Pleading, the leading authority on criminal law, states:

"If a person attempts to rob or murder another in or near the highway . . . and is killed in the attempt the slayer is entitled to an acquittal for the homicide is justifiable."

"The killing need not be in self-defence but may be in defence of another against whom open or property service felony is threatened."

Another authority, Halsbury's Laws of England, states:

"Where a forcible and violent felony is attempted upon the person of another, the party assaulted or any other person present, is entitled to repel force by force and if necessary to kill the aggressor. The use of deadly force is justifiable only if it is to prevent the felony and is from serious violence or from a reasonable fear of it."

Commenting on today's news, a lawyer says: "In this case I consider that shooting to wound would be justifiable in self defence against robbery with violence. But shooting to kill would only be justifiable in the last resort, if there were no other way to prevent death or serious injury of those attacked."

Crowbar raiders snatch £5000

Crowbar raiders forced away an iron grill protecting the rear window of a Paisebars Avenue, Burkhampton sub-post office today. Then they prised open the safe door and escaped with £5000 worth of stamps and postal orders.

WEATHER—Bright periods.

Forecast until noon tomorrow for London and S.E. England: A cold day becoming cloudy towards dusk as a fine trough with rain or sleet moves in from the west. Winds light, mainly northerly, becoming south-east and moderate. Rather cold, max. temp. about 40deg. (4C). Outlook: colder weather with further outbreaks of sleet and snow. Tonight's forecast: London and S.E. England: Cloud with slight rain or sleet clearing, mainly southern areas during early morning, with frost developing. Cold. Barometer falling today. Barometer at noon: 29.77in., falling. Lighting-up time: 4.11 p.m. to 7.31 a.m. tomorrow. Sun rises 7.55 a.m., sets 3.52 p.m. High water London Bridge 11.25 a.m., 11.46 p.m.

The Daily Telegraph
and Morning Post

4 a.m.

No. 33943. LONDON, TUESDAY, JUNE 9, 1964. Printed in LONDON and MANCHESTER. Price 5d.

HUSBAND OF DAME MARGOT SHOT

'Political argument' in Panama

3 BULLETS IN CAR: CONDITION SERIOUS

SCOTT FRANCIS
Daily Telegraph Correspondent

PANAMA CITY, Monday.

DR. ROBERTO ARIAS, 46, the Panamanian diplomat and husband of Dame Margot Fonteyn, the British ballerina, was shot three times and seriously wounded in his car in Panama City today.

He was taken to Santo Tomas Hospital, and given an immediate blood transfusion. One bullet was reported to have pierced his lung, and a doctor described his condition as "very bad."

Police said the shooting, in a suburban street, followed an argument between Dr. Arias and a political colleague. Dr. Arias, a former Panamanian Ambassador to Britain and the son of a former President of Panama, was objected to Panama's National Assembly last month.

The man with whom he was said to have been arguing was Alberto Jimenez, an alternate candidate in last month's election. Police said Jimenez had fled.

Dr. Roberto Arias who was shot three times and seriously wounded in Panama City yesterday, photographed with his wife, Dame Margot Fonteyn, the ballerina, in London. He is reported to have been in an argument with a political colleague.

Siamese twin dies after separation

ONE of the French Siamese twins, Bernice and four days old in St. Barthelemy's Hospital died last hour of operation yesterday morning, some six hours after surgeons separated the pair.

U.S. CLOSER TO 'HOT' WAR IN LAOS

CYPRUS hunt for British major

CORNED BEEF CARGO SEIZED AT SEA

COMMONS CLASH OVER RELEASED STOCKS

Evening Standard

FRIDAY, MAY 25, 1963

Silent masked robbers make a lightning swoop on treasure from Rothschilds

£250,000 LONDON BULLION RAID

Gang flee in van with 40 gold bars

FORTY bars of gold worth between £250,000 and £280,000 were stolen today by a three-man gang in a lightning raid on the bullion broking firm of Sharps Pixley and Co. in Paul Street, Finsbury.

Mac's son-in-law for Moscow

By **PHILIP MARSHALL**

DAILY Mirror

Saturday, October 28, 1978 9p

Hero shot in £1m swoop

DEATH OF A DRUG BUSTER

Daily Mirror

3d. Saturday, May 22, 1963 No. 18,484

'The Big Buyer' pulls off greatest-ever coup

GHOST SQUAD HUNT £250,000 GOLD RAID GANG

TWENTY picked detectives last night formed a "Ghost Squad" and merged into London's underworld in a search for £250,000 worth of gold bars snatched in The Great Bullion Robbery yesterday.

By TOM TULLETT and JOHN SMITH

Vanished

Screamed

AFTER THE ROBBERY

THE Sun

WHY DO TV'S SEXY STARS FALL FOR THEIR DOCTORS?

See Centre Pages

£7M GUARD IN BLAZE TORTURE

By STEPHEN GORDON and STUART DENNING

THE gang who made Britain's biggest-ever cash haul doused a quiet with petrol and threatened to set him ablaze.

Terror as gang poured petrol on him

Carole: I've been so silly

Carole and Mike pictured after their engagement

IS THIS A CUP FINAL DREAM?

CUP SPECIAL—PAGES 26 AND 27

Angry seamen hijack ship in Navy row

By CHARLES RAE

FURIOUS seamen last night seized a cargo ship . . . in a tit-for-tat action against the Navy, who took over a strike-hit troopship.

Twenty seamen stormed aboard the Blue Star-owned SS Browning as it docked in Harwich.

And they warned: "We hold on to this one until our ship is released."

Seventy Navy sailors, disguised as civilians, took control of Falklands troopship HMS Keren last week at Wallsend-on-Tyne.

It followed a pay dispute among merchant seamen needed to man the vessel on its way to the Falklands.

HIGH SIERRA !

The Ford Sierra is Britain's best-selling car . . . only five months after it replaced the Cortina. It sold 20,905 in March, claims Ford, displacing the BL Metro.

How the Curtain Road crooks pulled

THE £7 M

Tea-up guard gave gang their big break

By MICHAEL FIELDER

CROOKS were able to net £7million Britain's biggest-ever cash raid beca... thirsty security guard wanted his mo... cuppa.

The hooded gang were waiting when the ... strolled to collect a bottle of milk left be... loading bay outside the London HQ of S... Express.

They pounced on the startled officer — th... guard on duty — and bundled him back in... building early on Monday morning.

He was blindfolded and held prisoner...

The Great Easter Heis... underway.

The gang — three — acted military precision once the... in the HQ in Curtain R... Shoreditch, East London.

They overpowered and folded six other Security H... staff when they arrived.

Then the gangsters... criminal genius to work c... the sophisticated time-locks... vaults containing bundle... bundle of notes.

Vital

The jubilant crooks e... with a fortune in used £5... £5 and £1 notes—leaving... more than £1million in silv... copper because it was too...

Scotland Yard detectiv... certain the robbers mus... been given vital help by s... inside the security organi...

The vaults would no... have been closed on a Bank... day Monday. But the gang... have known they would be... — manned by a skeleton s... specially to take in cash... the Daily Mail Ideal Home... bition.

The vaults were also b... with bags of money col... from businesses throughou... gon over Easter and being... until it could be banked.

Kettle

All six or seven member... the gang would have had t... for more than an hour no... to load the massive haul... getaway trucks.

The raid began at 7am... thirsty guard decided to... himself a morning cuppa.

He put the kettle on... walked from the reception a... which is equipped with a... circuit TV access — to se... one of the nearby loading b...

As he crossed part of a... courtyard, where the... armoured trucks are kept, h... grabbed by two gangsters.

Detectives believe... raiders scaled... perimeter wall duri... night — possibly b... ladders—and had... lying in wait fo... guard.

The firm's pr... surrounded by 30ft... walls scanned by... lights and TV came...

But the raiders... over the wall and...

● NINE tea chests brimming with 1½ tons of banknotes . . . this is the cash-and-carry headache that faces the Curtain Road robbers.

● The gang would have had to use some mighty muscle - power when they made their getaway with their £7 million money mountain.

● Experts reckon a mere £15,000 in mixed notes weighs 7lbs and £1million tips the scales at 4¼cwts.

TREASURE IN CHESTLOADS

e most sensational banknote robbery of all time

CUPPA!

Security Express Limited

Warning

The Company accepts no liability
unless negligent for loss of or
damage to vehicles and articles
in them

*" We accept no liability" . . . the ironic warning
on the wall of the Security Express HQ.*

E GREAT NKNOTE BBERY

rd without being

took the captured
back to the recep-
tres—through two
security doors—
ked for the other
arrive.
in Road is full of
o premises which
shut for the Bank
and the streets
eserted.
eng's plan worked
lockwork. Each
r of the staff was
and had slinky
slipped over their

Tipped

believe the raid
anned by a crimi-
termind who spent
picking a team of
alts.
 have been tipped
a known crook
ned The Ginger
d been recruiting-
in East London
ast London
shut for the past
aths.
night Yard detec-
under Central
r Squad boss Com-
Frank Cater
hecking the files on
-time crooks cap-
pulling off such
ational robbery.
were looking par-
r for the expert
ith was cracked a
y network raised
the toughest ja

Mole

he most important
'facing Comman-
te and his hand-
squad of 30 men
ht was: Who is the

believe the tip-off
buld be a present
of Security Ex-
or a former em-

detective added:
to be someone very
the day-to-day
ons of the com-

apply wine bottles
und at the scene of
forensic experts
ay—but were not
to have belonged
raiders.

After the raid . . . Security Express staff and one of the firm's famous vans—with notice ringed

IT'S PURE MAGIC, SAYS BUSTER

Buster . . . "wish I was in on it"

By SUN REPORTER

GREAT Train robber
Buster Edwards yester-
day described the
Security Express hijack
as "pure magic."

Buster, who runs a
flower stall outside Lon-
don's Waterloo station,
said he was green with
envy at the size of the
gang's haul.

First

And he added: "It was
absolutely beautiful—the
best news I've heard for
ages.

"I only wish that I'd
been in on the job.

Buster, who got six
years for his part in the

theft of £2½million from a
Glasgow-London express
in 1963, went on: " The
train job was famous
because it was the first
of its kind.

" But the lads who did
this latest one deserve all
the credit.

" When a job comes off
that well it can only be
described as pure magic.
I'm green with envy at the
skills involved.

" I can't see those lads
getting caught. They're
obviously a bright bunch
and provided everybody

got a fair share they
should be well away."

SECURITY at the hold-up
firm was "a joke," according to the landlord of a
nearby pub.

The publican claimed
that Security Express men
drinking in his bar regu-
larly talked about how
easy it would be to pull
off " a job."

Guard

But a former guard,
Dave Tierney, said pre-
cautions . included four
sets of locked doors and
double-checks on security
passes. He added: "Get-
ting in was the work of
master crooks."

Blaze torture

Continued from Page One

a married man in his
future.

A STAGGERING
reward of £500,000 was
offered yesterday to nail
the supergang.

The golden carrot—un-
equalled in British
criminal history — was
put up by underwriters at
Lloyd's, who insure Secu-
rity Express.

TICKLE

My Laurie Haggar a
director of the loss
adjusters called in by
Lloyd's said : "We must
recover the money as well.
We hope we can tickle
someone enough to lay
them all the way."

Detectives last night
waited for an underworld
supergrass to rise to the
bait.

But the gang are cer-
tain to put out a "con-
tract" on the life of anyone tempted to squeal.

THE Sun

Friday, April 8, 1983   15p   TODAY'S TV: PAGE 14

Five little sisters die in blaze

By DAVID GRAVES

FIVE little sisters were killing yesterday when a horror-blaze swept through their home.

The girls, daughters of a clergyman, were being bathed by their mother when the tragedy happened.

Mrs Jo Olumide left the youngsters, aged between two and nine, to pop downstairs for a moment.

Then she saw a sheet of flame leap from an upstairs room.

The terrified woman ran outside to get help, but by the time she arrived back the house in Frogmore Avenue, Hayes, Middx, was a blazing inferno.

Police spokesman said: "There was nothing Mrs Olumide could do but watch. She is in deep shock."

Charity

Firemen found the bodies of four of the girls huddled together in the bathroom.

The fifth sister was rushed to hospital but died an hour later.

The dead girl's father is the Rev Olly Olumide, chaplain at a psychiatric hospital in Southall.

Mr Olumide, a West Indian, is well known locally for his charity work.

TWO brothers, Richard Knowles, 10, and Karsie, two, died yesterday when a fire broke out in their bedroom.

A third brother, Mark, five, jumped to safety from the window of the house in Penrith Crescent, Ferry Fryston, Castleford, Yorks.

YARD HUNT £7M TOFF!

PRINCE CHARLES has gone down with the classic naval ailment . . . the mauled mitt. His right hand is sore and swollen after being heartily gripped by thousands of husky Aussies.

The prince used his left hand when he and Princess Diana (above) visited Perth yesterday.

Picture by ARTHUR EDWARDS

Charles gets a real big hand!

- Gang of 14 called their boss Paddy One
- He was a military type with posh accent

By MICHAEL FIELDEN and STUART HIGGINS

A GANG of 14 supercrooks—led by a "toff" with a posh accent—carried out the £7million Great Banknote Robbery.

The exclusive information was revealed last night to The Sun by one of the security guards held up at gunpoint by the raiders.

The guard said the team—who used phoney Irish accents—acted with military precision.

They knew every detail of the vaults and even the names of staff before they raided the Security Express HQ in Curtain Road, Shoreditch, East London, on Easter Monday.

CONTACT

The guard, who asked not to be named, told The Sun how the toff called himself Paddy One.

And in a dramatic de-

MOVE AND WE BLOW YOU AWAY
—Pages 4 and 5

velopment last night an underworld contact gave what is believed to be the real name of The Toff and his alleged lieutenant to The Sun.

The contact told us: "He's no push, he could have been through military school."

The Sun immediately passed the names to Scotland Yard.

Robbery squad boss Commander Frank Cater said: "This information is extremely interesting.

"We shall be following it up straight away."

The Toff was said to be a middle-aged man who lived in the Canning Town area of East London until he mysteriously vanished three months ago.

He is thought to have a

Continued on Page Four

made a mental note of his name for the future. Half-way through the trial I considered Buster's case was not going very well and had a word with George Stanley. 'I don't like it George, I'm going to pull one of the jurors and try and get Buster a new trial.'

He was shocked. 'You can't do that! That would be illegal – and not only that, you'd go to prison.' I told him I didn't care, I was worried sick that Buster would go down for thirty years. He told me not to worry. Bernard Caulfield wouldn't let us down.

When it came to Tommy Butler, true to form he never helped one bit and he even tried to get Frank Williams to double on us. During the trial when Frank Williams was about to enter the witness box to give his evidence, Butler grabbed hold of his arm and whispered in his ear: 'We can't let him slip, Frank.'

But Frank was a man of his word and went along with our defence. When Bernard asked him what scale or position Buster would be on the train gang ladder, Frank replied: 'On the bottom rung.' Buster got fifteen years which was half of what the others got so it didn't turn out too bad, at least not if you say it quick and you aren't the one who has to do it. Buster did eight, and the others between twelve and fourteen out of the thirty.

Some time after his trial, Bernard Caulfield came to my pub the Prince of Wales with some friends, and we had a drink. He was a very nice man. I followed his progress and found him to be a very fair judge. He could dish it out with the rest of them, but he did show compassion and humanity when he had to sentence someone, not like Melford Stevenson and Sir Frederick Lawton. They were dogs, as I was to find out at a later date.

June had no money left over after all the expense of the trial and what they had spent to live on the run in Mexico and Germany. Buster had also been ripped off by a guy who had an office in the City. He was a right smooth operator and had a young German girlfriend. We nicknamed him Hunchie because he was short and had the start of a hump on his back which would have got worse as he aged. He conned Buster for £20,000 in 1964 and that was a lot of cash. To help June, Alf and I paid Hunchie a little visit. He was full of the usual shit but I was not prepared to listen and told him so. We gave him a week to come up with the money and left him alone for a few days. Then we picked him up on another day in Hyde Park and kidnapped him for few hours before dropping him off at his Chelsea home. It was just to let him know that we knew where he lived and to give him a reminder about paying the money he owed Buster.

It turned out that Hunchie was a right rascal and owed a string of debts. People were queuing up to be paid. Before I was due to visit Hunchie again, I got an excited phone call telling me Hunchie was dead. I asked my informant how it happened and he said that he was found in his bath having suffered a heart attack, or something like that. There was no chance of money from him now, so I got in touch with Peter Wickman from the German magazine *Stern*. We organised a feature article which was sold to the Sunday newspapers here and in Germany and made June £25,000 so it helped her out until Buster got home.

I have to say this about coppers in those days: they never took it out on your wife like they do today. Tommy Butler, for all his faults, behaved like a gentleman around a lady and wouldn't dream of nicking them like today's police. If she loves him, a wife will stay with and support her husband no matter what he has done. Most wives I have known are strong and loyal to their men and suffer with them every inch of the way and are still there waiting for them when they come home from a long sentence. I take my hat off to you, ladies. You are by far the stronger of the sexes. I love you all.

· 12 ·
'Give Me a Name'

My brother George was lying close to death in the surgical ward of St Thomas's Hospital, London. He had taken the full blast of a double-barrelled shotgun aimed at his groin at point-blank range. Although heavily doped up he was still in agony after four operations. His upper thigh had been so badly wounded that there was talk of amputation. George and I had always been close and now I shared my brother's pain. His eyes were like deep, black holes in his pallid face. He looked like death. I felt anger, sorrow, and the urge for revenge as I watched his suffering. A policeman was at his bedside and I asked for a moment alone with my brother. I bent down and whispered in George's ear: 'Give me a name.'

George's eyes turned to where the copper had been. Satisfied he was out of earshot, he uttered: 'Ginger Marks.'

George was shot on 17 December, 1964, in a reckless, foolhardy attack. The assault was over in minutes but the repercussions continued for years, jeopardising the liberty of innocent people, dividing friends and destroying families. His assailant was George 'Jimmy' Evans who is only alive today because of the cowardly way he used his accomplice and friend Tommy 'Ginger' Marks as a shield, avoiding being shot himself. My brother George, who is one of the chaps, stuck to the time-honoured code of the underworld: he told police nothing. The comeback was our business.

Evans was a safe-blower who worked with his own little firm which included David Norman, a man called Sams (who knew George), and Tommy 'Ginger' Marks who was a good friend of Evans. He was also involved with Joe Wilkins who ran escort agencies in the West End. To give you a small insight into his character, Evans had a monkey which he dressed as a policeman and, to the amusement of his friends, he'd whack this poor animal with a rubber truncheon. 'Hit the copper. Hit the copper.' Evans was not only violent but an insanely jealous man. Pat Evans, a lovely lady who was his wife, was terrified of him.

He was gun mad. Firearms were an obsession which he continually indulged in. He'd talk about every gun that was ever built, giving all their technical details.

My George and Pat Evans fell in love shortly before the shooting. Their feelings for each other were genuine and deep and they are still together now, more than thirty years later. When they first met, both were married with children and homes of their own so they used to meet at George's flat in Cable Street, Stepney. But Evans got suspicious and started spying on her. Shortly before 17 December, 1964, he saw Pat driving George's car and challenged her. She told him the car was a repossession and she had borrowed it but Evans searched the glove compartment and found an electricity or phone bill belonging to George showing his home address: 12 Bland House, Lambeth Walk. He knocked at the door but George wasn't there. He was told to try the betting shop in Nunhead Lane, again without success.

A couple of days later, George went to look at a car showroom in Rotherhithe, just by the tunnel. Sams and Evans happened to be there and Sams pointed George out to him. (There had been some confusion because there was another George Foreman living in Essex at the time.) On Thursday 17 December, 1964, Evans hid in the boot of Pat's 'repossessed' car when she drove to George's flat. He jumped out just as she was about to enter the flat and pushed her inside. Slamming shut the door he pulled a knife on her and demanded to know whose flat it was. Pat said it belonged to her girlfriend but Evans didn't believe her. In a rage, he kidnapped Pat and drove her to the house of David Norman, who was a loyal friend, and asked to borrow a tool. He was given a single-barrelled shotgun.

Norman was told to keep Pat away from the telephone and to stop her if she tried leaving the house while Evans drove back to Cable Street to confront George. My George was standing outside the flat talking to several other people, one of whom had called the police after hearing the fracas involving Evans and Pat. By this time, however, the police had gone. But with so many witnesses about, Evans was not prepared to use the gun.

Instead, he returned the firearm to Norman and went off to borrow a double-barrelled shotgun. He cut down the barrels with a hacksaw and then drove around to Marks's flat in Stepney. The three of them then went to George's marital home in Lambeth Walk. Norman was the getaway driver while Evans and Marks went to do the business. Evans hid the sawn-off shotgun under his coat. By this time it was dark and he removed the bulb from the landing outside George's front door.

Marks, wearing his usual hat and glasses, knocked at George's door. Fortunately his wife and kids were not in. George opened the door to him and Marks gave him a moody name, pretending he was looking for someone else. A few minutes later there was a second knock on the door. George opened it and this time Evans came out of the shadows: 'Hullo George,' he said, and blasted him with the shotgun at point-blank range. The impact sent George the full length of the hallway.

Fortunately, hearing the shot a Polish neighbour investigated and found George in a pool of blood and he quickly rang for an ambulance. Evans returned to his home and told Pat he'd killed George. She was kept a virtual prisoner for the next ten months.

Evans and Marks hadn't anticipated the strength of

the Foreman brothers. After a few enquiries, Evans now feared the comeback.

Marks, on the other hand, was gung-ho about the possibility. He was seen sitting in the middle of a room with a shotgun across his lap saying: 'Send the fucking Foremans across here, I'll deal with them.'

Soon after the shooting I was tipped off that Evans's firm were going to rob Attenborough's, a jeweller's in Bethnal Green Road on 2 January, 1965. My information was that they were coming five-handed: Evans, Marks, David Norman and two others whom I didn't know. David Norman and the fourth man would break in while the fifth man and Marks would keep watch. Evans would blow the safe. Their point of entry would be through St Matthew's churchyard which joined the rear of the jewellers' shop.

By now I knew that Marks lived in Redman's Road, Stepney, and waited for him with Alfie and another man who was a solid chap and identified each member of Marks's firm. He then left us to our work. Alfie and I followed Marks, first to Attenborough's, then to Norman's flat where they collected more tools and finally back to Marks's flat in Stepney. After half-an-hour or so, Marks and Evans drove to the jeweller's in one car, and Norman and the fourth man followed them in another. The fifth man had been left at the bus-stop opposite the shop.

Alfie was at the wheel. He reckoned we were sussed and turned off just before we got there to avoid further suspicion. We later learned that the men were concerned about our car and had talked about it. Marks said it was a police car. He claimed he knew that because he had the registration number at home. We drove around the block and past the bus-stop where the five of them were talking and then turned into St Matthew's Row and parked in Goldman Close where we could watch the road. We waited a few moments in the car. Neither Alf nor I spoke. We just watched. Suddenly our luck was in. Marks and Evans began walking towards us down St Matthew's Row. Alf's hands gripped the steering wheel. They strolled past us without looking and turned left into Cheshire Street by the Carpenter's Arms public house on the corner. Alf started the motor and slowly drew out. My right hand closed on the .38 revolver and I wound down the passenger window with my left. Alf gently eased the car forward and drew alongside the pair as they walked past a school playground adjoining the pub. I leant out, my gun at the ready: 'Ginger!' Marks stopped in his tracks. Unsure of who we were and startled by the recognition, he stepped towards us. I let fly a hail of bullets.

There was no sound from Marks but Evans reacted instantly. He crouched behind Ginger and gripped his shoulders using him as a shield. The pair of them performed a macabre dance in the street trying to avoid the volley of bullets. Ginger took most of the bullets although one entered Evans's coat missing him by a hair's-breadth. Evans could no longer support his shield. He let go of Marks's shoulders. The man dropped to the pavement as Evans ran away. I dived out of the car and stood over Marks with my gun pointing to his head. He didn't move.

Alf tore after Evans in the car. Panic-stricken, Evans banged on the door of the Carpenter's Arms pub which still had its lights on. Nobody answered. He ran back up the road and dived under a lorry in Wood Close as Alf chased round again. He pulled himself up off the ground and hugged his body to the underneath of the lorry so he couldn't be seen from the road.

Marks was still lying on the ground. We picked him up and slung him into the back of the car and tore off in the direction of Vallance Road. It was pitch black and without street-lighting so we knew we would not be identified. The Carpenter's Arms pub customers had come out when they heard shots but quickly went back inside. This was the East End and people didn't want to see anything that was not their business.

When he thought the coast was clear, Evans came back to look for Marks. All he found on the otherwise empty road was a pair of spectacles and crumpled hat at the spot where Marks had fallen. He collected Ginger's things and ran to the churchyard and told his firm that Ginger had been shot by: 'Someone in a car.' The four of them drove back to Cheshire Street to have a last look. Evans, who was now in a state of frenzy, drove round the corner to Vallance Road and knocked up the Kray Twins telling them what had happened. Reg and Ronnie told him: 'If you've any trouble with the Foremans, you get on with it yourself, don't come to us for help.' Until then I had no idea he had been friendly with the Twins. But it wouldn't have made any difference. They knew the sort of person I was and no one could have stopped me from making a comeback to avenge my brother.

Evans and his firm then drove to Ginger's wife Annie to break the news. It was now the early hours of Friday. Annie broke down uncontrollably when given the glasses and hat, the last memento of her husband she would ever receive. Pulling herself together, she phoned Ginger's brother Walter (Terry) who immediately came round and together with Evans, went out looking for his brother. Again this proved fruitless. Checking with hospitals in the area they were told nobody had been admitted with gun-shot wounds.

They returned to Annie's just before dawn and rang the police to tell them that Annie had received an anonymous phone call informing her that Ginger had been shot in Cheshire Street. When the police came to interview her, Annie gave them Ginger's glasses, but as they were leaving her home, one of them picked up Ginger's hat and put it on his head as if it belonged to him. He was politely told by Ginger's daughter to leave her dad's hat alone.

During the daylight hours, police searched the area around Cheshire Street and found blood spots, spent bullets, and a cartridge. A bullet had entered the brick wall bordering the playground next to the pub and from its height, they reckoned Ginger had been shot in the stomach. Detective Chief Superintendent Townsend was put in charge of the case.

Losing Ginger did little to damage Evans's appetite for the bit of work his firm had set out to do. Two nights later they were back at the same spot trying to break in again. It wouldn't have needed the brains of Lloyd George to work out that you would now be under round-the-clock surveillance as the star witness in a potential murder inquiry. To expose your firm to the risk of capture by attempting a robbery at the scene of the murder just two days later was sheer madness. No wonder they all got nicked.

In fact, Evans himself was interviewed as a possible suspect in Ginger's disappearance. His home was searched and a shotgun found. Describing the 'murder' car, he said it was red with the first three letters of the numberplate reading: 'BLA'. He purposefully misled police because those three letters were the same as on Ronnie Everett's red Simca. The car I used was nicked and rung specially for the job and Alf and I destroyed it immediately after.

Police continued their efforts to solve the mystery over Marks's disappearance. More than forty owners of cars were interviewed and in the absence of a more mundane motive, there was speculation of gang warfare. Police were told by one witness that Ginger had cheated someone out of their share in a cigarette robbery and was expecting trouble from that source. He was also wrongly linked with the Great Train Robbery.

A publican claimed Marks had asked him to look after a gun and on 18 January, Ronnie Everett's car, registration number BLA 876B, was stolen in Romilly Street, Soho. He reported the theft at Tottenham Court Road police station. Although this had no bearing on what happened, it was to figure prominently in the future when Evans tried to implicate members of my firm who were innocent of involvement.

All the firm and my personal friends and known acquaintances were questioned by police during their routine inquiries. But unknown to us at the time, Evans had already put several of us in the frame: me, Alfie, Jerry Callaghan and Ronnie. A south London informer who had served in borstal with Evans had given him a list of names of my close friends and associates in case of reprisals and it was in Evans's interests to convict as many of us as possible.

Evans seemed to live a charmed life. He and two of his accomplices were charged with breaking and entering Attenborough's jewellers. His accomplices were each jailed for six months at the Old Bailey, while strangely the case against Evans only got as far as the magistrates' court, and he was acquitted.

In February 1965, Evans was charged with shooting my George who still refused to identify him. It was only his own mouth that got him nicked. He was bragging to people about what he'd done and word got back to the police. While on remand in Brixton, he told an old friend of mine from the East End and a good pal of the Twins, Colin 'The Duke' Osbourne, that George Cornell, who'd been rowing with Ginger shortly before his disappearance, had killed Marks. Cornell was shot dead in the Blind Beggar pub in Stepney a year later.

Evans was again acquitted on 9 April, 1965 both of shooting George and of possessing a shotgun which was found in his home. He claimed he was continually being hassled by police for not cooperating over Marks's disappearance (which was hard to believe). In the meantime, police enquiries about Ginger widened. French police were asked to interview two drug smugglers who were convinced that Marks grassed them on a drugs deal in return for police favours and assistance to get a US visa. In an exclusive *News of the World* article on 11 April Evans claimed he had not shot George and that Marks's disappearance had no connection with the shooting. The newspaper offered a £5,000 reward for anyone who could provide them with Marks's whereabouts.

There was also continued speculation which has lasted to this day over what happened to Marks's body. It has been suggested he was disposed of by a bent undertaker, buried in a motorway, or set in concrete and dumped in the Thames. It was none of those. . .

I owned the Prince of Wales pub at the time and police were slipping in and out keeping watch on me. Their operation was dual: undercover and open. One PC and WPC pretended to be a courting couple and began using my pub every day. You could spot them a mile off. They watched me round the clock and waited for me to make a move. Cossers would come in to the pub and say: 'Aren't you worried Fred with your back to the door?' When I said there was no reason for me to worry they intimated that there was going to be a gang war.

After Evans was acquitted, and as time went by, I used to go over and plot up on him. I wanted to do him badly. At the same time I didn't think it was worth going to jail for a mongrel dog like him. But I kept watch nevertheless. He had about nine lives and I kept thinking he was going to run out of luck. I once missed him coming out of a club belonging to Joe Wilkins at the back of the Strand. I got a phone call tipping me off that he was there and went around with a tool. I hoped I'd catch him outside the club but missed him by seconds. The street was very dark and I had apparently walked past without recognising him. Afterwards I remembered a guy giving me a funny look as he got into his car and drove off.

I then tracked him to a block of flats in Hackney and sat there night after night waiting for him to come home. He never stuck to a routine, arriving instead from different directions, even climbing over walls. Above the entrance to his block was a flat roof with a railing. A perfect spot to conceal yourself. I slipped on an old boiler suit over my clothes, a balaclava to hide my face, and got up there and waited with a rifle and silencer. Early one morning as dawn broke and people began moving about, I packed up, took my gun to pieces and got into my car. As I drove towards Bethnal Green Road, a car came up in front of me. It was him. And he got me in an instant. His eyes were everywhere. He was like a hunted animal. He knew he had escaped death by inches and it was only a matter of time before his luck ran out.

Years later, I was told that police had asked both Evans and David Norman if they would give evidence against me. They refused. Meanwhile I was arrested together with the Krays as an accessory to the murder of Jack 'The Hat' McVitie and sent for trial at the Old Bailey on 28th February, 1969. In April the same year, after I had been convicted of being an accessory after the fact of murder and sentenced to ten years, I faced a second murder rap, this time over Frank 'The Mad Axeman' Mitchell (I was acquitted of this charge in 1975). Nine months before my release I was charged, this time for the Marks murder. Shortly before this, Evans had again been approached by a detective who told him he knew who shot Marks and the reason behind the shooting. The policeman intimated that he knew it involved Mrs Evans and that it wasn't a gangland feud or a revenge attack for grassing other villains.

All the time I was serving my sentence over McVitie I had no idea police were still investigating me over Ginger Marks's disappearance. The crucial turning-point came in 1972, when Evans was charged with the murder of a young Scottish carpenter. Apparently on 28 July, 1972, he killed an innocent young man who was larking about with a group of friends. They had surrounded Anick Webb's car (Evans's French common-law wife) after she stalled at the exit of a car-park. Evans, who was driving his own car in front, jumped out and chased after two of the men, stabbing William Fernie, a twenty-one-year-old Scottish carpenter who died instantly, cradled in his girl-friend Pamela Lawrence's arms. Evans was charged with murder and Anick Webb was arrested the following day in Plymouth but released without charge. Evans was acquitted of murder but found guilty of manslaughter at the Old Bailey in February 1973, and jailed for seven years. While he was on remand awaiting trial, he was again seen by several officers of the law and asked to help in the Marks affair.

Other problems were also getting on top of him now. Anick Webb wrote to say she was fed up with him being in prison – he had been on remand for six months. She wanted to end their relationship. Evans wrote to her and said he had sold his soul to these people to be with her, and that he would soon be out.

After he was sentenced to seven years for the stabbing, he discovered he was to be sent to Albany Prison on the Isle of Wight and immediately protested. He demanded another prison because Alfie Gerrard was serving four-and-a-half years there and Evans said he knew he was a friend of mine. The request was refused. At Albany, Evans got a friend to point out what Alfie looked like and then confronted him. Suspecting Evans might be bugged or looking for witnesses to make up false verbal statements, Alf walked away saying he didn't know Evans. I knew what was going on in Albany Prison at the time because no one can have police visits without the rest of the prison population finding out. I had many good friends doing time there during the same period, among them Mick Regan, Roy Hilder and Alf Gerrard.

From my Category A cell at Wormwood Scrubs, I

organised someone to screw Anick Webb's flat and find those letters in which Evans said he had sold his soul to the devil. I got the originals and made a number of copies.

In 1974 Evans finally cracked and told police he wanted to see them. Evans named four of our firm as being involved in Ginger Marks's murder: me, Alf Gerrard, Jerry Callaghan and Ronnie Everett. He'd already talked to the prison deputy governor and chief officer to ask how he could help police enquiries. His statement now was vastly different to what he had told them ten years earlier. In the fresh statement he confessed to shooting my George and said that David Norman was with him at the time. Marks, he claimed, was shot for boasting that he had supplied the gun and driven him over there.

Evans, after all the intervening years, was miraculously able to recall, and recognise, four people on that dark night in January 1965. He said Jerry was driving and Ronnie had stepped out of the car to stretch himself at one point before the shooting, and that he saw Alfie filling up at a petrol station at 2.30 in the morning after the killing. This proved to be untrue.

Checks were later made and it was found that the garage in question always closed at 11pm or earlier. Soon after this false statement was made, Evans got his transfer to Pentonville Prison.

Marks's brother Terry was interviewed but he refused to cooperate. He was old school and good stuff.

In November 1974, another prisoner called Baker with a string of burglary convictions who absconded while on home leave, made a statement to the effect that Alfie had said to him: 'I will make you a lump of bacon, like I did that cunt Marks.'

David Norman was arrested on 3 January, 1975 over an offence on which he had jumped bail four years earlier. He was charged with armed robbery and possession of weapons. Now questioned by the police about Marks for the third time over ten years, he suddenly remembered that a red car, an 1100 type, had followed them from Redman's Road, Stepney, to Bethnal Green Road. He also admitted accompanying Evans to my George's when he was shot, and to breaking into the jewellery shop in Bethnal Green Road. He said he had heard a shot and that Evans told him they had got Marks.

Ronnie Everett was arrested on 6 January, 1975 in connection with the murder of Thomas 'Ginger' Marks. Jerry Callaghan and Alfie Gerrard were arrested the following day and taken to Leman Street and Arbour Square police stations. All three were interviewed on 8 January in a question-answer session.

I'd nearly served my time for McVitie when they finally came for me. I had nine months left to serve out of my ten years, only to face another murder charge which could have put me away for life! Superintendants Chalk and Troon visited me in Wormwood Scrubs after the others were arrested. I was taken from the laundry block to the admin block. I was ushered into an empty room and the door closed behind me. Chalk and Troon suddenly entered from a side door. The moment I realised it was those two, I headed for the door, banging on it with my fists and demanding to be taken out of there. I yelled: 'Open this fucking door, you've set me up.'

Troon and Chalk, ignoring my protest, said: 'We want to ask you questions about the disappearance of Thomas Marks.'

My response was as before: 'I've got nothing to say to you. Open this fucking door or I'll smash it down.'

The screws finally got the message. The door opened: 'What's up, Fred?' the screw asked.

'Take me back to the laundry you bastards. You set me up!'

Some time later I was taken from the Scrubs to Arbour Square police station and a questionnaire was put to me.

197

I answered 'no comment' all the way through and signed every answer, initialled every page.

I was formally charged with murder and taken back to the Scrubs and put in the hospital observation wing (the rule is twenty-eight days in the hospital wing for all prisoners charged with murder). One day, to my amusement, my door was opened for breakfast and I saw a screw standing there in his white overalls with a food trolley. Next to him was a con with hair slicked back and a little Hitler moustache. He was wearing a prison shirt and tie, looking very dapper. I pointed my finger at him and said: 'I know you,' to which the little guy nodded his head like a toy dog. 'You're Graham, Graham Young,' and he was nodding his head vigorously and shaking with glee because I had recognised him. It was Graham Young, the mass-poisoner, who poisoned his own mother when he was eleven years of age and then poisoned his work colleagues when he was released ten years later. I said: 'Don't you get up to any of your tricks with my breakfast Graham!'

He replied: 'No, not you Fred.' I didn't know whether to keep him as a friend or enemy and tell him to fuck off because all the people he befriended were now poisoned. He would have made a brilliant chemist if he hadn't been such a nut. He was consulted about poisons by the Home Office because he had become such an authority in that field.

After surviving Graham Young's cooking and twenty-eight days round-the-clock observation, I was sent to Wandsworth as a Category A prisoner again. Maureen visited me and two screws sat beside us writing down everything we spoke about. I told her: 'Say no more, love. Just wait eight months until I finish my sentence and go to Brixton [on remand]. At least there we will have decent visits.'

When I arrived at Brixton, there were Ron, Alf and Jerry, all waiting to greet me. I hadn't seen them since they'd left for Australia around 1967 so it was quite a reunion. Also in the Cat A wing were all the men arrested for the £8 million Bank of America robbery in Mayfair, one of the biggest at the time. Among them was Johnny 'the Bosch', the best key-fitter in the business whose real name was Leonard Wilde, Peter Colson, John Mason (who was cleared of the robbery), Henry Jeffery, Micky Gervaise (who later became a grass), Jimmy O'Loughlin, Billy Gear and Stuart Buckley who was the insider. Philip Trusty, who shot a constable at the wheel of his car during a raid, was also there and later got a twenty. The Guildford Four who were on trial at the time, were also there. They came up before Judge Donaldson who was later to be my judge. I used to console the youngest of them, Gerry Conlon, and put my arm around his shoulder saying it would be all right, I knew he was innocent. In fact, the other prisoners were all convinced they were innocent. Otherwise there would have been little sympathy for bombers. Gerry told me he thought Donaldson was a very fair judge and this gave me a little comfort because we were the next to appear before him. But he rapidly changed his mind at the shock of being found guilty and being sentenced to thirty years. So much for Judge Donaldson!

At our committal hearing in Old Street Magistrates' Court, our defence lawyers were: Louis Hawser for Jerry Callaghan, Big Ronnie had Hutchinson, I had William Denny and Alf had Barry Hudson. All applications for bail were refused and we were committed for trial at the Old Bailey.

We came before Judge Donaldson at the Old Bailey in November, 1975. Evans, the first prosecution witness, admitted he had lied under oath at his own trial, and at a divorce court hearing. He also admitted that he had lied for money when he wrote his story in the *News of the World*.

When shown the original letter he had written to

Anick Webb which said: 'I have sold my soul to these people to be with you,' he became extremely angry and refused to answer counsel's question.

Louis Hawser QC, for the defence: 'Did you write that?'

Evans: 'I don't know where you got this, it is personal and nothing to do with you.' Unable to control his rage, Evans then tore up the letter in a frenzy.

Mr Hawser watched in amusement: 'Tear them up all you want,' he said, 'I have the originals here.'

David Norman's evidence did us no harm. He also denied hearing any comments made by Marks or Evans that night about the description of the car or the people in it, i.e. 'That's a police car, I have its number written down at home.'

Evans had said in his evidence that his response to that had been: 'Don't be silly. I've just seen Callaghan driving it and Ronnie Everett in it.' Neither of the two other burglars who had been convicted of breaking into the jeweller's were called to give evidence about the mystery red car.

Louis Hawser then asked Evans about guns. Evans became so engrossed talking about his pet obsession that he went on and on detailing all the different kinds of shooters without realising the effect this was having on the jury.

On the second day of the trial, Mr Justice Donaldson told the jury to discharge Ronald Everett.

After hearing evidence from other witnesses, the judge asked the jury if they wanted to hear any more. The foreman told the judge they'd heard enough and the trial was stopped. We were all discharged and no defence witnesses needed to be called. The remaining three of us walked free, much to our relief.

That afternoon we celebrated our freedom at the A & R Club in Charing Cross Road which was owned by Micky Regan and Ronnie Knight. The place was packed out with friends and relatives. Mick Regan showed himself to be a true and loyal friend for over thirty years. As he still is today. He is a man who commands immense respect. Mick and I shared many great times and many anxious moments when things looked bad. This is the true sign of friendship which no amount of money can buy. I would have done anything for Mick and still would, make no mistake about that. Mick has been retired for many years now but I think the average reader of true crime in Britain should be aware of who were the genuine chaps that held all the respect – in those days. Mick was part of that scene. God bless you and yours, mate.

Chief Inspector Chalk retired a year after the trial and Troon was later promoted to Detective Inspector. I heard of Troon many years later when he was called on to investigate political deaths in Nigeria. Apparently there was a power struggle between two political parties who were killing each other off. While he was out there somebody tried to poison him, but failed, and I thought at the time that the Devil looks after his own.

I make no apologies for my own role in this affair. Alfie and I were not innocent. We followed an underworld code which in its own way is as strict, if not stricter, than the statutory laws governing the general public. I have never killed anyone for money despite what the rumours say. When we were swiping gold bars and wages amounting to £50,000 and £100,000 in the early 1960s, why would we risk all our lives and liberty for chicken feed? That was never our style. There had to be a very good reason to kill, and that reason never involved money.

This episode, more than most others, showed who the true chaps were. My George might have died from Evans's attack but even in the face of death he honourably stuck to our code of not grassing who shot him. As a result, Evans was acquitted. But what about Evans?

He broke every code in the criminal world we lived in. He gave statements and evidence when he wasn't man enough to do his bird.

This is a person who wants and asks for respect with his own kind? No way. He will have to live with what he has done for the rest of his life. He's even going to try to grass me from the grave. He has left statements with his solicitor, Fellowes, in the event of his death saying that I would be responsible. He didn't mind going around shooting people but, when things got a bit rough, he just couldn't be a man and face the consequences – or stand and take the comeback. He did everything he possibly could to get rid of his enemies by sweet-grassing to start with and then, after his arrest for the killing of a young man, went all the way and committed the *ultimate sin*. He became a police prosecution witness.

Once a grass always a grass, and everyone should know what he did. How people can still talk to him, let alone do business with him, is beyond me and this latest remark applies to an awful lot of people. On reading this, they will know who I'm talking about. Think again, gentlemen. I rest my case, no more need be said, it's all over now. I can still sleep at night but I wonder if he can?

The question has been asked: Do I have any regrets about Ginger Marks and Evans? The answer is: Yes. I regret that I did not shoot the two of them that night.

· 13 ·
The Mad Axeman

Until I was arrested with the Krays as an accessory to the McVitie murder, I lived the life of Riley. All my legitimate businesses turned over vast sums of money and the firm continued with lucrative pavement work and bank and wages robberies. The Twins were in a different business to me so when they were offered work which was not in their line, they'd pass it over to me. I would do the same for them and we'd each get our cut.

The Prince of Wales pub had become a centre for socialising and business. Even my doctor enjoyed his visits there. But then Dr Fred Coffey, a lovely man, was very sociable. He was a tall, introspective man with a touch of Alastair Sim (the actor). Generally he was unflappable. I saw him get excited only once and that was when Maureen was about to give birth to Danielle. We had to race against the clock to get her to hospital in case the baby was strangled by the umbilical cord. We got stuck in a lift coming down from our fourteenth floor flat and he really lost his rag.

Fred was no alcoholic but like all Irishmen he loved his drink. The cellar at my pub was supplied by a friend who worked for ICI. He was a multi-talented chap and was involved in one of their hotels used by top executives as a weekend retreat. They had the best cigars, champagne, and liqueurs. Stephan La Fay would come over every month with cases of vintage port and Margaux wine, which I bought off him at a knock-down price. He was a regular presenter on the TV series 'Café Continental' and appeared on this programme with Helene Cordet, a very close friend of Prince Philip.

I wasn't aware of how wonderful wine could be until I met him. He taught me a lot about the different vintages, and Fred Coffey, a connoisseur of fine drink, loved my cellar and in particular, the brandies. I always gave him a twenty-five-year-old Camus brandy which he loved.

Through him I met a succession of other Irish doctors. Dr Steven Erner was a rugby international. He had a surgery on Gypsy Hill and helped deliver my Jamie into the world. Then there was Dr Leo Barrie who had a surgery in Peckham, another lovely man like the previous two. He gave evidence for me in the Mitchell trial. Leo was due to come to our home on the night Mitchell was shot and remove Maureen's stitches from an earlier operation. For some reason, he was unable to come but made a note in his diary that I had called from the Harley Street clinic where Maureen was being discharged from. When he gave evidence for me, confirming I had been at the clinic when the shooting took place, Judge Lawton went red and exploded. He told ushers in the court: 'Take that man back to his surgery and bring me his diary.' Leo couldn't believe it. They fetched his diary and scrutinised the details in case he'd written it in a different pen. But everything was in order and the jury were obliged to accept the evidence.

Whenever any of us got cut or hurt, Fred and the other doctors would attend to our wounds. Joe Carter once got a big stripe down his face when a guy on the Twins' firm cut him up at a party. That geezer was thrown off the Twins' firm for misbehaving with my friend. Dr Fred always did a neat job!

Fred loved a bit of excitement and was quite amused by what went on. He was a very trustworthy man and, being an Irishman, the authorities didn't matter to him. He didn't feel the need to report every incident that occurred.

One afternoon, on a robbery in south-west London, we had a bit of a run-in with security guards delivering money. All were well-padded and wore visors and crash-helmets. They were armed with clubs and liquid dye-guns. We were also tooled up. I had a .38 and a club around my wrist and Alfie had a shotgun. They sprayed dye at us as I ran towards them. I slipped and as I went down, a big guy in front of me whacked me on the nut with this big club which was like a long baseball bat. I had on a trilby hat which softened the blow a little bit, and I retaliated by battering him across the jaw with my .38 revolver.

As he came forward to have another go at me, Alf let him have it in the shoulder with his shotgun. It spun him around like a top. He was not badly hurt because we'd taken out most of the shot from the cartridge and replaced it with rice. It was used mainly to make a noise and frighten, rather than to injure people.

We managed to get away with a few bags and it turned out to be a nice touch. On returning to the Prince of Wales pub, I ran upstairs to the toilet. One minute I was having a piss and the next thing I'd passed out, hitting my nose on the cistern. Maureen was behind the bar and heard the thud so she and Ronnie Oliffe rushed upstairs to find me unceremoniously draped across the pan – not a pretty sight! Dr Barrie was called and their description of me led him to believe I'd had a heart attack. Later it all became clear. The bang over the head had given me delayed concussion.

That evening, we were due to go to the Dorchester to a dinner and dance to which I had been invited by Ronnie Knight and Barbara Windsor. Maureen was looking forward to it and I couldn't let her down.

But by then word had got around that a robber had been cracked on the nose during a raid (they got it wrong again, it was my head) – and here I was, at a top dinner attended by some of Scotland Yard's finest, answering the description of a man with an injured nose wanted for armed robbery! Worse still, I hadn't been able to scrub off all the dye which would have shown up under ultra violet lighting. During the dinner I got one or two long and hard looks but nothing was said.

I was always in the bath after that trying to get rid of the last traces of .dye, and the joke went around: 'Where's Brown Bread? In the shower again?'

Throughout a long career I was only set up once. And that was at a jeweller's in Holborn. We were told about this jeweller whose shop was on the first floor in a building next to a Lloyds Bank. He'd collect money each day and exchange it for a bag of uncut diamonds. It was suggested we take the parcel of diamonds and sell them to another jeweller. This sounded quite tasty so we said we'd have a look.

On the stairs leading up to the shop was a landing with a cupboard and we fitted it up so we could go in there all tooled up and wait for the parcel.

The day we were due to carry out the hold-up, Mick called me and Alf over to see him. He had a betting shop in Red Lion Square right next to a big old pub where we met to finalise our plans. Sitting at the bar as we walked in was Alec Eist from Scotland Yard's Flying Squad. Mick greeted him and asked what was happening. Alec replied: 'I've just been to a meeting at the Yard this morning. We've all been handed guns to foil a robbery, but fuck that, I don't want no shoot-outs. The Guvnor has said this is a right heavy firm involved so take no chances. You've all got to be tooled up.' He said they had been told it would happen outside the bank and that they'd been sitting there all week waiting for the robbers. What a lucky break! Prevention is always better than cure. We slipped him a monkey (£500) and stayed out on the piss with Alec all day to show our appreciation.

Alec Eist was a rebel cop. He'd stand on tables and sing and make a right pest of himself when he was drunk. But he was as much a crook as any of us and quite capable of doing anything. It was much easier to hold your hand out for a few bob than to have a shoot-out and he was a pragmatist. He had his ear to the ground and knew who was who on the London scene. Often he worked undercover and posed as a crook. He was a right rascal but you could live with him. At the same time, he also nicked a lot of people. He'd nick you as quick as look at you if it was safe to do so. But he was very good with us. If anyone was in trouble he'd work a bit of bail and try and help us in court. It was very easy for a copper to fluff his lines or make a pig's ear of the evidence without arousing suspicion.

In December 1966, the Twins were having terrible problems with Frank Mitchell who, for a very good reason, was known as 'The Mad Axeman'. They had organised his escape from Dartmoor on 12 December and came to regret their action almost immediately. To unleash him on the public was as irresponsible as taking the muzzle off a crazed rottweiler and letting it loose in a playschool. He was a backward, disturbed child living in a man's body of almost superhuman strength. It had taken thirteen coppers to hold him down in Marylebone Court and everyone was terrified of him. He had a fearsome reputation for slashing screws and inflicting violence on anyone who crossed his path.

Frank Mitchell was a typical product of the English penal system. Since the age of seventeen, he had been institutionalised in borstals, prisons and mental hospitals. He had been birched and received the cat-o'-nine-tails. During an earlier escape from Broadmoor, he broke into an elderly couple's home and threatened them with an axe which he deftly balanced on his knee while drinking tea with the petrified husband and wife.

Mitchell had been sentenced to life-imprisonment and had done nine years of his sentence. He now wanted a release date which the prison governor, though a sympathetic man, was unable to deliver. The Twins told him that once he had escaped, they would help him appeal to the Home Secretary, and the plan was for him to stay on the run for six months, petitioning the authorities for a release date, then supposedly returning to prison to finish off his sentence – it sounds ridiculous!

And the scheme was doomed to failure with someone like Mitchell. You couldn't trust him, and the Twins aged five years while he was out. He threatened to kill a dozen policemen rather than go back to prison. They were losing sleep and he was becoming a real threat. He wanted to go out at nights with a mask on his face, saying he wouldn't be recognised. He would demonstrate his strength by heaving up his minders by their belts and do 100 press-ups after having it off with his bird all day and all night. She once tried to escape out of the window and he pulled her back. From the time he stabbed Bruce Reynolds in a bath house in Wandsworth, I knew his reputation. He would pick up screws and crack their ribs in a bear hug, pretending to be friendly. Word got out that search parties looking for him after his escape would have shot him on sight.

Mitchell was holed up in a place near Canning Town where he originally came from. He'd wanted to see his parents who were nearby but the Krays dared not let him out of their sight and kept minders with him twenty-four-hours a day. Reg arranged for a girl to keep him quiet and brought in Lisa, a good-looking hostess to keep him company. She tamed him for about a week but then he got up to his old tricks again and became aggressive, pulling a knife on one of his minders and later arming himself with one of their shooters. The situation became even more harassing when he felt snubbed by Ronnie who wouldn't visit him.

The final straw came when Mitchell said of the Twins: 'I'll hold their mother responsible if anything happens to me.' Ronnie asked me over for a meet in Hackney and we had a private talk. There was no solution to this problem other than the decision a veterinary surgeon has to make when confronted with a mad dog that is a danger to everything and everyone else. Ron and I decided he would have to go. I didn't know Mitchell personally but Ron asked me if I could do him a personal favour. I agreed to help him just as he helped me and others on my firm many times before. Our meeting was on 23 December, the last day anyone was to see Mitchell again. Albert Donoghue, whom I knew and liked, was in the next room. He'd taken part in Mitchell's escape and helped mind him. While he was working for the Krays, he came to see me on a regular basis, bringing my share of money from occasional joint ventures in which we were involved.

Donoghue would play a key role in Frank Mitchell's disappearance whilst the Twins would stay out of the way (although he denied knowing Mitchell was going to be killed in a recent book he wrote: *The Krays' Lieutenant*).

The operation to get rid of Mitchell went smoothly. It was a shame that more than two years later, Donoghue decided to grass on us. There was no need to do that, he did not have to name names, although I have some sympathy for him in as much as the Twins wanted him to take the sole blame for Mitchell's death. It was a dark winter's night, almost pitch black, when Donoghue coaxed Mitchell from the house to the back of the waiting van, with the engine running. There was no way he could have seen anybody else in the van. All he had to say at a subsequent trial was that it was too dark to identify anybody and that he returned alone to the house. Donoghue told a number of lies about the incident although his description of the killing itself was fairly accurate. The worst thing was that he said I had done it for money.

As I've emphasised before, this was never the case. I

had no need to kill anybody for financial reward. Mitchell was a problem, a threat to all of us. I took part in his killing as a favour to the Twins. There was no financial incentive whatsoever. Donoghue and others on the firm used to bring me money all the time from the Colony Club and other West End interests. And when Charlie Kray and some associates got nicked in Nigeria, I helped them out with £5,000 to secure their release. So to claim he handed over £1,000 after Mitchell's disappearance is an insult.

Judge Lawton, who tried me on the Mitchell case more than two years after the event, asked about 'grassing'. Detective Superintendent Leonard 'Nipper' Read told him that the criminal world had its own rules of conduct.

Read: 'There is an association of criminals in the same echelons,' he explained.

Lawton asked him: 'For criminals in the First Division, what would you say was the sin of sins against the world in which they live?'

Read replied: 'The sin of sins is, in the parlance of criminals, to grass.'

Lawton: 'Would you put Donoghue in the First Division?'

Read: 'I would put him in the bottom half of the First Division.'

Lawton: 'He will have to keep his eye on the relegation.' Ha ha ha.

Lawton's joke about this may have brought a laugh in the courtroom but outside it was serious business. Until the Krays and I had been arrested, nobody wanted to give evidence against us. It was only when they were convinced we would be safely locked away for many years that some people agreed to talk to police.

Read told the court that Donoghue would know about grassing being the sin of sins and said his life in prison would be most uncomfortable. 'For this reason I have taken certain steps . . .'

Donoghue was charged with conspiring with Billy Exley and 'Mad' Teddy Smith to effect Mitchell's escape from Dartmoor Prison. He was further charged with harbouring Mitchell between 12 and 24 December, 1966 and of murdering Mitchell on 24 December, 1966. Kenneth Jones QC, prosecuting, said no evidence would be offered on the murder charge as it was proposed to call him to give evidence at a later stage. Donoghue, he said, took Mitchell some clothing and told him he was being taken to another place. He took Mitchell from the flat and, shortly after, shots were heard coming from the direction Donoghue and Mitchell had taken.

Alfie Gerrard was on his toes in Australia in April 1969 when the three Kray brothers and I appeared at the Central Criminal Court charged with killing Mitchell. We all pleaded not guilty to the charge and the Krays were also charged with helping Mitchell escape from Dartmoor.

Several others were charged with conspiring to help Mitchell escape and with harbouring him. The jury were told they would be kept under police surveillance which of course always looks bad for the defendants in a case.

The Crown Prosecutor Kenneth Jones QC outlined the case against me. He said money was handed over to the killer by a man named Albert Donoghue who had seen the shooting, been involved with Mitchell, the Krays and others, and had himself been accused of Mitchell's murder but who had decided to make a statement to the police.

Mitchell had been serving a life-sentence for robbery with violence and was killed in a van outside a flat in Barking Road, in the East End of London on 24 December, 1966, twelve days after being sprung from Dartmoor while on an outside working-party. He was taken to a hideaway flat where a young nightclub hostess was ordered to comfort him and sleep with him and he found himself in a very nearly hopeless position. He was subject to a life-sentence and had escaped from one prison on Dartmoor to a flat in Barking which in many ways must have become like a second prison. He was entirely dependent on others and obviously this couldn't go on. Something had to happen. It was then that Mitchell was murdered by Foreman and Gerrard.

On the last day of Mitchell's life, 24 December, Jones continued, Donoghue arrived at the flat and told The Mad Axeman he was going away. Mitchell said he wanted to take the girl, of whom he had become very fond, but Donoghue said she could follow an hour or so later. Mitchell and the girl packed their bags. The girl was then paid off with an envelope containing about £100. Donoghue, who had left the flat, then returned to collect Mitchell. Mitchell kissed the girl before he left to indicate his affection and left with Donoghue.

The girl saw them turn the corner into Ladysmith Avenue, there was a pause and then she heard three or four muffled bangs. Perhaps they came from inside the vehicle as they were very muffled. They certainly came from Ladysmith Avenue. She thought they were shots. She asked someone to see what had happened but she was restrained from leaving the flat. What she had heard, according to the prosecutor, was the 'act of murder'. It was the shooting of Mitchell in a vehicle in Ladysmith Avenue.

About five or ten minutes later, Donoghue came back to the flat and said they must all clean it up. He then made a phone call and the girl heard him say, 'The dog is dead'. Jones suggested this could be an oblique reference to the fact that Mitchell was dead. He said Donoghue then took the girl by car to see Reginald Kray who told the girl that if she ever said a word to anyone, they would get her. He said this coldly and calmly and deliberately. It was a clear threat to her.

Jones alleged that Ronnie Oliffe and Jerry Callaghan

were also by the van (this was wrong: there was only me and Alf from my firm). It was alleged that Foreman and Gerrard shot Mitchell as soon as the van doors were closed and that a gun was used with a silencer. Gerrard's gun had no silencer. There were four shots, said the prosecutor. 'Foreman fired twice more into Mitchell's chest and head until he must have been dead. Donoghue was dropped off, and he made a telephone call to Reginald Kray to tell him what had happened. Mitchell's murder was planned by Ronald and Reginald Kray. When Donoghue took him from the flat on Friday evening, 24 December, he was taking him to his death. Afterwards Donoghue had gone to Ronnie and been required to repeat details of the murder, telling him exactly what had happened.' The prosecutor alleged (wrongly) that Donoghue then went to my pub in Lant Street and paid me £1,000 on the Twins' instructions. At the same time he said he had a discussion with me about the final disposal of Mitchell's body which had disappeared off the face of the earth.

William Henry Exley told the court he was a minder at the Mitchell flat in Barking. On the night of the alleged murder, he was at a party with Reggie Kray and others when Donoghue came in and said: 'The other fellow's gone.' Reggie and Donoghue went outside into the passageway and he followed. He overheard Donoghue say: 'They gave him four injections in the nut but he was still moaning.' He thought they said there was some in the body as well.

Cross-examined by Reg's QC, Paul Wrightson, who asked Exley whether he did as he was told by Reg, Exley said in a raised voice: 'I slept with a loaded shotgun for four months. They wanted to come and get me in the same way they got Jack the Hat. They shot and wounded Nobby Clarke, Donoghue and Jimmy Field.' Calmed by the judge, Exley admitted he had been convicted of shooting with intent to murder. He denied that the murder vehicle belonged to him. He told the judge he was in prison and that 'if I live long enough, I will get released in October.'

Mitchell's hostess gave evidence in court as 'Mrs C'. She said she was taken to the flat from a club where she was working by a man named Donoghue. She spent several nights with Mitchell and once she tried to leave and got a spanking from him. 'He was trying to protect me,' she said. 'If I had got out of the flat, he would not have been able to protect me.'

Another witness (Mr B) said Mitchell was in his flat with a man called Scotch Jack, whom he later knew was called Dixon. He said Frank Mitchell stayed in his flat for eleven to fourteen days and while there Mr B was a general errand boy. Asked if anyone else visited Mitchell, Mr B said: 'Yes, Ronald, Reginald and Charlie Kray, a man called Cowley and another called Dixon and Albert Donoghue.' He said on the night of the alleged shooting, Mitchell left the flat with Donoghue and Cornelius Whitehead at about 11pm, shortly after that he heard about three or four bangs as though a motorist was in trouble and all his tyres had burst.

Donoghue's evidence, given on Tuesday 22 April, 1969, was potentially the most damaging: he described how he had collected Mitchell at the Monkey's Fist pub in Dartmoor and brought him back by car to London. Foreman was going to take him to the country where he would spend Christmas with Ronnie Kray. After that he was to be put on a boat and sent to the continent somewhere. 'A meeting was arranged by myself and Foreman for the evening so I could prepare Mitchell for the trip. I met Foreman . . . I went back to Mitchell's flat. I told him we were leaving and he became agitated when the girl could not go with him. I told him we would arrange for her to follow. I went out at about 8pm and saw a dark blue van in Ladysmith Avenue with one of the men standing by the back doors. I went back and collected

Mitchell who shook hands with everyone and made a fuss of the girl before walking out.'

Asked by the prosecutor when he first knew that Mitchell was to be shot in the van, Donoghue replied: 'When the guns opened up.' He said he saw two men pump about twelve bullets into Frank Mitchell. 'Frederick Foreman and a man called Gerrard were sitting on the left. Foreman told me to go to the front of the van and tell the driver the route.

'As I walked up and got in the van, both doors closed and two guns started firing as the van drove off. I spun around and saw Mitchell on his knees, clutching his chest. The guns were just blasting away at him. One was a small revolver which Gerrard had. The other was a black automatic with a silencer. It was Foreman's.

'Mitchell fell back on his shoulders. His knees were up. Mitchell started making noises from his throat. Foreman held the gun about a foot away from Mitchell's chest and fired three shots. The material of Mitchell's coat was jumping up and down.'

Donoghue added that Mitchell made some more noise and Gerrard said: 'Give him another Fred, I'm empty.'

Mrs C, the blonde nightclub hostess said she had stayed four nights with Mitchell and had been given a brown envelope containing money on the evening of the last day. She said Mitchell had been given a long scarf by Albert Donoghue. She and Mitchell had grown to like each other during their four days and nights together and they had kissed goodbye when he left. Then she heard bangs like gunshots. 'I shouted out, "Oh God! They've killed him. They've shot him".' She heard three, four, or five shots fired, the sounds coming from the side of the flat. The sounds did not echo, they were muffled. About five minutes later Mr Donoghue came back in the flat and made a telephone call. She was taken to a party after Mitchell had left although she had wanted to go home. 'Reggie, Connie Whitehead and Albert Donoghue would not let me go home and I stayed the night at the party with Albert.'

On 24 April, the judge directed that the Krays be found not guilty through lack of evidence. The case against me continued. Terry Spinks the Olympic gold-medalist boxer was called to give evidence and said he had been drinking with Ronald Oliffe on the night he was alleged to have been driving the van in which Mitchell was shot. Spinks said on 24 December 1966 he arrived at the Log Cabin, a club in Soho, at about 5pm and stayed about four hours. Oliffe and his brother were there and dropped him home in his cab at about 9.30pm. Terry said he was a friend of mine and the second time he met Donoghue at the Stork Club, he came across to his table with three other men and said he recognised him as the man with Foreman who had thrown him out of the pub. 'He picked up an ashtray and hit me across the eye with it. He said the matter was not finished and he was going to burn down Foreman's pub.'

A number of witnesses were called by my QC, Tom Williams, Labour MP for Warrington (his junior was Ivor Richard who became Labour leader in the House of Lords in 1992), who testified I was at the Prince of Wales on the night in question. I had a further alibi: that I had visited my wife Maureen in a Harley Street clinic on the night Mitchell was killed. To prove this, I tried to get a statement from a nurse who had since emigrated to Australia. I sent Maureen down under with a top detective agency, Pinkerton's, but Maureen was arrested the minute she set foot in Australia. They then took the nurse into protective custody and said she was in danger of being nobbled, when Maureen only wanted a statement from her. The nurse confirmed that she remembered I had asked her for a cup of tea or coffee but wouldn't say it was on that particular night. It may have been the day before. When Lawton gave his summing up, he put doubt into the jurors' minds that these might have been genuine events occurring on a different day. I have never spent a more anxious time until the jury came back and announced their *not guilty* verdict on 16 May.

It would have been very unsafe to convict on the evidence of a man who was himself implicated in the crime. Even the prosecutor said that everything that happened in the van at the time Mitchell was allegedly killed rested on the evidence of Albert Donoghue. My defence brought seventeen witnesses to establish bias by Donoghue and four alibis as to my whereabouts.

Prison officers at Leicester told me that if I was indeed guilty of the crime, I had performed a public service and should be awarded a medal the size of a dustbin lid. That's how much terror Mitchell had struck into everybody's heart. When Mitchell climbed into the back of that van, it marked the end of all his troubles.

· 14 ·
Muddy Waters

Although his conduct of the case was disgraceful, Judge Melford Stevenson will never know how accurate some of his remarks were when summing up in the Kray trial in March 1969. Before sentencing me to ten years for being an accessory *after* the fact in the McVitie murder case, he said: 'The needs of justice sometimes require that truth should be dredged from very muddy waters. When you start that kind of dredging, what you may bring up from these muddy waters may be very disagreeable indeed.'

Well that worked both ways. I agree that some of the things we did then were murky but I was not happy about the administration of criminal justice. Before Melford Stevenson sentenced me, he asked the crown prosecutor Mr Jones QC what the maximum was. He said he was thinking of giving me and Charlie Kray life-imprisonment. Mr Jones told the judge the maximum was ten. It had been changed from life only a year before our arrest. 'But,' added Mr Jones, 'I'm only looking for four to seven.' Stevenson thought he'd wear the mantle of the almighty and savaged me as best he could by giving us the maximum sentence.

I had nothing to do with the McVitie killing. My role in this never-ending saga, which I now hope to put to rest, was a very limited one. I got rid of the body for two reasons. One: because it had been put on my doorstep and threatened my own safety, and secondly: as a favour to the Krays.

Dumping Jack 'The Hat's' body on my doorstep was stupid. I was one of the last people who had a public showdown with McVitie when he caused trouble in my 211 Club in Balham. It would have been very convenient for the police if he'd been found dead on my side of the water. It put me in great jeopardy. Not only was I charged over his disappearance, but I found myself in the dock of the Old Bailey with the Kray firm who faced *two* murder charges: George Cornell's and Jack McVitie's.

The two cases were tried together. For those who were not involved with Cornell, this was an affront to natural justice. You became 'guilty' by association and that same jury who watched you in the dock now had to decide about you in a second trial. If ever there was a miscarriage of justice that was one!

Cornell was shot in the Blind Beggar on Mile End Road on 9 March, 1966. He and a bookmaker friend, Albie Woods, had visited Jimmy Andrews who'd been shot in the leg and was recovering in hospital. Cornell was connected to the Richardson firm and had called Ronnie Kray a 'big fat poof' behind his back so he was a marked man. It was claimed that Ronnie boasted to associates about killing him: 'I put a couple of bullets in Cornell's head. I took his fucking head off,' which was not true.

McVitie had worked for the Krays but was eventually regarded as a liability. The Twins said of him: 'His big problem was he liked to drink a lot, but he couldn't hold his drink. He got nasty. McVitie started to let us down. He went into the 211 Club in Balham High Road which was owned by our friend Freddie Foreman. McVitie was drunk, so Freddie told him to leave and he did.

'He upset another friend of ours, Ron Oliffe, in a club called the Log Cabin, in Wardour Street, which the boxer Billy Walker had an interest in with his brother George. Then he misbehaved himself in our club, the Regency. He took a gun out and fired a couple of shots at a fellah called Tommy Flannagan. Thank Christ he missed. Then he cut a fella with a knife in the basement, walked upstairs and wiped off the blood on his knife on the dress of a woman who was having a drink at the bar.'

McVitie was killed by Reggie Kray at a party in Blonde Carol Skinner's flat in 71 Evering Road on Saturday, 28 October, 1967. His cousin, Ronnie Hart, who later gave evidence against all of us, was present. As far as I can make it out, and from what the Twins told me, it was not premeditated murder but a spontaneous action that resulted from Jack's behaviour at the Regency Club which the Twins minded for the Barrys, one of whom was in the dock with us. Jack 'The Hat' had shot the place up and the Barrys demanded to know why the Twins couldn't keep 'this cunt out of here'. The Twins called Jack to the party in Evering Road where they were going to chastise him. The Lambrianou brothers, Chris and Tony, were despatched to the Regency to bring him over to Blonde Carol's. But the whole thing got out of hand. The Barrys had supplied a gun with a faulty mechanism. It would not shoot but it was intended to scare him. I think they forgot there were other ways to skin a cat.

When he came to the flat, Reggie went through the motion of shooting him but of course the gun didn't work. Instead they were going to give him a good battering. But it went too far when someone brought Reggie a carving knife from the kitchen which he used to stab McVitie. He plunged him in the body. I can confirm that there were no injuries to the face or neck as has been reported. The fact that there were a lot of people there – more than a dozen witnesses – is additional proof that it had not been premeditated. If Jack had played his cards right he could have walked away from that flat, but he was so high on amphetamines that he became brave. He even took his coat off and challenged them. This is when Ronnie told Reg: 'Kill the bastard.' If, however, they had intended to kill McVitie from the start, they would have done it differently to that. Looking back on it now, the lawyers could have emphasised this point more: that it was not a premeditated killing, rather a fight that went wrong. Those harsh sentences of thirty and twenty years resulting from this gangland fight would never have been applied today. Ronnie Bender got twenty years for cleaning up blood stains!

The Lambrianous and Ronnie Bender dumped the body on my doorstep in Bermondsey, just down the road from the pub. Ronnie had a go at them: 'You fools,' he roared. 'You went and dumped it right there on Fred's doorstep knowing he had a row at the 211 Club a few months earlier!'

McVitie was wrapped in Blonde Carol's bedspread – the cleaning tabs would have traced it back to her flat immediately if the police had found the body. The corpse was slumped in the back seat of the car which had been parked outside a church in Bermondsey. Afterwards, Charlie Kray was woken up and taken to a safe house in north London where everyone was stowed away. Like Charlie, I'd also been in bed that night and neither of us knew what had gone on. Tommy Cowley then came over to my pub between 2 and 3 in the morning to knock me up and tell me that they'd dumped Jack 'The Hat' down the road not far away. I didn't see who was with him because whoever it was, had parked round the corner. Hart swore in court that it was Charlie, but in fact it was Tommy Cowley. It would not have been sensible to go out between 2am and 5am, before there was any traffic on the road.

At about 5am, a few hours after Cowley left, I went out to look for the body. The Lambrianous and Bender couldn't remember exactly where they'd dumped McVitie so I drove around the streets searching for the car. I spotted this battered old Zephyr with a different-coloured wing, with broken lights and only one windscreen wiper working. It was all locked up so I had to force the window open with a screwdriver. I could see McVitie lying across the back seat. Fortunately, it was a horrible winter's morning, pissing down with rain. I had a set of keys and found one which would fit the ignition but I could hardly see a thing as I drove away. Alf tailed me in a backup car and I drove with the body in the back all the way up to Camberwell Green and garaged it in a lock-up. I took a liberty with myself doing that. It wasn't daylight and I could easily have got pulled for a number of reasons. I transferred the body to a van and disposed of McVitie's Ford Zephyr motor in a wreckers' yard and no trace of it was ever found.

On the following Monday I drove his body down to the coast with a backup motor minding me off. And that was the end of Jack 'The Hat' McVitie. We had a friend on the coast who wrapped him up in chicken wire attached to weights. Our contacts with certain fishermen who'd helped us with smuggling had been kept alive and they were now called in to help out again. As with Ginger Marks and Frank 'The Mad Axeman' Mitchell, Jack 'The Hat' McVitie was buried far out at sea away from the fishing lanes, deep beneath the 'muddy waters' Justice Stevenson spoke of in his summing-up to the jury. We had been told by American contacts that bodies weighted down in this way would never find their way to the surface but would slowly be disposed of by crabs and other deep-sea dwellers. Many people prefer burial at sea.

I was protecting the Twins. The rule of thumb was, where there is no body, there is no evidence and therefore no conviction. Before McVitie, the one exception to this rule that I could remember took place on an ocean liner when a steward was convicted of the rape and murder of a young woman called Gay Gibson. After killing her, he pushed her body through a porthole into the ocean and she was never found. He was convicted in spite of the lack of evidence.

For our part, we felt fairly safe once we had properly disposed of a body. But I felt very bitter about Hart involving my friends and it seemed very odd that Tommy Cowley walked out of the case at the early stages. He was a ginger-headed little geezer who thought he was something special because he worked for the Twins. He was a collector. A nothing. If he hadn't been with them he would have been annihilated for his flash behaviour. Tommy had also brought the Mini car used by Reggie Kray to drive away from the scene of the murder. He parked it near my pub with tell-tale blood stains in it. They wanted it cleaned and washed up, which it was. A few days later they picked it up again and took it to a black cab depot near Vallance Road. Witnesses who spotted the car there were called to give evidence at the trial. Tommy Cowley was a slippery little fucker whom I never liked and one of the first to grass to Nipper Read whom he secretly met in Wandsworth prison library in the dead of night. He was on remand with us in Brixton, a couple of cells along from Charlie, myself and the Twins. On returning from a court appearance, Tommy was transferred to Wandsworth Prison, and we never saw him again.

I was also surprised that John Barry, whom I later met in prison when he was awaiting trial for armed robbery, had also given evidence against us. Even one of the Mills brothers from Ladbroke Grove, one of the respected families, gave evidence against us which was very disappointing. Another was Charlie Mitchell (no relation to Frank Mitchell). He too gave evidence for the prosecution at Bow Street Magistrates' Court and was never seen for years until he turned up in Spain. He was battered by a Spanish doorman and drowned in his own blood.

On the day the Twins were arrested I went to their flat in Bunhill Row, Clerkenwell. There had been nothing in the news so I wasn't expecting any bother when I took the lift to their floor. As I got out of the elevator, the whole landing was full of policemen. The Twins' front door was off its hinges and leaning against the wall. The police were all standing about. I walked straight through them and past as if on a mission. I didn't know where I was going and it was a long corridor. They would be watching me so I didn't want to head for an exit. Thankfully they were local cossers and hadn't recognised me. As I got to the end of the corridor, I rang at the door of one of the flats. It was opened by a young married woman. 'Excuse me, love,' I said. 'There's a bit of a problem up the end at Mrs Kray's, do you mind if I step in for a bit?' She invited me in for a cup of tea. I told her I was sorry to intrude and explained that I had called to see the Twins and not picked a good time.

She told me the cossers had been there and smashed the door down. 'There's hundreds of them, but you can stay as long as you like,' she said. We chatted for a while and then she showed me the exit downstairs which I used to get out of the building. Fortunately I managed to slip the net and didn't return to my house or to the flat above the pub but went straight on my toes again. I didn't want to disappear in case the Twins needed my help but I was told to fuck off by Frank Williams. He said I would be better off keeping out of it.

I kept in touch and stayed at a hotel for quite a few weeks. Apparently Nipper Read was very keen to arrest me because Hart and one or two of the other witnesses wouldn't give evidence while I was at large. But I didn't know that at the time otherwise I would have made sure I stayed well away, although I would have had every copper in the world looking for me. Eventually I was arrested in my pub after going there to see if everything was all right. I met with a few friends, Micky Regan, Patsy O'Mara, Ronnie Oliffe and after they all walked out I left the pub to walk over to my Mercedes. As I got in they sprung me. Read, Cater and a copper called Ian

St John: the murder squad. They took me to Tintagel House where I was formally charged. Nipper Read was an unassuming type and didn't employ any bullying tactics. In fact both Read and Cater were quite polite to me.

One of the police officers said I was a bonus to the Twins. They knew I would move heaven and earth to help anybody. At one stage there was a suggestion that I was implicated in the Cornell case. It was claimed that I delivered the guns to the Twins at a party and that one of those guns was used to kill Cornell. Thankfully the court accepted it was untrue, nevertheless I was made to sit in the dock for six weeks with people like the Lambrianous whom I'd never seen before.

When I complained, I was told by my QC to keep quiet and not to make a fuss and upset the judge. He would carry on with the trial with or without me. The lawyers promised they would try and get a severance of the trial so that the Cornell case and the McVitie case would be tried separately. Neither me, Charlie, Tony Barry, Ronnie Bender or the Lambrianous were involved with Cornell yet we had to sit through the Cornell trial without our names being mentioned at all. At one stage Judge Melford Stevenson even tried to hang numbers around our necks like Nazi war criminals. I shouted out: 'What's this, a fucking cattle market? Or are we fucking Nazi war criminals? I'm not putting that around my neck,' and tore it up and threw it in the air resulting in an awful commotion in the dock. Screws were leaning over trying to quieten people down and there were a number of scuffles and chairs going over. At one stage it got quite ugly in the dock and the judge relented about the numbers. I spread further chaos by changing seats with Scotch Pat so they didn't know who was who. He had been twenty-four stone and had reduced to twelve. Scotch Pat and Fat Wally had been in bed with a barmaid and the question had been asked if the bed had been constructed with scaffolding because their combined weight of about sixty stone would have been too much for any bed in the UK. The trial was a complete farce.

Even the way we were brought to the court each day from Brixton prison was prejudicial to our case. We were bundled into a 'meat wagon' (prison van) and locked inside rabbit-hutch cells – they were like empty cupboards with nothing to hang on to and driven at high speed with motorbike escorts and a fanfare of sirens and klaxons blasting away until we reached the Old Bailey, making it look like we were all highly dangerous enemies of the state. Fumes would escape into these hutches and most prisoners were sick in them.

Each day a different route was used although you could hear us coming for miles. One time a police outrider went skidding along the road and we all tut-tutted saying what a shame it was. But there was no need for the break-neck speed. The drivers were intent on beating their record (under ten minutes) in getting from Brixton to the court. It was frightening and we used to give the warders a lot of verbal over the way they treated us on the journey. They'd race through red lights and police ahead would stop traffic. The only light note to this was when we drove down The Cut near Blackfriars, and past my old favourite pie and mash shop. All the staff knew me because I'd patronised the shop with my family and had once tossed out four pests who were drunk and being silly and the staff were delighted. Now, when we drove past their place, they were all waiting to cheer and wave to me as the prison van blasted its way down the road.

In his summing-up, Judge Stevenson said: 'No one disputes the fact that Cornell was murdered. That he died as a result of a shotgun wound in the Blind Beggar. In the McVitie case there is no body. There is no clear, undisputed evidence of his death, and the prosecution say that his death is a matter you are forced to infer from the evidence they have been able to call. The witness Ronald

Hart called for a closer consideration than anybody else in the case . . . the suggestion is made that Hart is really the murderer . . . we start on the fact that he is himself a self-confessed murderer. He has admitted joining in the violence as a result of which McVitie is said to have died. He has implicated a large number of people in the dock and that excites dislike in all of us. The dislike of what we used to call a sneak.'

The jury delivered its verdict on 4 March, 1969 after retiring for six hours and fifty-five minutes. The trial had lasted thirty-nine days. We were sentenced the next day (my 37th birthday). I was found guilty of being accessory after the fact of McVitie together with Charlie Kray and Connie Whitehead. Later, Charlie and I were taken separately from our cells to the solicitor's room where further charges were made. Nipper Read, Cater and my defence counsel had heads bowed and looked very glum. Nipper Read said, 'I understand it's your birthday Fred – I have some very bad news, we are charging you with the murder of Frank Mitchell. Have you anything to say?' I looked at my lawyers (Tom Williams and Ivor Richard). They just shook their heads so I replied, 'No Comment!' I was returned to the cell where Charlie and Connie Whitehead were waiting anxiously. Charlie was next to be charged with the Mitchell murder and came back visibly distressed.

Ronnie Kray was found guilty of the murder of George Cornell and Jack McVitie. Reginald Kray, Christopher Lambrianou, Anthony Lambrianou and Ronald Albert Bender were also found guilty of McVitie. Anthony Thomas Barry was found not guilty of the murder and discharged. John Alexander Barrie, a Scotsman who was not in any way connected with the London Barry family, was found guilty in the Cornell murder. All he had done was to discharge a gun in the ceiling, and for that received a twenty-year sentence.

The Twins were sentenced to life-imprisonment and

Melford Stevenson recommended they be detained for a minimum of thirty years, the longest murder sentences ever passed at the Central Criminal Court. He said to Ronnie: 'I am not going to waste words on you. The sentence is that of life-imprisonment. In my view society has earned a rest from your activities.' Reggie was handed out the same treatment and Charlie, like me, got ten years. Donoghue, who admitted guilt and grassed on us, got two years for the same offence.

There was a curious sequel to this case. On 20 January, 1970, three men were sent for trial at the Old Bailey from Bow Street Magistrates' Court. They were accused of conspiring together between 2 December and 12 December, 1969, to defeat the course of public justice by attempting to persuade Ronald Hart, by threats and inducements, to make a written statement that differed in material particulars from the evidence given by Hart on oath at the Central Criminal Court at our trial which had ended on 5 March, 1969.

Understandably, there had never been a case quite like it. Two of the men, Derek Higgins, a private investigator, and Alexander Thomson, my solicitor's managing clerk, were both ex-policemen working on the case for my appeal. The third man, Kenneth Prater, was a journalist. All were respectable people gathering evidence for Brendan Quirke, my solicitor. They had arranged to see Hart – at his suggestion, to question him about the evidence he had given in court. After my trial, Maureen got a call out of the blue from Ronnie Hart. He said that he had told a pack of lies at the trial and was now under a lot of pressure and needed money to get away, but wanted to put things right first. Maureen was too clever to take this at face value. She told Hart that if he wanted to talk about my case, he should ring my solicitor and gave him the number. Hart said he would ring again and this time she had Higgins there to record the conversation. Hart repeated what he said before but kept asking for help. Maureen then came to see me at Leicester Prison to discuss his offer. I told her I didn't trust him one bit. If he had been prepared to tell lies at our trial he was probably just trying to set us up for something now, I warned. My lawyers felt they were on the verge of winning my appeal and were quite excited by the prospect of getting a statement from him. The worrying thing though was the way he said he wanted money to go away. He asked: 'How much will you give me to go away?' and other leading questions like: 'Will I be all right with Fred afterwards? I know what I done to him but I will say whatever you want me to say. How much will you give me?' At the meeting, the three men were set up for a police bust. Holes had been drilled in the walls of the room from the adjoining house so police could listen in and bug the conversations. During the meeting, DCI Frank Cater arrested Higgins and Thomson. The original charge of conspiracy without details of the accusation was withdrawn at the request of the prosecution.

At their Old Bailey trial in May, the prosecutor John Leonard claimed that Hart was threatened by one of the accused and that the journalist had asked Hart to provide 'loopholes' so that the Home Secretary could be petitioned for my release. It was alleged that Hart was told by the accused that I had 'access to the proceeds of the Great Train Robbery'.

The men, rightly, pleaded not guilty. Mr Leonard said that Hart had given evidence in the trial to the effect that once McVitie had been stabbed, the Krays gave orders for the body to be taken 'over the water' for disposal by 'Freddie'. After the trial, Hart and his family were given a secret address in Essex but Prater the journalist traced him and introduced him to Higgins and Thomson. The prosecutor said the impression was given that they were planning a French TV film on crime in London. After their first meeting, a '£5 note was left on Hart's table for his trouble'. Higgins was reputed to have said: 'Foreman is a rich man and you will not come to any harm . . . If Foreman has to sit for ten years thinking about the man who put him away he is bound to get him when he comes out.' Hart was allegedly offered £500 or the cost of fares for his wife and family to emigrate or take a holiday to Australia. Another meeting was arranged but only Higgins and Thomson arrived. The prosecutor said the journalist got 'cold feet'. A two-hour interview at that meeting with Hart was recorded on tape by the police. But after just one-and-a-half days of the trial, the judge ordered their acquittal. The Common Serjeant Judge Griffith-Jones said: 'there was no doubt that the defendants were employed in various inquiries and to see whether anything could be properly done to submit "something" (fresh evidence) to the Home Secretary regarding Foreman.' Nevertheless, the men were not reimbursed for the money they had deposited towards their legal-aid costs. Griffith-Jones said, bearing in mind the tapes and transcripts, they had 'brought matters upon themselves'.

His view was not shared by the press. The *Sunday Times* took up the cudgel and described the proceedings as THE CASE THEY HAD TO DROP. The newspaper said the case: 'represents an amazing piece of back-tracking by the Crown in two hazy areas of British law – conspiracy and the perversion of public justice. On the charge sheet these two were linked together and resulted in what is thought to be a unique indictment . . . there have been many cases in which it has been alleged that people have tried to sway the evidence of prospective witnesses *before* a trial but never *after* a conviction. It is significant that the original charge had to be amended three times before the trial and that the Crown seem to have had considerable difficulty in preparing the indictment.'

Originally, the charge had simply been: 'conspiring together to defeat the course of public justice'. At the committal the prosecution added the following details:

Britain bags Foreman

Hard man . . . Freddie Foreman, who was flown to Britain yesterday

Eileen Sams . . . ordeal

Nat West allowed innocent Eileen to face a theft charge

● THE National Westminster Bank allowed an innocent woman to face a theft charge — because the true villain was a member of their staff.

● Restaurant manageress Eileen Sams, 23, went through a year-long nightmare after being accused of stealing £2,000 she deposited in a NatWest night safe.

● Yesterday, as Eileen was cleared, the bank was blasted by a judge as "deplorable."

Full story — Page 5

COSTA CROOK SLUNG OUT SNARLING

Sun news special

By MICHAEL FIELDER

COSTA fugitive Freddie Foreman was thrown kicking and cursing out of Spain last night to face questioning in Britain over a £7million robbery.

He was flown into Heathrow in manacles after an astonishing battle with Spanish police at Malaga airport.

It took SEVEN burly cops to shove the snarling and struggling hard man on to a London-bound jet.

TWO needed hospital treatment

after 58-year-old Foreman, clad in blue shorts, shirt and plimsolls, lashed out on the tarmac.

He screamed: "I'm not f***ing going, I'm not f***ing going."

WORRIED

The expulsion of Foreman — one of Britain's most wanted men — was first in a series of deportations expected in a crackdown on Costa Del Crime fugitives.

Ronnie Knight, ex-husband of Carry On star Barbara Windsor, was said to be "dead worried" at his luxury villa near Fuengirola after hearing that Foreman had been booted out.

Knight, who is fighting expulsion in Spanish courts, is wanted in connection with the same Security Express robbery.

There is also a warrant for the arrest of Knight's wife Sue, alleging she handled stolen money.

Holidaymakers watched in amazement as Foreman — former henchman of the gangster Kray Twins — launched into his frenzied struggle.

The super-fit ex-boxer, arrested earlier at his

Continued on Page Two

£70,000 LOTTO See Page 10 ● **£31,000 BINGO** See Page 24

Hunt for the toff

Continued from Page One

wife and family still living in the district.

The guard told The Sun boss:

A TOTAL of 14 men made up the gang — each with a pre-planned role in the cash robbery of the century.

SECURITY was so slack that one of the floodlight bulbs in the Security Express 'yard has been dead for six months.

INSIDE information was so good that the gang even knew the name of one of the guard's pet dogs.

ADDRESSES and car registration numbers of all the wives, Security Express staff—were known to the raiders.

ONE of the guards had guns pointed at eight different points of his body—including his private parts—during the gruelling ordeal.

The Sun's underworld contact obtained the gang was handpicked by The Toff.

He said a secret training camp to carry out dress rehearsals

THE GREAT BANKNOTE ROBBERY

FREE!
AUTOMATIC COFFEE MAKER

FREE

MOVE AND W

The Sun reveals th
terrifying threat o
£7 million raid gan

AN AMAZING account of the £7million Great Bank Holiday Robbery has been given to The Sun by one of the guards who was forced at gunpoint to 'let it' happen.

He gave us the following minute-by-minute exclusive story.

Yet it all began as just another routine day when supervisor Greg Counsell arrived at the fortress-like headquarters of Security Express.

He took over from the nightwatchman just after 7am and brewed himself an early morning cup of coffee.

There was little to do. He was the only employee on the premises and he could afford to put his feet up and read The Sun.

It was Bank Holiday — a traditionally easy shift — and the staff anticipated a quiet and uneventful day.

But within 3¼ hours, 38-year-old Mr Counsell was at the centre of a terrifying robbery ordeal.

At 10.15 he was brutally snatched in the yard at the security firm's HQ in Curtain Road, Shoreditch, London, by the gang who had hidden behind a gale.

It was 'the beginning of a nightmare. He became the gang's puppet as he was held at gunpoint and ordered to co-operate or die.

Pressed

At 11.37 the first of his unsuspecting workmates turned up and walked into the carefully-laid trap.

The first of the seven to arrive was burly air footer, "Taffy" Jordan.

He was unaware that Mr Counsell had the barrels of two shotguns jammed in his belly as he pressed the entry button.

The other workers arrived in dribs and drabs because it was an 'inside-shift' designed only to cover a handful of special deliveries.

When the gang was satisfied that every employee was inside the yard, at about 1.45 they moved in the vaults.

Within a backbreaking 30 minutes they had lugged the colossal £7million fortune to waiting getaway vans.

By 2.30 the operation was over.

Britain's biggest-ever cash haul had vanished into thin air, leaving barely a single clue behind.

Drilled

In an astonishing minute-by-minute dossier The Sun has pieced together the terror, the drama and the ordeal of the Bank Holiday crime of the century.

We can reveal that the gang was a small army of FOURTEEN men equipped with brand new weapons.

They acted like a well-drilled army unit under the orders of the well-spoken gang boss who called himself Paddy Oree.

They had remarkable knowledge of the layout and intricate alarms at the security firm's premises and even

called staff by their christian names.

They warned that they knew the home addresses and car registration numbers of all eight staff held captive in the ordeal.

Plucky supervisor Greg Counsell was named by workmates as the hero of the four-hour gunpoint drama.

They said he coolly bargained for their lives by persuading the gang to let come Bank Holiday robbery—

He told them that if they did not have the captives there would be looked on as folk heroes —but if they pulled the trigger there could expect no mercy.

We have learned that real hero became increasingly concerned about penny-pinching cutbacks and a feared an easy target for villains.

Pounced

One example was that floodlight bulbs in the Security Express yard had been dead for almost six months without being replaced.

And it was staff cutbacks which led to just one man being on duty —in charge of more than £3million—when the gang pounced.

They grabbed 38-year-old Mr Counsell as he made a morning cup of coffee on Easter Monday.

He was walking from the reception area to his control room when a huge security door inside the firm's yard swung open.

The shocked supervisor told detectives he was then confronted by a firing squad of masked men.

They surged towards him brandishing shining new weapons, ranging from pistols to sawn-off shotguns.

The bandits, all

dressed in black from head to toe, pinned him against a wall, forced his head down on to his chest and rammed a gun barrel against his right cheek.

They had sneaked into the yard under cover of darkness and had hidden by the dustbins behind the security gate.

Police believe they simply clambered over the 12ft high perimeter wall and slipped, unnoticed—past the prison-like closed-circuit TV cameras.

Bundled

Staff said a child could have scaled the perimeter wall and no one would have trouble finding a blind spot past the cameras.

It's Mickey Mouse security — just a joke," said one worker.

Mr Counsell, who had seen no sense of the raiders since he started work at 7am, told police he thought at first he was the victim of a prank by a gang of children.

He was about to tell them to clear off out of the yard when he realised it was no joke.

The bandits, most in balaclavas with eye slits and one in a bizarre monkey mask, bundled him back into the building.

Jammed

He asked the gang what was going on and one of them told him: "Just keep quiet and no one will get hurt. Keep calm, no one is going to hurt you."

As the gang spoke, Mr Counsell feared that he was a prisoner of IRA terrorists.

They all talked with Irish accents and called each other Paddy One, Paddy Two and so on.

But, as the bandits

mumbled their accents slipped and Mr Counsell told police he then became convinced they were cockney crooks.

Mr Counsell was marched out at gunpoint back to the firm's reception area, his eyes constantly watching plaster to prevent him getting a single glimpse of the raiders' faces.

"When he asked the gang where they were going, one of them snapped: "Shut your mouth. We know what we are doing."

And for the next three—hours he was forced to play out the most gruesome role of his life.

The tape was torn from his eyes and he was ordered to sit in his normal chair, but held a soundproof glass screen—and believe as if nothing had happened to his colleagues arrived one by one.

Trussed

They arrived cheerily for the Bank Holiday shift and nodded good morning to Mr Counsell —unaware that two hooded men were crouched behind his desk with guns levelled.

As each man arrived they were jumped on in an instant.

Despite the hidden terror Mr Counsell stayed cool as he pressed a button to let his colleagues in.

Once inside they were grabbed by the raiders and blindfolded.

At one stage Mr Counsell overpowers all one of his workmates in the yard behind him and arrived. One of gang poked into victory with a gun, forcing he was not to alert his pal.

He was ordered "Keep a straight face in future we will have your brains out."

But Mr Counsell was forced to go through this sporting ordeal time after time as the firm's staff came one by one to their fate.

All the time to tied to chairs, their action—filling one man over the phone to operate the controls and answer the phone.

And, as well as being held up with the shotgun, a bandit constantly plastered pressed a gun barrel against his right cheek for 45 minutes.

The gang took the ringing of each victim until his colleagues arrived.

squire

They were seen due to clock on with the boys —relatives—perhaps cash from the Mad Issel House business.

So detailed was intelligence, they knew the name of dog owned by the guards and a name experiment John Atkinson, pointed a gun—

The white squire was stage master at the raid, would handle called One.

Mr Counsell police in a that the toff had a racy bearing and he was known as an officer.

He said the man used to secret if the the raid but it lapsed into a de-dat voice.

The raid had to have all told there was the value.

Carted

Once the staff all held captive gang began them one of the one of the room. Loaded to a world."

"One of the gang ringleader be the leg to was moving of mate thinking of action.

The new from one group specially recruited the big job, to sure all the alarms to ensure the security poor britain and pules with THIS

SUN EXCLUSIVE
By MICHAEL FIELDER and STUART HIGGINS

'They had been in training.. they shifted cash like hell'

Freddie, Jimmy Lane and John Parry – south London bookmakers.

John H. Stracey, Johnny Cheshire, Freddie, Nicky Carter etc. in 1958.

Janice and daughter Marsha.

Waggy Sullivan, Baunchie, George, Peter Cowles,
Bertie Somers and Jessie Pigott.

Teddy Haynes, Ronny Olive, Butcher Payne at the 211 Club.

Janice, Teddy Dennis, Freddie and Pam Dennis at Oslo Court.

Ronnie Kray's funeral in 1995 – Alex Stein, Freddie, Laurie O'Leary as pallbearers.

Freddie and Joe of Bobby's Bar, Tenerife.

Roy Hildes and wife Sue.

Freddie and George at Alcazaba, Marbella.

Patsy O'Mara; a good friend.

Family group – top row *(left to right)*: Herbie, Wally, George, Bert.
bottom row *(left to right)*: Freddie and parents.

Freddie, George and Pat in Alcazaba, Marbella.

The Eltham Boxing Club at Chris' restaurant, The Red Pepper, Puerto Banus, 1987.

Mo and Danielle with children Santi and Freddie.

Left to right: Patsy Pitts, Stevie Rich, Freddie and Roseanne Pitts in Marbella.

John Mason, Freddie, Johnny Cook, Ronnie Olive, Billy Corbell, Mary and Micky Regan, Dell Rudell and Joan (Dell's wife).

Frank, Freddie and Ian; a business meeting.

Albert Donoghue – Krays' lieutenant.

Selwyn Cooney after
shooting at the Pen Club.

Harry and Barbara Dance –
good friends.

NEW GYM IS A HIT

London's latest gymnasium is opened and it's congratulations for the proprietor. Left to right, Terry Spinks, Teddy Waltham, Tim Riley, Fred Foreman, Reg Gutteridge, Dave Charnley, Mark Rowe.

IT was like Old Home Week when Editor **Tim Riley** declared open the Borough Boxing Club gymnasium at the Marshalsea, near St Georges Church, Southwark, on Friday last.

The Board of Control was represented by Secretary **Teddy Waltham**, Reg Gutteridge made a short introductory speech welcoming " anything that helps the game, and the Chaps, Past, Present and Future were well pleased with their tour of the premises.

Terry Spinks, Olympic Gold Medallist; two of our best lightweight champions since the war, **Dave Charnley** and **Tommy McGovern** and former Brixton middleweight **Ronnie King** were among the company.

Old-timers

Old timers **Joe Rolfe** and **Ernie Mills** met **Neville Axford** and **Peter Indaco** of a later generation.

Mark Rowe was with trainer **Bill Chevalley** and **Arthur Ward** brought along young Scots featherweight, **Johnny Cheshire**.

Amateur referee **Don Chandler** was happy to meet so many old Fitzroy clubmates, Charnley, McGovern, Rowe etc., and the chairman of the new premises **Freddie Foreman**.

Manager **Arthur Boggis** was impressed with the amenities, and the new Swedish Saune Bath, it takes off three pounds per sitting, was inspected with admiration. Manager **Don Cornwall** and **John Parry**, promoter, made early bookings.

From Balham's 211 Club came **Bernie Colman** and Joe and **Fred Scala** with enough nosh for a battalion of soldiers.

Former Champion

Teddy Haynes, former Midland middleweight champion, and Ronnie King will be in control of the coaching.

The Manor was well represented by Bermondsey featherweight, **Phil Lundgren**, **Jimmy Revie**, the Brixton banger, promising young amateur lightheavyweight, **Johnny Branch** was there with **Alf Hewett Junior** and **Dave Barry**, honorary coach for the Fisher Club brought along young **Kieron Murphy**, who said he would be in the top amateur ranks next season.

That Man About the Rings, **Ray Bartlett** was there, of course.

The Party went with a swing with Mrs **Fred Foreman** making everybody feel at home and, with her staff, keeping the cup that cheers in circulation.

Herbie in full regalia.

The real Charlie
Bronson!

Alfie and children.

Alfie and Nicky.

George and Pat.

'by attempting to persuade Ronald Hart by threats and inducements, to make a written statement that differed in material particulars from the evidence he gave at the Old Bailey Kray trial.' The 'threats and inducement' were omitted on the indictment and before the case opened the defence applied to quash it by suggesting it disclosed no offence in law. Judge Mervyn Griffith-Jones did not accept this but agreed to an alteration in the wording of the indictment so that the final version read: 'attempting to persuade Hart to make a false statement . . .' The jury was told the police had set up the meeting when Hart contacted them after he had been approached by Higgins and Thomson to talk about the Foreman conviction. The police recorded the two-and-a-half hour conversation from a vacant house next door. On the morning of the second day of the trial the prosecution asked for a one-hour adjournment. This was granted and at the end of it, prosecution counsel made the surprise offer of 'no evidence'. The explanation for this was quite simple, The *Sunday Times* said: 'For the case to succeed the prosecution would have to prove that Higgins and Thomson believed Hart's evidence at the trial to be true and they were therefore trying to persuade him to make a "false" statement. If they had merely tried to discover if he had lied, they were committing no offence and therefore it would not be right to leave it to the jury. For this reason, no evidence was offered.' The *Sunday Times* was surprised that in view of the cost it would have taken to bring this prosecution to trial, it was remarkable they proceeded without more careful examination of their chances of success. The newspaper said the plain facts were that the two former policemen appeared to have been acting quite lawfully in carrying out the instructions of a reputable firm of solicitors, Quirke and Co. 'Furthermore such inquiries are carried out regularly by solicitors and bodies like Justice and the National Council for Civil Liberties and from time to time by newspapers and it has always been accepted that prosecution witnesses may be interviewed in such circumstances.'

Mr Brendan Quirke wrote to the president of the Law Society: 'It is a sorry day when the managing clerk of a responsible firm of solicitors who was acting properly, regularly and in consultation with counsel can be arrested and thrown into prison and detained for fourteen hours.' Thomson, his clerk, was not allowed any contact with his solicitor. The *Sunday Times* commented: 'One can only ask why the police brought this prosecution. The effect of it could only be to deter perfectly legitimate inquiries. In the circumstances the judge's decision that the two defendants should pay towards their costs seems completely unjust. Bearing in mind the fact that these men will receive no compensation for their loss of business it seems a particularly harsh one.'

After the failed prosecution of Higgins and Thomson, on 13 June police went to Hart's Harwich home apparently by chance and found him bleeding heavily from deep cuts in his left arm. Hart had apparently tried to kill himself and wrote a letter saying he had been 'under constant worry and pressure' over what was going to happen to him for telling the truth. Based on what Hart told Higgins and Thomson, a petition was sent to the Home Secretary asking for my case to be reopened.

But the authorities focused on fighting my appeal. Fresh statements against me were made by Chris Lambrianou. He thought that by now telling the police everything, he would do himself a favour. He'd been sentenced to life with a recommendation of fifteen years. He filled in the gaps about all the details: taking McVitie through the Rotherhithe tunnel and leaving the body in the car near the church. He tidied the case up for the prosecution. Afterwards, my solicitors said it would be better if I didn't see his statement. It was very damning for me. That clinched it as far as they were concerned. My appeal was thrown out. But his statement did him little good. At the end of the day, he didn't get any remission and served his full fifteen years. Tony Lambrianou was a different class altogether. He had the bottle to drive the car with McVitie's body in the back seat and the sense to keep his mouth shut afterwards and do his bird like a man.

I felt sorry for Ronnie Bender when he was sentenced. He got twenty years, five more than the Lambrianous, for annoying Melford Stevenson and disrupting court proceedings. Melford Stevenson had annoyed all of us by putting on a great show for the jury whenever something was said in our favour which he disagreed with. He'd sit up and contort his face in a way which undoubtedly influenced the jury. Ronnie Bender got his own back by blowing his nose very loudly whenever the judge spoke. Stevenson would glare at him, but got his revenge at the end when he dished out five years on top of what the others got. So much for impartiality and treating people equally. But in this case the government really felt they had nailed the 60s gangs and cleaned up London. The Richardsons were first, followed by the Krays, the Tibbs and the Dixon families. If I had got off the charges, Charlie Kray would also have to be acquitted and that was the last thing the government wanted.

· 15 ·
Table Four

On Saturday night, 21 December, 1991, six screws, a
senior officer and a deputy duty governor were held
hostage by masked prisoners at HMP Full Sutton, in
York. I was asked by other prisoners to help resolve the
situation. During the five-hour siege, the deputy came to
within a hair's-breadth of having his throat cut with a
pair of garden shears and the six prison officers were in
danger of being battered to a pulp. The atmosphere was
charged to the point where it was ready to explode into
violent blood-letting. Outside the prison doors, armed
police officers, wearing visors and padded jackets, were
wielding tear-gas, clubs, and riot gear, were impatient to
rush in and put their sticks about. It was strange you
could never recognise them – they must have been
brought in from other prisons. (Later I found out that
the government use the SAS to do the dirty work.)

I was caught in the middle with 300 angry prisoners
around me, some of them inciting fellow inmates to kill
the screws. As frequently happens with these situations,
the Home Office was brilliant at covering up the incident
– to this day, the press and public are unaware of what
happened. During the riot, thousands of pounds of public money was wasted and I put it down to the obstinacy
of those in authority.

While serving time I made many friends among chaps
in prison and I owe a debt of thanks to an articulate and
clever pal called Norman Parker for defining the meaning of the phrase 'one of the *chaps*'. Norman wrote:

Parkhurst Tales (published by Smith Gryphon) and defined the term 'chaps' which I have used on the first page of this book:

'**Chaps**, an almost mythical grouping of criminals whose ethos includes: professionalism in the pursuit of crime; loyalty to others of their kind; hatred of and non-cooperation with authority; and courage. Many aspire to membership, few qualify.'

Chaps who are sent to prison always remain the same. I have always come out of prison the same way as I went in. It has never changed me. That is what makes villains 'chaps'. They don't graft or grovel to people. They just get their heads down and get on with it. And they are better prisoners to have because they keep a steadying influence in prison life. And the people who run prisons, the governors and prison officers, usually appreciate their level-headedness. They stand for common sense and fairness, but in sticking to these principles, they can just as easily be sent down the block as they can be instrumental in saving lives of prison staff. In either case they expect no thanks. All they expect is to be treated in a civil and fair manner, a basic courtesy that should be extended to everybody, regardless of their status. What the authorities have not yet woken up to is that taking a man's liberty is sufficient punishment. You don't have to take his dignity as well. A short sharp shock is much better.

Joe Martin is probably the longest serving prisoner in Britain. He was jailed for eighteen years, but he's been inside for thirty-two! It seems like the Home Office has been interfering with the judge's recommendations again. The killing he was accused of was accidental. He might have lost a little remission when he once tried to escape, but to keep a man locked up for so long is unacceptable. By coincidence, some of my mates, Joey Martin, Tommy Wisbey, Bobby Welch and Georgie Stevens, were all involved in that escape bid from

Leicester security wing. When I arrived, Bobby had just undergone a simple cartilage operation to his knee in the prison hospital. But complications set in and he has suffered great pain ever since and can only get about with the aid of two walking-sticks. He is a lovely man and a good friend and I am sorry to see him suffer all these years after that prison operation, but he may well talk about that one day in his own book.

George was a real character. His pet budgie, his only friend in life, flew away. He was in an adjoining cell to me and drove me fucking nuts calling out to his budgie and continually asking me if I could spot it. From our cells we could only see the top of a tree across the prison walls, the highest in the country, and I told Georgie that if he was up there, other birds would eat him. He spent hours calling to his little friend. The next day Maureen visited and to shut him up I asked her to buy him a budgie. Maureen, who hates birds through a traumatic incident in her childhood, went to great pains to buy him a pair which he named 'Maureen' and 'Fred'. This was a great sacrifice for Maureen whose phobia about birds which wouldn't normally bring her anywhere near one of our feathered friends, let alone walk into a petshop to buy one.

The thing about being one of the chaps is that you acquire a high profile. The screws see the way other prisoners treat you and that identifies you as a high-profile prisoner, which has its good and bad points. The good points are that you get respect, while the downside is that you prejudice your chance of parole.

So while I was commended at Full Sutton for defusing a powder-keg situation, it did me no favours regarding early parole. The six officers were held hostage in D wing over an incident that could have been solved within minutes. A prisoner from up north had received a visit on the Saturday afternoon and word spread that he had been beaten up afterwards. The prisoner's pals demanded to see the prison officer in charge to make sure their mate was all right. By 7.30pm the situation had become so volatile that I was called to try and straighten things out. I went to the main office on the wing to make some sense of what was going on as the prisoners refused to be banged up in their cells until they were sure nothing had happened to their pal.

The prison governor was not on duty that night. I told his duty governor that all it needed was for one prisoner to go down to the block and see if his mate whom they thought had been beaten up was all right. If he was, they'd all go back to their cells. But the duty governor refused. He said he wasn't going to have prisoners dictate to him. The situation became more charged.

Among the prison population were a large number of political prisoners who helped stir things up. Next thing we knew, the authorities called for one of the visiting magistrates who sat on the prison board, to come in as a negotiator together with the number five governor, an ex-priest. It was all a waste of time.

The prison exploded. A lot of angry and frustrated prisoners broke into the kitchens at about 11pm and grabbed kitchen knives and any other tools they could lay their hands on, including the garden shears. Some disguised themselves in home-made balaclavas and began smashing up toilets and sinks. By now, the prison authorities had a full-scale riot on their hands.

A few of us London fellows were trying to be sensible while the northern boys were foaming at the mouth. I even tried to get authorisation for a signed note from the prisoner to say he was not injured which would have appeased the men. But it was not allowed.

At midnight the screws had to run the gauntlet to a back room. Some of them were as young as my sons and they were really frightened, on the verge of tears. They were pleading: 'Don't leave us Foreman, stay here!' The corridor outside was crowded with prisoners wanting to have a go at them. I told the cons to calm down. 'We're looking at a ten stretch on top of our bird,' I said.

As I say, there were a lot of paddys trying to incite the riot and disrupt the prison system. People had their own motives and you found yourself being manipulated by a number of sectional interests. On top of that I was being put up as the number one rioter. The prison governor and several POs were now talking on the telephone. One screw turned to me and said: 'Foreman, you are now in control of the wing,' and handed me the telephone to speak to the prison governor.

Outside, the riot troops eagerly awaited a chance to get at us. They were only stopped because of the ridiculous design of the doors. They opened inwards and the prisoners had jammed them tight with furniture from cells. There was no possibility of escape but quite a lot of damage had been done. I had to wrestle a couple of mad paddys to stop them cutting an officer's throat and getting us all extra bird.

Eventually someone was allowed to go down to see if the 'injured' prisoner was fit. There wasn't a mark on him. It had all been one gigantic fuck-up.

I then negotiated with the authorities for an undertaking that there would be no recriminations. I told them that providing no prisoner was arrested or charged, everyone would return peacefully to their cells. Both sides honoured the undertaking. But none of that should ever have happened. Apart from the financial loss, several men nearly lost their lives, all because the men were not given proof that a fellow prisoner had not been assaulted. Once again, the taxpayers were the losers, and the incident was hushed up to save embarrassment to the prison service and the Home Secretary.

Thank God an old pal of mine wasn't there at the time. The notorious Charlie Bronson is a legend in British prisons up and down the country. A brief rundown of his record explains why. Charlie has spent more than twenty-five years in prison and has been moved over 135 times to sixty different jails. He's ripped off about six prison roofs, taken some five hostages, and assaulted about twenty screws. He arrived at Full Sutton just after the riot. I'd met him a few times over the years and we had mutual respect for each other. His real name is Peterson but he changed his name, saying he was the 'real Charlie Bronson' and prison authorities should recognise him as such. He is built like a brick shithouse with the strength to match and once did a record 2000 sit-ups with a medicine ball.

Originally he began a four-year sentence after ripping off a series of council house roofs over a row with his girlfriend. But because of his behaviour in prison, he ended up doing fourteen years inside. He is now institutionalised. At present he is in top-security Belmarsh jail after taking a prison doctor hostage at Winson Green.

I had the pleasure of his company for about two months at Full Sutton. On one night two brothers badly upset Charlie after trading verbal insults with him across the yard. Frustrated, Charlie smashed up the furniture in his cell. In the morning, at opening up time, everyone stepped out of their cells into the corridor, yawning and scratching their bollocks, when out jumped Charlie into the passageway like Rambo. He was stark bollock naked, covered from head to toe in black shoe-polish and only wearing a bandanna around his head. Wielding a table leg in one hand, and a broom handle sharpened into a spear in the other, he raged down the passageway. As he did so, all you could hear was cell doors clanging shut as other prisoners stepped back into their cells a bit lively at this awesome sight. Charlie's tantrums resulted in four assaults on screws and one fractured skull which he'd cracked with the table leg. Some two hours later, while he was still on the loose, I asked to see if I could deal with him together with another young lifer called Mark Edmonds who was also a pal. We found Charlie crouched in a small recess ready to do battle. Preparing for a counter-assault at each end of the wing was the mufti in full gladiatorial regalia. We coaxed Charlie into the bathroom, got him into a nice hot bath and began scrubbing the boot polish off, while I scolded him like a naughty schoolboy: 'You fucked up again Charlie. I thought you liked it here. You are with nice people, we have a drink of hooch over weekends, you sing your songs, [he did a great impersonation of Louis Armstrong singing 'What a Wonderful World'] and now you've fucked up.'

After we'd made him presentable, Charlie said to me: 'Don't let *them* take me down the block, Fred, you take me.' So I spoke to the PO and they were quite willing to let me and young Mark escort him down the block without any aggravation. Obviously Charlie is a sick man and needs help. But the prison system has brutalised him.

He was later moved to Parkhurst where he upset some of the chaps who I think might have overreacted, bearing in mind Charlie's reputation. Charlie, in his crazy way, had decided to dig a fish pond near the running track. As prisoners ran past, dirt was falling back into the hole which upset Charlie. He jumped out gesticulating and calling them 'Fucking LGs', which means London Gangster and is fighting talk used by non-Londoners. As a result Charlie was served up severely by a number of the chaps and he got himself stabbed. He lost six pints of blood and was in intensive care, but survived and is still up to his old tricks. I'll always have fond memories of Charlie but on that occasion he stepped out of line when he should have known better.

I have spent too many years in prison. But compared to some people I haven't done badly. Most prisoners I knew didn't look on prison as a reforming institute. It was more a breeding ground of information, like university. A place where you learnt all the tricks of the trade.

That's why they don't work. They just teach you better skills and show you your real vocation in life – doing something you're good at like thieving. They leave men bitter and twisted and break up families. Children forget their parents and the whole family unit breaks down. Long sentences have never achieved anything.

I began my sentence for McVitie at Leicester. We were dispersed from Brixton to different prisons around the country. The Twins and Charlie Kray were sent to separate prisons: Ronnie to Durham, Reg went to Parkhurst and Charlie to Chelmsford. Whichever prison you go to you are bound to know people. At Leicester, apart from Bobby Welch whom I've already mentioned, I ran into: Charlie Richardson, who was doing a twenty-five over the torture trial; Billy Gentry, serving a seventeen for armed robbery, Tony Dunsford, a double-lifer; and Nobby Clark, also a double-lifer who looked like the old film actor John Caradine. While in prison, both Tony and Nobby had killed again. They found Nobby dragging a young guy down a corridor with wire flex around his neck attempting to hide him in a cupboard. I'd known Charlie and his brother Eddie, and Billy Gentry prior to arriving, and got on okay with them. But I also met other prisoners like Micky Kehoe who was to become a friend for many years after.

Leicester special wing, occupying an isolated high security corner of the prison, was to be my home for the next four years. To reach our quarters, visitors would be brought through a series of passageways and gates and then made to sit across a large table. No physical touch was allowed and two screws sat next to you with notepads, listening to every word you said. Prison life was extremely limited. The only time we left the wing was to go to the sewing machine shop and a small, caged exercise yard. We were completely isolated and never saw other prisoners in the main wings. There were only eight prisoners at any one time, year in year out, and you got sick to death of seeing the same faces. The security was unbelievable.

One of the madmen in our section was Arthur Hosein. He and his brother Nizam kidnapped and murdered Mrs Muriel McKay, whom they mistook for Anna Murdoch, wife of media tycoon Rupert Murdoch. Hosein would walk around singing: 'I want to be a millionaire . . .' He was completely round the twist. We'd play football and he would snatch the ball and run away with it, giggling and laughing. He wasn't special wing material and everyone despised him for what he'd done. He wasn't accepted as one of the chaps. It was only a matter of time before one of us knocked him out. That honour eventually went to 'Hate 'em all Harry'.

Hosein had grown his thumbnails to an extraordinary length and filed them to a razor-sharp point. He slashed his own brother Nizamodeen across the cheek when he'd made statements to assist the police. The other cons in the wing were concerned about his 'lethal' weapons. An opportunity arose one day when Arthur volunteered to cook one of his curries. I booked out a pair of scissors and grabbed his arm under mine and cut off both thumb-nails: 'You can't cook food for us, Arthur, with dirty fingernails.'

Arthur protested loudly: 'No, no, no Mr Freddie,' but it was too late. I had cut him down to size.

Living in such close quarters resulted in tensions and fights. Charlie Richardson had a good row with Ronnie Bender providing us with good entertainment. People fought each other for no reason at all. Eight prisoners crammed in a small space was bound to have this effect. You get on one another's nerves and the slightest little thing upsets you. Every few months, a new face would appear and you'd drain every bit of information and news out of him. It was a disappointment when an old face returned because you wanted somebody new.

Reggie Kray arrived at one point in exchange for

another con. After a few days he had a few heated words with Peter Hurley, a strong and fit young guy. I stepped in just before the row started, to make sure Reggie didn't get hurt, and was glad I acted quickly. Hurley grabbed a knife from the kitchen sink and I managed to grab his wrist and arm before he had a chance to do any damage. Reggie than sank a few left hooks into him and that was the end of the row. Reg was grateful to me for what I did, but then Pete Hurley, a bank-robber from Liverpool, wasn't a bad kid and I felt sorry for him. He was out of his league.

Other faces to pass through included police-killer John Duddy, who was arrested with Harry Roberts. John often spoke to me about the incident and used to shake his head, saying: 'As the police car drove away, I went down on one knee and fired a shot through the back window and it hit the copper in the back of the head. How unlucky can you be? If I'd tried it a million times, I would never have pulled it off. It was a total freak shot. Even Annie Oakley couldn't shoot as straight as that.' He said it had been a reflex action and not a premeditated act. Afterwards he lost the will to live and just wasted away and died in prison. He knew he would never get out.

Conditions were medieval. You couldn't see daylight because of the extra bars they put on windows and the whole unit had a ridiculous number of bolts on every opening door. The cells had no heating. In winter you were given a jug of water which would turn to ice by your bedside. That's how cold it was. Prisoners named the wing the 'submarine'. When you woke in the morning your nose would be frozen. As a Cat A prisoner, you were shifted around to different cells, sometimes up to three times a week. Just when you'd arranged everything and cleaned up the cell, they'd tell you to pack everything up again. It was soul-destroying. Then they would also knock on your door every fifteen minutes during the night. A red light was left on all the time and if they couldn't see your hands above the sheet they'd flash the light on and off. I'd throw my boots at the Judas hole where faceless screws peered at us like perverts at a seedy sideshow. It was mental torture. All through the night they would kick the door. When they'd finished with your cell, you'd hear them kicking at the next cell door. It was an extreme case of sensory deprivation, the kind of torture you think only goes on in third world dictatorships.

During this period of time we had many important visitors to the wing. The then Home Secretary (later to be Prime Minister) James Callaghan paid us a visit and we complained to him about our conditions and treatment. Charlie Richardson was well up-front and had plenty to say. Like a typical politician, Callaghan agreed wholeheartedly with us and promised to change things. As he left the security gates, he turned and waved to us promising: 'I won't forget you lads.' I was there for another two years. Nothing changed.

But a more sympathetic visitor was Lord Hunt. He'd been made chairman of the parole board and was a well-respected public figure who had climbed Mount Everest. He visited me in my cell for a chat and discussed a book I was reading called *The Anatomy of Britain*. He mentioned that it had been written by a friend of his. I felt he was very dissatisfied with his job because he was powerless to implement his ideas. I asked him if he went on future expeditions could he find room for me? We had a chuckle over this remark and before leaving he shook my hand and wished me luck in the future. A regular visitor was Lord Longford and one Christmas we even had a visit from a bishop in full regalia with crook and robes. He said prayers and blessed us all. He was a nice old boy and his compassion was appreciated.

One of the problems with prisons is the constant change of staff and governors. A new governor would change everything the previous governor had done and you had to start all over again. You would be given new routines and different rules and they twisted things round to suit themselves. In Leicester, we went on a hunger strike for twelve days over Cat A visits. We were joined by special wing prisoners in Durham, Parkhurst and Chelmsford. I lost a stone in weight and it was the first time I could see my ribs since I was sixteen. The governor would get screws to fry up onions in the wing in an attempt to seduce your tastebuds. But we held out and stood firm.

The authorities had decided that visitors would have to be photographed and checked out by local police station officers. During visits, we were also required to wear sterile clothes which would be left in reception, and then submit ourselves to a strip search. During the visit, there was to be no physical contact with wives or friends, even children would not be allowed to sit on your lap. The whole thing was so stressful and upsetting you dreaded the entire procedure. We won our hunger strike but the victory was short-lived, because years later they got all their own way again and reverted to the same old rules.

After more than four years segregated with eight people, I was moved to Wormwood Scrubs in west London. John McVicar, the so-called 'No. 1 public enemy', took my place in Leicester. The change to the Scrubs was dramatic. It was like being dropped in the middle of Waterloo Station in the rush hour. All of a sudden, even though I was still a Cat A prisoner, I was in D wing surrounded by 300 men.

The hierarchy in this prison centred around Table 4 and I was able to exert quite a lot of influence here. So much so that at one point, Table 4 was mentioned in a governors' report, publicising the fact that they were giving some prisoners more leeway because they were a steadying influence on the rest of the prisoners. But in spite of us being a calming influence in the wing, we were

not immune from being sent down the block if we misbehaved.

The diners at Table 4 included: Buster Edwards,
Jimmy Hussey, Gordon Goody, Roy Hilder, Frank
O'Connell and Alan Gold. We selected who we had on
our table. Dining took place in the centre of the landing
at the bottom of the staircases in D wing, home to the
long-term prisoners. There were television sets on opposite walls at each end of the wing but little else. All you
had were a few shops to work in, an engineer's, laundry
and the gardens. A concrete exercise yard with goal-
posts, lay between the wing and laundry building. On
the other side of this was a patch of grass which we
laughingly described as the 'bowling green' and a tiny
aviary and you never ventured far from there.

Although it was a Victorian prison, it had not been
built on the star system as most of the prisons were.
These allowed for the governor's office to be in the
centre from which he could survey down every wing. For
some reason the Scrubs was built on a different system
being made up of four separate blocks and no connect-
ing corridors. Each block had its own exercise yard. The
kitchens were in another block and when food arrived it
was freezing cold. It had to be put back on hot plates and
re-heated. Nevertheless, the food was really bad and you
got cold meals all the time. Prisoners seemed to be permanently hungry. The meat was so thin it looked as
though it had been cut with a razor blade. The prison
authorities were again courting disaster. A hungry man
is an angry man.

We were always sorting out problems at our table. At
one time we had a row with all the black guys because
they were getting out of their pram. Other problems
would arise over currency or snout, as well as incidents
of bullying and intimidation. The victims would air their
anxieties at Table 4 and you would see other prisoners
watching us, looking for tell-tale signs. Usually prisoners

were seeking a bit of protection. Somebody was taking liberties or wanting to beat them up and they looked to us to resolve their problems. You could hear young prisoners on remand hollering and screaming in other wings.

By exercising a controlling influence we were helping the prison authorities, so we also had to show them our authority could work both ways and that we could create problems as easily as we could solve them. That was the only power we had and we needed to exercise it, as I had to during a repeat of a Muhammad Ali vs. Fraser fight on television. We were all mad-keen boxing fans in our wing and were watching the fight which was scheduled to finish at 8.30pm. Bang up time was half-an-hour earlier although on special occasions they would give prisoners the extra time. However, it meant the screws would be late going home. On this occasion the screws wanted to go home and bang us up early, though with several hundred men intent on watching the fight, a little diplomacy to keep them happy would not have been a bad thing.

One insensitive screw came over from another wing and turned off the set just before 8pm. I got up and turned it back on. The screws walked away growling and standing around ready for another showdown. Then another hard-case turned off the telly again. I turned it on again and nobody would budge. It caused a right scene at the gate because there was a change of shift due and all the screws would have to stay behind. In the end they backed down but were raving mad at me. They didn't want a full-scale situation on their hands but the next morning I was called down by the governor and read the riot act. It was all right when I kept things peaceful but they weren't so forthcoming in return. I was threatened with a 'sojourn' to Parkhurst or Durham.

Soon after I had arrived I was sent down the block for three months for attacking John Barry who had grassed on us in the McVitie trial. It was just before Christmas

1973. Barry was on remand for robbery and I saw him in the yard. Frank O'Connell (he was doing fifteen for armed robbery), and two other prisoners, one a lifer, and myself were being escorted across the yard to the book-binder's. I spotted Barry playing football. He was still in remand gear and hadn't been weighed off. I got the ball and dribbled it for a little and then kicked it towards Barry and chased after it. I covered the yard in no time and he knew I was coming for him. The screws told me to come back but I ignored them. As soon as I got near I jumped him. The screws came running over and we all wound up in a big pile in the yard with Barry under-neath. Frank pulled a screw off me and despite people holding me, I was still trying to batter him. I managed to sink a couple into him and ripped off his shirt and jumper in the mêlée. He was shouting at the top of his voice: 'I knew it was you, Foreman.' Typical of his kind, he was still grassing me up. He still couldn't keep his mouth shut.

I was dragged away and thrown down the block. Nothing happened to him. Wheeler, the prisoner gover-nor, was livid. He had virtually guaranteed Barry's safety when he was sent there from Wandsworth. Other friends of the Twins had threatened him there and that's why he finished up in the Scrubs.

Three of us, me, Frank and the lifer, were sent to the block and were brought in front of the governor every week so he could determine how long we'd stay there. I argued with him, asking why he had flaunted Barry in front of me when he knew he was a prosecution witness. I stayed down the block all over Christmas and the New Year. You only got number one diet down there and my old mate from Leicester, Micky Kehoe, ran the gauntlet down the back of the punishment block to climb up to my cell window and pass food in to me.

Back at Table 4 after the punishment block, I con-tinued helping young guys and protecting many a kid from being molested, often by just showing friendship to them. Roy Hilder, one of the chaps on Table 4, had been a customer in my pub and met Sue, his wife, there. They made a lovely couple. I used to keep my eye on him and at one point he had a confrontation with the biggest black man you'd ever seen. Roy had to stand two steps higher on the stairs so he could punch him in the head. I stood behind the black guy. When Roy saw me there, he chinned him, really knocking him out. Another black guy who was formidable was called Daly and had done a bit of fighting in his time. He ran around the exercise yard shadow-boxing with lead weights in his hands. Another inmate, a fellow called Proudfoot, had a confrontation with him while I stood by. Proudfoot was a scouser. Skinny and tall with no muscles. Most of the time he just lay in his cell smoking pot and listening to Eric Clapton. He was a throwback to the 60s but like all scousers he loved his football and was quite a good goalie. On this particular day he went for a high ball just as Daly was shadow-boxing his way around the perimeter of the exercise yard. The two ran into each other and the ball went over the bar. Proudfoot had saved the goal. But by now Daly was growling and went for Proudfoot, who looked at me and the signal I read in his eyes was Help! Help! He was a beanpole next to this gruesomely built ex-fighter who was solid muscle from head to toe. 'I'm with you,' I told Proudfoot. In prison it's always a one-to-one. You never gang up unless you think a pal's going to get hurt. If it's a no-good bastard, you let him get battered. I encouraged Proudfoot to have a go. 'Go on,' I said, 'give him one.' As he shaped up to him, Proudfoot threw a right hander and pole-axed Daly spark out. Nobody could believe it. When he tried to get up, Daly's leg went into a spasm. I was laughing. 'See what you can do!' I told him.

Proudfoot's chest swelled as if to say: 'Don't mess with me.' I couldn't stop laughing. This pot-smoking, pallid and weak-looking beanpole, the type you kicked sand in the face of, knocked out Marlvin Hagler with one punch!

Norman Parker had also wanted to do Daly. He came to me one day and said: 'Fred, I have to have a row with Daly. I want to do him.' Now Norman had already killed two people and was asking me to get Daly in the recess and knock him out. He knew what I was capable of and told me: 'If you can knock him over, I'll plunge him and finish him!' Was I hearing right? I asked him incredulously if he really wanted me to be an accessory to murder just before my release. Norman, being slightly paranoid, had not liked the way Daly looked at him but I told him not to wind himself up and defused the situation.

Table 4 resolved another potential disaster in the Scrubs in about 1974 when prisoners rioted over food and conditions. The food situation in the Scrubs was stupid. I picked up a bit of ham one day and it was as thin as tissue paper the way it was cut. Everyone was hungry and the food atrocious. I threw the ham at a gold-braided prison chief and it stuck to his face like clingfilm. I told them they had to do something about the food. Not only were we getting cold food but it was inedible. If food is all right the prison runs well. This followed riots in other prisons, including Parkhurst from which both Frankie Fraser and Martin Frape were afterwards dispersed. Frape joined us in D wing in the Scrubs and now found himself in the middle of another riot. Prisoners at Parkhurst had tried to hang screws and cut their throats. About 300 D wing prisoners refused to go in their cells and all the other wings camped in the yard. Some prisoners had got on to the roof of our wing and we were feeding them for about three days. The whole prison was on red alert and surrounded by armed mufti wearing riot gear. Now the rioting prisoners began settling old scores and were fighting each other as well as trying to rip the prison apart. Me and the others on

Table 4 were eventually able to talk some sense into everybody and resolve the situation.

One of the hardcases in the Scrubs was a flat-nosed geezer called Catino – we called him the 'Cat' for short. He was unpopular with other prisoners and had battered a few people with a can of beans in a sock – one of the weapons used in prisons. Cat claimed he was a post office bandit which gave him some standing. At the time there was another prisoner who'd been done for rape although he protested his innocence. This fellow and his secretary used to pull girls in bars and clubs and take them home for little caning sessions which he'd administer on their bare bottoms. He'd then take photographs revealing the marks and weals, but they were never brutally raped and were half-willing participants in his sex games. One girl screamed and then another and that was how he came to trial. He was a businessman and felt really hard-done-by getting seven years.

While in prison he built up a scrapbook library on sex offenders so you could check out everyone's background. We never accepted him because of what he had done, but one morning he came to our table full of excitement to show us a picture of Cat in the *News of the World*. There was Cat posing for a boxing photograph wearing his shorts with the headline: The Beast of Bedsitter Land. Now we knew what he was really inside for. He was doing a ten for attacking young students by knocking on their door and as soon as it was opened, he'd chin them and rape them on the spot. On the following Saturday morning we had our usual football match. He was on the opposition team and I was full-back. He came on with one of his hard tackles. As he raced for the 'dropped ball' his left foot came up between my legs and caught me on the inside of my knee. Instinctively I cracked him on the jaw with my right and gave him a left hook on his way down, catching him in the mouth and knocking out a couple of his teeth. The screws took him to hospital but nothing was said. He never grassed me up and the screws said nothing because they wanted him to get a seeing-to. I wound up with a couple of stitches in my knuckles.

At the time, my Danni and Jamie were attending the Italia Conti school which was then in south London. Danni's classmates included present-day stars like Tracy Ullman, Sadie Frost, Lisa Maxwell, Patsy Kensit, Bonnie Langford, Lena Zavaroni and the Neves sisters, Vivien and Tracy. I used to bring the girls home when we lived in Dulwich and also went to all their concerts at Conti's. Now they were having trouble at north Lambeth underground near the school. Young yobbos barracked the girls and put hands up their dresses. It was all getting out of hand and the school wasn't able to control it. I was told of the problem and got Danny Oliffe to go there on my behalf and sort it out. He found out who the troublemakers were and went round to their father's, one of whom was a local newsagent. He told the geezer: 'If you don't stop your kids molesting the girls, we'll come and batter the fuck out of you.' The Shreward family who owned the school were very pleased that the problem had been resolved so quickly though they never knew how. They were very good to us when Maureen had difficulty in paying school fees for both Danni and my Jamie and gave us a fair bit of leeway.

Shortly before I was moved from the Scrubs, I battered a certain screw. I attacked him because of the way he mistreated one of the Angry Brigade prisoners who were not dangerous people but misguided students rebelling like most other kids. This screw was notorious for his ill-treatment of prisoners. He used to terrorise all the young prisoners and the borstal boys in the other wings and he was often drunk and causing trouble. On this particular night, one of the Angry Brigade, a nice lad who was very studious and intelligent (he got most of the answers right on Bamber Gascoigne's quiz shows) was off to education classes. He was running a bit late and came down the staircase with all his books, calling down to the main gate to let them know he was coming. But just as he got to the gate, the screw locked it and said he was too late which meant he would miss his lessons for that week. The lad remonstrated with the screw who was pissed again. The screw was feared by prisoners and other screws alike. He used to fling his hat to the floor and challenge people to a fight.

I watched him as he grabbed the kid and his books and slammed him up against the gate. The books were sent flying and before I knew it I was tearing down the wing towards him. The other screws standing there warned me: 'No, no, don't do it, Foreman.' I took no notice and ran past them and leapt at him. He came down with my flying tackle and I knocked him half-way down the wing. I then got on top of him, wrestled him on to his back and sat on his chest. I was about fourteen stone in weight. Pinning him down with my body I then started battering him until Frank O'Connell and Jim Hussey came up and pulled me off. The screws didn't interfere but Jim and Frank stopped me from beating him up really badly. He had big claw-marks down his face and a black eye. There was no way he would have got up if I hadn't been pulled off him. They got him to his feet and, pointing his finger at me, he screamed: 'You're nicked!' The next morning I was up in front of the governor.

Outside a large deputation of prisoners were waiting and they warned that if I was punished, there would be a riot. The authorities knew I was under pressure having been seen by Troon and Chalk and that I was about to be charged with the Marks murder. It was only a matter of time before I was slung back to Wandsworth to face the trial. By not punishing me they had defused the situation. Under normal circumstances I might have been charged and wound up with a two stretch on top of my ten, but on this occasion nothing happened.

A few months later I was shipped to Wandsworth – 'Wanno' – again. Some of the screws were sad to see me go because I helped keep a happy equilibrium at the Scrubs. I was put into the mailbag shop for the last six months of my bird and then straight back to Brixton on remand for the Marks murder trial. Going to Wandsworth was like returning home with all the old faces there. Micky Kehoe, Tony Baldassari, Ronnie Scrutton, Billy Murray and Charlie Dale were all there. Since I'd last seen Micky, he'd been out on licence and committed further armed robberies so he finished up doing eighteen years. Tony Baldassari was just starting a ten-year stretch. Ronnie Scrutton was also beginning an eighteen, Billy Murray was on the tail-end of a life-sentence for robbery. Tony Baldassari was a pal I'd known all my life and had told me, when we were sitting together in prison sewing the mail bags: 'When this sentence is over, that's my lot. I couldn't face any more long sentences, Fred.' When he finished that sentence, he committed another armed robbery and was surrounded by armed police – rather than face more time he decided to burn the money and blow his brains out.

Ronnie Scrutton was another armed robber and part of a very active firm. He came from a big family in north London and could sew a perfect mailbag. He'd spent many years practising! I refused to sew any mailbags and rather than see me on a charge, he'd sew some for me. He had been one of my customers at the Walk Inn and whenever he'd had a good touch would walk around with bottle of scotch and gin, topping up people's glasses. Billy Murray was doing life for shooting a security guard but that was accidental as they'd already got their loot and were driving away. Charlie Dale was another face and cut the cloth for the mailbags. I knew him and his brother Johnny Dale, who was a friend of mine for many years, got himself a bad name and was shot in the back. Two Irishmen were charged with attempted murder but were acquitted.

On his release from prison, Micky Kehoe got married and went into the printing business although he kept certain other, more profitable, interests alive. He did very well but suffered a cruel death. He was out on his motorbike and was knocked over by an ambulance. He had overtaken it to avoid a police escort for the Queen and while he lay on the ground, a police outrider accidentally ran over his head and killed him. The Queen stopped the cavalcade and asked after him but to no avail.

It would have been the highest insult for Mick to be killed by a copper after all the years he suffered in prison. It was a tragic departure just when he was enjoying his life. We were very sad when Ronnie Scrutton, who was well into his eighteen-year sentence, died of a heart attack while doing press-ups in his cell. He was a well-loved character and a terrific spender. Micky Kehoe and Ronnie Scrutton were of the old school. Armed robbery was their game and they were definitely two of the chaps.

· 16 ·
Snookered

After I had served my ten stretch for Jack 'The Hat' and been acquitted of Ginger Marks's murder, I tried to get my life and finances in order again. Most of my assets – the pub, betting shops, flats and houses were sold while I was in prison. All that was now left was the twelve-roomed house in Dulwich. It was a nice place with plenty of room for the family and the back garden looked out on to a wooded area which made you feel you were in the heart of the country. It was lovely and Maureen had decorated it in style.

I had to get into something to earn a living, so my friends Micky Regan and Ronnie Knight put up £10,000 for me to invest in some pool tables, and together with my pal Ted (Ginger) Dennis, we started up a new business. At first it was hard work but it soon grew and we were able to repay the money and own the business ourselves and things began to look good again.

All the people I had known in south London were under one wing when I came out. They were united and gave each other support. We were a formidable force of chaps. The Richardsons and the Krays were gone and it was just us and the Bermondsey firms and nobody was rowing. We had a virtual army. Some 300 to 400 people came to my homecoming party in the Angel pub. Everybody was there. I had bought a complete set of new clothes for my big night – naturally my wardrobe was all out of date. I spent all night saying 'Hello' and shaking hands with old friends, but I was really uncomfortable around the feet and I whispered to Maureen, 'I'll be well pleased to go home and get these bloody shoes off, they're killing me!' When finally I did get them off, I found I'd left the cardboard packing inside – silly bastard! Over the next three years we had a golden era but then petty quarrels began to threaten our unity. Civil war finally broke out when I fled Britain and went on my toes to America after a customs officer was killed in a multi-million pound drugs raid.

Ted Dennis and I had sixty pool sites taking in up to £3,000 a week. It was a good living and we got our sons to help us: Ted's Gary and my Gregory. Jamie would help occasionally when he was not busy in theatre or doing a TV series and my niece Barbie also did some part-time work for us. It was a good business and most of all, a straight business. Then one day I received a phone call from one of our sites saying that a copper had called and taken our pool table away. This had also happened at several other pub sites. The bloody cossers were nicking all my pool tables with the cash inside and storing them at Camberwell nick!

Ted and I went to see our solicitor, Tony Block. We met with police and asked the officer (the same one who'd charged me with the Marks murder) what he thought he was playing at. We showed him all the bills and receipts for the tables, cues, balls and chalk, and told him to get off his arse and 'put the fucking tables back' or he'd be the one to get nicked. This was costing us time and money when we were totally legitimate. Perhaps if we'd had the chance to buy some tables off the back of a lorry things might have been different, but we hadn't.

The police had to admit defeat and it was worth watching the fat cossers puffing and panting as they carried three hundredweight of slab-filled tables back to where they got them from. Ted and I were used to handling them but the police had no idea and made hard work of it.

While I was busy with the tables, Maureen went into the antiques business with Ronnie Oliffe's sister Mary who had a stall at Bermondsey market every Thursday. I put a bit of cash into the stock and they built up their little business, at the same time picking up bits and pieces for our home which was looking better and better.

We progressed well from here. My Danielle and Jamie were at the Italia Conti school of acting and Gregory was in the music business managing groups and helping me with the pool tables. I went into partnership with my George in a bar of the Hotel Ellerslie in Crystal Palace. It was very successful and banged out every weekend. The owner was Billy Howard's ex-wife Jan and she was on her own now and needed to put the hotel on the map to boost the takings. There was a lot of building work to be done so we pulled in Johnny McAvoy, a builder and brother of Michael who was later convicted of the Brinks' Mat robbery, and Mick Regan to finance and enlarge the basement into club premises. We also sold a share to Brian (Little Legs) Gifford who was a bit of a mover and had other businesses like a car showroom, warehouse and another club in Bloomsbury. Brian had wanted to get on the firm with me for years and now that he had, he gave me a share of the car showroom and we were flying.

With all the money coming in, we bought Jan's share of the hotel when she wanted to sell out. I invited my old pal Micky Regan to invest and later we sold it on to Bill Best and his brother Dave so we all made a nice profit.

Once a month at the Ellerslie, we'd go on the piss with my Ozzie mates who formed the most successful shoplifting gang in Britain. Ronnie Oliffe introduced me to them when I wanted to buy some tom for Maureen. They were led by Ozzie Bruce and were all characters in their own right. Cadillac Jack, Billy Hill and the Bush-ranger were part of the team. They helped me out when I was inside doing my ten by employing Jamie. Part of their operation was an illegal spieler in Earl's Court and Jamie was given the job of board boy, chalking up the winners and prices in the day's racing. They'd treat him generously with tips whenever they won a bet, knowing that Jamie was taking home the money to Maureen and helping with the expenses.

Another face who occasionally came into my club to drink was the actor John Bindon. John had a reputation for violence as well as being a ladies' man. He charmed society beauty Lady Vicky Hodge and had an affair with her which went on for more than ten years. As an actor he'd won small parts with famous names like Michael Caine and Ryan O'Neal. He also appeared with Mick Jagger in *Performance* and with The Who in *Quadrophenia*. Home TV series like *The Sweeney* inevitably cast him in the role of a villain and he acquired instant fame after holidaying with Princess Margaret on the Caribbean island of Mustique where he was a guest of Sir Colin Tennant. The pair were said to get on famously. He poured her champagne and lit cigarettes for her while she was spellbound by his cockney background and capacity for storytelling. But he was best known for hanging five half-pint beer mugs on his manhood. He was very fond of pulling his dick out and showing it off. It was like a baby's arm with an apple in its hand. Even Princess Margaret was not spared the sight of his manhood. While he was photographed naked on the beach, the princess strolled by barely concealing a smile.

One Sunday in early November, 1978, Ronnie Oliffe and myself were having a drink at the Ellerslie when there was a disturbance at the entrance hall. A chap called Johnny Darke had arrived and was drinking with his pals outside the main clubroom. He had a few words with Brian Gifford and chinned him. It's the old case of kick the dog and you kick the master, so Ron and I went out there to sort it out. A few punches were thrown and one of the offenders went over the stairs into my car-park. It was not a major incident because it was a hands-up job and they didn't want any real trouble with me. The row was with Brian Little Legs. But the golden rule is that you never make trouble in a man's place of business where he is trying to get a living. So I said to Little Legs after we got them out: 'Come on, get some tools and we'll go and give it to them.'

He didn't want to know and said: 'It's only a right hander Fred, forget it.'

Word travels fast and next weekend, who comes down the club but Johnny Bindon and a little firm from Fulham. Johnny said he had heard about the row and that he also had words with Darke but had done nothing about it because Darke had said he was a pal of mine, which was not true. I didn't have anything to do with him.

John said: 'I've got this for him,' and put his hand under his coat. I thought, 'Oh no, he's going to pull out his dick again', but instead he pulled out a wicked look-ing hunting-knife.

I told him: 'You do what you have to, John,' and sure enough, some weeks later they clashed at the Ranelagh Yacht Club and Darke was knifed to death.

John told the court that he had been drinking with a mutual pal of ours, Roy Dennis on 20 November, 1978, when Roy screamed out: 'I've been stuck.' Dennis was bleeding from a knife-wound and was followed across the floor by Johnny Darke.

John Bindon told the court that Darke attacked him with a knife: 'I felt a sharp blow to my back near my kid-neys. I looked down and could see the knife under my right arm. Darke sat astride me with the knife. He was quite calm. I was stabbed again. I felt weak and my head was spinning. Blood was pouring out of my chest and eye. Darke was standing a few feet away with the knife still in his hand. He was saying something like: "I'll cut your head off." Then he came towards me and swung his arm with the knife in it. I thought I was going to die. It was quite obvious he was coming for me again. I held my arm out with my knife in it. I was trying to keep him off me. But I can't remember feeling resistance to my knife when it entered Darke. But I was expecting to drop down any minute. The next thing that happened people began separating us. Friends patched me up and put me in a car. They thought I'd better lay low so I flew to Dublin. Sometime later he gave himself up and faced trial for murder. It was proved self-defence. Much to his surprise, after a long trial, John was acquitted.

Apart from the drinking club my George also had the minicab firm in Peckham and his 'Shush' clubs. Once again we were enjoying life after prison. But the winds of change were blowing our way once more. I used to visit Ronnie Oliffe's spieler in the Old Kent Road where the poker schools were really heavy. One chap who used the club was an old friend from the East End and a good pal of the Twins, Colin 'The Duke' Osbourne. While to many he was known as the Duke, to close family he was known as 'Pasha'.

The Duke lost a fortune over a period of time. On some days he'd go down for more than £50,000 at a spiel in the Old Kent Road, so he had to be into something big to have that kind of money.

Nearly a year after the Darke killing, in October 1979, I was in my George's minicab office in Peckham when the Duke called. Johnny Fitz was still with us working the radio control desk when I got the message. He'd been phoning all over to reach me and asked if I'd meet him as he was in a bit of trouble and needed a flop to put his lorry down. Unknown to me, a large consignment of cannabis was stored in a specially concealed floor of the container, and also unknown to me, the lorry had been bugged by Customs. Wherever it went it was being monitored, so at the end of the day, when it settled in one spot, the authorities knew that it had reached the end of it's journey.

Eddy Watkins, we called him Scatty Eddy, was the driver. I'd known him for some time as he'd worked at the Blue Plaice for Alfie Gerrard as an assistant cook and now owned a good garage and several lorries. Apparently he'd been doing a profitable cannabis run for some years.

When the Duke asked me to meet him urgently on Blackheath Common, it was also to link up with Scatty Eddy and the lorry. But as we were there talking to him, Eddy warned us that we were surrounded by surveillance teams. I was angry about that because it meant that we were probably being photographed and I had no wish to be deeply involved in their enterprise.

Nevertheless our first thought was to get Eddy away safely. I told him to drive through the Blackwall Tunnel and pull the vehicle across the other end of the tunnel to block it off and then run up the last 100 yards so nobody could follow him. He was devastated because he saw his whole garage and lorry business going down the pan, not to mention the years in prison. I told him that it was not the end of the world. He would live to fight again. But nothing seemed to cheer him up. I didn't know at the time that the lorry was packed with £2.5 million of drugs. He had invested all his money in this last parcel so it was no wonder he was very depressed.

The Duke and I waited at the other end of Blackwall Tunnel but he never turned up. We reckoned the silly bastard had gone through the Rotherhithe Tunnel instead, so we drove down to Whitechapel and parked opposite Bloom's restaurant on the other side of the roundabout. Eddy had driven directly there hoping to save his investment but he had plenty of unwanted company. He was surrounded by Customs and police officers and there was nothing we could do. Reluctantly I drove back to south London and dropped the Duke off in Bermondsey.

I then drove home and sat there with a cup of tea and a bacon sandwich watching television. When the news came on I nearly dropped the cup and saucer. Scatty Eddy had shot a Customs officer dead. We never even knew he'd had a gun. It was completely out of order. He would only have had to serve a five-year stretch as there had been no robbery and sentences for drugs were not as bad as they are today.

He must have panicked in Stepney. He'd parked in a side-street and jumped out of the lorry wearing an anorak in which he'd concealed a loaded Beretta pistol. He was spotted by Peter Bennett, an undercover Customs Officer and detective John Harvey from Hampshire's drug squad. The officers were ordered to move in and arrest him. They ran towards him and the Customs Officer grabbed him by the arm. Eddy shot him in the stomach. He'd fired through his coat so the officer didn't realise he was armed. The other copper chased Eddy as he tried to run away and brought him down with a rugby tackle. Eddy shot at him but grazed his own stomach. A pensioner passing by then whacked him on the nut with his walking stick and he was arrested.

Now everything would be magnified out of proportion and all those involved would get hammered. The whole weight of the law would be on them and instead of smuggling a harmless drug there was now a murder charge to consider. No Customs Officer had been murdered for a couple of hundred years since the wrecking crews in Cornwall. They would now be turning London upside down like lunatics. The only thing for me to do was to put a lot of time between events.

All the people closely involved with Duke and Eddy were arrested but as I had played virtually no part in this enterprise, no one mentioned my name at that stage. Unfortunately Eddy was very much the architect of his own downfall. He'd come out of Maidstone prison in 1976 with no money and built up the drug run with the

Duke, making a lot of money very quickly. But he made the mistake of talking about it to another prisoner who grassed about their conversation. Later he brought attention to himself when at a hotel meet he lit a celebratory cigar with £20 notes. From that moment he became a marked man. Police and Customs set up Operation Wrecker to catch the Duke's gang. They very quickly learned that the cannabis had come from Pakistan and had been welded into legitimate containers carrying goods for large companies and watched the runs for eighteen months. Duke's big spending didn't go unnoticed either. His firm had imported more than £10 million of cannabis in three years and this accounted for his high rolling activities in spielers.

The police began looking for the Duke and I. Eddy was given life with a twenty-five-year recommendation. After serving twelve years he overdosed in his prison cell. Others involved in the drug-running were sent to prison for various periods of eight, five and three years. While their trial was on, the Duke and I were in hiding. The Duke was in Bermondsey and I was in Dalston. I told the Duke I would get a passport for him and he grew a beard and changed his appearance. But he was dead before I could help him. To my dismay, I was telephoned and told to buy a newspaper: the Duke had been found lying on a football pitch on Hackney Marshes on 1 December, 1979. He was all suited and booted and laid out on the ground. He had committed suicide and left a note taking full responsibility for any evidence that was found. It was a very sad note and he lodged it with Tony Block to be used for the defence. After he killed himself, friends took his body to the Marshes and laid him out, rather than face police questioning about the safe house where he had stowed. But the Duke need never have died. His passport came through a couple of days later and he could have been away with me.

As soon as I got my passport, I left England for

Tenerife and rented a flat in Los Christianos for six months. It was very hard putting all my interests up for sale, including the house in Dulwich. It had been a lovely and happy house and just when we got it right, we had to sell. Maureen never flinched and sold it to be with me. The kids came as well and we treated our stay as an extended Spanish holiday until my new passport for America was ready. Staying there also gave me time to grow a beard and change my appearance because I had to return to London for my passport and attend to business. Friends had arranged another new passport for me, and to my surprise my new identity was in the name of George Newbury, an old Fulham face who got seven years for attempting to shoot Charlie Mitchell.

So there I was, landed with the identity of one of the chaps. The last person in the world I would have wanted to be at that time, but I had to use it. One minute I was in business flying on all cylinders, the next, I had to lose myself and disappear off the face of the earth. It's not easy having to sort everything out when you are a wanted man, so it was a tearful goodbye to my family. I said I'd see them in six months or so when I had settled in America and they could join me. Jamie had to come sooner because police wanted to arrest him as well. They'd seen him driving me about London after I'd lost my licence and jumped to the wrong conclusion. They also thought if they nicked him, I'd give myself up, which I would not have done as there was no evidence to hold him. It was safer for Jamie to come and stay with me.

I experienced further heartache while still on the run in London. Just before going overseas I was told my father had died in December, 1979. Nobody had been able to get in touch with me before his death because I'd been hiding in Dalston and, sadly, I was unable to visit him in his final hours. Six months later, while I was in America, I got the news that my mother had also died. It was a tragic year.

· 17 ·
America

My first mistake before leaving for the States was to buy a single, rather than a return ticket. Perhaps it reflected my inner feelings. I wanted to get away for good. But in practical terms it meant that when I arrived in New York 'nerves a'jangling' I was stuck for several hours in the immigration department. They didn't like Brits coming over on one-way tickets. That might not have been such a problem if I hadn't been using the name of George Newbury who had form as long as his arm. Apart from the seven stretch for shooting at Charlie Mitchell, he'd got a string of other convictions from robbery to assault. Standing there with my beard and false papers which were being scrutinised all the more carefully because of the ticket, made me just a little anxious. But I kept my nerve and somehow they didn't pick up on the convictions and let me through.

I breathed a sigh of relief as an old Glaswegian pal, Joe McClean met me at the arrival lounge. Joe had moved to America fourteen years earlier and had married an American girl, Joanne, who worked for the Bethlehem Steel Company in Allentown, my new home. Joe worked for Paula Arlen, a slot-machine and video game concern run by Dave Rosen, a lovely man who was well-connected with New York families and was known as Mr Philadelphia. He owned whole streets of houses and gave generously to charities and other good causes. Joe and his wife took really good care of me and made me feel one hundred per cent welcome.

Allentown was a great little place surrounded by beautiful Pennsylvanian countryside, very similar to England. Billy Joel wrote a song about it. We were conveniently situated at the apex of a triangle close to New York, Philadelphia, and Atlantic City. I felt very much at home there.

For the first nine months, I helped Joe run his business, learning all there was to know about it. In many ways it was very similar to what I had been doing in London with the pool tables, and which my partner Teddy 'Ginger' Dennis was still running in my absence. A great and loyal man is Teddy. He looked after Maureen and Danni until they could join me and continued giving me a cut in the takings. Here in Pennsylvania, Joe and I and Mr Rosen went all over the state finding sites for game rooms, and bars who wanted to take our machines.

Joe and his gofer, Herbie Catts, had also taken me around the nightclubs and sights around Allentown. It was really impressive. They also found me a luxury apartment in the Olympic Gardens, a prestigious place with nice mod-cons where you could rent all the furniture you needed. They smoothed everything for me. The garden was beginning to look lovely again.

Soon after I arrived, my Jamie came to join me. I felt really bad about that because his career as an actor suffered as a result of him having to go on his toes. He'd been doing really well with TV, stage and commercial work. He'd just auditioned for a French produced film *Quest for Fire*, about a family of half-apes, half-humans in the Stone Age. It won awards for best film around 1979 in the Cannes Film Festival and they'd badly wanted him to play a starring role. He was rehearsing for the part shortly before the customs drama but obviously lost it when he had to join me.

On his arrival, Jamie went straight to the George Washington Motel from where I was meant to pick him up the next day, but my people in London had not got in touch and the result was that Jamie spent nine days waiting for me. By the time somebody told me, he was down to his last dollar wondering what had gone wrong. He wouldn't have been able to pay the motel if I hadn't come when I did. The annoying thing is that I'd been driving past this motel for days wondering when my son would arrive and he'd been there all the time! We almost cried with delight when we saw each other. We cuddled and kissed. I love my Jamie to bits and never feel embarrassed at my show of affection for him. Now that one of the family was with me, things were a lot more settled.

Before you could open a bank account, you needed a social security number and for some reason I was given one straight away. I then opened an account with the First National Bank where the manageress was Nancy Beck, a tall, blonde, lovely English girl who missed the company of a well-mannered British gentleman and I made sure she knew nothing of my past. We built up a friendship which lasted throughout my stay. Jamie in the meantime had formed a relationship with a beautiful blonde girl called Betsy who worked for a large stock-broking firm. Jamie and I look back with fond memories of the lovely Betsy.

I began to invest money in video games and leased premises in Hamilton Street, Allentown. Dave Rosen helped me out. He was so well-connected and a brilliant businessman. He taught me a lot about running an enterprise. He would say to me: 'Always when you open a new business, just say to yourself, location, location, location. And never close a door on someone. Always leave it open just a bit to give them an out and they can also come back in.' This was good, sound advice from a man who knew everyone and had so much experience of life.

The apartment I rented was fine for Jamie and me but not big enough for the family and I wanted Maureen and Danni to join us once they'd sold everything off. Maureen had already emptied the bank accounts except for one in which there was a small amount of £75, which she had overlooked. This money was to show up at a later date and be used against me to help secure a conviction when I stood trial for the Security Express robbery.

For the moment I was sitting pretty. I had nearly half-a-million dollars sitting in the bank and bought about forty vending and video machines and rented a shop for a games room in Allentown's high street (Hamilton Street) as well as putting machines into several bars and clubs. I also bought a Chevrolet truck and Chrysler Cordoba car and still had enough left over to build a brand new Georgian-style house with swimming pool and large grounds with cherry trees. It was all tastefully furnished with lots of guestrooms. Jamie and I went out together working every day and finding new sites and meeting new people. We made lots of friends and connections. Some Italians, who had nightclubs in the Balearic Islands off Spain and were connected to a New York family, gave me a lot of help so I did a few things for them in return. I met a lot of solid people from Philly (Philadelphia) and Atlantic City which were only two hours' drive from Allentown. I would also drive up to the mountains and find sites in summer camps, bars, hotels, and restaurants for my machines.

If a site was too large or I had too few video games or machines to fill the place, then Joe and his firm would fill half of it with his machines and I would get fifty per cent of their takings and do all the repair work and collections. In the meantime, Maureen and Danni arrived. Maureen was happy with the new home and Danni got a job with the Allentown theatre company, appearing in several Shakespearean productions. Gregory was still in London doing his own thing and coming to visit us every now and again with his new wife Lisa. A number of our close friends would also come to rest up and take it easy for a month or two. The only drawback to our happiness in America was that unbeknown to me, Maureen and

Danni missed their friends and family in London. So much so that they would sometimes cry at night.

I tried to make it more homely for them and even bought the girls a Maltese terrier whom we called Pasha after the Duke. Things couldn't have been better for us. Apart from all the capital and property we owned, we now had a tidy sum of cash in the bank.

I was getting reports from back home each week on how different businesses were going, from spielers to clubs and minicab firms and little drinkers like the Shush clubs. There was restlessness among the firms who had been strongly bonded whilst I'd been in London. It worried me and it was disappointing that I couldn't go back to help sort out their problems.

When I was there, all the south London firms would go to boxing shows which were regarded as major events. The venues were held at good hotels like the Kensington Palace and we'd come fitted out in evening dress. While I was away, a lot of silly jealousies and squabbles resulting in tension between the different groups began to arise and came to a head one night at one such boxing event. Ronnie Oliffe, Paddy Onions and all the Bermondsey people who used to drink in my pub and had supported me, were at this show with Alfie, Jerry and Peter Hennessey. They were all good, solid chaps but sat at different tables raising money for a charity. The boxing show was run by Beryl Gibbons, who was the licensee of the Thomas-à-Becket, and the only woman boxing promoter in England. She took over from her husband Tommy, a boxer and promoter, who had previously died from cancer.

During the evening, an argument broke out between Peter Hennessey and Paddy Onions. Neither Micky Hennessey nor I were there otherwise I'm sure it would not have happened. But all of a sudden the argument sparked off a fight, splitting loyalties of the different factions right down the middle. Paddy had come out of the kitchen and grabbed Peter Hennessey round the back of the neck and stabbed him about a dozen times in the back. While he was on the floor, chairs and bottles were smashed over him. Peter was a good friend of mine and there is no way he should have been treated like that. If he'd been a wrong 'un he would have deserved it but he was one of our own. Good company and a well-respected thief and one of the chaps. In addition, all his family were friends of mine. Similarly, Paddy Onions's family were also friends of mine as were Ronnie Oliffe's. We were all connected in one way or another and such a split should never have occurred.

The result was that Peter Hennessey died and a couple of people, including Paddy, were arrested some time later by police. Another kid, Jimmy Colman was also arrested. Although hundreds of people were present at the venue, nobody saw anything and Paddy and Jimmy were acquitted for lack of evidence. Nobody, not even the waiters, would give evidence against anyone. They were good, solid south London people. But the damage had been done and the dangerman was now Mick Hennessey, Peter's brother. The others knew he wouldn't stand for what happened. No way. Now everyone was on tenterhooks wondering what was going to happen and where it was going to come from. When and where was the comeback?

The sensible thing for survival is to hit before you get hit. I'd helped Micky before when he stabbed and killed Dicky Horne at a party. Horne had put a glass in the face of Bernie Hennessey, another of Micky's brothers. So there was little question that he was likely to carry out a revenge attack for Peter. Micky Hennessey was a man of few words. He'd come round to my house, read the paper, then suddenly get up and say he was popping out. In the two or three hours he'd been with me, he'd not said two words. People were a bit frightened of Mick, and Paddy Onions's mob were not at all happy. Mick was driving down Bermondsey with a pal when they struck. Two men on a motorbike drove up beside him as he stopped at traffic lights and blasted him with a shotgun.

The assault nearly took Mick's head off. The motorcycle roared off. Mick's pal took him to hospital and police came to see him. He was lying there with this big hole in his neck and they were round his bedside telling him he was dying and to tell them who was responsible. He told them to fuck off and mind their own business. It was touch and go but he survived.

I felt frustrated over here in America when I heard the news. But there was nothing I could do from there. My mate Micky Regan then asked if Micky Hennessey could come over to visit me. This further divided south London and put Mick Regan in the middle, too, because he had been friendly with both sides. We had all been unified and ours was still the main firm, so over he came. He needed a lot of convalescing to rebuild his strength. He stayed with me for a month or two.

Although Jamie was still with me, things had got a lot better for him in London and he was able to slip back without being arrested. By now they realised he had only been driving me about because I'd lost my licence and they had nothing on him.

Mick Hennessey had been thinking deeply about what to do. He enjoyed the States and came out working with me. But now he'd made a decision. He said: 'I can't let it go, Freddie.'

I responded: 'You've got to do what you have to do. I wouldn't insult you by asking otherwise. Your brother has been killed and I can't ask you to stop. But do me one favour. Leave my little mate out. Ronnie Oliffe had no part in it. I blame Paddy for this. He kicked it off and done the villainy. What you do about that is up to you. No one could have asked me in George's situation to leave it out.'

Some time later, Paddy was shot through the window of his house. A bullet lodged in his jaw. The gunman was suspected of being a guy called Davie Barry from up north. Sometime later Paddy was shot and killed outside his wine bar. He died on the pavement. People hoped the whole situation was resolved and the thing could now be laid to rest, but it wasn't. Dave Barry was taken into police custody and while he was there he was suffocated, supposedly, while resisting arrest. People in south London were still tooled up and it was a situation where everyone was trying to wipe each other out.

There was also unrest between the Philadelphian and New York families who were engaging in deadly internal warfare. They were all trying to get a bigger cut of Atlantic City's casinos and the media used to publish a score card: how many bodies were found in car-boots or wearing concrete overcoats. I'm afraid the Philadelphia side who helped me when I arrived, were on the losing end and suffering badly. The families even took over local TV stations and named intended victims over the air waves.

The Balliteri family in Allentown became good friends of mine. I used to frequent their nightclub and we did some business between London and the States on precious metals and other ventures. There's nothing like sharing a bit of money to bond friendships. They also owned car-sites and I bought several motors off them.

When I emptied cash from the machines I had to be careful of the hold-up firms, usually Puerto Ricans or blacks and that got a bit scary so I asked for some help. They supplied me with a .38 revolver for backup.

Jamie and I had our little rows with gangs of blacks and Puerto Ricans. We punched a few of them out and stuck the gun up noses when necessary. Jamie became very adept at taking care of himself. I once had to bar a couple of guys who were battering the side of one of my machines saying: 'It ate my quarter, man.' That sort of treatment wrecks the mechanism and these were expensive machines. The two guys I had barred came back a few days later with some friends and I thought we were going to have some trouble.

They came up to me and the best approach was to confront them head on. I told them: 'I don't want you in here any more. Now fuck off!'

To my surprise they said: 'Okay Mr Fred, no problem.' That was easy, I thought. As I turned to walk away I realised why they'd backed down. For standing behind me were three massive Hell's Angels all dressed in black leather, standing with feet apart, defiantly chalking their snooker cues. They were praying for the opportunity of a good row. I'd never seen anybody tooled up so openly. They carried huge hunting-knives in their belts and down their boots and, while they looked threatening with their leather hats, studded belts, tattooed and muscular arms, they were good as gold. They never gave me any trouble and I welcomed them on my premises. They loved Jamie and his English accent. We taught them cockney rhyming slang and phrases like: 'Leave me out', 'count me out', 'drop me out', which they loved mimicking.

The police never gave you any hassle but when they'd come into the games area looking for someone, we'd watch a line of cops march in single file, never guessing who they would arrest. They'd march past a group of Puerto Ricans and blacks and suddenly turn around and pounce on one of them, cuff him up, and drag him off to the nick.

I was probably the only white guy in Allentown able to drink at an otherwise all-black bar around the corner from my shop. I'd put some machines into their premises and the guy who owned it let me set up a little card spieler which I bankrolled. There was quite a lot of poverty around and I'd occasionally give some of the younger boys $5 notes. You could see they'd not eaten for days; typically they would make straight for Wendy's or McDonalds. All the black and Puerto Rican girls called me 'Poppa Fred'. I was like a father figure to them.

In the summer, the city fathers would arrange concerts at which big bands like Count Basie's and Woody

Herman and his Herd played in Allentown Square. The black community would arrive and set up chairs hours earlier to get a good pitch. When I came on the scene, they'd wave: 'Down here Poppa Fred', and give me a front-row seat.

We were always being asked to barbecues and parties by neighbours and friends and I reciprocated their generous hospitality. It was now 1981 and everything was going smoothly. But in spite of all the comforts, Maureen and Danni still missed England. When I said we could go back for a short holiday which would also give me the chance to sort out some business, they were over the moon. I asked Joe to take care of the games rooms while I was away. Pals had told me that it would be a lot safer to come back now as the heat was off. My George Newbury passport presented no problems at Heathrow and I spent about two weeks seeing friends and family and being very discreet about my arrival.

After seeing all the opportunities in America, and seizing them, it took a little while to acclimatise to Britain again. I'll never forget going to Miami where two things struck me as summing up the American way of life, both of which were pertinent to my philosophy. One was the name of the hostelry overlooking the harbour: the Last Chance Bar and Restaurant. The second was the name of a luxurious yacht gliding up to the restaurant: it was called *One Hit*.

I'm not advocating that a young man should turn to crime, but let's face it, what chance have you got if you have no qualifications or education? So that must be the key: education and jobs to earn a living which all governments should provide. In all the years spent in prison I never once met a prisoner who had been educated at Eton, Oxford or Cambridge – funny that . . .

Back in London I had a meet with a few friends on a Friday afternoon: Micky Regan, Teddy Dennis, Roy Hilder, Ronnie Knight, Bimbo, a well-known entrepreneur, and many more. We were at the Martin Harris Club in Gerrard Street, Soho, where Ronnie Knight's Sue was working as a barmaid. A fellow called Franie Daniels was also there. I and many other people respected him over the years for his involvement in a robbery at Heathrow airport in the 50s. All his conspirators were arrested at the time and got up to fifteen years' imprisonment, but after a fight with police he is said to have escaped by hanging on to the underneath of a police van. Later, in 1974, he was arrested but acquitted of the murder of Scotch Jack Buggy who was killed in a Mount Street, Mayfair, gaming club. His body, wrapped in a carpet, was found by two off-duty policemen fishing off Seaford, Sussex. What a coincidence.

They talk about a Freudian 'slip of the tongue' but Daniels made his slip when he put a hand on my shoulder just like cossers do when they're arresting you. While I was drinking with the chaps, I felt his hand grasp my shoulder. 'Welcome back, Fred. Nice to see you again,' he said. At the time his mode of greeting didn't reveal his treachery and it was only thirteen years later that someone told me. Daniels had gone upstairs and was overheard making a phone call outside the men's toilet during which he said: 'They're all in here and he's wearing a beard.' He was the grass.

I had not been in touch with Ronnie Knight since I'd left for the USA and he was very surprised at seeing me there. When he walked in he said: 'Now I know why the whole of Gerrard Street is alive with coppers.' That was my cue to make a run for it. I went outside with Mick Regan who offered to walk me down the road. As we got half-way down Gerrard Street, the Old Bill came running round the corner in line formation just like a rugby team. I managed to side-step and dodge between them and ran up towards Shaftesbury Avenue only to see more cossers looking down at me. Mick was already under arrest as he had no need to run or try to escape. Next I ducked into an alley that ran behind some Chinese restaurants right into a van blocking my exit and, before I knew it, I was surrounded by police levelling guns at me. One of the coppers was so nervous his hands were shaking. He screamed at me to put my hands up. I was handcuffed and they started walking me back towards Shaftesbury Avenue.

Even though I was handcuffed to two coppers, one of the heavy mob kept poking his gun in my back. I refused to go any further saying: 'If that cunt trips over I'll be dead with a hole in my back.' They then took me into a doorway of a shop and called for a police van. As we were waiting to be collected, Teddy Dennis and Bimbo, whom we'd left drinking in Martin's Club walked by. They were signalling an offer of help and also wanted to snatch back a telephone number Bimbo had slipped into my top jacket pocket which could have been incriminating. With so many police around, rescue was impossible so they pretended to attack me. Teddy went for me: 'That's him, the flash bastard,' and the pair starting to fight with me, pulling at me and causing panic with the coppers attached to me.

Holding my handcuffed hands up, I said: 'Go on, fuck off the pair of you.' It was a nice try to get me away but without bolt cutters it wouldn't have worked. They did manage however to retrieve the phone number. What a lovely gesture from these solid old boys. They don't come any better than Ted, Mick and Bimbo.

Mick and I were taken to Holborn police station and kept overnight. The next morning I was taken to Southampton Magistrates' Court and Tony Block, my solicitor, rode his motorbike down from London to see me.

The police charged me with importation of cannabis and I was remanded to Winchester as a Cat A prisoner. At my trial in Winchester Crown Court, my defence counsel, John Gray QC told Mr Justice Bristow that I had very little to do with the Customs incident and pleaded mitigation on my behalf. The prosecution brought up all my past involvement with the Twins and my record of ten for Jack 'The Hat' and so on. An unrecognisable photograph of me talking to Duke Osbourne and Eddy Watkins on Blackheath Common had been produced. In spite of that, the judge, a very decent and fair person, said I had suffered enough already through losing my hotel, pool table business and my home. In view of the fact that I had already spent six months in prison, he gave me a two-year suspended sentence at which I was highly delighted. I had been treated fairly for a change and I thank the judge for his consideration and leniency towards me and my family.

Because Bristow had been so fair to me I felt a bit sorry about letting him down during my two-year suspended. If you're still alive Mr Bristow, I apologise if I let you down subsequently. It's not often you get treated with such civility. While I had been in custody, Maureen and Danni had nowhere to live so I found them a flat in Bermondsey Lower Road, on the Bonhomie estate, kindly provided by a pal in the nick. It was a temporary measure as our home was still in America. They were quite happy there and had their own street door. But police smashed it in one day and brought their dogs and a team of drugs squad officers. They searched the flat and all they could come up with was a joint the size of a thumbnail. They were charged with possession of cannabis and locked in cells overnight. The following day a kind-hearted copper at Tower Bridge told Maureen and my daughter Danni that I would be sent to prison for eighteen years.

On my release from Winchester I went with Maureen and Danni to Tower Bridge Court. While all the other cases were fined £10 to £15, he fined Maureen £35 for a dog-end. I often chip her about being a junkie whenever she starts on about my life of crime.

I was given permission to return to America to sort out my financial affairs and then came back and got on with the pool table business. I also began making trips to Spain in preparation for moving there permanently. I'd had enough of England. With money from America I was able to purchase a few properties in a Spanish development called the Alcazaba.

For the first time in my life I had to report to a probation officer. She was a nice young lady with an office above Camberwell Magistrates' Court and I got on very well with her. We even invited her to a benefit party for King's College Hospital in aid of the glaucoma department where my George had been treated for years. It was held at the Frog and Nightgown pub in the Old Kent Road and we raised £2,000 for the doctors and nurses. Some years later George was standing in the far corner of the bar getting a drink for friends when he thought that a few lights had blown, making a popping sound. The barmaid had ducked down out of sight under the counter as George held out his hand for the change. By now all the other customers and band were flat on the floor and George was the only one standing. Several men had come to the pub doorway and began letting go with handguns at people behind George including amongst others, Tony and Patrick Brindle. Fortunately they missed their targets and no one was hurt. The would-be hit men legged it back down the Old Kent Road, while the firm standing behind George ran out after them, dropping to one knee, Hollywood style, and letting go with their own shooters. Afterwards they returned to finish their drinks saying to George, 'You didn't lie down, did you George?'

As he can't see very well and didn't associate the pops with bullets, he replied: 'I don't get down on my knees for no one.'

A few minutes later the governor of the pub came out of the back storeroom with a decorator's ladder, climbed up the steps with a plaster board and trowel saying: 'I've got to get out of this fucking pub,' as he spread Polyfilla over the bullet holes in the walls. South London's a funny old place.

279

· 18 ·
Security Express

Eleven years before the start of the National Lottery, a cash sum nearly equivalent to today's weekly jackpot lay in the vaults of Security Express's HQ in Curtain Road, Shoreditch. The odds of an experienced team of bank robbers walking off with the prize were 14 million times better than the average punter now has of choosing six winning numbers.

Easter came early in 1983, and with it a cold spell. The temperatures on the morning of Easter Monday (14 April) were near freezing and snow showers had sprayed a fine mist over cars and buildings. As is normal on a holiday weekend, the City of London was a ghost town. Members of the firm, some of whom were hiding behind walls and buildings in Curtain Road during the night, were alert to every sound. They were there to make the most audacious crime ever undertaken in London's square mile: to rob the HQ of Security Express, aka Fort Knox, of £7 million in cash. The redbrick complex had twelve-foot-high walls, and steel-shuttered doors. Alarms and cameras were strategically placed around the entire building and it was considered impenetrable. The next most difficult job would have been an attempt on the Crown Jewels in the Tower of London.

The firm's operation had been carefully planned. Mistakes of past robberies had been dissected, particularly the errors made in the Great Train Robbery when some palm- and fingerprints were left behind. Escape routes had been planned, vehicles assembled, safe houses prepared, and route familiarisation practised. Tools were constantly in use so they were already at hand, but strict instructions had been given that nobody gets hurt. Threatened, yes. But no physical violence. Everyone involved would wear facemasks and gloves and everything brought inside the premises would be taken away. This included cigarette butts, apple cores, and even tissue paper. No clues would be left behind for forensic examination or DNA testing.

A watch had been kept on the Curtain Road, east London premises of the country's leading security firm for several months. A rough guide to security measures taken inside the building had been given. The gaps would be filled by staff who would be persuaded to assist. This weekend the vaults would be overflowing with five tons of cash in silver and paper money. The moment for the jackpot had arrived.

The firm entered the premises like a commando operation, with five men scaling the wall and secreting themselves in the yard at strategic points around the main building and behind a parked van, next to large garbage bins where they could avoid security cameras. Patiently they waited in the cold for the door to open – they knew from undercover surveillance that it would open. The opportunity came at around 7am, shortly after guard Greg Counsell took over from the nightshift man. The gang had watched the two men arrive and depart. Unbelievably for such a large establishment, only one man was on duty! This surprised even the villains, not to mention – later on – police and other interested parties. The guard had made himself tea and walked through the compound to fetch a pint of milk left at the front gate. Thinking he was perfectly safe he left open the door to the back of the building. But to his surprise one of the firm was on him. The others raced inside the building. Two members of the firm were disguised with monkey masks and the rest wore balaclavas. All wore boiler suits and gloves and were tooled up. Counsell did the sensible thing at the point of a shotgun and cooperated. He opened the glass doors of the main reception area, allowing the firm inside the building.

With the preliminaries successfully completed, the gang now had to wait several hours for the timelock to release some of the locking mechanisms on three of the main underground vaults. After that, it would require the cooperation of several guards holding passwords and keys before the vaults could be opened. A further seven employees were due to arrive during the course of the afternoon and they would have to be taken care of one by one and cooperate fully with the firm.

The second employee to arrive that day came soon after 1pm. Counsell was told to sit at his desk and not even look at the man. 'Look down,' he was ordered. A flicker of the eye, one little mistake, and he could give away the whole game. One of the firm lay concealed under his desk poking a shotgun into his bollocks to persuade Counsell he should follow the firm's advice. Each guard was wrapped up with women's stockings and a plaster put over their mouth and by 2pm, all staff had been accounted for. The task of waiting for the staff had been long and arduous and required strong nerves. The firm could not afford to make a single mistake.

Now came the delicate task of opening the vaults without setting off alarms. When turning a lock it had to be opened in a prescribed sequence. One wrong turn and the bells would ring. Keys also had to be put into locks in the right sequence. It would require the cooperation of two members of staff, each of whom held a required key. With time on their hands, the firm were able to rehearse the lock-opening procedure with the guards to make sure they were not given wrong information. The guards were told to repeat the methods and codes over and over again. Experience had taught the firm that by separating employees first, they would tell you everything, but not while others were listening. When they'd got all the information from the employees, they were made to lie down together. If any further problems arose, the man responsible would be taken out on his own and asked to repeat codes and numbers and procedures until they got it right.

They had to employ psychology. If one of the guards had made a simple error, or lied about procedure, the whole operation would have been doomed. At one point, keys to the main vault were missing. Lighter-fluid was poured on to a guard's legs and a matchbox rattled by his ear. The firm threatened to torch him if the keys weren't found. One of the guards quickly showed us where they were hidden. Threats were made but nobody was battered. They were all well-treated and offered cigarettes and a drop of tea although the firm did eat the guard's sandwiches. Phonecalls by customers to Security Express were answered and no suspicions were aroused.

Once the vault doors were open, the firm transferred the cash, (most of it came from the Ideal Home Exhibition), to trolleys and sent them up on a lift to loading bays where a seven-ton truck was waiting. The operation to move five tons of cash had only taken about an hour. All the men jumped into the trucks save for one who operated the electronic gates to let them out. He then had a limited time in which to run to the gate before it closed on him and just managed to get through in time. By mid-afternoon the firm was driving away with the cash jackpot.

As always in these cases, known villains were immediately checked in case they had any part in the robbery. Frank Cater who had worked with Nipper Read and was now a Commander of the robbery squad worked on the case with about 60 police officers. Initially 120 officers were assigned to the case and half-a-million pounds in reward money was offered. Unlike the Great Train Robbery there had been no gossip about this job and no evidence left at the scene. The job had been carried out with textbook professionalism. Unfortunately there is one thing that villains can never guard against, and that is the possibility of someone grassing, or a gang member boasting about his role and throwing money around in such a way as to attract attention to himself, thereby endangering his colleagues. None of the chaps would ever grass or be silly. However, a man I did not know and whose background should have been researched thoroughly to see if he could be trusted, blew the whistle some time later which resulted in the arrest of John Horsley, Terence Perkins and William Hickson, and two of the Knight Brothers, John and Jimmy.

The grass, Alan Opiola, was recruited by John Knight to help count and launder some of the money. Opiola was not one of the chaps but a motor trader who was friendly with Knight. He rented a van to transport some of the money which was traced back to him. He should never have been recruited because he turned Queen's Evidence and served three years in protective custody for his treachery. John Knight and Terry Perkins, were each sentenced to twenty-two years.

It had been all too much for Opiola. He told police how he stared in disbelief when he saw the rows of banknotes, four feet high and five feet wide stretching across a bedroom floor of his Southgate house. Before he turned into a Judas, he was paid £25,000 for his help. Another part of the haul was counted at Horsley's home in Waltham Abbey, and he hid nearly half-a-million behind a panel in the wall of his father's room. Horsley also offered to grass but he changed his mind.

The police put a surveillance team on Horsley, Billy Hickson and Terry Perkins. Questioned about the other two, Horsley implicated Hickson immediately. Horsley got twelve years, Jimmy Knight eight, and Hickson got six for handling £30,000 of the money.

Detective Superintendent Peter Wilton was in charge of

enquiries and extended them to Spain and he was able to examine deposits in Spanish bank accounts and the purchase of property. Unfortunately in my case, with all the money I had coming over from America, it looked as though I had profited from the Security Express proceeds in the same way as police had suspected Ronnie Knight, who kept a high profile on the Costa Del Sol. Shortly after the police inquiries, the Madrid-based news magazine *Tiempo* wrote a well-informed six-page cover story about our lifestyles and listed properties allegedly bought with the proceeds of the Security Express robbery.

I thought it was time I left England when Johnny Knight was arrested for the robbery nine months after it had taken place. He never thought he'd be nicked and had volunteered to delay going on holiday to Portugal so the Yard could interview him. I wasn't going to take any chances. Innocent or guilty the police would have kept you locked up for months before a trial and I'd made arrangements and property purchases in Spain well before the robbery. Micky Kehoe drove me to the airport and I was away to a life of glorious freedom. All my investments were now in Spain as I had sold my house and business in America and transferred the funds over. Now I could take it easy and live off my rentals and the money I had made. All was lovely in the garden again but it was only to last an idyllic six years.

The Eagles Country Club and properties kept me busy but not to the extent that I couldn't party. Almost every day was party time in Spain. I'd go out of my house, meet a friend I knew and we'd be off to various bars drinking and enjoying ourselves. Sometimes you were out enjoying yourself so much that you didn't get back home until the next day. I felt safe in Marbella because I had done nothing wrong in Spain and had entered the country legally and there was no extradition treaty at that time which could be used against me.

Apart from my Eagles Country Club I was also vice

president of the Marbella Boxing Club which was run by Ricardo Cruz. We had a licence to put on a boxing show, Spain vs. England, and invited the Eltham, South London Boxing Club to take part. We put on the fights at the Marbella Football Stadium. It was a terrific night's entertainment which ended as a draw for the two countries and everybody enjoyed themselves. Every fight had been a cracker.

The licence we held was for only two promotions a year so we had one to go. I invited Frank Warren – his uncle Bob was a face from the old days – to come over with Ernie Fossey to promote a show at the Puerto Banus bullring.

When Frank came over, we dined at my expense with the Spanish Minister of Sport and also the Minister for Tourism at the Don Pepe hotel. We were joined by my old pals: hotelier, boxing manager and promoter Jack Tricket, Vinny Scarfo, a reputable car dealer, and Nat Busso, an MC and referee, all from Manchester, and we laid plans for a future fight venue. I didn't hear from Frank for quite a while, when out of the blue Micky Duff arrived in Marbella with his entourage and arranged a world title fight between Lloyd Honeyghan and Gene Hatcher with Frank Bruno and Gary Mason on the bill.

Scotland Yard wouldn't give up trying to get me back. Another factor which gave me occasional trouble was the fact that other villains had found the good life in southern Spain and were not prepared to keep their heads down and enjoy themselves without making their presence known. Whenever there was national publicity about anyone wanted by the British police, the spotlight would turn on me. I've already explained how once the Spanish were told about me, they'd haul me in for questioning whenever there was a major incident in Andalusia.

Efforts to extradite me continued and, when things got too hot, I would make for the hills until things cooled down again. While I cannot plead innocence I feel very strongly about the way the authorities went about the case. If you go down that road then you are on the way to a dictatorship and you expose the ordinary person in the street to the whims and prejudices of police and other authorities. There was little if any evidence against me but the British police were out to get me and they eventually succeeded, through using the press and media and getting on side with police in Spain. Only recently a judge in England threw out a case against somebody who was illegally brought back to London from Poland, to face serious charges. He said because that person was returned illegally, and against his will, it was not proper that he should face a trial. That set a precedent which should have been applied to my case.

The press in both Spain and England named us the 'Costa Crooks' and 'Famous Five'. Scotland Yard said they wanted to interview me, Ronnie Knight, Clifford Saxe, Ronald Everett and John Mason for the Security Express robbery and the £26 million Brink's Mat bullion robbery in November, 1983. Again there was no hard evidence but it planted guilt, and by repeating it often enough, which the press did, the general public could be excused for accepting it as a truth.

Spanish authorities were also affected by the Madrid magazine labelling us 'Robbers of the Century'. How can you get a fair hearing with publicity of this nature?

Apart from the problems with police we had a lot of good times with lovely people enjoying a drink with their ladies and everyone was very polite to each other. A lot of family and friends would visit from time to time and my Jamie also had a lot of showbusiness friends who came by. Recently I read some malicious account that Freddie Starr was gay. Freddie used to come to my home in the Alcazaba and to our parties and believe me, he was all man. No way was he a poof, although none of us have anything against homosexuals. I've employed lots of them over the years who are still my friends to date.

But to make a false allegation is like calling someone a grass and that makes my blood boil.

One geezer, who took a liberty and didn't know how close he came to getting a good hiding, was Roger Cook, the investigative TV reporter. I nearly obliged his masochistic streak when he buzzed my flat with a helicopter, trying to take sneak photographs of me, and later knocked on my door demanding to see me. I was on the point of going out there and clumping him but was held back by Maureen. Taking her advice I let the Alcazaba security chase him off the premises.

Spain holds many poignant memories for me, two of which involved close friends of mine. Ding Dong (Dell Rudell) was accidentally killed on the waterfront at Puerto Banus. He had been on a golfing holiday with three others in the late 70s and after a good drink at Joy's Bar on the harbour, got into his car, switched on the ignition which caused the car to lurch over the harbour wall straight into the marina. He must have left the car in gear. The other golfers got out but it was too late for Dell.

One of my saddest incidents, which was beyond belief, involved Jimmy Allen, a friend of mine for over forty years who was due to leave Britain and come over to be with our friends in Marbella. Before he was able to do so, he was murdered in a cowardly attack.

Jimmy was a millionaire who'd built up a very successful business in scrap-metal, cars, plant-hire and commercial vehicles. He loved engines and knew all about them. He was the sort of man everyone invited to their homes. He'd only been in Spain a few days and already he'd been a guest on an ocean-going yacht worth millions, talking to the owner about its engines. Whenever he came to Spain we'd meet up with him and his wife at Tony Dalli's Italian restaurant in Marbella.

They were great times. At the restaurant a piano accordionist would play his favourite tune: Neil Sedaka's 'Hungry Years' and we'd meet up with the chaps and talk about old times.

Before his death in 1986, Jimmy had sold one of his yards for more than £600,000 and had taken a cruise with his wife, leaving his son Billy in charge of the business. Billy had been the apple of his father's eye. He'd been at the scrap-metal yard since a small boy and his father spoke proudly of him at every opportunity. As far as his father was concerned he couldn't have put a foot wrong.

After their cruise, the Allens returned home to find some problems with their business. Not long after this, Mrs Allen died unexpectedly. One morning Jimmy made his wife a cup of tea, and on returning to her bedroom he discovered she'd passed away in the night. Grief-stricken, Jimmy came to Spain to convalesce.

We looked after him. Without his wife, he was a broken man. I would take him out and even spend the night at his flat talking him through his trauma. He couldn't sleep. We made the mistake of going to Dalli's and when they played 'Hungry Years', tears streamed down his face. Slowly he began to return to his old self and wanted to buy a flat in the Alcazaba.

Jimmy needed to return to England – his son Billy had sold the family house, unbeknown to him, so he'd booked into a hotel. The day after his arrival there was a knock at his hotel door. The man who stood in the doorway claimed he had had a slight prang with Jimmy's Mercedes, and could they settle the damage without going through the insurance company. Jimmy turned to the bedside table to write out his details when, without warning, he was pushed face-down on the bed and smothered with a pillow. He lost consciousness, only to be awoken by his son Billy. Billy then took his father to hospital and lied to the doctors about Jimmy's deluded state of mind.

Jimmy discharged himself a short time after and went to stay at a friend's bungalow in Essex. He was attacked again – this time fatally. His head was smashed by an iron bar while he was asleep – again his son Billy was first on the scene!

I discovered later that police had received information that I may have been involved in his death over a 'drugs deal that went wrong'. Police came to interview me: two Scotland Yard detectives flew to Spain. They told me: 'Fred, we know it's bollocks [about my involvement] but can you help us in any way?'

I told them that the bastard who did this deserved all he got and that Jimmy had been my pal for forty years. I'd like to know who killed him myself and if they found out, to drop me a line.

My son Jamie was also questioned by police because it had been alleged that he was trying to sell Jimmy's gold Rolex watch, which was entirely untrue. Jamie couldn't believe it: He said: 'Romford murder squad phoned and asked me to call by regarding the death of Jimmy Allen. They intimated I could make a few calls first, to my father for reassurance, so I spoke to several people in Spain, including my father.

'They sat me down and asked me how long I'd known Jimmy and the family. They also asked me if I had ever met anyone outside the gates of Barking cemetery at 11pm on a certain night. I didn't even know where the cemetery was let alone meet anyone there. They also asked about the watch. I told them: "Not in a million years. I'm an actor, not a fence."

'Police told me there was some talk about exhuming Mrs Allen's body but I didn't know if she had been cremated or buried.

'The police believed me. They knew our people *never* talk to police but on this occasion I'd been given the green light to talk.'

Billy was sent for trial and accused of hiring a hitman to murder his father and also for defrauding two million pounds from his father's company. Strangely, the jury was not told Jimmy had died or in fact been murdered –

only that a hitman (Anthony Smith) had been approached, but did not take up the contract. The jury found Billy, not guilty of hiring a hitman with intent, but guilty of fraud and sentenced to seven years. I still find it very difficult to accept poor Jimmy's fate and hope that one day his murderer will pay the price.

* * *

Now Spain was behind me. I was back on the plane to England. Had I been dreaming? Did all these things really happen in my life? The aeroplane shuddered as it dropped altitude. People were shaking me, telling me to sit up. I was waking up again, my head was in a fog. There was a dull pain in my wrists from the handcuffs. All the passengers got off the plane leaving me and the three Spanish coppers. Suddenly I was surrounded by four members of the robbery squad. Christ! We're back in London!

Scotland Yard's heavy mob, the robbery squad, arrested me on the plane. A skinny, young uniformed copper was with them and they asked him if he wanted to be famous. He swelled to twice his normal size as they handcuffed me to him. I looked out the window at the welcoming party. The police had been working overtime in stage-managing my return. But try telling that to a jury. Press and TV were in a wide arc waiting for me to step off the plane.

After they were satisfied the press had got their photographs, and the uniformed cosser had got his moment of glory, I was bundled into a van and sat between two fucking huge robbery squad officers. They put the uniformed copper in another van and he was jumping in and out of it directing traffic. I was then taken to Leman Street police station near Shoreditch where Henry Milner arrived out of the blue to handle my case. I awoke next morning staring at the cold sterile white-tiled walls. My back ached from the hard wooden bench. The reality of my predicament set in. I appeared at Bow

Street Magistrates' Court the next day where I was remanded in custody and sent to Brixton Prison. My life of luxury, enjoying endless days of pleasure shaded from the sun by palm trees around a swimming pool, was now a distant fantasy.

I was sent reeling back in a time capsule when they took me to Brixton. I was put in the cottage, the small wing where I'd been with the Kray brothers in 1968. It had its own little exercise yard separate from the rest of the prison. Vicky Darke, a nice boy who'd represented England in karate was there. He'd been nicked for armed robbery. Mark Rotherwell was another inmate with whom I was friendly. There was also a black guy called Ferdinand who claimed he was an ex-mercenary but was really just a sadistic killer. He had two fellows pleading for mercy on their knees in a nightclub but stabbed them both. One died, the other was saved only by the skill of a surgeon. There was a little Canadian guy we called The Bear because he was hairy all over like a teddy bear, two IRA guys, and Charlie McGhee who was in for shooting a copper and had got a recommended twenty-five years. Between us we had one bath, the same one, stains and all, which I had shared twenty years earlier with the Krays.

Charlie McGhee used the black guy's bath water out of turn but thought nothing of it. Later, while he was playing cards, Ferdinand borrowed a pair of scissors from the screw and stabbed Charlie five times in the back. 'That's for using my bath,' he said as Charlie lay bleeding on the ground. One of the chaps smashed Ferdinand over the head with a heavy wooden chair and laid him out. Ferdinand was a dangerous bastard and I later found out he used to terrorise a family I knew who owned the Red Pepper restaurant in Puerto Banus. It was owned by Chris, a good friend of mine. (I'd eat there regularly as it was the best in the port.) Both Ferdinand and Charlie McGhee were eventually transferred to Albany Prison and, some time later, the black guy found himself surrounded by the chaps on the sports field, one of whom was Charlie. Ferdinand was jerked about a dozen times and his nose was also sliced off in the knife attack. Because he was eighteen stone, his blubber saved his life. He got his just deserts for murdering innocent people.

At Brixton, both Mark Rotherwell and Vicky Darke were fitness fanatics so I used to work out with them. We had a couple of chairs and a broom handle with buckets of water for weights at each end. But for some reason, the governor stopped us from doing this harmless work-out. Mark and Vicky also used to wrap cloth bandages around their hands and spar with each other at karate. They were two great lads. I was sad when Vicky got eighteen for the armed robbery and missed his company when he was transferred. We met up again in Full Sutton. Mark was convicted of being an accessory to murder. After his release he got a job on the door at the Ministry of Sound nightclub but the newspapers did a piece on him and he was sacked. They never let you forget your sins.

When I first arrived at the cottage (the most secure wing in Brixton prison), I stepped out into the small exercise cage and was walking around on my own, a solitary figure, when I heard voices calling my name from one of the cell windows overlooking the yard. You couldn't see faces inside the cells, just a wrist and hand sticking out through the bars waving at you. I looked up to the window and asked who it was. If it wasn't two of my old pals! Tommy Wisbey and Jimmy Hussey informed me they'd just been weighed-off for a ten and seven years. We had a laugh about our situation, gave our regards to the families. Both were being moved to Parkhurst that afternoon. I said I might see them later.

About a week later, I heard a commotion early in the morning, keys rattling, doors banging, and someone was put in the empty cell next to mine. I was opened up and taken out for exercise and on my return saw this prisoner who looked very familiar. We stared at each other for a second or two, and he said: 'Is it Fred?' I pointed a finger at him: 'Gerry? Gerry Conlon!' It had been fifteen years since I had last said goodbye to him at this very same prison. He was only half-way through his sentence but had aged considerably with the amount of bird he had done. His father had died after he had served only five years of his thirty-year sentence. We gave each other a big hug to celebrate our reunion. But I had still better news for him which he wasn't aware of. 'Great news, Gerry,' I said, 'You're home on Thursday.' He couldn't believe me. I asked him who was here with him and he told me Paul Hill and Paddy Armstrong, who was in a cell down the end of our landing. I told him to get Paddy but we couldn't get Paul because he was up on the next landing. They came into my cell and sat on my bed while I made a cup of tea. He still couldn't quite believe it but said: 'Now I know why the screws have been so bloody civil to me for a change.' I told him again that the radio had said he would get one court appearance and be released. When they heard the 4pm broadcast confirming what I'd said, Gerry and Paddy leapt up from the bed and jumped up and down in the air like a footballer who'd just scored a cup-final goal. Full of emotion, the pair held each other as tears streamed down their faces. The next day they were released, and rightly so.

While I was still there awaiting trial for the Security Express robbery, I received the news of Charlie Wilson's murder in Spain. Charlie, his wife Pat and their family had been old friends for many years and I was very upset. Even more so when I read an article originating from Spain on information from a well-known conman who goes under the name of Joe Flynn. The article alleged that I had arranged Charlie Wilson's murder from my cell in Brixton over a drug deal that had gone wrong.

While writing this book, two suspects have been inter-viewed by police. One of them is in the process of being extradited to Spain from Britain where he is serving a prison sentence. Another suspect has been shot in the back. The man who put the contract on Charlie, Roy Adkins, was shot dead in Holland. Adkins's close friend Micky Blackmore went to Holland on his release from Maidstone to reclaim Adkins's money was also shot dead.

In the meantime, I have not forgiven this mongrel dog Flynn for getting money by causing distress to Charlie's wife Pat and other members of her family as well as my own. Maureen and Pat had been very good friends as well and this cast a slur on all of us. Pat Wilson immediately issued a strong denial, saying the article was completely untrue and that I was a personal friend of Charlie and his family and that this was a malicious article written by someone unscrupulous enough to cash in on lies. In her words: 'Freddie was a friend of the family and a complete gentleman.'

I'll never forgive that bastard for causing so much upset to a grieving widow in an extremely turbulent and tragic time and I hope I run into him one day. In the meantime if any of my friends would like to say a little word in his ear to explain to him where he went wrong, I would be eternally grateful.*

*NEWSPAPER REPORT – Duncan Campbell, *The Guardian*, 26 March, 1997:

'The man widely believed to have killed great train robber Charlie Wilson seven years ago has himself been shot dead . . . the Roff killing was the latest in a feud that began on 23 April, 1990 when a tall young man on a mountain bike arrived at Wilson's home near Marbella in Spain, shot him twice and fled, probably with the help of a getaway driver. Wilson's cousin, Norman Radford, said then: "Charlie's death has upset a lot of big names out here. They are not happy men." Roff, from a south London criminal family, escaped in May 1988 with two other prisoners described by Scotland Yard as "dangerous and potentially violent" after over-powering their guards on a prison coach in Essex en route from Albany prison on the Isle of Wight to Blunderston in Suffolk. One of his co-escapers, William Edmonds, was also questioned about the Wilson killing.'

· 19 ·
Farewell to Arms

In normal circumstances, the case against me for the Security Express robbery would never have come to court. The evidence was too flimsy. The prosecution case depended on the alleged confession to Spanish police, a defunct bank account holding £75, and deposits of money whose source they could not prove. A damning scenario for defendants is when armed guards are put around prison vans bringing you to the Old Bailey. What must a jury think when they see television and press photographs of police sharpshooters? A steady build-up of articles about my friendship with the Krays and my past convictions and even acquittals were other factors which must have influenced the jurors. Then, at the trial itself, police told the press how: 'A tight security net was thrown around the Old Bailey . . . and jurors will be guarded by police throughout the five-week trial.' One juror was taken off the case because of claims of 'nobbling'. We certainly didn't do any jury 'nobbling'.

My crime was more to do with upsetting the establishment who are much more concerned about property than they are about human suffering. Laws were made to protect the wealth of the rich, to keep the world safe for millionaires. I was a professional and honest thief who represented a threat to them and that is why they've always tried to put me away and keep me inside for the whole term of my sentence.

I don't blame them, but I am fully aware of what the press can do. They all have their connections with police officers and get their stories from coppers who feed them little titbits of information. It's been that way ever since I can remember. I know that police computers would have been alerted each time the parole board sat to review my case and sure enough, as regular as clockwork, there would be a rehash of an old and damaging story about me in the newspapers and bang would go any chance of parole. So I never held my breath when it came around.

By comparison with other crimes, my nine-year sentence for handling money from the Security Express was harsh. No one was hurt or injured, no poor people suffered. Women and children were not molested or hurt. No old lady was robbed of her life savings by some unscrupulous solicitor or conman, yet I was made to serve nearly all my sentence. Why? Because I hurt the establishment who have shares in companies like Security Express and in the insurance companies who had to pay out.

That's why I received nine years. Violent rapists and sex offenders have got much less. Other prisoners sentenced to ten and twelve years were all out on parole while I was still serving my nine. With such inequality I am surprised that the authorities can't comprehend the anger and bitterness of so many prisoners. One of the reasons I have written this book is to counteract the number of misleading stories about me in the past. I want to set the record straight.

My trial opened at the Old Bailey in March 1990. I was charged with robbing security guard James Allcock of £6 million, receiving stolen cash of £363,280 and using a false name to obtain a passport. One of the first prosecution witnesses was Captain Domingo de Guzman of the Guardia Civil who had spoken to me in Marbella in November 1988 through an interpreter. My Spanish lawyer Mrs Susana Fernandes, who was present at the meeting with Guzman, testified at my trial that I had *not* made a statement, as the Spanish police had alleged. Michael Worsley QC, the prosecutor, admitted to the court that my guilt hinged on the 'alleged confession' and the fact that I 'suddenly came into an enormous amount of money'. All Scotland Yard's heavy mob knew me to be someone who does not talk to police or make statements. To do so in Spain would have been suicide as I was fighting extradition proceedings at the time. The prosecution also knew that I was not skint because of the money I had from America, and although I deposited large sums in the Allied Irish Bank in London, the source of this money could never be proven.

While awaiting trial my Jamie went on his toes to Spain because police wanted to arrest him simply because he'd deposited money into my account. Until that time, Jamie had been working regularly on TV and for commercials so now it meant that while I was awaiting trial he couldn't get acting jobs in Britain. The day after Maureen's visit to me at Brixton prison, police burst into my son Gregory's home at 5am demanding to know where his mother was. Fortunately, he didn't know where she was as she'd booked into an hotel. But we had to get her out of the country because they wanted to arrest her, too, in connection with the robbery.

On 4 April, 1990, exactly seven years to the day after the event, I was found not guilty of the robbery but the jury found me guilty of handling the cash and of the passport charge. The next day Judge Stephen Mitchell QC passed sentence. He jailed me for nine years for handling, a further nine months concurrent for the passport charge, and a concurrent year's prison for breaching my two-year suspended sentence at the Winchester trial. The judge told me: 'I disregard the fact that, due to your resourcefulness, you were able to escape justice for so long and were able to enjoy a life of relative ease and security in Spain.' As if that wasn't enough, police were reported in the press as saying that they had received a tip-off that I'd offered £1 million to the underworld to spring me!

At my appeal, where I had been led to believe we

would win because of the weaknesses in the prosecution's case, I was handcuffed between two large officers and led into court in front of all the appeal court judges. My barrister John Matthews QC argued that I should not have been charged with both offences: robbery and receiving: and as I had been acquitted of robbery, it followed that I should also have been acquitted of the receiving charge. The court deferred judgement, sending me back to Full Sutton to await their verdict. It took them about a month to search the law books for a precedent, which they found in a remote case in Hong Kong, rejecting my appeal on 12 March, 1991.

Theft and handling—alternative counts
FOREMAN [1991] Crim.L.R. 702, C.A., No.90/ 2141/S
The appellant was charged with robbery (the Crown's primary case) and, in the alternative, with handling (by receiving) proceeds of the robbery. The jury were directed to consider the robbery count first and to consider handling only if they reached a verdict of not guilty of robbery. They acquitted of robbery and convicted of handling. The conviction was upheld. The acquittal of robbery meant that the appellant was innocent of that charge: applying *Att.Gen. of Hong Kong* v. *Yip Kai-foon* [1988] A.C. 642 It mattered not that the jury may have reached their conclusion because they were sure that the appellant was not a robber, or were not sure that he was, or somewhere in between. Where there are alternative counts of theft and receiving the Crown do not have to make the jury sure that it was not a case of theft before there can be a conviction of receiving.

Archbold News, 27 September, 1991

They had to go all the way to Hong Kong and dig up some poor fucking Chinaman to blank my appeal!
In the first week of December 1991, the Tribunal

Supremo (Supreme Court) in Malaga, Spain, confirmed
the decision of the Sala de Lo Contencioso. Adminis-
trativo of the Tribunal Superior de Justicia of Andalucia,
overruled my deportation by the civil governor Francisco
Rodriguez Caracuel. After everything that happened they
now confirmed I was wrongly expelled from the country.
The Spanish High Court said my extradition: 'Does not
abide by the rules of the Judicial Order' and 'overrules the
extradition of one accused in the "Robbery of the
Century", ordered by the Governor.' My solicitor J.
Carlos Ramirez accused the Spanish police and Governor
of 'kidnapping, torture, and illegal deportation', and insti-
tuted a lawsuit against them which is still going on.

After my trial in Britain, I was sent to the familiar surroundings of Wandsworth Prison and met up with my
old pals Tommy Wisbey, Patsy Sullivan and Dogan Arif.
I used to have pool tables in the Arifs' clubs and drank
at the Connoisseur, their place in the Old Kent Road.
Dogan was doing a ten for drugs. He'd been wrongly
convicted of the charge, having been the victim of a mis-
taken identity, but stuck to our code by not revealing
who the other person was. When we were together at
Wandsworth, I questioned him one morning about a
scratching noise during the night and asked him if he was
trying to dig his way out. Perhaps it was a black guy
between our cells trying to escape, he suggested. We
couldn't question him outright as it was none of our
business so I had another restless night listening to this
scratching sound. This went on for about a week until I
spotted the cause. A large sewer rat managed to squeeze
under the cell door and gamely waited only a few feet
away ready to snatch the left-overs from my food tray.
We looked at each other and finally he panicked first,
eventually finding a gap through which he could wiggle
his fat little arse through and escape. I then plugged the
gap with my towel. He never visited me again. Later I
was moved from Wandsworth to Full Sutton where I met

Mehmet, another member of the Arif family, who was doing an eighteen-year sentence for armed robbery.

In April 1991, Maureen visited me there and wanted to stay at a local hotel for a week so she could make multiple visits. She was then a woman of sixty. In spite of that, she was arrested in connection with the Security Express robbery. The police took her to London and put her in the cells for the night.

It was disgusting because they left her in limbo for over a year while they were deciding whether to charge her with handling the proceeds of Security Express. At the end of the day they never charged her. None of this helped our relationship in difficult times.

While in prison and since, I have undergone terrible feelings of guilt and conflict over Maureen. Guilt because after all these years of being with her, I left my wife, and this subconsciously affected me in my dealings with other people. I knew what the problem was. I felt that people would no longer respect me after walking out on her. It also affected my self-esteem and made it difficult to cope. I was looking to find reasons to punish innocent people to assuage my own guilt and to destroy any relationship and chance of happiness because I felt I had lost the one thing that I had strived for all my life – respect.

I hurt the one I loved in order to destroy what we had together because I stopped respecting myself. I was looking at ways of punishing myself by trying to end a relationship with a lovely person whom I love very much. At the same time, I tried my hardest to make Maureen and the family come to terms with what I had done and to reassure them that I still loved and cared for them. Inside, I was hurting as much as they were but I had made my choice of whom I wanted to live with. If your heart is with someone else you will drive those around you nuts and be a pain in the arse.

I can't live a lie. I have only a certain number of years left to live and I feel it's only the beginning of a new phase in my life. I'm still reasonably fit and well and not ready for the pipe and slippers. The grandfather bit is all right and I like to be Poppa Fred to my five grandsons and see them as much as possible. But it takes time to adjust. I was on my own a long time and Maureen and I spent many years apart. She was obviously looking forward to my return and starting life again but I just couldn't face life as it was before I went in for my last stretch. I had to change direction and then fate stepped in at the right time when I was in Spain and met Janice. We had no control over the situation. She changed my life and I haven't regretted one single day of it because she has made me extremely happy in every way possible and has stayed loyal and solid by my side since we first met.

After two years of being a Double A category prisoner I was decategorized and sent to Maidstone (back to slopping out again). I had been in prison since August '89, my first parole was due around June '93 when, as I expected, something would happen to jeopardise it. Sure enough, an article appeared in the *Sun* newspaper stating that the murder squad were about to interview me in Maidstone Prison regarding the shooting of three men. A few days later the police from Ruislip murder squad arrived. One of the coppers was named Dave Thomas. They were very polite and did their interview in a civilised manner, obviously knowing that these three shootings had fuck all to do with me. The first name they put to me was Roger (the growler) Wilson, Tommy Roche and a chap named Don Urquhart. It was said that he was a friend of mine and was seen frequently in my company. To be honest, he may have been in my company while having a drink at the Eagles Country Club with about 300 other people, but I had most definitely no business interests with either him or Tommy Roche. In my experience I knew that time would tell and that these three murders would be totally unconnected. Subsequently, I have been proved right. At the time I took it in my stride – they were just going through the process of elimination – and with my reputation, my name was always going to be stuck up. So I never held my breath, as I had never been allowed early parole before, why should this time be any different?

When I arrived at Maidstone, who was the first one there to greet me? Reggie Kray – with a handful of phone cards and a box of chocolates. We hadn't clapped eyes on each other since 1970, when we were together in Leicester special wing. We were both very excited at seeing each other after so many years. I thought when I looked at him of all the years that had past, all the experiences and adventures I had on the outside and all of those years Reggie had been locked away. It made me very sad. It was an emotional reunion. Later that same day I met up with Terry Perkins who'd been kicked out of Blantyre House Prison in Kent and moved back to Maidstone. Poor bastard, he'd been jailed for 22 years for the Security Express robbery, the very same robbery that I had been acquitted of. He was near to the end of his sentence and about to be moved to Latchmere House which is supposed to be the flagship of the British penal system. Everyone wants to get there at the end of their bird.

Unlike some prisons. At Blantyre House Prison, for instance, prisoners were expected to engage in some very odd practices. The governor encouraged grown men to do the Hokey Cokey holding hands with screws. I mean to say! And if you weren't prepared to accept the 'Blantyre House Attitude' you were out on your ear to another prison. They would never accept me, thank God!

Britain's flagship prison – Latchmere – did not impress me either. While I was there, they prevented me from attending the funeral of Buster Edwards, even though he was like family to me. Nevertheless I was allowed out to work five-days-a-week, returning to the prison at night.

I already had guilt feelings, as no doubt most readers of this book will have had when someone they love dies and you didn't find the time to visit them before. I drove by Waterloo Station when Buster was still alive without stopping to see him. It was always so difficult to park there. But why didn't I take the trouble to stop and speak to him for just a few minutes? Maybe I would have realised he had a problem and was depressed and managed to do something about it. Unfortunately I was still at Latchmere and on my outside work duties. I had to return to prison each night so every minute of the day was accounted for. Yet, if only I had made that extra effort I wonder if he would still have been alive today. He was the godfather of my children and I was godfather to his children. Such are the guilt feelings we all have when someone is gone and it's too late to put right.

Governor O'Neill of Latchmere House got me to sign a letter saying I would not attend Buster's funeral while I was out on the work scheme. All my family were there and it was my Jamie who read the eulogy, not Roy James's son as was reported. Everyone praised Jamie on his oration and for his tribute to our dear old friend Buster. Prison authorities must think we are made of stone. But we are all very ordinary humans with the same feelings as everybody else. In Maidstone Prison, like many others, we raised money for charity. Here we helped a little girl called Chelsea get an operation, so none of us was without compassion. In all the prisoners raised about £700 from their meagre wages (£4 per week).

The excuse given by the authorities for refusing me permission to attend Buster's funeral was that they did not want to attract publicity. However, unknown to the authorities, I still went to the flower pitch and paid my respects. That was on the day of the funeral. I mingled with the crowds and waited for his procession to come through Waterloo. I watched my family drive by in the cortege and felt unbelievably sad that I couldn't be with them.

A little later, I was on the receiving end of a further injustice at Latchmere which made me very angry. In preparation for my release in May I was still on outside work duties. These involved collecting money for a cash-and-carry firm called Bootleggers and delivering it to them the following day. One night I came back to the cells with my collection which amounted to nearly £400. There was a search of the cells and they slung me out for breeching the prison charter by having too much money, even though they had authorised my job!

With only five months left to serve, I was shipped out to Wayland in Norfolk, a big security prison, so now I was back to square one. Fortunately for me a warder serving at Norfolk, PO Clitheroe, knew me from years before and kindly arranged for my transfer back down south. PO Gibson from Springhill, my old prison in Hertfordshire, kindly offered to accept me from Wayland Prison but the governor would not have me back. Was it because of my birthday party where the boys presented me with a cake in the shape of a Security Express van?

Mr Clitheroe then phoned Janet Wallsgrove, assistant governor to Mr Jones at Maidstone who readily accepted me. They are the most humanitarian governors I have met in the prison system. I should have got parole like everyone else but didn't. It will take me a long time to forget the woman responsible for sending me to Wayland. She grounded me for two weeks as my punishment which I accepted as a man. But at the end of the two weeks, she shipped me out in handcuffs to Wayland Prison in deepest Norfolk and informed the parole board of her actions. They later refused my parole.

On St Patrick's Day, 17 March, 1995, I was standing outside my cell door in Maidstone prison when I heard a con say that Ronnie Kray had died. It came as a shock to me as I was only talking to Reggie the day before and Ronnie had sent his regards to Joe Martin and myself. Also Reggie had phoned Ronnie every day and there was not the slightest hint of any danger. When Reggie had asked him about his condition, Ronnie said: 'Hang on a minute, I'll call the doctor.' Ronnie was more concerned about the £50 in stamps that he owed Reggie and said that he would send them on to him as soon as he could, so no one suspected what was to happen.

I asked to be taken over to Reggie's wing and comfort him in his hour of need. It was an emotional time for Reggie, Joe and myself. As soon as Reggie saw me, he burst into tears and I hugged and comforted him as best I could. He asked me to be a pallbearer which I said would be a privilege. We'd had a long friendship that stretched over more than forty years. A lot of water had passed under the bridge since then.

A jug of green hooch appeared from nowhere (after all, it was St Patrick's Day). In sad situations like these, a drink helps a great deal. I said: 'Just think about it Reg. Ronnie knew on what day to go. All the chaps up and down the country will be in pubs and clubs saying, "Cheers Ron, you're at peace now. No more troubles or worries."' I told Reggie that he must be strong and survive and carry on with life and live for both of them because as long as he lives, they will not be forgotten.

I stayed with him all day. Governor Jones was coming over to see us after lunch so Joe and I were able to stay with Reggie over the bang up. The chaps kept us happy with more jugs of the green stuff and believe me, it was needed. Reggie would show us a catalogue of some watches and point out one he had ordered for Ronnie. It was a very sad day. I shall never forget how every minute there was a gentle knock on the cell door and another con would come in and pay his respects and then leave us alone.

After lunch – we were not hungry but sandwiches came by the plateful: tuna, ham and more green stuff. We three huddled together, talking about old times. How funny Ronnie could be without knowing it.

Governor Jones called us all down for a chat. He is a good man who was always helpful and understanding. He asked us how he could help. I was a little angry and told him: 'It's a bit late now, Governor. Reg needed help a few days ago when his brother was taken ill and he needed arrangements to visit Ron.' Reg was told that Ron had an ulcer and no one dies of an ulcer in this day and age. We can't accept the cause of death, nor the way Reg heard it – from another con who was listening to the radio. His brother Charlie saw it on TV and I said it was a common courtesy for families of hospital deaths or car accident victims to be informed first, but not the families of prisoners. I have seen dozens of prisoners get visits from the vicar or a governor to break bad news, but never such a disgraceful lack of sensitivity or compassion to a man who has lost his twin brother. When Reggie was allowed to visit Ron at Broadmoor, even after twenty-seven years they were like Cat A visits. When Reggie visited Ron at Broadmoor, they still had two screws outside an open cell door whereas all the sex offenders, rapists, child molesters and murderers had open room visits. Because the visits were so bad, Reggie hadn't been down to see Ronnie for several months, so there was more guilt there. They had found the visits too upsetting for each of them as Reg had received a three-year parole knockback.

I asked the governor if the truth could be told regarding the way Reggie and his family and friends found out that Ronnie had died, which he agreed to do. I saw his statement and we were all satisfied with his report. He also said he would try and organise for me and Joe to attend the funeral but would have to confirm this with the number one governor and get his agreement. I was told that higher authorities had refused permission for me to attend the funeral even though I had only two months left to serve of a nine-year sentence. They said it would attract adverse publicity. Reggie wanted me to be a pallbearer but even then the authorities would only allow me to go in handcuffs, the same as Reggie. 'How the fuck am I able to carry a coffin while handcuffed to a screw?' I asked. I told governor Jones they must be joking and that this was going to cause serious problems in the nick. Mr Jones contacted the parole board and talked them into the only sensible solution left: to give me two months' parole. Hardly a large concession.

The Ronnie Kray funeral was held at St Matthew's Church, St Matthew's Row. A few doors up from the Carpenter's Arms, the pub once owned by the Krays, and the corner of many memories.

When we buried Ron, we buried my past.

· 20 ·
Show Some Respect

Since my release from Maidstone in March 1995 I have been kept very busy writing and promoting my book, meeting and talking with old friends, and slowly getting back into the London scene. Since the episode with Duke Osbourne and 'Scatty' Eddie Watkins in 1978 which preceded my three-year exodus to America I had only spent one year in London. Then in 1983, the year of the Security Express robbery, it was a case of 'on my toes again'. At the age of fifty-two, I moved the family to Spain where I spent the next seven years until my 'kidnap'. The consequence of this abrupt departure, was a trial and a nine-year prison sentence. When I look back over the last 18 years, I realise now how little time I have actually spent on the streets of London. After getting the feel again of moving around my home town, my conclusions are that although there is a lot of money being pumped into commerical business and different enterprises, the poor are still poor and the amount of homeless people on our streets is a disgrace. Even after all the hardships we suffered during and after the war years I have never witnessed such poverty and desperation. People, especially the young, needs a sense of achievement to give them a feeling of self-worth. I don't see that in the vacant eyes of these poor kids forced to sleep in shop doorways.

From the slow monotony of prison life, where you are conscious of every minute of time, once out in the free world all the clocks and events seem to increase at a rapid pace: the Grand National, Boat Race, Cup Final, Christmas, where did the year go? Prison is like a time capsule; you come home and still think and live in the past. The pubs we used to go to have been pulled down – in fact whole areas have been demolished and turned into supermarkets. A short-cut turns into a dead end and I'm constantly having to rely on the A-Z to get me out of trouble. You just don't know where the fuck you are.

When you get released you think all your troubles are over and the future looks great. But you don't know what destiny holds. This has been especially brought home to me recently by the dramatic events which led to the death of four men I served time with. Prison has a way of bonding friendships when men and women are sharing hardship, pain and sorrow – it brings us all closer together. So when you hear of a tragedy involving one of your old friends, it hurts inside. One such event was the shooting of Lionel Jeffries.

Lionel was a very enterprising little fellow; we used to call him Hiram Holliday as he looked like a Jewish bank clerk. In May 1987, Lionel, John Queen and Bobby Knapp hijacked a Post Office security van. They transferred 17 bags of money to their getaway car. They'd stolen £1,000,000. Unfortunately, sometime later, all of them were arrested and sentenced to fourteen years. But they did their bird like men; proper people; three of the chaps.

Lionel was already at Springhill with Micky Reilly and Pat O'Sullivan when they got the news on the prison grapevine that I was arriving on the Friday from Maidstone. So being that they were already ensconced in the top huts, otherwise known as 'Park Lane' (two beds in a small room the size of a broom cupboard), they organised that for a 'niffty' (£50) to another prisoner – who was out within a few months – he would vacate his place, moving down the hill to 'The Bronx'. The Bronx was not exactly what you'd call a 'des res' – in fact it was old 1942 airforce huts; 12 beds separated by a curtain with a small cupboard. Even though I'd still been pissing in a bucket at Maidstone, it was in my own cell and there's a lot to be said for one's own privacy. Unaware of the arrangements that Lionel, Mick and Pat had made for me, I was totally amazed at the reception I got. On my arrival, I was confronted with the governor, and Chief PO threatening to put me on the first bus straight back to Maidstone for bribing and forcing a prisoner to vacate his hut! Obviously the guy had got a pull and spilled the beans so to speak. So despite their efforts I still had to spend the next three months down in The Bronx until a place was found in Park Lane.

Anyway, we were all on the garden party: Lionel, Mick Reilly, Pat O'Sullivan, Dave Bullen and myself. After a back-aching week of hard but satisfying work, planting beds of daisies and pansies in front of the big house that was the main administration block of the prison, we all stood back to admire our work – the pansy beds looked really lovely. Then disaster struck. The next day Lionel came rushing into the hut frothing at the mouth, 'Someone's ripped up all our pansy beds!' This was a case of life and death. Several accusations were thrown about, old arguments and enemies dissected. Who could, or would, do such a terrible thing, to us of all people? Lionel came to the final conclusion, 'It's a certain team down at The Bronx . . . Get the tools out!' (He could be a vicious little bastard when put out.) Then along came the garden screw, surveying the scene of devastation, noting our angry faces and clenched fists. 'Those fucking sheep have got through the fence again!' Not being country boys, we hadn't noticed the little round balls of black shit lying around the pansy beds for all to see. The evidence being obvious, the case was closed. So our next job was mending the fence at the bottom of the field. Meanwhile, Lionel threw stones at the sheep. It's amazing how every little incident in prison can be magnified out of all proportion.

Lionel Jeffries had always had a good name, was a stand-up guy, and honourable where business was concerned. He was always a good money-getter and had plenty of bottle. Unfortunately on his release he started to move around in dangerous circles. If he got in trouble with money, then I'm sure he would pay it back. But I'm afraid time ran out for Lionel. When he went on a meet to talk to those involved, he was blasted to death by two black guys on a motorcycle in Kensington High Street. Whatever the reasons are, or were, I think in his case the people overreacted. They could have given Lionel more time to settle his debt – he did his bird like a man and had never fucked anyone for money as far as I knew. And to be shot down by two imports from Jamaica is an insult to the name of most London ex and present criminals, who do their own business, not hiring Yardies to do their dirty work. It leaves a bad taste in the mouth. A large number of chaps are not too happy about what happened to Lionel. It may sound strange to the average man in the street. But the chaps always gained respect, and took a certain amount of pride in putting their own liberty at risk when settling an old score. Lionel did not deserve to die by the hand of two black men, who leg it back to Jamaica after the dirty deed is done.

Back at Springhill, Micky Reilly, who had been fitted up by drug officers to a ten-year sentence, fought his case for two years and eventually won it at the appeal court. Pat Sullivan got parole and Dave Bullen went to Latchmere. I followed Dave after a few months. But during my stay at Springhill there were a number of other prisoners due for release. One was a good friend of mine, Micky Williams, but I will tell you about him later.

Another was Laurence Gibbons. I had known Laurence for many years and did bird with him at Full Sutton and Maidstone. He got ten years for a drugs offence. It took four years before his appeal and acquittal. So eventually, like Micky Reilly, he too walked out a free man. A car dealer by trade, on his release Laurence left London to start a new car site in the coastal town of Margate. He had acquired a partner by the name of Richard Hilton, a face from that area. The car front was large, specialising in American motors and expensive models such as Rolls-Royces and Mercedes. They had even ventured into a gold and jewellery shop business together. Everything in Laurence's garden was rosy, until 'when that old wind blew in the seeds of weeds and all was ugliness' (an old Chinese proverb).

On the fatal night Laurence and Hilton had been drinking heavily and a silly row started. Laurence challenged Hilton to a 'straightener' outside the house where they had both been living with their families. Laurence led the way, But Hilton didn't fancy his chances. So he took hold of a *Crocodile Dundee* knife from above the mantelpiece, just to give himself an edge so to speak, and stabbed Laurence in the back and stomach several times. Then, realising what he'd done, he helped Laurence into his own Roller, drove to the nearest hospital, dumping him outside and doing a runner.

Hilton later gave himself up to the local police and was eventually charged with manslaughter after two trials, the first being stopped when Hilton sacked his defence team and the judge awarded him a new trial. He got himself acquitted on a case of self-defence. So it was a very good result for Hilton, but not for Laurence or his wife Julie and their two kids, Amy and Danny. If it was an accident, between two business partners, why didn't Hilton do the right thing, and see that Laurence's loved ones were provided for? As it stands, he took Laurence's life and all his assets, leaving the family nothing.

Back to my old mate, Micky Williams. Micky had been thrown out of Springhill when I met up with him in Maidstone. He was a lovely man, kind and generous, big and strong (about 18 stone, 6ft 2in), with a very happy disposition and an extremely infectious laugh. After his

313

release, Mick made a bit of money and was doing OK. He had a nice flat just off Westbourne Grove, and also a penthouse apartment in Majorca where he spent a few winter months of each year. All was fine and beautiful in his garden until, when getting out of his car one night, he was surrounded by three black muggers. They were after his Rolex watch. Two attacked him from the front but Mick put up a fight and was holding his own. Then a third mugger came in low from behind, grabbing both of Micky's legs in a bear hug. Mick was pitched off balance, and he went crashing face down, bouncing on the pavement. All three of his attackers then sat on his back, tearing the watch from his wrist, then ran off with Mick chasing after them. But Mick wasn't built for speed. Exhausted from the effort of fighting all three of them, Mick didn't know the damage that had been done to himself. Apparently, he had torn the main vein (aorta) to his heart: a result of the whiplash action of crashing face-down. He didn't know how serious this injury was, and thought it was just bruising. I went to see him, and we tried to find these muggers, but with no luck.

Mick decided to have a few weeks' holiday in his penthouse in Majorca. But after only a few days he had to return home. He was feeling really rough. Although he didn't know it at the time, his torn vein was leaking out blood internally. Back in London, he went straight to the Wellington Hospital in St John's Wood, where on examination the doctors operated immediately, cutting him open from chest to abdomen, and leaving a scar similar to a zipped-up track suit.

My first visit to see Mick gave me a terrible shock. He had lost four stone and looked dreadful. I said: 'Just wait until you get well mate and we'll go and find those bastards who did this to you.' So Micky went back to Majorca to rebuild his strength. Then, out of the blue, I received a phone call, informing me that Micky had a heart attack while he sat on his settee watching a video.

He was dead – it was over very quick. I rang his old number to speak to his wife, but there was Micky's voice: 'Sorry we're not in but if you would like to leave your name and number we will get right back to you. Now would you get off the line there's a train coming, ha ha ha.' That oh-so-familiar laugh. It made my eyes fill and a lump come to my throat. I had got his answerphone. It almost brought me to tears, but instead my feelings turned to anger. Those three muggers had took a man's life away for a poxy watch. A good man who was worth more than those three put together.

I was moved to Latchmere House, the flagship of the penal system. After several months of community service you are allowed out on licence to work during the day and return to your cell to be locked up at night. For this privilege you're deducted £40 per week out of your earnings. Here I met many old friends that I had spent time with during my travels from prison to prison. It's the same for most prisoners serving long sentences. We all have to take the same route and gradually get closer to the gate and freedom. One such chap was Dave Ewing. He was a lot younger than myself, but we had met up over the years, never on the out, only in different prisons. Dave was a nice kid and I liked his politeness and respect. I would often loan him a score to go to work with, and he always paid me back. Which was more than a lot of other guys did. Dave had suffered since he was a young man. When his father got ten years, they gave Dave a three-year borstal. From then on he went down that slippery slope; one conviction after the next. Another factor that didn't help, and I know affected Dave a great deal, was what happened one night when he was asleep in the bedroom of his council house. A fire started. In the house were Dave, his mother and two little girls, his sister and niece. While Dave was helping his mother to safety, by climbing out the upstairs window and dropping to the ground, along came his father who rushed into the house and carried one of the little girls out. Then against firemen's and neighbours' advice, his father ran back in for the other child. This time he never came out. When the fire was extinguished and the smoke cleared, they found Dave's father at the top of the landing, still cradling the little girl in his arms. Both were dead. Although Dave's father had a criminal record and was looked on by society as a bad person, he was a man, and a brave man at that. He risked his own life to save two little girls and paid the price. But unfortunately that was not to be the end of the suffering for this poor family.

While in Latchmere, Dave got a job as a motorbike courier. He was over the moon. He had all the leathers, and most importantly for him, something he'd never owned before, a driving licence! In fact he was so proud of it he kept getting it out and showing it off to everyone. He saw this job as his last big chance to really make a go of things on his release. It was great to see him so happy and determined to turn his life around. So you can imagine the shock I got when I learned that for some unexplained reason his life was snuffed out as he left an off-licence after buying himself a six pack. He had been shot in the chest by a police officer from an armed response unit. The officer responsible has been charged with murder and anything I write or say now would be *sub judice*. However, although it's the first time I have known a police officer to be actually charged with murder while on duty, I fully expect it to be another whitewash. It will be very interesting to see, and I hope to give you the result of the episode before the end of this book.

I have been asked many times: 'What makes a young man, or a not-so-young man do the things that I have done?' I said at the beginning of this book that it was my craving for respect. But as well as demanding respect, I believe that I have always shown respect to those who deserve it. This is one of the reasons that I felt compelled to add this new chapter to my book. Because it seems to me that no one is showing respect for anyone else these days. You may find this a bit ironic coming from a man like me, who has admitted to doing the things I have done. But I have never heard before of young boys raping girls in the playground, stabbing their teachers, beating up their mothers and fathers. What the fuck is going on?

In my youth we stole to put things into our homes to make things comfortable for all the family, not by carrying the TV out the back door to sell for drugs. Modern criminals are shooting each other at the drop of a hat, not even one at a time; it's like a shooting gallery. And it's not only criminals. What sort of message is society sending out? When an armed police officer can shoot an unarmed man, on suspicion of nicking a car, human life counts for fuck all. I really think there should be a real change in direction. Whatever the government has been doing to this country for the last eighteen years, I tell you now it's not working. People can't see the wood for the trees. Their civil liberties are gradually being taken away. And what amazes me more is that the British people are standing for it. The unions have been crushed, there is no platform from which people can speak up and demand better conditions, better wages, better housing. I haven't noticed any new homes for the poor – for private enterprise, oh yes, for those who can afford it. I have to admit that I have never been interested in politics before. I always got my own living the best way I could, regardless of which government was in power. But now I find myself becoming a socialist. I truly believe there can be a better future for all of us who live in this country, and I hope that the next generation will teach their young the real meaning of respect.

Perhaps it's the wisdom of age or just self-preservation, but there comes a time when you feel you have no more time to give them, when you focus on your existence and realise how precious and fragile your life and liberty is. I've lived all my life hard and fast, and have paid the consequences for that. I make no excuses for what I have done or ask anyone to condone it. If I'm honest, in looking back, I would probably do the same things all over again. When you have to put bread on the table, drastic times call for drastic measures. As my old pal Alfie Gerrard used to say when the firm came up with problems, 'There's nothing a few grand won't cure.' And he was right. If one of the chaps had a touch, everybody shared in his good fortune; the old, the young, family and friends. The pubs, clubs, and with a few of them, the bookmakers too! There's no feeling to compare with being able to pay all your bills, treat the family, book a nice holiday in the sun, and walk down the street with a spring in your step, your hand in your pocket feeling a wad of notes: a feeling of elation inspired by your own achievement and self-worth. It's like winning the lottery and being released from prison all at the same time.

When the chaps went to work we didn't go out with the intention of harming any member of the public. The less violence used, the better. In most cases we were gone with the money before they knew it. I must admit that some people had a few traumatic hours while being wrapped up. But I can't remember any staff or workers going to hospital for treatment. Several coppers, yes, but that's their job. That's what they got paid for.

In the criminal world, as one old score is settled, new grievances arise. New people are arrested as old prisoners are released. It's a neverending vicious circle. As far as I can remember it's always been that way and it will never change. Like the landscape, the London crime scene is constantly changing. The armed robber has been wiped out, the 'jump-up' is a thing of the past, TCs (traveller's cheques) and 'carding up' have been made so difficult with all the new technology that people won't take the risk. It seems that the only game in town is the drug scene. It's like America in the 20s when they introduced prohibition – the more you make something hard to get, the more people want it. Then it's a case of supply and demand. I noted in the *Times* recently that last year Rizla, the cigarette-paper manufacturers, trebled their profits. Now you can't tell me that more people are smoking Shag or Old Holborn. It's just that more people, young and old, are rolling a joint. If they want it, let them have it, and make it legal. To lock people in a cell, and dish out all these horrendous sentences for petty drug-related crimes will be looked on by future generations as inhumane. Comparable with sending a young pickpocket to Australia for stealing a handkerchief or loaf of bread. Some people will always have addictive personalities. If drug users are not strong enough to break the habit, help them. Treat them the same as you would with any illness. It will only run its course when each individual educates him or herself, because knowledge is the only way to progress. However, hard drugs are a totally different ball game.

The drug scene is unlike any other illegal occupation, and to any young criminal who is contemplating a dabble in this type of enterprise – think hard. There are big profits to be made, I agree. But, you are also gambling with your life. If you happen to get ripped off by someone else and can't repay the money you owe, then the buck stops with you. It's a case of pay or be paid. It all sounds so easy until something goes wrong. Then you better have some good answers ready. But with certain individuals you don't even get a chance to plead your case, or have a sit down. I think if a case is genuine then give a man a chance to put it right. As in the old saying 'you can't get blood out of a stone', nor can you get money back from a dead man! I wrote earlier that you should never close the door, but always leave it ajar, for a man to come back in. A man of respect doesn't get it from the barrel of a gun. It comes from not taking liberties with other people, or allowing other people to take liberties with you; of being able to face up to whatever hardship confronts you, and stand on your own when your time comes. You don't earn respect overnight. It's a long process of confronting the trials and tribulations of life; and of being judged by the way you shape up and handle any given situation. You're constantly under scrutiny by other people in the so-called 'underworld'. The slightest misdemeanour will spread like wild fire through the prison grapevine. The stories are retold and sometimes exaggerated out of all proportion. So a man has to handle himself with a certain dignity in the face of adversity. It's a relief and some kind of comfort to know that when you are arrested for whatever crime, and you stand in the dock, you stand alone.

I suppose you could say I'm of the 'old school'. However much of a cliché it may sound, I believe in 'honour amongst thieves'. Thankfully there are still many young criminals around that think as I do. Pulling strokes and playing dirty games only lead to guilt feelings and in some cases, nightmares. So pick your company carefully. As the saying goes: 'If you sleep with dogs you'll get fleas.' Remember that bad deeds have a funny way of catching up with you when you least expect it. They talk about the long arm of the law, but the old firms still have a long reach . . .

Epilogue

Now that my career is over, I hope that I can relax and enjoy all the simple things in life that have been denied me over a number of years. In putting the record straight, in a manner of speaking, I take this opportunity to thank all our old customers and associates for their help and support over the years and to deny all those rumours, prevalent at the time, that we watered down the gin. Not true. The vodka, *yes*. And some of the staff were not completely honest when it came to handling money. Lots of them actually thought it was their own. Imagine! Some even got their money mixed up with mine. Never mind, as the song goes: 'You've got to give a little, take a little . . .'

We can't have it all our own way. Look at Maxwell, Levitt, Clowes, Leeson and the BCCI bank. Once the ball starts rolling they can't stop it. We had one enterprising barmaid who on her first day at work found two 'dodgy' £20 notes in the till. Of course she didn't know who she took them off. Couldn't remember the customer. Needless to say, she only lasted the day. One of our other barmaids who worked at a different pub during lunchtimes, thoughtfully deposited the 'dodgies' into the other pub's till. We paid her £20 for her trouble and cut our losses.

Over the years we have had many legal and not-so-legal businesses. One of the legal businesses was the Ellerslie Hotel where one of our partners was Brian 'Little Legs' Gifford who had his head blown off while in bed by a person who is no longer with us. This happened after we had parted company. The word was that he had handled somebody's tom (jewellery) to sell and they weren't too happy with the sale price. There you go, sticky fingers again. Is it worth it? Why can't people play the game and save all the aggravation? They don't want just a few slices of bread, they want the whole loaf.

Getting back to the hotel, we had fifteen unmarried mothers for whom the council paid rents of £40 a week. We spent a great deal of money on that hotel. Each of the mums was given a television set (which their boyfriends nicked and then sold) and we built a club and bar downstairs. This was in 1978 when Dave Best ran the hotel so we had a nice little earner. At the weekends, the bar was packed. Now what real harm is there in having a little drink after time? Other countries let you drink round the clock if you wish, so it's the old story.

Dave Best entertained two undercover policemen for fourteen nights. They said they were 'electricians' and he was summonsed, fined, and we lost our licence. Without the club licence it wasn't worth the effort so we sold it to Watney's Brewery and had to pay £25,000 capital gains tax.

They were strange old times. You never knew what was around the corner. For example, the builder who did the work for us was Johnny McAvoy. He died of a heart attack and his brother Micky was sent down for twenty-five years for Brink's Mat. 'Little Legs' was shot, our customer Johnny Darke was stabbed to death at the Yacht Club by Johnny Bindon who in turn died at an early age.

Life is too short to be taken seriously. Enjoy it while you can. When I was in Maidstone, a mutual friend of Johnny Bindon and myself, Alan Stanton from Fulham, was doing a ten-year sentence with me. Alan and I used to have our visits on the same days so I had the chance to see him and lots of other visitors. It's like a social meeting for cons. On most London prison visits you may see as many as a dozen people that you know, as well as your own families. It makes it more enjoyable and helps to keep the visits happy and cheerful. That's why London prisoners and their families are happier when they are kept down south. But it seems that the authorities take pleasure in moving you as far away as possible and northern prisoners are sent down south to places like Parkhurst and Albany. On the other hand, London prisoners like me are sent to places like Full Sutton and Durham. It just doesn't make sense to me why they make a mother with little babies travel from one end of the country to the other on the whim of some shiny-arsed thirty-year-old office worker at the Home Office. If you ask me, it's spite. They just play around with people's lives.

Getting back to Alan Stanton, he used to say to me after our visits how worried he was about Johnny Bindon. It was very sad to see a man who'd been big and powerful reduced to a thin, drawn figure. John was dying and on each fortnight's visit he had wasted a little more. But the next thing I knew was that Alan himself had been taken to hospital with a lung infection, caused through the working party cleaning the roof and walls of pigeon crap that had been caked solid over many years. Pigeons shat all over the roofs and sills of our windows and the dust from their droppings can be lethal inside your lungs. Alan was dead inside two weeks and, tragically, Johnny Bindon, who nobody expected to outlive his best friend, attended Alan's funeral.

I'm a great believer in fate. Que sera, sera ('... What will be, will be', as the song goes). None of us are immune to bad luck. That's why I hate arguments and silly rows. Life's too short for all that crap. Enjoy life while you can and love each other. There's great satisfaction in making other people happy and giving them a good time. Charlie Kray is a fine example of this. For those of you who haven't had the good fortune to meet him, let me just say this: Charlie's a party animal, he loves to socialise and in fact it has turned into a full-time occupation for him. Now we all have our crosses to bear but Charlie had more than his fair share. For starters, can any one of you imagine what it is like to be the elder brother to the Twins? The worry, the stress, the sound advice that was continually ignored. The abuse when things didn't go as planned. The betrayals by family and friends. The hardship of going to prison for ten years when you were innocent. Then all those journeys from one end of the country to the other, visiting his brothers in different prisons for over twenty-eight years. I ask you. Not many people could have stood up to that sort of pressure without cracking up completely.

Yet Charlie, God bless him, has always greeted people with a smile and a warm handshake. I hope and pray that very soon now his brother Reggie will be set free and then Charlie will be able to lead a normal life.*

British prisons under the Tories, Michael Howard and Anne Widdecombe will be in a complete turmoil this summer if the above mentioned are still in power. I have never been a supporter of the Prison Officers' Association, who fight to hold back any form of human rights or progress for the prisoner. No one who has spent years as a prisoner in places like Wanno (Wandsworth), 'their main stronghold', would argue about the brutality and strict routine of a prison run by screws, for screws' benefit. All they want to do is lock you up 23 out of 24 hours per day. Any other privilege such as work, visits, gym, baths, education or exercise is carried out with scorn and resentment. Not only 'Wanno' but many other prisons

*Unfortunately, after a nine-month undercover police operation Charlie, at seventy years of age, faces 12 years of incarceration. It seems the police would go to any lengths to lock away a Kray. Their mentality is such that perhaps they fear, as Reg's 30-year sentence draws to a close that on his release, the two brothers will go back into business.

throughout Britain are run on exactly the same hostile regime of non-cooperation. People like Michael Howard are trying to set the prison system back 25 years. He will turn this country into a police state if he has his ideas turned into law. The only man who has ever made any sense regarding the penal system in my view is Judge Stephen Tumin. I hope and pray that one day a future Home Secretary will listen and act on this man's advice. If they don't, then it will be the prisons running with blood, not the streets, as a well-known politician once said.

Apart from my family, there are many other friends who have suffered and stood by me through all these turbulent years. I sincerely thank them. There are also many people from the legal profession like Peter Hughman, Tony Block and Henry Milner who've worked hard for me. I would also thank barristers and QCs who include Tom Williams and Ivor Richard, my defence team in the Cornell, McVitie and Mitchell trials; William Denny, my QC in the Marks case; and John Matthews QC who defended me in the Security Express robbery trial. Justice Bernie Caulfield also has my thanks and I won't forget how fairly treated I was by Judge Bristow at Winchester Crown Court.

My outlook on the future has changed considerably. I'm no longer looking for fortunes or to become involved in big business. To be honest I want to do as little as possible. I need a little time to sort out my life, but if I'm needed I'll always be there for my family and friends. They all know that. So my last message is to all the chaps who are still doing bird and whom I may have spent time with over the past forty years. I can't mention everyone by name. The list would be endless. Just remember that they can't stop that old clock going round and your day will come when you walk out through those gates, like many before you. Don't waste your time in the nick. Get fit, read everything you can, and try to educate yourself towards a better life. The old ways have gone. Computers. Now that's the best advice I can give. There must be a clue there to have a good touch. I think I might have a chat with Mr Levitt. He's the expert on how to make millions without getting any bird. If things go wrong we could all handle a few weeks' community service, couldn't we? Now try and stay out of trouble chaps, and don't do anything I wouldn't do.

    God Bless.

    Freddie.